Books by David Harris

THE LAST SCAM

I SHOULDA BEEN HOME YESTERDAY

THE LAST SCAM

a novel by
DAVID HARRIS

Delacorte Press ◆ Seymour Lawrence

Published by
Delacorte Press/Seymour Lawrence
1 Dag Hammarskjold Plaza
New York, N.Y. 10017

Manufactured in the United States of America

First printing

Designed by Judith Neuman

Library of Congress Cataloging in Publication Data

Harris, David, 1946–
The last scam.

I. Title.
PS3558.A6435L3   813'.54   81-5582
ISBN 0-440-04674-2   AACR2

To the original Henry Amazon,
may he remain forever safe,
and to my wife, Lacey Fosburgh,
without whose support and understanding
this book would never have come about

.

PROLOGUE·JUNE·1977

Henry Amazon, a Vietnam veteran and
small-time dope smuggler, decides to
smuggle one final shipment of high-
quality dope across the Mexican border
before quitting the dangerous business.

Henry Amazon noticed smoke on the far side of the ridge when he was still a long way away. The single greasy strand was almost hidden behind the slabs of early morning glare lifting off the Pan American. Barely visible black specks seemed to be swirling in it. Amazon guessed some Zapotec was burning off a new cornfield over there and brought his eyes back to the asphalt.

Henry Amazon had been driving his Toyota Land Cruiser south on the Pan American Highway for two days. The long-legged American had regularly scammed back and forth along the same route for almost nine years. The trips south were always empty, and the ones north always full. When all was said and done, none of them had amounted to much more than ready cash to blow, operating capital left over, and a reason for Henry Amazon to go south again. This morning he'd left Puebla, his last stopping place, at 4 A.M. As usual his southernmost destination was Oaxaca, one state over and some five hours farther down the Sierra Madre's Pacific slope. Henry Amazon calculated he would be there in time for lunch. His eyes didn't return to the smoke until the Pan American had climbed halfway up the ridge's steep north face.

This time the sight made Amazon nervous. The smoke was rising in tight coils, and the specks turned out to be buzzards, wheeling in and out of the sooty corkscrew with lazy swoops. The presence of those carrion birds changed the *gringo*'s take altogether. Whatever was burning up ahead was either already dead or close to it. Henry Amazon noticed sweat on his palms as he approached the crest of the ridge, and he had to remind himself that he was an innocent American, traveling under a valid tourist permit. His only outstanding violation of Mexican law was a single joint of *mota,* wrapped in cellophane and stashed in the top of his sock. To ease his nerves, he carefully extracted the contraband and flung it into roadside oblivion. Just in case, Amazon told himself. Buzzards could mean trouble. Henry Amazon made a point of trusting his premonitions, and in this case they had turned decidedly ominous.

At the crest the Pan American dropped quickly into a mile-long corner where two ridges intersected and the asphalt slithered along a sharp cut in the face of a mountain of pale green and rust-colored rock. The rise on one side reached a thousand feet, and the drop two thousand more on the other. The roadbed's apex was three hundred yards of flat two-lane with an inside shoulder wide enough to park three trucks side by side. Amazon's eyes went to the wide spot as soon as he entered the cut. At the moment it was occupied by two military transports and a civilian sedan. The sedan was parked across the flow of traffic. The source of the smoke Amazon had spotted was somewhere directly below the roadblock, deep in the descending *barranca* and still out of sight. He stopped his Land Cruiser next to the Judicial Federal agent waiting with the detachment in the flat. The agent was wearing a yellow polyester leisure suit.

"*¿Qué pasa?*" Amazon asked, motioning at the drifting soot.

The Judicial Federal agent ignored his question. He wanted to see the American's papers. When Amazon produced them, the agent said he would have to examine the vehicle as well. Henry Amazon obliged by getting out and opening the Toyota's rear hatch. Rather than stand there and watch the Federale's search, Amazon walked over to the highway's narrow inside edge to see for himself what all the smoke was about.

On the flat's drop side a bare three feet of crumbling red rock separated the asphalt from a forty-five-degree grade that tumbled for almost half a mile through tangles, tamarinds, and twenty-foot spired cactus. When the drop finally bottomed out, a lower ridge quickly rose on the other side. A succession of such descending ridges ran off to the West as far as Amazon could see. The smoke was rising from the smoldering remains of a Volkswagen van littered over an outcropping a hundred yards down the slope at the *gringo*'s feet. All the car's various pieces were charred, and flame was still licking around what had once been its tires. The Kombi had been rented the day before in Oaxaca by one Norris Levenseller alias The Patchoolie Kid. At the time Amazon first saw it he had no idea who the driver had been. He did notice a faint odor of marijuana on the edge of the rubber smell.

Henry Amazon and the *gringo* known as Ramón Ramón had first dubbed Norris Levenseller "The Patchoolie Kid" because of the stinking brown oil he used to rub on the back of his freckled neck and enormous mane of red hair. Amazon and Ramón had still been best friends and partners then. They had hired The Kid as a driver a year after entering the smuggling business and promoted him to a twenty-percent partner shortly before the trio had gone their separate ways during the disastrous rainy season of 1972. Afterward The Kid had turned free lance and begun making solo runs north, piled high with Oaxaca tops. His last one had ended barely four hours earlier. Coming into this corner, The Patchoolie Kid hadn't seen the roadblock until it was too late to do much but go for it along the narrow inside edge. Ten yards from the barricade, a soldier shot The Kid's face away, and he and his rented Kombi sailed off the drop at forty miles an hour. When the Volkswagen finally came to rest on the outcropping below, it immediately broke into flames.

Only the dregs of the fire were left when Henry Amazon arrived on the scene. By now a dozen flesh-faced buzzards were gathered halfway between the wreck and the edge of the roadbed where Amazon stood. The *zopilotes'* principal interest was in two smoking chunks of the demolished Kombi's driver that had fallen through the windshield. As Amazon wondered who the poor son of a bitch had been, one buzzard suddenly flapped off its perch, swooped toward the smaller of the two smoldering hunks, and seized it in his beak. The *zopilote* could only manage several waddling steps with the sizzling meat before the heat broke its grip. At that the rest of the flock plunged down, rolling the first buzzard in the dirt and kicking the smaller meat over the edge of the outcropping. Several of the awkward birds squawked down the slope after it. The others turned and swarmed on the second and larger helping.

Their feast was interrupted by a pistol shot. As the birds lurched upward, making a clumsy black smear over the *barranca,* Henry Amazon whirled around to see where the gunfire had come from. The Federale in the yellow leisure suit was standing five feet away, tucking his weapon back in his belt.

"*Zopilotes,*" the Mexican muttered.

With no more comment, he returned Henry Amazon's papers. The Federale expected the gringo to get under way immediately but first Amazon had a question.

"Who was it?" he asked, motioning with his head in the direction of the wreck.

The Federale didn't like questions, and his answer was initially two words long. "*Un traficante,*" he said. Then the Mexican thought to translate and added four more. "A trafficker in drugs."

"*¿Un gringo?*"

The Federale looked Amazon over several times before responding with a question of his own.

"May I inquire why the *señor* is so interested?" the Mexican smiled.

Even though Amazon grinned back, his asshole was squeezed tight enough to grip a dime sideways. "Just curious," he shrugged.

Without waiting for more questions or answers, Henry Amazon

strode back to his Land Cruiser and was quickly moving south again.
The clouds in that direction were thundering and turning black on
their undersides.

Henry Amazon didn't find out who the buzzard food had been until
the next day when he encountered Ramón Ramón at the Fontana
Restaurant in downtown Oaxaca. The afternoon rain had descended
early, and the street outside was slick. Amazon stood in the entrance
stripping his wet poncho off and spotted Ramón. The Fontana's tables
were laid out on the tile walkways surrounding an inner courtyard.
Ramón Ramón was by himself, hunched over the back table on the
right. Left to his own devices, Amazon might have ignored his former
partner, but Ramón noticed and motioned for him to come join him.
Things had not been easy between the two men for years. The
dissolution of their partnership in 1972 had been followed immediately by Ramón's running off with Wanda Lamar, Henry Amazon's
girl friend at the time. It had taken a while for Amazon's bitterness to
recede to its present state of truce. He didn't see much of Ramón
anymore, but when their paths did cross, both of them were usually
civil. During his latest stay north of the border, Amazon had heard
stories about Ramón's having killed a narc in Albuquerque. Ramón
Ramón was eating squid salad when Amazon sat down across the
table. This June the Arab-faced Ramón had a thick, shovel-shaped
mat of black whiskers perched on his face.

"¿Quiubole?" Ramón grinned.

"Same old same old," Amazon answered. Then he asked about
Ramón.

Ramón Ramón explained that he was "laid back at the moment,"
letting his action "cool off." He passed the information on with an
air of mystery as to exactly why, but Henry Amazon already knew his
secret.

"Makes sense," Amazon offered. "I hear you splattered a badge up
in Duke City."

Ramón's brown eyes snapped up from the squid in front of him, looking violated and shifting from side to side to check if anyone had overheard. Then Ramón Ramón changed the subject. "Have some," he said, pushing the dish toward the middle of the table for Amazon to pick at. "They're fresh."

Henry Amazon passed on the squid but got the rest of the message and dropped the subject. He'd just come in for soup and didn't have much appetite. In the course of explaining why, Amazon told Ramón about what he'd seen at the roadblock on the Pan American the day before.

Ramón speared a piece of salad with his fork and casually laid the news on his former partner. "That was The Kid," he said.

"What?"

Ramón Ramón finished chewing and looked back at his plate. "That was The Kid," he repeated.

The Patchoolie Kid's freckled features flashed quickly across the inside of Henry Amazon's head. Patchoolie had been nothing special, but Amazon had liked him enough that he found Ramón's casualness disturbing. He knew there was no love lost between The Kid and Ramón but expected that all would be forgiven now that Patchoolie had been snuffed at the hands of the Judicial Federal. Whatever else, they had been through a lot together once. Looking back on it, Henry Amazon would realize he should have known better. Sympathy had never been a major part of Ramón's action. He made a point of keeping score in life, and after The Patchoolie Kid's colossal fuck up on the Mitla airstrip in 1972, Ramón had dismissed Patchoolie as a zero. Neither time nor The Kid's descent into *zopilote* pickings changed a thing in Ramón's eyes. He'd been expecting as much for years. The only surprise was that it had taken so long to happen.

Learning of The Patchoolie Kid's sudden end was much more of a shock to Henry Amazon. Having seen The Kid reduced to broiled chunks the day before only magnified his sense of loss. His throat went tight. "Jesus," he muttered, "not The Kid."

Ramón started laughing as soon as he heard the words. "Come on,

Enrique," Ramón jibed, "get your nose out of your shorts. 'Not The Kid' my ass. You know the sucker was cruising for it. He never could take care of business as long as you knew him." Ramón interrupted himself to make a foray into the back of his mouth with an index finger, attempting to dislodge the shreds of squid stuck between his teeth. He sensed Amazon's mood and took pleasure in rubbing it the wrong way. "You knew it'd end like this. You had to, *mano*. What he did out in Mitla musta taught even you that much. I shoulda offed him then and saved the Federales the trouble. It had to happen sometime. Cop to it."

Ramón Ramón looked straight at his former partner, mutely offering him a chance to disagree. When Amazon didn't, Ramón sucked on his beer and continued.

"He was dumb, Enrique. Too dumb to do much but scam pissant loads and catch bullets when we hired him, and he only got dumber since. Sharks eat the slow fish, and that's how the *chamba* works. I ain't gonna miss him myself. I'll tell ya straight. I got too much else goin' to lose sleep over some *pendejo* motherfucker with no more sense than a teenage rock." Ramón stopped talking to fork more squid into his blank face.

Henry Amazon wanted to slam his fist on the Fontana's table and remind Ramón that The Patchoolie Kid had rescued Ramón's own ass on the highway outside of Mazatlán not so many years ago. He saved his energy instead. The relationship between Amazon and Ramón had long since dwindled into two acquaintances who knew each other too well to get along any better. Words would change nothing. He'd been around this merry-go-round with Ramón a hundred times before.

Amazon wanted to let the subject drop, but Ramón was having too much fun rattling Amazon's chain to stop yet. "You know," Ramón continued with a mouthful of seafood, "he was a lot like you, Enrique."

Henry Amazon let the statement hang in the air for a long time but finally couldn't resist the bait. "Yah?" he asked with an edge of irritation. "How's that?"

"You're both penny ante," Ramón laughed. "To the core."

9

Henry Amazon exhaled a whoosh of disgusted air in Ramón's direction. It was the same old shit. Amazon only found words to say after standing up to go. "I don't believe you, Ramón Ramón," he finally snapped. Ramón's name was said with great derision. "You're a real bastard."

Ramón leaned forward with his elbows on the table, grinned as he hit on his beer again, and snapped back. "The only difference between you and me on that score is the real part, *compadre*. You ought to be, but you just can't get up for it. You're still just play-acting. Nine years, and you haven't changed. You're a soft touch, Enrique, and the buzzards 'll most likely end up chewin' you just like they did The Kid."

Henry Amazon turned on his heel and split.

Ramón knew he'd pushed too far but made no move to retract anything. He just wasn't built that way. Instead Ramón laughed as Amazon huffed away, muttering "asshole" under his breath.

Outside, Henry Amazon paused in the cusp of dry air under the restaurant's overhang to light a cigarette. He would always hold Ramón's attitude that day against him. Henry Amazon had lived the last decade in a perpetual present tense, but that all began to change after Ramón told him about The Patchoolie Kid. As he walked back through the rain to his Land Cruiser, he was already thinking about who he and Ramón had once been. The image of how Ramón had hardened in the meantime revolted him. Amazon had the desperate feeling that he'd end up the same way if he hung around the business much longer. That desperate sensation would stay with Henry Amazon for the next year before eventually congealing into a decision to go for broke and get out.

When it did that, Henry Amazon would risk everything on one last scam.

JUNE·1978

1

On the first Monday in June 1978 Henry Amazon once again followed the southbound Pan American as it descended into the outside edge of the Oaxaca Valley. He could have drawn a map of the place blindfolded. The valley, fifty-five hundred feet elevation, was shaped like a lopsided three-cornered star with the city of Oaxaca at the star's axis. One arm pointed northwest to Puebla, another almost due south toward Puerto Angel on the Pacific, and the third southeast toward Tehuantepec and Salina Cruz, both on the Pacific as well. The Valley floor and the surrounding Sierra Madre del Sur were dotted with Indian villages. The Oaxaca Zapotecs he did business with knew Amazon as El Tortuga, The Turtle, a nickname he'd had for almost as long as he'd been coming south. June was the first full month of regular rain, and if everything went as Amazon planned, he would be both rich and retired before this rainy season was over. The sky turned gray after he reached the relative flat thirty miles from the Oaxaca city limits, and a sheet of falling water hammered on his Land Cruiser's roof and whistled under its treads.

The downpour came and went in ten minutes. The number of buses on the wet road multiplied the closer Henry Amazon came to the city. The number of burros diminished, and the highway broadened. Dump trucks piled with loads of green rock ground along in the right-hand lane, splashing clay mush at the Indians waiting on the shoulder. Amazon eventually took the turnoff into the center of town and was startled by the detail of soldiers stationed at the entrance to the Pepsi plant on the corner. They hadn't been posted there when he was last in town two months earlier.

Another truckload of troops passed Amazon in the next block as he waited to turn left into the courtyard of the Hotel Modesto. A private was riding with his feet dangling over the back lip of the truck bed. His Belgian machine gun rested on his thighs while he flung pebbles at the mangy dog pack milling under the streetlight. The dogs scattered, and the private's helmet fell off as he tried to get in one more good throw before the truck passed the Pepsi plant. Amazon continued to watch in his rearview mirror until the Army detachment had turned onto the highway toward the barracks on the city's far corner. The troops were just another form of buzzard, as far as Amazon was concerned.

The forty-year-old widow behind the Modesto's front desk recognized the American when he walked into the sparse hotel lobby to register. He came to town for a few days, three or four times a year.

"*Qué milagro, señor Enrique*," she welcomed. "You back in Oaxaca so soon. How long you stay?"

Henry Amazon looked up from the registration form. "Only tonight," he smiled. "Tomorrow I have some friends to see on the coast."

Those were just the first of many lies the *gringo* Henry Amazon would tell in the city of Oaxaca and its surrounding highland valley during the next month and a half.

The next lie came the following morning when he passed the desk on his way to the dining room.

"Buenos días," the widow greeted him. "You sleep well?"

"Si, muy bien, gracias," Amazon lied.

In fact, Henry Amazon had slept poorly. It had been 3 A.M. before he finally dozed and then only to dream one of those dreams he had never quite learned to live with.

In it Henry Amazon was back at a bivouac near the Qua Viet River where he, Ramón Ramón, and ten other grunts had been dropped the day before. Amazon was walking across the compound when the first incoming artillery fire vaporized the supply tent. With his ears full of the gook cannons stomping after him, Amazon ran for a bunker where Ramón Ramón was crouching in the doorway.

In those days Ramón's name had still been Jerome Whitehurst, but in the dream he was Ramón Ramón, all the way to the tag sewn over the breast pocket of his fatigues. As Henry Amazon threw himself down short of safety to avoid flying shrapnel, Ramón's voice came into sharp focus.

"Go for it, motherfucker," Ramón Ramón shouted. "Go for it."

Amazon started back on his feet to make a run at the doorway and then woke up. It was 5:30 A.M., and he'd seen the last of sleep for that night.

He was the first customer when the Modesto's dining room opened at seven thirty. He wolfed down his meal. In a few moments of chit-chat at the desk later while paying his bill, he learned that the Army had recently increased its activity. The widow explained that the detachment Amazon had seen at the Pepsi plant had become a regular feature two weeks ago after a bomb had been found strapped to the plant's front gate.

At half past ten Henry Amazon steered his Toyota Land Cruiser out of the Modesto's courtyard and turned right for the Pan American.

Amazon drove southeast only as far as the Sports Palace and then turned right at the EL CENTRO sign. After buying a *Carteles* from the paperboy on the corner, he headed downtown looking for a pay phone. The first one he found near Juarez Park didn't work, and neither did the one across from the fried-rabbit stand. Finally a phone near the School of Medicine took his twenty *centavos,* but there was no answer at the number he dialed.

Henry Amazon was trying to reach one Jesus Mapassa Guiterrez, a thirty-eight-year-old Zapotec from the village of Tolapan who had moved into the city six years before. In recognition of his sexual appetite, Jesus Mapassa was known as El Chorizo, The Hot Sausage. El Chorizo had both a truck and a garage, and Henry Amazon would need both in the coming weeks. For the moment he only planned to talk to Mapassa about renting the storage space. He needed it immediately.

Henry Amazon had quickly gone through two other unsuccessful partnerships after splitting with Ramón Ramón and then turned solo for a long time. Just the year before, Amazon had given up working alone and brought a Chihuahua *mestizo* named Zorro CeAttle into his business for a twenty-five percent share. Zorro was due in Oaxaca the next day with an empty load car. The last one of those they had loaded up had been lost at the border, *mota* included. Amazon was leery of letting this one out in general circulation before putting it to use. Better to park Zorro's wheels until the time came to head north with the goods.

Chorizo's was the only garage Amazon knew of, and he cursed the fucking sleazy Mexican phones for missing him. Amazon figured to pass time for a couple of hours and then call again. With that in mind he headed out the four-lane Periférico that circles the city.

As he did so, Henry Amazon's luck took a quick turn for the better.

Jesus Mapassa Guiterrez alias El Chorizo was skimming along at forty miles per hour in the opposite direction on what had all the earmarks of a sausage run.

Chorizo's 1968 Ford pickup was lowered a bit in the front end and painted orange with thick black tiger stripes tapering back from the grill for half the length of the hood. Henry Amazon didn't know the woman pressed up against the Indian's side but right away guessed what they were up to. El Chorizo was driving the Ford with his left hand while his right was out of view and up the woman's skirt, playing with the hair bushing out from under the elastic edges of her drawers. As Henry Amazon pulled up next to them at a stoplight, all the *gringo* could see was that the woman was holding on to Chorizo's arm with both hands.

"*Yo no creo,*" Chorizo shouted, spying Amazon and pulling his other hand back into the open. "Tortuga, you're back with much quick."

"I need to talk to you," Amazon shouted back. "*Ahorita.*"

Chorizo pulled into the first side street past the light where they parked a dozen yards apart. Chorizo told his woman to wait and walked back to prop himself on Amazon's running board.

"What's your thinking got in it?" the Indian asked.

Jesus Mapassa Guiterrez alias El Chorizo was five and a half feet tall, and his most prominent feature was two silver teeth side by side in the middle of his upper jaw. The mustache above them was thick, and his skin murky and mud colored. El Chorizo's polyester pants and shirt were standard city Zapotec, but he had long since given up the traditional *huarache* sandals for a pair of alligator boots that he spent a great deal of time and energy keeping the mud off of during rainy season.

"I need your garage," Amazon explained. "It's for a car."

Chorizo lifted his eyebrows and flashed his teeth.

"It won't be loaded most of the time," Henry Amazon continued. "I just don't want it being seen around. *Comprende?*"

"*Si,* I understand. But you got to pay two rates *amigo.* Load and unload. It's better that way."

Henry Amazon immediately offered instead to pay five thousand *pesos* in front, forgive the one thousand Chorizo still owed him from February, and lay another two thousand on the Indian when the load was in the car. If he had to let it sit more than five days loaded, Amazon would pay another five thousand and for sure move it after ten.

17

El Chorizo figured he could count on a second offer and just looked troubled.

The *gringo* knew what Chorizo was thinking.

"I got no more offers, Sausage. That's the one and only."

In response the Indian's voice rose and grew a whine around its edges. "*Chinga,* Turtle, you got to do more. That Chrysler you and the Mexican left here with got you too much rich."

"The Chrysler never made it, *mano,*" Amazon snapped back. "Everything got lost. *Todo.* I don't got no more *dinero* for your garage than what I told you up front."

El Chorizo let out a long silver whistle. "*Qué lastima,*" he finally muttered. What a drag. With that thought, the Indian seemed to lose himself in space.

"Okay." Amazon finally smiled, putting a lot of compromise in his voice. "I got one more thing to add."

He paused until Chorizo looked at him.

"I'll also make a down payment on the use of your truck. Not this one, but the Dina flatbed you keep out at your wife's cousin's place. I may want you to run it north for me, but I don't want to make no deal about it now, *sabe?* What I will do is give you a *pistola* to keep the truck free for a week; then I'll come and make an offer. If you don't like the business I offer, you give the piece back and we're square. If I don't offer you any business besides the garage, you keep the piece. If I do and you take it, the gun's yours along with whatever else we agree on for driving."

The Indian stared away in the direction of his pickup with the woman in it and fumbled with the pack of Winstons rolled up in his sleeve. After lighting one and blowing out a stream of smoke from his nose, Chorizo looked back at the *gringo* again.

"What kinda piece you talking about?"

"Forty-five. Seven-shot, automatic."

"With bullets?"

"The works."

"*¿Quantos?*"

"*¿Quantos qué?*"

"Bullets."

"A hundred rounds."

"One fifty, and I keep them even if I don't like your business."

Amazon agreed immediately.

"When do I get it?" Chorizo continued.

"Tomorrow morning, when I bring the wheels."

El Chorizo's face broke open in a flash of teeth. While he grinned, Amazon pulled five folded one-thousand-*peso* notes from his shirt pocket and stuck them out the window. Chorizo took the offering, unfolded it, and rolled the bills into a stick between his fingers.

"Make sure you're home between seven and twelve," Amazon added.

The Zapotec flashed his teeth again. "*No problema, compadre . . .* I . . ." For a moment Chorizo faltered into silence. His eyes were being pulled back to his pickup.

When the woman in the cab caught Chorizo's gaze, she winced and made motions as though she ached something terrible, rubbing her worn bouffant in the tassels dangling in the Ford's back window so that the bleached tuft in the middle pressed against the safety glass.

"*Bueno,*" the Indian finally said, turning to his business with the *gringo*. "I'll be there." Chorizo then excused himself from Henry Amazon and began walking quickly back to his truck. Halfway there, Amazon called out to him. "*Compadre . . .*"

Chorizo stopped and turned his head.

"I just want to know one thing."

"*¿Si?*"

"Do you wash your finger before you go home to your wife?"

El Chorizo burst into laughter and was still chuckling when the *gringo* pulled away from the curb and onto the Periférico headed for the Pan American again. El Chorizo advanced at a slow rumble in the same direction. When the woman asked what was so funny, he told her it didn't matter. It was a *gringo* joke she wouldn't understand. The Indian still had his rolled-up thousand-*peso* notes between two of the

19

fingers of his right hand and used them to begin nudging at the mound of fur in the woman's pants again. When they reached the highway, Chorizo's pickup turned left and north while the *gringo* went to the southeast, outside of town.

It was a little past noon, and Henry Amazon's energy had already begun to flag. He knew he needed to sleep and wanted to get out in the countryside to do it. The city of Oaxaca sometimes made him feel exposed and greasier than he liked to be.

When Henry Amazon woke next to the road toward Mitla, it was late in the afternoon and clear. His Land Cruiser was hidden from the Pan American by a stand of cypress trees, and he had slept in a state of total unconsciousness, sprawled across the front seats with his knees jackknifed in the air. The smuggler woke with an oatmeal head, out of sleep but not quite anywhere else yet.

At first he stayed horizontal and let his mind drift back to the Fuenteses' dirt floor four years before. There he had lain looking across the hut at the bright doorway where a half dozen Indians maneuvered to get a glimpse of the *gringo* who had been carried in after his fight with the Huavis. El Chorizo had been one of those who had managed to wriggle into the front row. The semiconscious Amazon had noticed the light glint off his silver teeth. Jesus Mapassa alias El Chorizo had been working as a small-time fence in stolen radios then and had ridden the bus out to the village to visit his cousins two doors down from the Fuenteses. Chorizo had returned the next week with some *mescal* for the recuperating *gringo*.

Amazon had cemented their friendship two weeks later when they had run into each other by accident on the *zocolo*. As they talked, Wanda Lamar walked by on her way to the market, and the American introduced her to El Chorizo. By then Henry's feelings for Wanda were dead and buried. Wanda Lamar was a Barnard dropout and at the time was living off her trust fund in a tiny room over the courtyard in the *posada*, deep into her native stage and wanting to have a Mexican baby real bad. She soon became the first and only *gringa* Chorizo had ever laid. He did so repeatedly until Wanda finally missed a period and left town on the Veracruz bus, saying she wanted to have her first child in the Yucatán. No one had seen Wanda in Oaxaca since.

At the same time Chorizo was duffing Wanda, he had also been helping Amazon put together a load and get back in business. Most of the weed had been fronted to the *gringo,* and the week after Wanda had disappeared toward Veracruz, Amazon had returned from the *Estados* to pay everyone off. With the proceeds of a few more errands like that, El Chorizo had bought his pickup, and his career as a sausage hound had flourished. Henry Amazon's business was a good thing that stumbled into the Zapotec's life, and the *gringo* was sure Chorizo wouldn't put it in jeopardy.

Henry Amazon rubbed the sleep from his eyes and sat up. He had to force himself into the present. It was time to move. After lighting a cigarette, he turned onto the highway headed back for the city, looking to find dinner and a place to spend the night.

Later, in a tiny plastered sixty-*peso* room with two beds and no windows along the back wall of the south valley Pachuco Courts Motel, Henry Amazon scanned the Tuesday morning paper that he'd bought ten hours earlier.

The daily's front page was dominated by a photograph of General Fernando Vega Cortez de Corriente, the governor who had assumed office with the imposition of martial law six months earlier. The *Carteles* had been having one of its usually spotty press runs that morning, and General Cortez de Corriente's image was blurred around the edges. Even so, it was apparent he had an unusually thin neck. The General's pale jowls spilled over his jaw, and the ice-cream-cone taper in the almost invisible neck made Cortez de Corriente's head look like a scoop of vanilla balanced between two shoulder boards. The man to the right of the governor was indistinguishable but, from the shade of the newsprint, appeared to be a *mestizo.*

He was helping Cortez de Corriente announce the completion of construction on the new city market. The building was on the edge of town, near the river and designed to replace the ancient existing market, two blocks from the *zocolo.* The old structure was characterized as an "eyesore" in the General's press release. Cortez de Corriente's office had assured the *Carteles* that the Indian commerce from the old structure would be moved soon in order to "alleviate the downtown squalor from visitors' eyes." The new market had taken a year to build and was as yet unoccupied.

After finishing the General's comments, Amazon's eye fell quickly to the front page's bottom right-hand corner. A short story there indicated that one Juan Montez Palencia, an officer in the Judicial Federal's special effort to stop drug trafficking, had been found shot to death near Mihuatlan, where the pavement ends on the Puerto Angel Road.

2

Montez's killing was the first news thrown into Agent Purdee Fletcher's lap when he arrived at the Oaxaca Airport on the regular Mexicana Tuesday morning flight. Late as usual, the 727 touched down about the same time as Henry Amazon had found El Chorizo on the Periférico. Except for the airline's service crew, the only person at the runway edge was a Federale wearing a purple shirt opened at the collar. His face was thin, and his sunglasses seemed to be built right into his cheekbones. The Federale was there to pick up three *gringos*.

Fletcher, Agent Ray Bob Wissle, and Emil Grimes, the contracted chopper pilot, were the reinforcements the Drug Enforcement Administration had promised the Mexicans two weeks earlier at the Operation Condor meeting in the Distrito Federal. Purdee Fletcher was the agent in charge and led them down the ramp to the airport's Tarmac pavement.

Purdee was forty-six and had once been wiry. Gradually the chunks of fat under his belt had solidified into a roll, and now he had

something of a pear-shaped look. Fletcher wasn't much on formality and insisted that everyone call him "Purd" or, even better, "Ole Purd," which is what he called himself. He also called himself "the best goddamn investigator in all of narcotics enforcement." That he should have ended up here with those skills was a constant sore point.

The Federale approached Purd as he stood at the base of the ramp, looking for his welcoming committee.

"*Señor* Fletcher?" he inquired.

Fletcher responded by thumping the Mexican on the arm. "Call me Purd, *amigo*. You must be Pissaro Cruise."

"Pizarro Cruz, *señor*," the Federale corrected, "and no, I am not he. I am Senior Agent Lazero Garcia Huahilote, Judicial Federal."

Fletcher had been expecting Oaxaca's head Mexican to meet him and was somewhat taken aback. The thought that these fucking greasers didn't have the sense to know whose ass to kiss flashed across Purd's mind, but he decided to let first impressions slide until he got the place sized up better.

"The *Jefe* sends much apologies," Garcia continued in English that sounded as though it had been practiced during the drive out from town. "He has encountered much trouble and must send me in his place. He says I should bring you there to meet him."

"Where?"

"At the ... how you say? The place they keep the bodies."

"The morgue?"

"*Sí*," the Federale agreed, "the morgue."

As they walked toward the car, Garcia explained that Montez had been found shot to death earlier that morning. No suspects, but *traficantes* were the generally accepted theory. Purdee then introduced the rest of his crew.

"This is my pilot, Grimes," Purd started, motioning at a skinny twenty-seven-year-old wearing a navy-blue baseball hat, jeans, and jogging shoes. Grimes's eyes sat at the back of his sockets, surrounded by smudges that gave him a raccoon face. "And this," Purd continued, "is my partner, Agent Wissle. I just call him 'Hog' myself."

24

Being called "Hog" didn't bother Ray Bob at all. Although he'd only had the nickname for the week and a half since he'd been assigned to Purdee, the junior agent had already taken a liking to it. The twenty-four-year-old Texan had been stationed in San Antone for the two years before his transfer to the Condor task force. All the old Customs boys waiting for their pensions to ripen in the office there told endless stories about the exploits of Ole Purd Fletcher in Manila during the war and how Purd had later collared the biggest nigger violator in Watts, one on one.

"You're a big ole boy," Purd had told Wissle when they first met, "so I'm gonna call you Hog. You got the look of a real porker." Purdee Fletcher had then punched Ray Bob's enormous arm as if to confirm the title.

Later, when Grimes had asked him where he got the nickname, "Hog," Ray Bob had bragged that "Ole Purd gave it to me." That Tuesday in June Hog Wissle's view of his senior partner was still couched in a rookie's hero worship.

Hog and the pilot Grimes sat in the car's backseat while Purd rode shotgun next to the Federale.

Unlike Wissle, Emil Grimes suspected Purdee Fletcher didn't know his ass from a hole in the ground. Grimes spent most of the ride into town staring out the side window and ignoring the front seat conversation. When they reached the Periférico and turned left past the cardboard and sheet-tin huts of the squatter town along the river bank, Grimes's eye picked up a wide gray haze lifting off the settlement. Washing was hung out on the nearby bushes, and the chopper pilot detected a wisp of roast corn aroma floating on top of the pervading smell of hot coals, stale urine, and donkey shit.

All that Purdee Fletcher knew about his Federale counterpart, Pizarro Cruz, was what Condor chief Norton Longbeem had told him in Mexico City.

Talk around the station there was that Cruz had been moving up the ranks at a rapid clip for a man with so little family juice. After a stint at the International Police Academy in Washington, D.C., Cruz had arrived in Oaxaca two months ago as second in command of the station. The head Federale at the time was a *huero* named Castillo who had cornered the post two and a half years earlier by virtue of an uncle in marriage who was in charge of the Distrito Federal's Department of Immigration.

When Longbeem and the Ambassador had insisted on a shake-up in Oaxaca at the Mexico City Operation Condor meeting in May, Mexico's attorney general had immediately offered to sack Castillo and move Cruz into the station's chief slot. All the Mexicans had wanted in exchange was a pilot, two *gringo* agents, and appropriate "operational expenses."

Cruz's first raid as station chief had been an empty-handed fiasco. His second, two days before the new *gringos* finally arrived, had been a modest success. In Mexico City Longbeem had told Purdee Fletcher to make it real clear to Cruz that they wanted better numbers and didn't want to wait all fucking year to get them. Norton Longbeem had described Cruz as a "cement face."

Purd had to agree with the description when the two finally met at the Oaxaca coroner's department. Cruz kept his shades on inside the building, and though exposed, the rest of his coffee face showed little. When his features changed, it was only into momentarily stiff creases meant to pass for an expression of one sort or another. He and Fletcher left the others in the room with Montez's corpse while they retired to an office to talk in private.

Purd passed on Longbeem's "numbers concern" as soon as they were alone.

"Ole Purd's ass is on the block right along with yours, Pissaro," the American explained. "My *jefe* says we got to produce or go home, and I can tell you right now Ole Purd is one producin' son of a bitch." Purdee started to punch Cruz on the bicep but stopped short of actually touching him. Something about the Mexican's face warned Purd against it.

Cruz watched the wave of the *gringo*'s fist near his arm and smiled a smile that came out shaped like a rectangle. The Federale allowed in English as how the problems down here so far had all been the leftovers of his predecessor. "Corooption," Cruz amplified. "Castillo was a crook and maybe left some crooks behind. Montez had been one of Castillo's men. It is believed that his corooption led to his death. Or so is our latest theory." The Mexican looked at his pointed shoes for a moment and then raised his shades back up to Purd's face. Cruz flashed his boxlike smile again. "It is of course a sad affair for the Judicial. Since it is a murder and outside of our official jurisdiction, the case is in the hands of the State Police. From what we know, this man was certainly taking the payoffs from the lawbreakers in San Rafael. My men found this stuffed in his mouth," Cruz finished. With a quick motion of his hand, the Federale dug a cellophane-wrapped package the size of a finger out of his cream leisure suit and extended it to Purd.

The American fumbled with the wrapping before stripping it off. Inside was a cluster of marijuana buds. The shriveled leaves were sticky and had a slight gold color around their edge. Holding the sample up to the light, Purd could see tiny red hairs on the face of the leaf.

While the American examined the *mota* head, Cruz examined the American. The *gringo* looked past his prime but still cagey. Behind Purd's veneer of boisterous comradeship, Pizarro Cruz saw a lot of frustrated ambition. It automatically made the *gringo* his adversary. Cruz himself had not wanted agents from the Americans, only a pilot and money. The *gringos* would bring with them an independent line of communication with Mexico City Condor that Cruz could not control. His authority was only now taking root at this station, and the Mexican resented the challenge. There could be only one bull goose here, and Pizarro Cruz, like Purd Fletcher, was the kind who liked most of the credit for himself.

When Purd returned the *mota*, Cruz smiled, checked his watch, and discovered it was time for lunch. He said he would be pleased if Purd

27

and his men would join him and several of his agents for something to eat. There they could talk more.

Fletcher said it'd be his and Hog's pleasure, but they should leave Grimes at the hotel. Emil Grimes wasn't really a cop, the American cautioned, only help hired on a three-month contract to jockey the Mexican's birds.

When the two *jefes* rejoined the others in the main autopsy room, the group was making random pidgin small talk and idly staring at the body on the slab ten feet away.

The late Montez lay on his back. The fatal bullet had entered at the bulge in the rear of his skull and exited somewhere around the bridge of his nose. The exact location was uncertain. The slug had apparently been notched and had splintered on its way through the contents of the head, leaving a small cavern in the middle of the former Federale's face. Secured by a stringy piece of gristle, the bulb of Montez's nose flopped sideways and lay against one of his cheeks.

"*Nos vamos,*" Cruz snapped.

Garcia Huahilote opened the door for his *jefe,* and the rest of the Mexicans fell quickly into line.

The only additional information Purd ever collected about Montez's murder was over lunch. Between the soup and the braised shrimp, Cruz made an offhand mention that his men had found Montez in Mihuatlan two hours after he'd been shot. From then on, the case was never mentioned again.

It wasn't until Purd and Hog were back at their rooms in the Casa Trocadero that Cruz's casual comment resurfaced. After consulting his map and finding that Mihuatlan was sixty-two kilometers outside the city, Purd began wondering how Cruz's boys had been so quick to discover the body in the dark, hidden in a gully, one hundred meters off the road behind a cornfield. Not to mention how they were so sure it was two hours in the first place. Purd made a note in his mind to tell Longbeem, when he put through his first weekly report over the phone that Cruz's version of the killing stank. In the same thought he remembered to add that, of course, Ole Purd wasn't wasting any time on it. It was, as Longbeem was sure to say, "lunch bucket stuff."

"Look, Purdee," the American in charge of Operation Condor had hammered at him in his Mexico City office the day before, "let's be sure you got the rules straight. I want to run through the drill one more time." Longbeem had paused to let Purd know to listen hard. "We got a real tender deal going here, friend, and I do not want you fucking it up. We not only got Washington on our necks but greasers all over us too, and the greasers are real sensitive about who owns the turf we're all working. The Drug Enforcement Administration is in the United States of Mexico to help the government suppress narcotics traffic, not organize Mexican affairs. These boys like to collect their dues and handle their family matters their own way. You get my drift?" Just in case Fletcher didn't, Longbeem had spelled it out. "Whatsoever the Mexicans do to or with each other, the violators, or the evidence is their business. Leave all the lunch bucket stuff alone. If not, your dick's in the meat grinder, and I won't be able to help."

Norton Longbeem hadn't needed to remind Purdee Fletcher that Ole Purd was hanging on to his job by a thread. After the grand jury in Miami, Longbeem had saved Purdee from early retirement during the official housekeeping by requesting the Southeast Region to transfer Fletcher to Operation Condor to do fill-in legwork. Norton Longbeem had been the only friend Purdee had left in a position to help. Longbeem had done so because the two of them had entered the Customs Service together twenty-two years earlier, and both had survived the reorganization that made their wing of Customs part of the new DEA. Immediately upon Fletcher's arrival in Mexico City his old friend from way back had told Purd that this was his last rescue. Ole Purd Fletcher either made good marks on this one, or he'd better plan to hurt his back, cash in his sick leave, and take an early option on a stucco one-bedroom in Retirement City. Longbeem had added that he was sure that Purd would be able to find a little night work as a security guard on the side. Purd got his drift.

After thinking it over some more, Purdee Fletcher changed his mind completely and decided not to mention the Montez thing to Longbeem at all. Better to stick with the situation at hand.

The only live fish Cruz had on his line were the prisoners from the San Rafael raid two days before. Cruz had already arranged to take the *gringos* to see them as soon as the Chief of the State Police returned to the City Prison after *siesta*.

For a while Purd just sat in his room with the blinds drawn against the afternoon sun. He disliked being forty-six. Since his career's momentary collapse after the Miami grand jury investigation, he knew there weren't many more years before he was going to drop even further off the pace and get left behind. Chasing bad guys was a young stud's game down at the level where he was playing. He wanted out of the daily performance demands, but the only direction immediately open to him was out altogether, and that terrified him even more. Purdee always said with a certain amount of pride that he just hadn't been enough of an asskisser to advance through the echelons. It was a logical explanation why an agent with as legendary an arrest record as his own had failed to advance up the ladder, but it wasn't true. In private Purd had to admit that he had kissed a lot of asses over the years, but it hadn't been sufficient to keep his own anything more than simply afloat. He viewed his present assignment as a case in point. He was in exile and knew he would have to earn his way out of it.

These greasers all seemed young and slick to Purd, and he wondered if they joked about his unkempt clothes and roll of fat. He knew he was going to have to carve out a little respect in their eyes but didn't really feel up to it.

Eventually, he just decided to let the subject go for a while and left the dark to lay by the Trocadero's swimming pool and drink *cuba libres*.

Hog Wissle had gone wandering around downtown and on his return to the hotel joined his partner by the pool. As the afternoon wore on, Purd told the junior agent a little of what really happened in Manila and, when asked about it, claimed it had been three niggers in

Watts, not one, as everyone generally believed. The number two nigger, Purd added, played in the outfield for the Los Angeles Dodgers. Hog Wissle was impressed.

Hog himself had spent his two years since Agent Training running a team of marijuana-smelling dogs at San Antonio International. He had applied for transfer to Operation Condor with much the same spirit that had once moved him to send away for the Tropical Island Treasure maps advertised along with magic tricks and surplus Italian weather balloons in the back pages of *Saga* and *Argosy*. His first day in town Ray Bob Wissle already felt like he was in the movies.

Garcia Huahilote and his boss Pizarro Cruz didn't pick Hog and Purd up until after seven thirty. The State Police *jefe,* they explained, had been delayed and was only now scheduled to arrive at the City Prison. Ordinarily Cruz would not have waited for the State Police to visit a prisoner, but the State Police *jefe*'s family owned Mexico City's Cobraa Works, S.A., as well as the Chiapas Mining Company, and were often mentioned in the Mexico City gossip columns as dining regularly with the President himself. The *Jefe* might have been insulted if important *gringos* came by while he was away. Besides, Cruz was in no hurry. He expected to get little more out of the three Indians he still had locked up.

All in all, Cruz's second raid had netted 418 kilos of *mota,* the three Indians guarding it, the woman cooking *tortillas* in a nearby hut, her sister, and a boy herding goats across the road. After threatening the women and the goatherd with something close to death if they didn't tell him the next time strange things were going on in the neighborhood, Cruz had released them. His men and the State Police had questioned the remaining three guards for two days. On the previous evening, Cruz informed the *gringos* as they drove for the City Prison, the one they'd caught with a gun had finally given the name of his Mexican boss. Actually, it was a nickname, "El Tasajo," The Piece of Meat. El Tasajo was known to the Judicial Federal as one Gabriel

31

Bolero Penitente, a small-time local hustler who'd once done time for thieving. Cruz had his men kick the door in at El Tasajo's mother's house, but she said she hadn't seen him in weeks.

As dark was settling onto the city, Garcia turned his car into the prison headquarters. A half dozen of the State Police's detectives were lounging around the courtyard inside, waiting to get a look at the new *gringos* in town. Hog Wissle nodded in their direction when he got out of the car and then followed Purd to meet the *Jefe*. Purdee Fletcher knew the Mexicans were watching but chose to ignore them. Most of the detectives were brown and carried their pistols tucked into the front of their pants.

Their *jefe*, Jorge Palomino Cobraa, was much paler and only thirty years old. It was difficult to be a Cobraa and fail, and Jorge Palomino was confident, short, fat, white, and jovial. Like Cruz, he had been at the International Police Academy. After a polite amount of police small talk, the *Jefe* summoned a detective called Ox into the small cubicle where the *gringos,* Cruz, Garcia Huahilote, and the deputy *Jefe* sat around his desk.

Ox was the biggest greaser Purdee Fletcher had ever seen, nearly the size of Hog and positively looming over the shorter Purd. The *Jefe* told Ox to get the Indians ready to be talked to, and they would be in presently.

When the group from the *Jefe*'s office first saw the prisoners, Ox had the three Zapotecs facing the wall and standing at attention. When the first one in line slumped his head to the left, Ox slammed his fist into the Indian's ear. When he whimpered, he brought the heel of his size eleven cowboy boot down on the suspect's bare foot. Afterward the Indian stood both straight and silent. Only the way five of his toes curled off the ground gave any indication of discomfort. His face had snapped shut.

To be questioned, the Indians were walked one at a time down to the end of the hall and taken through a steel door into a room with a bulb hanging from the ceiling. Ox first brought the second and then the third Indians in line for their turns, but Cruz and the *gringos* didn't have much interest in them. Both were farmers who grew their family's corn supply during the day and picked up a little cash income by guarding the *mota* hut at night. Both knew no more names than each other's and that of the Indian who had told them about the job and was now standing outside in the hallway, first in line. He was the suspect everyone was interested in. Ox only kicked the others around so that number one would have some screaming to listen to for a while.

Number one Indian was already in fairly rocky shape. His right eye was closed from the interrogation the night before. When this last suspect was finally fetched, the first thing Ox did was throw him against the wall. When he came back on the rebound, the giant detective punched the five-foot-tall Indian's lights out with a right in the middle of the face. One of the *Jefe*'s men brought some water to bring him back around.

Purdee Fletcher then strolled forward with his partner Hog a step behind.

The senior *gringo* could feel the eyes on his back and thought he heard a snicker amongst the Mexicans. For a few seconds he just stood in front of the Indian, trying to push through his inertia. Finally Purd asked Ox to stand the man up, and Ox jerked the Indian to his feet.

The *gringo* then talked at the Indian with a soft edge on his voice. The suspect tried to look at the giant black Florsheim wing tips on Purd's feet, but Ox jerked his skull back so the Indian was eye to eye with his interrogator.

"Son," Purd said, "I just want to know about the Americans who came out there where you and your friends were arrested." Then he called Hog without taking his eyes off the Indian.

"Hog?"

"Here," Hog answered.

"Tell him that in Mexican."

Hog translated, and the Indian replied that he had never seen any *gringos*.

33

Purd said that this Piece of Meat must have been selling his shit to somebody, but the Indian claimed that he didn't know anything at all about that. He had just been given a gun and told not to let anyone mess with the hut.

"Well, son," Purd continued in his easy and polite manner, "I'd like to show you some pictures and see if you've seen any of these folks anyway."

While he paused to let Hog tell the Indian what was happening, Purd fished several snapshot-sized photos out of his coat. There were ten of them, to be exact. "The Big Ten" was what Longbeem had called them in the Condor briefing. It was all part of the Condor idea, the station chief had lectured. "Get the honchos out of circulation." These photos were the big violators authorities on either side of the border knew about but either had no goods on or couldn't locate. However they got handled was less of a question of procedure than end results. All of these violators figured as major *gringo* movers of Mexican narcotics. Longbeem had spoken "major" in capital letters and paused for emphasis. It had been needless for Purd to ask if nailing one of these ten creeps was worth a lot of points.

Patiently, Purdee Fletcher held each one of the faces up for the Indian's inspection. The Indian shook his head no each time.

"You never seen any of these *gringos*?"

The suspect shook his head again.

"You sure?"

The Indian dropped his chin and looked at the ground. He told Hog that he was sure.

Purd grasped the suspect's chin between his fingers and pulled it level again.

"Are you sure, son?" he repeated. "This is very important. I don't want you making any mistakes. Tell me yourself. Say I sure. I . . . sure."

It took a while for the Zapotec to understand what the *gringo* wanted. When he did, he tried to mimic Purd as best he could. "I . . . chure," the suspect stammered.

While the sounds were still in the Indian's mouth, Purd cocked his right foot and brought the toe of this giant wing tip full force into the suspect's groin. The Indian immediately fell over on his side and began to puke. Ox moved to pull him back up but Purd motioned for Ox to let him alone.

"I like to let mine have a little room to move," the *gringo* explained.

With that Purd ran a series of kicks along the Zapotec's rib cage. The watching Mexicans made no sounds whatsoever, and Purd knew he'd caught them leaning. They'd figured him for a candyass because of the way he'd started, and his surprise attack had left them a little stunned. The *gringo*'s reluctance had melted and was rapidly being replaced with frenzy. He was going to punch this doper's ticket so bad that even these bean-eaters' dicks would shrivel.

The Indian squirmed and rolled on the dirt floor trying to escape, but Purd followed, thumping his heel against the Indian's lower vertebrae. When the suspect wriggled into a corner, Agent Fletcher planted his wing tip in the crack of the Zapotec's ass three times in swift succession. The Indian screamed in Spanish that he swore on the Virgin and his own blessed mother that he had never talked to a *gringo* or even seen one. "I chure," he began to rave. "I chure. I chure."

"What?" Purd roared, dipping with surprising quickness, hauling the Indian upright.

"I chure," the suspect mumbled.

Purd slammed the Indian into the wall. On the rebound he put his foot in the suspect's groin again. The pain drove the Indian unconscious for the second time that night.

The *gringo* agent's chest was heaving, and Purd paused over the mute body to spit out a gob of brown-flecked mucus. Almost as quickly as it had come, the strength was beginning to fade out of his arms. The air smelled of bodies and was so quiet everyone's breathing could be heard. Purd was losing his appetite for the interrogation and calculated that he'd impressed the Mexicans enough for one night. With practiced calm, Purdee Fletcher lit a Camel cigarette with his oversized Zippo lighter that had a palm tree and the words *Miami Beach* engraved on one side. Then he asked the *Jefe* to have a couple men bring this creep back around.

When the Zapotec had been revived, Purd stood over him.

"Son," he threatened in the same gentle drawl he'd first started with, "you and me gonna get to know each other real good in the next few days." Then Purd turned on his heel and looked at Hog.

"Tell him that in Mexican. Ole Purd's through with him for the night."

Cobraa, Cruz, Garcia, Huahilote, and Ox were all leaning against the wall near the door. The rest of the *Jefe*'s men had crowded into the doorway to watch how Purd went at it. The consensus amongst them was that this *gringo* must have some *chingadera,* the way he'd muscled that piece of shit Cruz's men had dragged in two days before.

When they were all out in the courtyard again, Purd suddenly felt the sweat that had soaked through his coat at the seams. He also noticed a tremor in his arms. Before getting into Cruz's car, he bent over and used his handkerchief to wipe the flecks of puke off his shoe, all the while trying to steady himself. Purdee Fletcher could sense the thickening night stuffed against the lining of his lungs.

During the drive back to the Trocadero everyone agreed that it was sure to rain soon.

3

The promised rain didn't arrive until the villages woke at their usual 5 A.M. on Wednesday. Sheets of water were thrashing back and forth across the Pan American when Henry Amazon passed along the highway at seven. He took the Tehuacán cutoff out of town and turned right into the storm's full force.

As the Land Cruiser climbed steadily out of the valley, creeks sprouted on the road's shoulder and boiled downhill in a soup of cinnamon mud and rocks. A rain cloud was sitting on the crest of the approaching ridge, and visibility dropped to fifty feet when Amazon passed into it.

The grade reversed after five minutes, and he felt the nose of his Land Cruiser point down. Almost immediately the road broke through the cloud again. On this side of the ridge, rain was sporadic and largely confined to drizzle. Most of the switchbacks were covered with rocky slush and small uprooted plants. The storm had spent itself here, and within ten more minutes Amazon could see the sun. The warm light lifted a wispy fog off the pavement.

Henry Amazon finally stopped when he reached a spot where the descending road made a sweeping right-hand curve and a wide turnout and tourist vista overlooked the first fingers of the next valley. Down there clumps of haze huddled along the flattening angle of the grade. Amazon and Zorro CeAttle had arranged to meet at this vista when they had last seen each other three weeks earlier. It was eight fifteen now, and Amazon was the first to arrive.

At eight twenty-eight by his watch he picked up a glint of sun reflecting off a windshield close to where the grade commenced. In another fifteen minutes he could make out the outlines of a four-year-old Ford Galaxie he had bought in Albuquerque and registered under the alias Jorge Luis Lacandone during the last week of May. Jorge Luis Lacandone was the name on the American passport Henry Amazon had bought for Zorro when they first started doing business with each other the year before. At the time, Amazon had figured CeAttle would be easier to hide posing as a Southwest Chicano than the outright Mexican he was.

Zorro finally splashed the load car to a stop fifteen feet from his partner and stepped out with his shades on. From a distance the Mexican looked like half the population of San Diego, Tucson, or San Antone. That Zorro was some kind of *mestizo* was obvious. Just what kind was hard to locate.

His mother was a brown Chiapas Mixtec woman who'd arrived in the state of Chihuahua and married Zorro's dad, a day laborer and stevedore from a yellow-skinned strain of Yaqui cut by centuries of passing *conquistadores*. The skin Zorro ended up with was a dirty plywood color. His cheekbones were high, but he was bigger than most Indians ever get. That morning he was wearing tan slacks, kid leather boots, and a green polyester shirt covered with a bright yellow leaf pattern. Amazon was in his usual jeans and Western shirt with imitation pearl buttons.

The two partners gave each other a quick hug that wasn't quite as close as it was made to seem.

For his part Henry Amazon was still a little pissed about the loss of the Chrysler. His first question was whether Zorro had brought all the equipment that Henry had sent back across the border with him.

"*Todo*," Zorro answered.

In that case Amazon said they'd better get out what they would need right away. In the trunk were two walkie-talkies to supplement the CBs in both the Ford and Toyota, four pistols, one thousand assorted rounds of ammunition, and truck plates from the Distrito Federal, Guanajuato, New Mexico, and Chihuahua. After pulling out the forty-five and ammo for El Chorizo, Amazon selected a snub-nosed thirty-eight for himself.

Henry Amazon didn't bother with small talk before leading his partner onto the asphalt headed back for Oaxaca. The storm in that direction had been blown north and off the ridge, but the sky was still slate-colored and dropped flurries of spray here and there in one-minute installments. The only traffic the two encountered until they were well down the Oaxaca side of the slope was a delivery truck from the López Warehouse and the third-class bus headed for San Lupe Sosola. The Lopez truck was speeding in the opposite direction with two used refrigerators for San Juan Bautista Cuicatlan, but Henry Amazon and Zorro CeAttle had to caravan along in the Sosola bus's greasy exhaust for several minutes while the pavement wound through the foothills to a stretch suitable for passing. The bus was a shade of red with an orange trim and had FAITH IN GOD AND FOREVER stenciled in yellow Spanish under the passenger windows. The vehicle itself was named "El Tiburón," The Shark, in foot-tall letters on its front door and had pointed white teeth hand-painted along the length of its pomegranate-colored muzzle.

In some respects the last scam Henry Amazon had planned was no different from the others. He would put it together as he went along, and as usual he told no one, including Zorro CeAttle, any more than he thought they ought to know.

This approach worked fine for Amazon, but it was disgruntling for his Mexican partner. Under any circumstances Zorro CeAttle was suspicious; the *gringo*'s hidden way of doing business only further blistered his fears. Zorro had been harping on his exclusion regularly until he'd lost the Chrysler and a hundred thousand dollars worth of Grade-A leaf on the El Paso bridge. Since then, Zorro had only mentioned the subject once.

Henry Amazon had responded the same way he had the first time the question had ever come up. Tough shit, he'd told the Mexican. That was just the way it worked. Being a twenty-five percent partner didn't make Zorro an executive, and Amazon himself had dropped the one big happy family model of moving dope when he and Ramón Ramón parted company in 1972. In the same breath Amazon had launched into his familiar argument, pointing out that Zorro never had to risk his ass without knowing exactly how he was going to do it. That ought to be enough. Zorro had been making good money until his latest fuck up with the Chrysler, and this hustle would make him rich if he'd spend a little less time asking for more and concentrate instead on holding his end of the action up.

Before they arrived in Oaxaca, all the *gringo* would tell his partner was that their final scam involved two loads, driving one north and then fetching the second with an airplane.

At the time Henry Amazon was still figuring out the details himself. The economics of the scam were exceedingly tight.

The loss of the Chrysler had come close to wiping Amazon out. To get himself in a position to abandon the game, Henry Amazon had been forced to mortgage half of the projected first load to Fat Albert from Jersey City for fifty-five thousand dollars. Fat Albert had also agreed to buy the other half at three hundred dollars a pound. If Amazon and the Mexican could get a thousand pounds of the weed into the U.S., he figured they'd clear enough to pay for a second run with a plane. The profits of the second load would keep Amazon cruising for a long time. He planned to fill the plane with boxes of what the Indians call "The Kind." Figuring he could cram in 1,250 pounds and sell it at 1,250 dollars a pound, Amazon had watched 1,500,000 dollars light up on his pocket calculator. It was a magic number, and Amazon had passed it on to Zorro because he guessed the greed it induced would keep the Mexican off his back. Henry Amazon knew his plan had two big problems in it and wanted to wrestle with them by himself.

The first was The Kind.

This brand of leaf was a commodity in notoriously short supply. Fat Albert called it "scene," short for *sin semilla,* "without seeds." "Scene" can't just be planted and left to grow. It has to be cultivated, separated, nursed, and watched with a careful eye. The male Kind are destroyed at a young age, and as the females reach maturity, they secrete increasingly thick coats of resin onto their leaves in hopes of attracting pollen from their long-since-expired suitors. At harvest time, as much as nine months after planting, number-one virgin Kind has no seeds at all, and its leaves dry light green, spongy, soaked with resin, and laced with tiny red hairs.

Henry Amazon only knew three places he could get together as much Kind as he planned to carry, and the scam was only possible if at least two of those came through. One was an Indian called Rascón and his people deep in the mountains. The second was Monroe Jessee's old partner Gomez Gordo, and the third was still a secret. Amazon had told no one about it, and only he and the old man called The Cockroach from outside the Fuenteses' village knew. The old man had been tending a patch of Amazon's Kind for close to a year on the side of a *barranca* hidden in the next ridge over from the Indian's house. If it hadn't been busted since Amazon had been north, The Cockroach's field would fill half of a two-engine Cessna aircraft.

The plan's second problem was of more immediate concern.

The *gringo*'s calculations had been worked out on the assumption that he could still buy the first load at somewhere in the neighborhood of twenty-five dollars a pound. Price was a day-to-day question, and if it had risen in the two months since he'd last been south, Fat Albert's money might not be enough. As Henry Amazon led Zorro CeAttle into Oaxaca toward El Chorizo's garage, he figured the cash squeeze would only get tighter.

41

Chorizo lived down a long dirt road in the State of Oaxaca projects on the city's northeast side. Most of the two-room concrete-block houses in that neighborhood had been built with a rush of money from Mexico City that had dried up a third of the way through the Master Housing Plan of 1968. The fields the subdivision had been planned for had been cross-hatched with a series of dirt and clay one-lanes but remained largely empty of structures. El Chorizo's section of houses had originally been sold without roofs, and each homeowner made his own. Scrap sheet tin and used lumber was the common style. One of the Master Housing Plan's widely proclaimed "progressive features" had been provisions for universal indoor plumbing, but the few pipes that had ever been laid had consistent problems that by now had culminated in a tendency to leak turds into the street during periods of heavy rain. When Amazon arrived at Chorizo's, the gray sky was still drizzling on that part of town.

Henry Amazon slipped his poncho on, stepped out, and went right for the garage built shanty style against one of Chorizo's walls. Once he'd wrestled its doors open, the *gringo* told Zorro to park the Ford and wait in the Toyota while he went inside.

El Chorizo was sitting at a table drinking a bowl of coffee. His wife was making *tortillas* in the corner, and their three children were swirling around the *gringo*'s long legs as soon as they saw him come through the door. Amazon was in no mood to fool with them.

"I got to run quick, *compadre*," the *gringo* explained to Chorizo.

The Indian insisted on offering his coffee anyway, but Amazon turned it down and motioned with his eyes that they should talk alone. Chorizo told his kids to stay put and took Amazon into the second room where the family's sleeping mats were rolled up off the slab floor and stored. Henry pulled Chorizo's forty-five and ammo out from under the poncho and gave him a quick two minutes of instruction in how the action worked. Then the *gringo* said he had to leave.

El Chorizo walked him to the door but no farther. He saw the Mexican sitting in Enrique's Land Cruiser, and he didn't care to get any closer. Soon after Amazon had introduced Zorro a year earlier, El

Chorizo had told him that his new Mexican partner was "some kinda son of a bitch" and still felt the same way.

Henry Amazon had passed off their problems with each other: they both fancied themselves stud goats and didn't share turf easily.

But El Chorizo disagreed strongly.

"No, no, Tortuga," the Indian had insisted. "Don't you see? This *cabrón* got devil eyes and don't trust nobodys. He's not the kinda *hombre* you want to be partners with. No way. He don't give a shit for nothin' but himself."

It was true that Zorro CeAttle had the look of distance and suspicion about him. His eyes were narrow and intense and unlike any Amazon had ever seen: the eyeballs were a smokey shade of violet that ran the gamut from gray to deep purple, depending on the light around them.

With eyes like that there was little doubt that Zorro had been the strange one in the CeAttle litter. None of his eleven brothers and sisters had been born with anything but eyes in the standard Mexican shade. Zorro claimed the color excited women and made other men's peckers shrink. The impact of his purple stare gave Zorro a little edge in any situation, and he played it for all it was worth, like every advantage that came his way. It was his habit to keep the eyes sheathed behind a pair of space-age-looking Foster Grant sunglasses and unleash them only at crucial intervals.

Henry Amazon had first found Zorro through his old friend Monroe Jessee in El Paso. Monroe knew Amazon was looking for a junior partner and had suggested Zorro, who was between hustles across the river. He had been running wetbacks into the ranches of Texas and New Mexico for the last five years with a succession of *gringo* partners, most of whom, according to Zorro, had ripped him off. Against some of his instincts, Amazon decided to take Zorro CeAttle on for a quarter of the action, even though the strange-eyed Mexican had never worked south of Durango. Zorro knew the Chihuahua border back, forth, and sideways and had a reputation for holding his mud real well in tight situations.

After El Chorizo's, the two partners stopped at an empty café on the Pan American toward Mitla and ate *mole*. They sat at the corner table, overseeing the door and the road outside. All signs of rain were rapidly vanishing. After the woman brought their order, Amazon laid out the plan in a quiet voice.

They had to get a thousand pounds of tops together as quickly as they could for movement north. Amazon figured the Indian Vincente in the *mescal* village would have the crop together that he'd talked about on their last trip down and would know of others. So would Heronimo and the Indian they called Gangrene in Maquilsocho.

Zorro added the name of the potter across the river to the list and then wanted to know about the second load.

"That's *sin*," Amazon replied.

Zorro made no gesture of recognition.

"You know, *sin, mano*. The Kind." Amazon smiled. "*Las virgenes astronadores . . .*"

"*Yo sé*," Zorro interrupted in a more serious tone. "I know what your talking is about. I was just wondering where you're gonna get this *mota* like that?"

"I got some ideas," Amazon said, thinking about Rascón. He was staring out the windows. "I know some folks in the mountain."

"When we gonna meet them?"

"We aren't."

"What you mean?" Zorro asked after a moment of silence.

"Just that." Amazon scooped some more *mole* into his *tortilla*. "At least not right away. Today you and me are gonna leave a message for one of 'em on the way to see Vincente. Then I'm gonna meet the dude alone this weekend while you hang out back in town."

Zorro thrust himself forward onto the checkered tablecloth and started to whip his shades off, but Amazon backed him down with a wave of the *tortilla*.

"Hold on, *compadre*. Before you go into your act, you oughta know that's just the way this *hombre* works. I don't have nothin' to do with it. This man and his people don't see nobody but the principal until delivery time, and the principal is me, by myself. It ain't no decision of mine. That's the way this Indian sets it up, and he don't do no changing. With what he sells, he don't need to." Which was only partly true.

He probably could have brought Zorro along to a meeting with Rascón. But it would have made Rascón more nervous than the *gringo* wanted him to be.

They left the café and headed farther southeast. After half an hour, they were in the foothills, climbing rapidly.

The Land Cruiser's radio was tuned to station XEOA where the *gringo* music hour had just signed off with a long cut from Linda Ronstadt. *The Scorpions of the Valley Show* with host Garcia Garcia Garcia was about to begin. Scorpions of the Valley was the show's house band, and they knew just about every song anyone in Mexico had ever heard of. After opening with a few jokes to loosen the live audience up, and a couple of hot and fast numbers from The Scorpions, Garcia Garcia Garcia introduced the show's main gimmick. Anyone in the live audience who wanted to could come up to the mike and sing his favorite song with The Scorpions as backup. Or, more accurately, whatever portion of their favorite song Garcia decided to tolerate.

Most were interrupted quickly by the host with a sharp put-down, the Scorpion theme song, and a quick message from a sponsor. The Indians loved it and rode buses from all parts of the valley to sit in the audience or stand three deep against the back wall.

On this Wednesday Garcia Garcia Garcia opened with a middle-aged woman from Suchilquitango who'd come to town to recite an hour of Hail Marys under St. Geronimo's statue in the Santo Domingo Cathedral. Fresh from church, the woman had come to sing a slow number about the *bebé* Jesus. Three bars into it, Garcia thanked her and her mother-in-law, signaled for a rush of *mariachi* from the Scorpions, and brought on an old farmer from San Pedro Apóstol. He got in twenty seconds of "The Ballad of Pepe López" before being replaced with the Favrito Corn Snacks ad featuring the plastic vampire in each bag. The live audience stomped their feet, whistled, and shouted joking Zapotec insults at the old San Pedro farmer as he took the stairs off of the stage and back to the cheap seats.

At the same time Henry Amazon turned the Land Cruiser off the Pan American to the right and onto a narrow dirt road. This was the way to Rascón's message place. Stones rattled off the car's underbelly as the road climbed up the lead edge of a ridge and then curved along its flank for at least a mile before dropping into a wide wash and up the other side. Amazon stopped at the bottom of the dip and got out, leaving the engine running.

There he immediately collected an armload of rocks from the belly of the wash and carried them over to a small plateau where someone had planted a short straight line of three maguey cacti, the kind *mescal* is made from. He constructed a low pile behind the middle plant and returned to Zorro and the Land Cruiser.

"How's he gonna know it's you?" Zorro asked as Amazon wheeled the Toyota around and headed back toward the highway.

"*¿Quién sabe?*" he answered with a shrug. "For all I know, he might have been watching us the whole time."

Zorro quickly scanned the short rolling hills and gullies and saw no one.

"The only thing for sure," Amazon continued, "is that he'll be where I can find him on Sunday. Right now we got to locate Vincente."

Amazon stopped talking and began to fiddle with the radio. After twenty kilometers along the Pan American they reached the wrinkled lane of clay ruts and boulders leading downhill to Vincente's. Garcia Garcia Garcia said *adiós* until *mañana* with a special *mucho gusto* to the folks listening in Tomoltopec and a quick mention of the Scorpions' favorite tooth powder.

It was easy to tell when they were finally near Vincente's. The place smelled like a pig that had been lying dead for a week.

Vincente's village was a *mescal* village, where mature hearts of maguey cactus were stripped, quartered, roasted, and mashed until they yielded liquor. The process produced a thick layer of fumes, and Amazon gagged, rolled the car's window up, and lit a cigarette.

After piercing the outside edge of the village, the road dipped between two ragged lines of *adobe* huts and deeper into the stink. A white dog with sores on his haunches launched himself out of the courtyard doorway and yapped after the Land Cruiser as the street narrowed and dropped into and across a stream. A double-axled Dina flatbed loaded with barrels of *mescal* was approaching from the opposite direction and the two vehicles met in the creek bed. Amazon pulled as far to the right as he could, and the truck inched by, splashing the side of the Land Cruiser with mud and *mescal* slop. The dog stayed fifteen feet away on the slope, barking his lungs out until the truck approached. Then with a succession of fierce howls he attacked the oncoming Dina's front wheel and was run over.

Henry Amazon and his partner stopped at the storefront *tienda* on the next corner. The sixteen-year-old girl behind the counter called to her father in the back room as they entered. An Indian came through the blanket that hung between his store and the rest of the house. He had a nose like the blade of an axe and recognized the *gringo* right away.

"*Qué milagro, Tortuga. ¿Quiubole?*"

"This and that," Amazon answered in Spanish. "How about a couple of Orange Crush, *muy helado.*"

The Indian sent his daughter to fetch the coldest drinks from the icebox in the family quarters and turned back to the *gringo.*

"*¿'Sta Vincente aquí?*" Amazon asked.

"No," the Indian said. "He's been gone all day, but he had a feeling that you would be coming soon. I told him that was too quick, but he was so sure. He said he saw you in his dream last week. He says he saw you coming and right away gives me something to hold on to for you in case he's not here the time you come by."

The storekeeper reached into the back of a drawer under the counter and pulled out a parcel the size of two fingers, wrapped in an old page from the Oaxaca *Gráfico*. Amazon accepted it in a smooth sweep of his left hand and bent to tuck it into his boot. When he straightened up, the Indian girl came back with their soft drinks. The storekeeper said Vincente would be there the next morning if Tortuga and his friend came before eight. Amazon told them they would and led CeAttle back to the Land Cruiser.

On their way out of Vincente's village, Amazon couldn't help but notice the dead dog sprawled in the middle of the street. He wanted to drive around it but there wasn't room, so he accelerated over the carcass's head and turned toward the Pan American.

When they were back on the highway again, headed downhill for the city, he parked on a thin turnout.

"Let's take a look at this shit," he said, laying Vincente's parcel on the seat between them.

Zorro unwrapped it carefully. Inside were two mature and full *mota* tops. Henry held one of them up to the windshield. The color was a little greener than he preferred, but there was only a smattering of seeds, and the hairs were fine and frequent.

"Nice hairs," he said.

Zorro agreed. The Mexican was busy cleaning several sprigs and getting his cigarette papers out.

After two hits on the freshly rolled joint the rush began, and Amazon felt his mind lift off and slowly hover over his head. For a moment he could think of little else but what a goddamn beautiful valley he was looking at.

"This place is so pretty, I can't fucking believe it sometimes," he told his partner, motioning with his hand at the view on the other side of the windshield.

Zorro peered ahead. "Sure is," he finally agreed, "except for that." He was pointing at a barely visible shape on the right-hand slope of the valley that Henry Amazon had missed in his first glance. One of the Federale's blue-and-white helicopters was buzzing in and out of the ridge line like a dragonfly.

The chopper swooped low over several villages, then rose in an arc pointed toward the Oaxaca Airport. The high-pitched buzz of the disappearing machine echoed off the foothills for a while, then stopped altogether.

Amazon started the Land Cruiser again while Zorro rewrapped the package.

"Let's cruise," he said. He seemed distant and preoccupied. Somewhere inside his head Henry Amazon already knew that Vincente was going to want more for his leaf than he could afford to pay.

4

          They arrived at Vincente's by seven thirty. Zorro spotted two more helicopters but otherwise the drive out was uneventful. The storekeeper told them Vincente was right down the street at Alejandro's *mescal fábrica*. At the tiny dilapidated liquor factory, gates were open and Vincente's Ford flatbed was parked inside. Vincente saw them as they pulled in and hustled over from the pit where Alejandro's crew had a batch of cactus hearts roasting.

"*¿Quiubole, Tortuga?*" the Indian shouted. "*Qué bueno.*"

Amazon grinned and said he was just in the neighborhood and had decided to look him up.

Vincente laughed. "*Qué bueno,*" he repeated. Then he got right to the point.

"*¿Gusta mi mota?*"

"*Más o menos,*" the *gringo* answered. "It's a little green, and the taste ain't nothin to write home about."

Vincente didn't understand, so Amazon translated, adding that he figured his sample was about 450-*pesos*-a-pound dope.

The Indian wanted to know how much that was a kilo, and when Amazon figured it out on his calculator, Vincente turned his head aside in disbelief.

"*Mano, mano,*" he wailed, "you got to know there's other *gringos* paying kilos at fifteen hundred."

Amazon figured that down to pounds on his tiny machine and got 675 *pesos* per. Bad news. Very bad news indeed. "Thirty dollars," he grimaced inside his head. "I knew it. He wants thirty bucks a pound. I fuckin' knew it."

He looked up from the calculator with a flat expression and started to argue, but then he saw Alejandro, the proprietor, walking toward them across the courtyard.

Vincente noticed him too. This wasn't the place to talk business, he said quickly. They should meet out on the road to Yagul in the afternoon, where it would be private.

When Alejandro reached the group, Amazon and Zorro only stayed around to exchange *mucho gusto*s with him and apologized for having to be on their way.

Back on the other side of the creek the dog was still in the road.

The two choppers Zorro spotted that morning returned to the airport two hours after takeoff with little to report. Their flight had been termed a "training exercise," designed to accustom Cruz's men and the freshly arrived Hog to operations in the air. Purd had declined to come along, saying that he'd been up in plenty of "those fucking eggbeaters" in his time and didn't need any more practice.

The training flight settled back onto the Federale corner of the runway at eight forty by Wissle's watch. The junior agent then headed for the suite of Judicial Federal offices in the middle of town. Borquez's Funeral Home occupied the street level. At nine fifteen Hog climbed the stairs and joined Purd in the room assigned them near the rear of the floor. Fletcher was in the process of turning the office into his kind of command post. The photos of the Big Ten that Longbeem had given him were already taped to the wall, so he could look right at the faces while sitting in his chair. He carried a second set in his pocket.

The Big Ten had assumed an overwhelming importance in Purdee Fletcher's scheme of things. If his career hadn't turned so bad in Miami, he would have had a desk job by now. His problem was to find a way to regain his perch. The Big Ten program seemed the most likely possibility. One score under it would wipe a lot of bad marks off his record; two would most certainly spell comeback itself. This Thursday Purd was in a mood to start clawing his way back to the top.

When Hog entered the office, Purd had just stapled a map of the state of Oaxaca on the bulletin board and was arranging his color-coded set of pins around it. The map and its bulletin board were on the room's back wall between the two desks. A long table ran along the right-hand wall. On it Purd had already assembled the radio.

Next to the receiver he had mounted a tape deck to record traffic. The tape wasn't running, but the radio was on and filled the room with static. Wissle, still excited by the morning's ride, wanted to say more, but Purd cut him short and began explaining the map.

After that Purd said that, of course, Hog knew all about those pictures on the wall.

Hog did, but before he could say so, Purd had moved on again.

"What's more important," he continued, "is the pictures over there." He pointed at the blank board on the room's left side.

Hog stared. "What pictures?"

"The ones you're gonna take," Purd grinned. Then he produced two Nikon cameras from his desk. Each had a case for a telephoto lens on its shoulder strap. "You must have learned to use one of these in training."

Hog was proud to say he'd been fourth in his class.

"Well, I want that wall covered with *gringo* snapshots, my boy, and I want good ones." Purd paced back and forth between his desk and the door as he talked. "Look for the high fast types—you know the number. Cruz says there's a spot called Gringo Corners on that square downtown where a lot of the flashier tourists hang around. If you get anything interesting, I'm going to send it up the line for Nort's look-see."

Hog was impressed that his partner called the top man in the whole Condor network by his first name.

Purd had expected him to be. He wanted to jack the kid up and make sure he would use that Nikon camera right. Purdee Fletcher made a mental note to report to Longbeem that he'd instituted a photo reconnaissance sweep immediately upon arrival. Then he told Hog to go get a Mexican, show him how to use the second camera, and get on the street.

Just as Hog opened the door to go, the radio static was interrupted by a quick burst of faint but clear *gringo* talk, sounding quite faraway.

"Breaker One Seven. Hear me, Bimbo. Straight and narrow and clear as a bell. Loosen up and push it. Over."

"*Bueno,* Ace Leader. I'll be eatin' your bumper."

As soon as the transmission began, Purd had instinctively sprung for the recorder. His first lunge fell short, and he almost ended up on his face. By the time he'd righted himself and reached the switch, the senior agent had missed the entire transmission except for the "your bumper" on the end.

After Hog's departure, Purd listened to the radio a while longer, then turned it off when he left to meet Pizarro Cruz at the City Prison for another go-around with the Indian who'd given the Federales the name "El Tasajo," their only active suspect to date.

When it was finally time for Amazon's afternoon meeting with Vincente at Yagul, dark clouds had begun massing to the east end of the valley while the sun continued to command the city itself. Amazon and CeAttle drove toward the gray sky, stopping along the way for a Pepsi and an issue of *Carteles*. They were early anyway.

The Yagul Road runs straight between the Pan American and the archeological site on a nearby cliff. Three quarters of the way along it, a small dirt track angles off the larger one and into a gully cut off from view by a stand of thick bushes and trees. The track was wide enough for a truck, and the gully was empty when they clattered in. Amazon stayed with the Land Cruiser and read the paper while Zorro climbed to the lip of the gully and watched the road through the neighboring cornfield.

Vincente's double-axled Ford flatbed eventually appeared, trailing a rooster tail of light dust and pebbles. The truck's cab was painted navy blue with a five-pointed phosphorescent orange star on the driver's door. The windshield was lined with gold tassels, and Jesus himself rode nailed to the plastic cross on Vincente's dash. The Indian pulled in behind the Land Cruiser and killed the engine.

After *mucho gusto*s all around and a little small talk, Amazon offered Vincente a cigarette and got down to business.

"What's this bullshit about fifteen hundred a kilo, *mano?*"

"No foolin', 'Tuga. It's what *mota* going for all over, not just with me," the Indian answered. Vincente came up as high as Amazon's shoulder. Near the gums his teeth were stained a deep brown color that paled to a light yellow the closer it got to the chewing edge. His upper lip was covered with scattered bristles of black hair that shook along with the rest of his lip when he talked.

"When we dealt two months ago you figured twelve hundred at the outside."

"For sure, *compadre,* but that was then. Now is now." It had been a hard year with inconsistent rains and the heat from the Federales was on its way up.

Henry Amazon finally interrupted. "I get your message," he snapped. "I get the fuckin' message." After a pause he spoke again in a much more conciliatory voice. "It's still a lot of *dinero* for a bunch of regular tops."

"You don't got to buy it," the Indian reminded him. Vincente's face had lost much of its smile for a moment. "Maybe somebody'll sell you at that too-much little price of yours, but I'm not the one."

Amazon's immediate calculation was that he had no bargaining room and changed the subject.

"You know anybody else with *mota*?"

Vincente said he had a friend with almost as big a stash as his own. His weighed out at close to 165 kilos, and his friend's maybe 20 kilos less.

"What does he want for his?"

Vincente offered that his friend didn't know much about the market and had told him to make whatever deal he could.

When he lapsed into silence, Amazon made his offer. He'd pay Vincente fifteen hundred *pesos* a kilo if the Indian would tell his friend that he only got twelve hundred and let the *gringo* buy the other load at that price.

Vincente thought about it for a bit.

"What's in it for me?" he finally asked. "I'm gonna get fifteen hundred if I sell it to you or somebody else."

"This," Amazon said in a flash of inspiration. He reached into his boot and pulled out the snub-nosed revolver he'd kept for himself.

The Indian hefted the weapon.

Gnats were buzzing in the gully, and the air was getting thicker all the time. The storm at the east end of the valley had broken and was advancing toward Yagul.

"Shit or get off the pot," Amazon finally broke in.

"What?"

"Is it a deal or not?"

"Thirteen hundred for my friend and a hundred shells."

"Twelve hundred or nothin'." Amazon could sense the momentum of the bargaining shifting his way and decided against letting up. "That's a real special pistol," he lied.

It took Vincente another three minutes to give in. Amazon said he would pay Vincente half when he'd seen the load and half when he accepted delivery. In the meantime he might want the Indian to hold it for a bit. The gun was payment in advance for that too. As for his friend, Amazon wanted to meet him as soon as possible. Vincente agreed and said the gringo should come to Mitla at eight.

The other thing Henry Amazon wanted was barrels.

"¿*Barriles?*"

"That's right. Just like the kind I saw against the wall at Alejandro's *fábrica,* only empty with one end open."

Vincente wanted to know what for.

Amazon said he wanted the Indian to pack dope in the barrels after he'd weighed it.

Vincente agreed, and Amazon sealed the bargain by sending Zorro CeAttle back into the rear of the Land Cruiser for a box of ammunition. As soon as he'd received it, Vincente drove off. His last words were that he and his friend would meet them in front of the museum.

The afternoon rain began shortly thereafter. The water fell steadily in thin silver streaks, forcing the east Valley's Indian goatherds and cruising red wasps to seek the protection of bushes and trees.

Money was on Amazon's mind for the rest of the day. If Vincente's prices were any indication, Fat Albert's loan was not going to stretch far enough to cover all the expenses. He was still doing the addition over and over again in his head that evening in Mitla.

Henry Amazon knew the village from the old days when it had been his and Ramón's home base.

At eight he parked in front of the museum, twenty yards from Mitla's main intersection, and waited with Zorro in the Land Cruiser. The crossroads had been churned into a clay mush by the afternoon rain. At the roofed marketplace across the street Zapotec women were beginning to pack their wares under the pale glare of a string of fifty-watt bulbs.

It was something of a special evening in Mitla. Frank Brown's International One Tent Circus had pitched itself in the square next to the market, and crowds of Indians were waiting under the museum awning and in the market doorway. After Amazon and CeAttle had been in the village for fifteen minutes, the hurdy-gurdy had begun warming up. At the sound Indians made their way to the ticket office and went on inside. When most of the Zapotecs were either in the tent or clustered near the door, the hurdy-gurdy signaled the opening of the eight-thirty show with a flurry of steam and whistles. About the same time Vincente splashed into the village with his friend next to him in the cab of his blue and phosphorescent-orange Ford. Amazon and Zorro stepped out of the Land Cruiser and stood under the museum awning, leaning against the wall, and the two Indians eventually did likewise.

The Zapotec with Vincente was named Flacco and wore a thin yellow plastic *serape* over his shoulders. Flacco was both taller and narrower than his friend and hadn't grown a mustache yet. His milk-chocolate face, like Vincente's, was dominated by a broad nose and eyelids that appeared to droop. Flacco's fingers pinched at the folds in his khaki pants. He had never done business with a *gringo* and was visibly nervous. Amazon told the Indian that since the two of them hadn't dealt before, Amazon was going to insist on seeing his goods before they went any further, just to be sure no one was jacking him off.

Flacco said they could come and look right now if they wanted.

Amazon said it was too early for that kind of business. It was better to wait a few hours.

With several more minutes of conversation, first between the smugglers and the Indians in Spanish, and then in Zapotec between the Indians themselves, they succeeded in scheduling a meeting at midnight on the San Dionisio Road. Amazon then leaned back against the museum wall with Zorro. The two Indians mounted Vincente's truck and churned back through Mitla's enormous puddle.

Amazon continued to count money in his head. Every time he did, the numbers came up red. If he had to pay Rascón what he figured he would for holding The Kind for him, Amazon was five grand short of what it took to get all of Stage One north. Like it or not, he was going to have to call Fat Albert again.

Amazon figured it might as well be sooner than later and told Zorro to wait for him in the Land Cruiser while he made a phone call. He thought to himself that he knew how to hook the Fat Man.

Mitla's one telephone was in a five-and-a-half-foot-tall booth outside the museum's office, where the switchboard was located. Amazon lined up behind a pair of old Zapotec women on the bench and waited for his turn. Both were simply calling as far as Oaxaca, where the line was always open.

Connecting Mitla with Jersey City took a lot more doing, and the booth stayed empty for five minutes while the operator struggled to get a line to Mexico City and then Mexico City struggled to get an international opening to Jersey City. Finally the extension in the booth rang and Henry Amazon wedged himself in and took the call.

"*Bueno*," he opened.

"*¿Señor Amazon?*"

"*Sí.*"

Henry Amazon listened as Jersey City in turn got Fat Albert on the line. The Fat Man grumbled but accepted the charges.

"What's goin' on, my man? You got to have a reason for calling." Albert's voice sounded like he was standing at the other end of a tunnel.

"I'm just down here on the vacation I told you about," Amazon replied, trying to disguise his words in a spontaneous code.

"Yeah?"

"It's quite a scene."

There ensued a long silence.

"You called me to tell me that?" Albert finally blustered.

"I mean a real *scene*," Amazon persisted.

The line went quiet again for a moment on Fat Albert's end. The vacuum was filled by crackles and the ever-present buzz of the Mexican phone system.

"Scene?"

"Scene."

Fat Albert seemed to have picked up the drift of what Henry Amazon was dangling in front of him.

"Lots of nice women?"

"Virgins," Amazon answered.

"You know how I like them . . ." Albert was beginning to sound greedy instead of pissed off.

"Sure do," Henry Amazon interrupted. "I was thinking about your ass when I ran into them. Thought I might bring a few of the girls with me for you to meet."

"You got my permission for that."

"Well, I need a little travel money for them too . . ."

Fat Albert didn't respond immediately.

"You know how it is, Fat Man," Amazon continued. "I ain't as rich as you."

"I thought I made it real clear the last time we talked that I'm out on a limb cashwise, my man."

"Yeah, I remember, but I figured you could always scrape up another five for our favorite kind of dish."

"My five buys what?"

Amazon could hardly hear now because of the sputtering of the phone.

"Five," the *gringo* shouted.

While Fat Albert thought it over, Amazon noticed the line of three more Indians waiting to use the phone. They turned their eyes away from his and looked at the cracks in the museum floor tiles. Henry Amazon's neck was beginning to cramp from stooping when Albert finally spoke up and agreed.

"You'll bring them with you when I see you next?" the Fat Man in Jersey City asked. His voice was trapped deep in the receiver, and Amazon strained to hear over the hurdy-gurdy down the block.

Raising his voice, he told Fat Albert to wire the bills to him at the Hotel Modesto, Oaxaca, Oaxaca, and rang off when he was sure that the Fat Man had understood.

For the moment, he felt he had his money situation well in hand. He and Zorro returned to Oaxaca and rented the two-room bungalow in the Hotel Modesto garden.

At eleven thirty that same evening, they turned off the Puerto Escondido Highway south of Oaxaca and began wheeling through the darkened streets of Ocotlán. On the other side of the village square a dirt one-lane led on toward San Dionisio in a winding path almost due east. A dog on the edge of Ocotlán raised a howl when the Land Cruiser passed; other than that the night was quiet and still. No wind was blowing at all. The road was soon in short rolling hills and then crossed the outskirts of another village. The dirt surface changed to cobblestone, then back to dirt. Amazon watched the odometer, and after fifteen minutes he knew they were close. He was looking for a stream.

Two miles later the road finally crossed it. The streambed was one of the few in the south Valley deep enough to merit a culvert. Amazon pulled over and turned the Land Cruiser's lights off. There were crickets in the air but not much else except the occasional pop of a firefly.

"Lock and load," he grunted at his partner.

Zorro spun the cylinder in his thirty-eight, and Amazon checked the action on a thirty-two automatic. Both tucked their guns into their boots before getting out. Henry then led Zorro down the eight-foot embankment with his flashlight and followed the shallow current upstream to a spot where a cypress had fallen over the creek. There Amazon sat down on a log and switched the light off. Zorro sat beside him.

"This is the place," Amazon whispered. It was so dark he could only orient himself by instinct. He couldn't see his hand in front of his face and only sensed Zorro's presence nearby. Amazon broke the monotony regularly by pressing the button on his watch and often the glowing green numbers read exactly as they had the last time he looked.

The heavy darkness made him tense and after a while he could taste terror on the roof of his mouth. Henry Amazon worried that Zorro would notice and told himself to get his shit together. This was no time to let the Mexican see any weakness. Zorro would pry at any cracks in Amazon's act with all the leverage he could muster. He sucked a little air into his lungs, latched onto his nerve, and told himself to wait it out. It couldn't be much longer before the Indian showed up.

In fact it was fifteen minutes.

Amazon jumped when he finally felt a hand on his shoulder.

"Buenas noches."

The voice belonged to Flacco. He had no idea how long the Indian had been standing behind him.

Flacco told the smugglers to keep their light off, hold on to the tail of his *serape,* and follow him. He led them down a trail along the side of the bank until the path seemed to die in the underbrush on the edge of the stream bed. The Indian pressed on through the branches and told the *gringo* to switch his light on.

The flashlight lit up the inside of a cave twisting into the green rock of the surrounding embankment. The space was six feet tall at its mouth and got shorter the deeper it went. Vincente was inside on his haunches beside a pile of burlap bags full of dried *mota* cuttings. The Indian had his new *pistola* tucked into his belt. Amazon gave Zorro the light while he opened one of the sacks at random. The tops in the sack were thick, heavily seeded, and had little in the way of hairs.

Amazon told Zorro in English they were hardly great but that they'd do and then turned to Flacco.

"They'll do," he told the Indian.

Then he wiped his hands on his pants and explained that Flacco and Vincente's *mota* would have to be loaded into barrels. Vincente answered that he could do that, but he would need *dinero* to get the barrels from Alejandro. Amazon pulled a wad of one-thousand-*peso* notes out of his jeans and peeled several off.

The Indian spoke Zapotec back and forth in the meantime. Vincente then said his friend wanted some too.

Amazon looked up from his roll. "That wasn't the deal we made."

"*Sí, yo sé, amigo, yo sé*. But this *hombre*, my friend, he's a real country Indian, you know? He don't know any *gringos* and is worried. *¿Sabe?* A little cash for his family to eat with be real good to make himself feel better." Vincente's gold grin flashed in the beam coming out of Zorro's hand.

Amazon counted out several more bills and thrust them all to Vincente with a warning that there was no more until they met the next Wednesday to pack the barrels and weigh the load.

Back on the Puerto Escondido Highway the night was still, and the streets of Oaxaca, when they arrived, were largely empty. At two thirty-seven, by his watch, Amazon stopped the Land Cruiser at the curb a block from the Modesto and pulled a bottle of *mescal* out of his duffel in the back. He took a long hit and then passed it to Zorro after taking a little more liquor in the palm of his hand and splashing it on his shirt and around the Land Cruiser's window.

When they pulled up to the Modesto, the iron grill across the mouth of the courtyard was locked. They had to wake the Indian who slept on the driveway behind the gate. At first the watchman grumbled about drunk *turistas* but quickly changed his tone when Henry Amazon slipped him a hundred *pesos* for his trouble.

5

Their luck continued to hold Friday morning. After waking at nine, they drove to Heronimo's village, out the Pan American toward Mexico City and down twenty-three miles of dirt road.

Heronimo greeted the smugglers at his gate and motioned them into the yard. Right away Henry asked Heronimo how he was fixed for leaf. He still had close to a hundred kilos, he said, of the same *mota* the *gringo*'d bought the last time down, and he produced a sample wrapped in a piece of newspaper.

Zorro examined the weed, then rolled a little up into a joint. He lit it, passed the stick to Heronimo, who took two deep hits, and passed it on to Amazon.

"You got your load close by?" Amazon asked.

"Close enough," Heronimo answered. "Why?"

"I want to see how much space it takes."

The Indian led them to an eight-foot pile of cut cane stacked against the far wall. He dug through the bamboolike branches until he reached a tarpaulin-covered mound. Then he motioned Amazon forward to look under the canvas. A pile of burlap bags stuffed with *mota* cuttings was arranged underneath. By Amazon's estimate the whole thing would stuff into the Galaxie's trunk.

When he asked how much, he wasn't surprised to hear Heronimo say fifteen hundred *pesos* a kilo—thirty dollars a pound. That had sure enough turned out to be the going price, just as Vincente had claimed, but with Fat Albert's additional cash on the way, Amazon didn't feel he had to buck the drift.

"I'll pay that," he said, "but I'm gonna want you to hold it for a while."

The Indian thought about that. His neighbors were starting to get wise; people down at the store were kidding him that the Federales would catch him soon. He claimed he couldn't keep the *mota* for more than three days.

"Three days is fine. We'll fetch it Monday night." He pulled a wad of bills out of his pocket and peeled off a twenty-thousand-*peso* advance, which Heronimo took with a faint smile and counted carefully. "Good," he said.

As they started back to the Land Cruiser, Heronimo told them that they should be *listo* on the lookout for a soda pop truck parked out on the valley roads. His cousin in Santa Lucía Apóstol had warned him that the Federales and their *chivas* had been using it to hide in while they watched the villages. "Remember," Heronimo said. "A soda pop truck."

Driving away, Amazon felt happier than a pig in shit.

Three days in the Valley, and he already had his first thousand pounds lined up and waiting for the ride north. Three contacts and three scores. He couldn't remember ever getting loaded up this quick since Monroe Jessee had finally been run out of business in 1971. Monroe had been the number one *traficante* in the Valley then, very close to having the Oaxaca *mota* market cornered. He had bought the cops and maintained a warehouse down the Escondido Road. All a wise *gringo* had to do in those days was pay Monroe Jessee, point his tops toward Mexico City, and drive. Gomez Gordo had been Jessee's junior partner then. Monroe had finally been thrown in the state prison off the road to Mitla in September of 1971, and it had cost him twenty thousand dollars cash to escape and make his way north to El Paso where he now lived and owned a wrecking yard. Monroe Jessee's empire had splintered after his fall, but Gomez Gordo had kept a good piece of the business and a hand in The Heat's wallet ever since. As a smuggler Henry Amazon was momentarily oblivious to much else besides a strong sense of professional pride.

Zorro shared little of that feeling. The Mexican continued to resent the role he'd been assigned in their partnership and couldn't hold it down any longer. His resentment broke into the open while Amazon was in the middle of explaining the plan for the next few days. They were going back to the Modesto where he'd drop Zorro off to stay while he went by himself to find El Chorizo and get that end of things into shape. They would meet back at the hotel, and then the next morning Amazon would go alone again into the hills for one, maybe two, days to see friends and meet Rascón.

"*'Stá malo,*" Zorro blurted. "Very bad. We're partners, right? What kinda partner is it for me to sit in a hotel while you do all the business? You tell me? *Chinga!* How do I know what you're doing? Huh? You tell me how I'm gonna know—"

"Zorro . . ." Amazon interrupted with a soothing sound to his voice. "Zorro, back off a little. We been all through this. Ain't no more to talk about."

"Shit, there ain't." The muscles in the Mexican's face twitched in aggravation. "You got me walking around after you like I was your dog or something. I'm just supposed to roll your *mota* and go where you say go. What are you talking nothing to talk about? I sit in the room all weekend, and I can't even go get a piece of pussy unless I walk to get it. How do I know you're not cheating me? What do I know about nothing but what you tell me?"

"Don't give me that bullshit," Amazon said. "You watch the *mota* and the money right down to the wire. Where's to cheat, *señor Chinga?* When'd I ever run any number on you? You tell me. Go on. Tell me. Name just one time."

Zorro kept silent, and Amazon went on in a rush of words. "While you're at it you can just tell me all the other *gringos* that would give you a full quarter of the action when you ain't even worked south of Durango. You tell me all them things. Then I want to hear the part about that last Chrysler again."

Silence ensued for a moment as each tried to get his anger in check. When Amazon started up again, his tone had less passion in it but bristled with finality.

"The way it is is the way it is, Zorro. You knew the arrangement when you signed on to this scam, and after this one I don't give a shit how you do your business or who you do it with. *¿Sabe?*"

Zorro stayed silent.

"If we keep this action rolling the way it is now," Amazon added in an attempt to lighten things up, "you're gonna have enough bread at the end to buy out Gomez Gordo himself."

Zorro stared straight out at the road in silence.

Amazon poked his partner on the shoulder. "It's gonna be real good, *compadre*. You'll see. It's gonna be more *dinero* than you ever had before."

"I gonna do my part," Zorro said sullenly. "You don't got to worry about that."

When they reached the edge of the city, traffic was stopped by MPs east of the Central Barracks as four huge Dodge transports pulled out along the road, loaded with infantry, and ground away through their gears toward downtown. When traffic resumed, Amazon followed the trucks at a distance until they split to the right while he and his partner continued along the four-lane Periférico. They were headed for the Oaxaca Hertz dealership to rent Zorro a car to use while Amazon was gone. The closer they got to the center of town, the more apparent it became that something was going on.

At first there were just a lot more Indians than usual along the edges of the four-lane, trying to sell mangos, bananas, or whatever else they might be carrying. After the Land Cruiser turned north and drew closer to the heart of the city, the crowds of Indians with goods to sell thickened until the vehicle was inching along in a huge traffic jam. There were far too many of them for the sidewalks, so the Indians strolled between cars in the street. Several Zapotecs held up baskets full of sunflower seeds and dried shrimp for Amazon's inspection, but he said no. All he could find out in answer to the questions he asked was that the Army was up ahead. The crowd around the Land Cruiser kept slinking slowly south toward the river, and fresh waves of faces took their place headed in the same direction.

After ten minutes of stop-and-start Amazon finally came in sight of the Army. A line of soldiers was moving in the same direction as the Indians in a phalanx spanning the entire two sidewalks and lane-and-a-half width of the street, shoving the back edge of the crowd with their rifle butts shouting for *los indios* to go to the new market with their goods. Most of the Indians said nothing and moved grudgingly. Those who did speak up jabbered in Zapotec that the real market was in the opposite direction.

One side of the Army formation had a hole in it for cars, and a lieutenant eventually waved the Land Cruiser through with an impatient motion. The Hertz dealership was in the next block, and Amazon stood in the street for a moment after he'd parked and watched the receding mob scene.

He still had no idea what was going on, and once inside the rent-a-car office, he asked Carlos, Oaxaca's Hertz dealer, why the Indians were in the street.

Carlos said it was all about the new market. None of the Indians had wanted to go over to it when it was opened for the first time on Tuesday. They liked the old market with its fifty-foot ceilings, Carlos explained as he copied the number from Henry's Colorado driver's license. The Indians claimed the lower ceilings in the new market made their fruit rot quicker, and it was too far from the heart of the city. Carlos said he really didn't know much about it and smiled an embarrassed smile, the way he always did when politics came up.

"So the Army is making them move?" Amazon pressed.

Carlos sluffed the conversation off. "It will all work out for the best. I'm sure there's no big problem," he said. "Would you like a Dodge today?"

"No way. How about one of those new Chevies you had last time?" The dealer grinned another embarrassed smile.

"We only got Dodges today. You know how it is."

Grumbling about what a piece of shit the Mexican-built Dodges were, he took one anyway. Then he gave the keys to Zorro and sent him on his way.

When Amazon was in his Land Cruiser again, another two truck-loads of infantry passed him in a rush. The retreating Indians had moved sideways on the east-west cross streets until they had found a north-south avenue without soldiers on it, and now, like water lapping around the edge of a dike, the crowd was flowing north again toward the old marketplace in a tide of baskets and handcarts. For the moment General Fernando Vega Cortez de Corriente's troops had been outflanked, and reinforcements were being thrown in to fill the break.

Except for more soldiers, Purdee Fletcher didn't notice anything different as he walked across the heart of town to pick up his developed pictures. The Federales had no film lab of their own, so the work had to be contracted out to Pastilla's Photo Shop on the Avenue Hidalgo, much to Purd's annoyance. Not only was the security of the whole arrangement bad, but it took a hell of a lot longer. This Friday morning Purd was in a particular hurry and fetched them himself. He had to make his first oral report to Longbeem at the Mexico City Condor desk, and he wanted to take a quick scan of Hog's latest snaps to see if he could add anything more before he put the call through.

The regular truckload of troops was parked a block from the *zocolo,* and the usual two privates with machine guns were outside the door of the Banco Nacional. As Purd crossed the *zocolo* on his return trip, an eight-year old sold him the morning issue of Oaxaca *Gráfico.* The newspaper's only mention of the market controversy was a statement from the General's office to the effect that the kinks in opening the new facility would be "ironed out shortly."

When he got back to the office, Purd arranged the fresh letter-sized photos on his desk and made a list of American license numbers from the photos Hog had taken on the San Dionisio Road yesterday for Condor Central to run through the computer. When the list was finished, Fletcher lifted his receiver and told the Federale switchboard to put through his call to Mexico City.

In five minutes Longbeem was on the other end, sounding a long way away.

"Nort?"

"You got it, Purdee."

"How ya doing?"

"Real short at the moment," Longbeem snapped. "We got a lot of shit poppin' down in Michoacán, so give me the run-through quick."

"Well," Purdee began, squirming in his chair and pushing the receiver against his neck, "we got here Tuesday, like you know and—"

"What?" Longbeem's voice was washed over with a wave of crackles and then faded in again. "Speak up. I can't hear you."

"I said we got here Tuesday," Fletcher shouted. He started to go on, but Longbeem interrupted again. The boss was clearly short on patience this morning.

"Don't give it to me that way, dipshit. I don't want a goddamn diary. Just the relevant categories. How have you got your manpower deployed?"

"Grimes is out with his bird, and Wissle is doing the photo recon. I've got him working the tourist spots and the roads out to where Cruz thinks shit is being grown."

"What about you?"

Purdee cleared his throat. "I'm doing the interpretation on the recon and liaison with the Mexicans, getting a look at their suspects, reading up on their—"

Longbeem interrupted again. He wanted to know what they had in the way of suspects.

Purdee told him about the Indian he'd interrogated in the City Prison during his first evening in town. They had the Indian's Mexican boss's name now and just the other afternoon had found out that this head Mexican had a woman who worked in a whorehouse called the Cozumel.

"What other operations does Cruz have cooking?" Longbeem sounded bored, and his questions came over the wire from Mexico City in tight clusters of syllables, cut short at their ends.

Purd then told the Condor boss about his meeting the day before over lunch with Pizarro Cruz, *Jefe* Cobraa, and the Army colonel friend of Cruz's.

After the introductions the head Federale had said that he'd brought everyone together to consult on the plans for his next sweep. He was calling it Operation Sunrise, in honor of the time of attack. Cruz had said he had reliable information about more warehouses and a field in the same general neighborhood of the south Valley as his previous raid. The head Federale was planning to go in at dawn on Monday. Cruz and Ole Purd himself were going to lead eight Federales and a truck-load of soldiers into the village and its warehouses. At the same time another eight Federales in choppers would take the field, a mile away and connected to the village by footpath. Cruz's number two man, Garcia Huahilote, would command this force with Hog Wissle as his liaison and backup. Everyone who needed to had agreed with the plan, and there had been lots of talk in Mexican about the disposition of the evidence that Purd hadn't quite picked up on.

The other end of the phone was momentarily blank as though Longbeem was scribbling notes to himself.

"You got anything else?" he finally asked.

"Well, yes," Purd said, he had some license plates he wanted run. Longbeem told him to hold on and put someone named Boswell on the line to take the numbers.

Fletcher started to make small talk with this Boswell, hoping to extract a little gossip about the Michoacán stuff Longbeem had mentioned, but he got nowhere.

"Come on, Fletcher," Boswell interrupted, "just give me the numbers. We're in a stampede here."

"Purd," the Oaxaca agent corrected, "Purd."

"Okay, Purd. The numbers, please."

Fletcher read his list in a flat monotone.

"We'll run them and let you know," Boswell promised when he was done.

Purd wanted to ask to talk with Nort again, but Boswell hung up before he could. The connection dissolved into static. What a snot-nosed asshole that Boswell character was. There had been a time when Boswell would have dealt with Ole Purd a hell of a lot differently. Now Purdee Fletcher was in the doghouse, but that, he swore to himself, would not last forever. When he regained the status he deserved, he planned to repay all insults with interest.

Ray Bob Wissle spent most of his Friday in the back of a Kombi. The sides of the VW van had no windows and were painted over with ads for Green Barrels, a lemony soda pop distinguished from sixteen similar brands by its barrel-shaped green glass bottles. Two Federales disguised as Green Barrels salesmen were in the front seat and did all the driving. He didn't mind working with them, but he still felt self-conscious in their company. He rode in the back on a packing crate in the middle of the Kombi's cargo space. Flats of Green Barrels were arranged between the giant *gringo* and the window in the back door—to all passing appearances the truck was full of soda pop. The wall of bottles dipped in the middle, and after they'd parked on the San Dionisio Road so that the rèar window commanded all approaching traffic, Hog rested his telephoto on the dip and had a clean shot of a four-hundred-yard stretch.

On a map the San Dionisio Road traces a clay wiggle between the Puerto Angel Highway due south and the Pan American moving southeast. The road connects eight or nine villages as it climbs from the flat Valley floor and up and over several ascending ridges that separate two of the star-shaped Valley's three points. The Green Barrels truck entered from the Puerto Angel side and set up two villages, a quarter mile past a cornfield, at a spot where the road topped a rise and had a turnout carved off to the left side.

A little after one in the afternoon the Mexicans in the front seat stopped playing cards and broke out the lunch they'd brought along. They offered Hog a cold beef *burrito,* and he took it, along with a fresh but warm bottle of Green Barrels lemon drink. He felt sleepy when he got back on his packing crate looking out the windows. It took him a while to notice the light column of dust rising on the far side of the corn patch. It was thin and wispy but definitely visible.

In a few moments a Chevy truck with a camper on the back came into clear view between the rows of corn on either side of the road. When it was still fifty yards away, Wissle shot off a few frames to capture the truck itself, shot a few more focused on the California license plates, and then switched to the faces in the cab. The truck was approaching at a fast clip, and the cab was bouncing too much for a sure shot. From this angle his best prints would eventually prove to be the two exposures when the Chevy had slowed somewhat in deference to the VW and was only fifteen feet away—close enough for him to see three people in the cab, two men and a woman between them. Hog swiveled on his perch and leaned forward to try and shoot a few more through the wall of Green Barrels between himself and the front seat as the camper passed by. Part of the Federale's shoulder was in the frame, but it was the best Hog could manage under the circumstances. When the camper's *gringo* driver came abreast of the two Mexicans up front in the soda pop truck, he was riding with his elbow out the window. The driver raised his arm in greeting and smiled an *"adiós"* at them. Hog snapped him right between the grin and the words, when his lips were just beginning to lift apart and speak. The driver was wearing sunglasses and a shark's tooth suspended by a gold chain around his neck. As he lifted his arm, the loose short-sleeved Hawaiian shirt he was wearing fell back almost to the ball of his shoulder, revealing a small tattooed heart with an arrow through it. It was almost a week before Condor Central would wire Oaxaca Task Force that L.A. had IDed the driver as one Bruno Sawyer, a.k.a. Beef Stew, a Malibu dealer of some repute in local circles. According to the intelligence files on him, Bruno serviced a lot of the Hollywood music industry on the retail level. The tattoo would clinch the identification.

The *gringa* female next to Bruno Sawyer alias Beef Stew was never completely identified but didn't look more than seventeen. In the photo only half of her face was visible on the other side of the driver. She was blond, and round designer sunglasses covered her one visible eye, its eyebrow, and a good portion of the cheek under it.

The third *gringo* riding on the shotgun side was invisible in this snap because of the angle of Hog's view. In the two of the agent's earlier frontal shots of the camper cab that turned out best, this third *gringo* was looking back toward the truck's right rear, and Hog had captured no more than the back of his dark-haired head. He too would remain unidentified for a while.

Two hours after Beef Stew and company passed, the Federales and Wissle decided to switch roads and set up again at a rest stop off the road to Zimatlán right before the asphalt ends. Here they saw no traffic at all, with the exception of two local buses.

By four the Federales with Hog had decided to relieve their boredom by smoking a little *mota*. The driver rolled it, and after his partner took a hit, passed the burning joint to the *gringo*.

Ray Bob Wissle had smoked evidence every now and then with several guys off the airport detail when he was in San Antonio, but none of it had been as good as this Federale's smoke turned out to be. After passing the joint twice, Hog felt his skin begin to tingle a little, and then, without warning, his mind got very loose. He refused any more and silently sat with his camera pressed up against his face, focusing and unfocusing on a flowering tree across the road. For ten minutes he just got lost down the lens somewhere.

Slowly, very slowly, he drifted back into the reality of where he was. Hog's mouth was dry, almost to the point of gagging, and full of cotton-tasting spit. He popped open several Green Barrels after fumbling with them for a while and handed two forward to the Federales. Then he drained two more himself.

Soon Hog realized he had to take a piss and asked the driver to open the side door so he could get out. Hog climbed through, banging his knee on the way. He limped over to a nearby knee-high stick bush, unzipped, and with great relief produced a solid yellow stream splashing down on the plant. At the same time, the Coyotepec bus blasted by, weighed down by what appeared to be half a village of Indians, including a dozen on the roof along with the bundles. Hog was somewhat flustered at being seen in that exposed position, but he needn't have worried. Those Indians that did notice him were only interested in the fact that he was a *gringo*.

Shortly after six, to Hog's great relief, the Green Barrels truck finally drove back to the city for the evening.

Until what later became officially known as The June Terrorist Attack, this Friday evening in Oaxaca proved uneventful.

The usual throng of young Mexicans with portable radios, French and *gringo* tourists, Indians selling sunflower seeds, and dirty shoeshine boys milled about the *zocolo*. The marimba players perched on a corner of the bandstand and collected an audience twenty deep around them. The rest of the crowd strolled through the square, looking each other over. The ring of streets around the *plaza* was full of cars and trucks, mostly just cruising to see and be seen. The best vantage points were the outdoor cafés among the *zocolo*'s outer ring of shops, and all the café tables were occupied. Some places didn't close until twelve, but by then most everyone who still wanted to party had departed either for home or one of the city's three respectable whorehouses.

Henry Amazon and Zorro CeAttle were back at the Modesto's bungalow asleep. Amazon was in the bed nearest the door and dreaming.

His dream started in a crowd of Zapotec women, jabbering in dialect and waving fruit, but then suddenly switched to the small restaurant inside the museum courtyard in Mitla. He wasn't sure why he had come in there, but no one else was sitting at the tables. All the flowers in the courtyard garden were blooming, and the air was full of a soft honey smell. After a while Beano Freezer, Leroy Alabama, Leroy's black bodyguard, and Beano's old lady all came in together. Amazon couldn't hear all of what they were saying to each other, but he did pick up that it was about Ramón Ramón. Henry had expected them to greet him, but they took seats three tables away without any seeming recognition. He still couldn't hear them clearly after they were seated, but he somehow knew the subject of discussion had switched from Ramón to himself.

About that time Wanda Lamar walked into Amazon's dream. She was looking the way she had when she called herself Judy Rosenberg and still had every intention of returning to Barnard and her anthropology major. The part of Amazon that knew he was dreaming also noted that it was all a long time ago—before Wanda had run into the mountains with Ramón, before she'd fried her brain on mushrooms, before she'd taken to fucking Mexicans and going barefoot like an Indian woman. Wanda was wearing jeans that were stretched tight over her ass and much too long in the leg. She had rolled them up to a thick white cuff over her *huaraches* and wore a blue work shirt with long tails. In his dream her hair was drooping in black loops over her shoulders and down her back. Apparently she was looking around for someone: Ramón? Himself?

He was starting out of his chair to call to her when a far-off explosion rocked the room he was sleeping in, and he woke up.

At first Amazon's mind was still full of sleep, and very little in the dark room around him registered. Light was leaking under the blinds in a single flat line along the floor tiles. As he shook the grains out of his head, he began to remember the thump that had startled him into consciousness. The hotel had momentarily shivered after the sound and then settled again. The sound itself had been short and sharp and quickly mushroomed into a loud boom that had echoed around the surrounding hills.

The official version of The June Terrorist Attack issued the following day reported that at twelve forty-seven, Oaxaca time, person or persons unknown had placed at least a dozen crates of dynamite in strategic locations throughout the new market that General Cortez de Corriente had opened barely four days before. Their detonation had completely demolished an entire wall and parts of two others. The roof, deprived of a good portion of its support, had folded into the building, releasing an avalanche of masonry and steel girders down on the slab and the surrounding homes, shops, and streets. Stray pieces of brick and chunks of plaster were reportedly hurled as far as the *zocolo* by the initial blast.

The *Carteles* was the first paper out on the streets with a Terrorist Attack special edition, and Henry Amazon bought a copy in front of the Sports Palace on his solitary way to the Fuenteses' village Saturday morning. Shortly thereafter he stopped at a *torta* shop to eat breakfast and read up on whatever that noise was the night before. To make the special part of this edition more than evident, the *Carteles* printers had done the entire eight-page run in purple ink.

The front page was covered with photos of an immense pile of rubble. Despite the enormity of the blast the only casualty had been a burro belonging to an old Indian charcoal salesman. The Zapotec had been riding toward his woman's house in the squatter town by the river when an enormous shock wave had blown him off his burro and onto the sidewalk. A six-foot flying piece of steel rebar had then impaled the riderless donkey, entering the left side of its belly, proceeding through his spine, and out the other side, pinning the beast to the wall of a nearby *refresco* stand. The *Carteles* ran several shots of

77

the donkey, first pinned to the *refresco* stand, then lying dead on the street with his Indian master squatting next to the carcass, and finally inset close-ups of the wound itself.

The second page was topped with more pictures of police and Army swarming over the remains of the new market. Several featured State Police Chief Cobraa and several more General Cortez de Corriente himself, inspecting the damage. The bottom half of the page was headlined "Terrorists Attack Progress" and carried no byline.

In it *Jefe* Cobraa and the General's office were the only quoted sources. Shortly after the attack Cobraa's police claimed to have found a letter stuck to one of the City Prison gates. In it a group calling itself Fuerza del Pueblo, Force of the People, took credit for the bombing. Cobraa added that little was known about this FDP except that it was thought to be one of those groups that had sprung up since the General had assumed the governorship and shut down the university after last January's riots. Mexico City was reportedly sending a special political officer to help in the investigation.

General Fernando Vega Cortez de Corriente's office issued a short statement to the effect that the market would be rebuilt soon. "The New Market," the statement closed, "will soon stand as a model to the dignity of Mexico and her people, a beacon of strength in the face of those yellow goats who sneak around at night, trying to breed fear and unrest."

All of this struck Henry Amazon as very bad news. He knew that when police began looking for people, they had a habit of running across a lot more than they intended. His own scam would be out there where The Heat was, and Henry Amazon did not like that at all.

Back on the road edge where he'd parked it was evident the Army was still worked up over the assault. The guard at the barracks gate had been doubled, and trucks were regularly pulling in and out on the way to and from the new market. Detachments were being sent to search the university as well. While Amazon stepped through the hardened clay ruts to his Toyota, an officer's jeep pulled out at the head of another caravan. Each truck had a dark-brown private manning the fifty-caliber machine gun mounted on the roof of the cab.

The *gringo* headed out of town toward the Fuenteses' village, with a dire premonition that the shit had only begun to hit the fan.

The Fuenteses' village was a special place for Henry Amazon. He felt safe there. That he had come to feel that way was pure happenstance. Amazon had never even been to the village until Cazadero Fuentes, a total stranger, had saved his life after the *gringo*'s fight with the Huavis, four years earlier.

It had all begun when Amazon had come down to the Valley looking for a load. Amazon had intended to collect five hundred pounds to run into Texas with a Ford Econoline van. He'd checked first with a farmer near Tepuxtepec who'd said things were real slim. The only immediate supply of *mota* the farmer knew of belonged to two Huavis camped outside his cousins' village eight miles away. The pair of coast Indians had claimed to have Grade-A leaf that they'd grown deep in the mountains and hauled in. When Amazon had found them, the Huavis had produced a small sample that had indeed been fine. The price had been right, and he had arranged to pick the Huavis up that night and drive deeper into the Sierra Madre to their stash.

At close to midnight Amazon had cruised up the winding dirt two-lane with the Indians in the van's cargo area. In a short while the road had a sheer four-hundred-foot cliff off to one side. The Huavis talked to each other in hushed Spanish behind him, but Amazon had picked up enough words to know something was up.

One of them had a six-inch sheath knife, and the other a two-foot stick. Just as Amazon had spotted the headlights of an approaching third-class bus in front of him, he had also picked up a flash of sudden movement in the cargo area to the rear.

The Indian immediately behind him plunged his knife at Amazon's spine, but he had instinctively leaned forward and twisted so the weapon had dug through the meat of his back until finally deflecting off the shoulder blade. At the same time Amazon had whipped the van into a breaking slide across the path of the approaching bus. The force of the turn had thrown the Indians against the wall of the cargo compartment. Smoke and dust churned out from under the bus's wheels as it rattled to a stop twenty feet away, with the high beams flush on the Ford's side doors.

Henry Amazon jumped out. The first Huavi out after him had been temporarily blinded by the glare from the bus. Amazon had side-stepped, seized the Indian's wrist with his right hand, the Indian's belt with his left, and run toward the edge. When he'd reached the four-hundred-foot precipice, he had pitched the Huavi over, headfirst. The Indian's final sound had been a high scream that lasted less than three seconds and echoed around the canyon for another twenty. The bus driver had begun pulling around the van as the second Huavi ran up with his stick. But the fate of his friend had made him hesitate and Amazon knocked him out with a left hook. He dragged the second unconscious Huavi to the edge and rolled him over as well. This Indian had made no sound at all as he fell. The only noise had been the last snorts of the bus as it pulled out of sight down the grade.

Henry Amazon's back was running with blood from the long gash left by the Huavi's knife. By the time he had driven back to flatter ground, the wound had left him light-headed and confused. At the fork in the road he took the wrong turn and ended up on a clay track that didn't reach the pavement until the Gelatao Road thirty-five miles away. Finally he lost control and drove off the road. He had tried to continue on foot but hadn't got very far. His last vision before he passed out was of fireflies lifting hastily off the alfalfa as he pitched forward onto his face.

Cazadero Fuentes had found Amazon the next morning when he went to his field to cut food for his oxen. The Indian had loaded the half-dead *gringo* on his burro and carried him to his house by the creek in the village. The Fuenteses nursed him until he was back on his feet.

Since then, Amazon had made a point of visiting the Fuenteses whenever he was in the Valley. The village didn't grow much *mota,* so it had rarely been a matter of business as much as it was pleasure and rest. During this weekend trip out there, Amazon planned to make his base at the Fuenteses' while he went to meet Rascón on Sunday and checked out The Cockroach's crop farther up the ridge.

Most of the smaller puddles along the road to the Fuenteses' village had dried up since the last storm had come through. After an hour Amazon reached a long, relatively flat strip of valley crouching between sharp ridges on either side. The far ridge had a cube-shaped bump in its crest where a Zapotec stone fortress had been overrun with five hundred years of dirt and brush. Halfway across this flat the Fuenteses' village spread out in all the accumulated *adobe* and wood smoke of three thousand Indians. It was late enough on Saturday afternoon that the fields were by and large empty. Amazon shifted down to first when he reached the village streets.

To get to the Fuenteses' house he followed the main road as far as the churchyard. On the way he had to pass Bernardo's store where Indians drinking *cerveza* were sitting at the tiny table inside and out onto the front steps. Among them Amazon spotted Tornado, the thirty-year-old son of Esteban Maldito, who lived on the Fuenteses' street. Amazon called at him Indian style, whistling a short deep sound followed by a higher and longer shrill note. Tornado, out on the front step, first recognized the whistle and then the face in the Land Cruiser.

"Can it be? *¡Qué milagro, Tortuga!*" the Indian exclaimed as he approached the window. "What are you up to?"

Amazon answered that he'd just been traveling around and thought he'd stop in and see the Fuenteses.

Tornado then wanted to know how the *gringo* himself was. "You still got all those people trying to kill you?" he joked.

Henry grinned. "What honest man doesn't?"

Tornado laughed aloud, a belly laugh, and stepped off the running board. "That's real good, Tortuga. Like a Zapotec."

Amazon pulled away from Bernardo's and continued until the huge pink Church of the Martyrs of the Cross loomed on his right. He turned down a street that had been cobbled in stretches with rough rocks. The Land Cruiser shook and bounced another hundred yards, and Amazon turned and parked where this last clay road dead-ended at the short bluffs overlooking the village creek. The Fuenteses' was the last house on the block.

Like all Indian houses it showed a flat, windowless wall to the street, broken only by a solid, if thin, steel door. Henry Amazon knocked loudly, then pushed the door open and stepped inside. "Old man, I've come to see you," he shouted.

The door led into a dirt courtyard where the family's three bulls were tethered to the back wall along with the burro. Chickens and turkeys ran free and began a storm of clucking and long gobbles when Amazon walked inside. Joaquina, Cazadero's wife, stepped out of the room where the family ate their meals and where she and her husband slept at night. It was also the room Amazon had been nursed in.

"Enrique," the squat barefoot woman greeted him. "It is too good." Joaquina's face was the color of old leather and split into a giant smile. Her hair was braided around the top of her head, Zapotec fashion.

Amazon grabbed her outstretched hand with both of his own and tilted his head forward in the symbolic bow that is the village Indians' traditional gesture of respect for elders. Joaquina kept smiling and led Amazon into where Cazadero and his neighbor, Hermino Juarez, were sitting at the table, discussing the strange boom they'd all heard the night before. They were also eating part of a watermelon that the neighbor had brought over. A group of chickens, waiting anxiously around the Indians' feet for falling seeds, scattered when Cazadero jumped up to greet the *gringo.*

"*Qué bueno,*" Cazadero shouted, waving his slice of melon in one hand. "The Turtle himself has come back."

Amazon embraced Fuentes and exchanged *mucho gustos* with Juarez. Like Amazon and most of the rest of the village, Juarez considered his neighbor Cazadero Fuentes to be an extraordinary Indian and was proud to share a melon with him.

The oldest men in the village said Cazadero had always been that way, even when he was an orphan child herding other families' bulls. When the men from Mexico City had come to the village during the Second World War to recruit Zapotecs to be taken north under contract to pick *gringo* fruit in California, only Cazadero, then a young man and very poor, had known enough to go. All the others had been frightened to leave the village for so long and had said that if they went, the *gringos* would send them off to fight. Cazadero spent a year in the Salinas Valley and returned with enough money to build his first house and marry Joaquina. He had also been the first one to realize that the tourists in Oaxaca would buy the village's traditional cane baskets; it was he who had started selling handicrafts to the shops around the *zocolo*. Now the baskets were half of the village's economy. Because of Cazadero's past wisdom, his advice was often sought by his neighbors about everything from dreams to marriage intentions. His fields were watched carefully because it was widely believed that he knew the most about the best planting times. When disputes arose, he was often sought as a mediator. In a sense it had surprised no one when four years earlier the word had got around that Cazadero Fuentes had found a half-dead *gringo* and brought him back to his house to heal. He had been known for doing things out of the ordinary. Amazon had been accepted in the village because Cazadero had taken him in, and, given the Indians' suspicion of outsiders, the ease of it all had been a testament to the respect in which Fuentes was held.

By *gringo* standards Cazadero Fuentes didn't look like a leader. He was short and thick. His cotton shirt barely buttoned across his belly, and he wore a stained gray fedora everywhere he went. Also, a stained gray Windbreaker jacket, brown twill pants, and *huaraches*. The jacket was a habit left over from his one winter long ago in the Salinas Valley. Cazadero always said he'd been cold ever since and still remembered life in the *Estados* with shivers. He'd been glad to come home but glad he'd gone too. One of the Indian's prized possessions was a picture of himself taken more than thirty years earlier and now kept in a box on the mantel. In it he was wearing a similar jacket and hat, in front of a painted backdrop of the Bay Bridge. "San Francisco, California, 1945," was written across the back. Cazadero's young grin partially concealed the fact that he had just begun to grow the mustache that now bristled every which way on his upper lip.

"*Siéntese*," he told Amazon.

Before sitting down again himself, the Indian asked his wife to send one of the daughters-in-law to Bernardo's for a little of their number one *mescal*. It was an obligation to drink when an old friend returned. Then he sat back with his elbows resting on the table.

"So was that you we heard farting last night?" Cazadero joked.

Juarez had come over to Cazadero's house to discuss the mysterious boom of the night before. Neither of them knew that the new market had even been opened, much less blown up, and they listened with amazement when Amazon summarized what he'd read in the *Carteles*.

"*¿Una bomba?*" Juarez asked in disbelief.

"*Muy grande*," Amazon answered with a sweeping gesture of his arms. "Too much big. Too much loud and too much trouble."

The Indian laughed, and then Juarez, anxious to spread the news to the village, excused himself and left.

The two friends then discussed how the *gringo* had been doing. The Indian knew Amazon was a smuggler, but it made no difference to him. Cazadero sympathized with his loss of the Chrysler and his problems getting along with the Mexican. Then Amazon asked about Cazadero's health, and they spent half an hour talking about the stomach problems the Indian had been having. When the *mescal* arrived, Amazon and Fuentes drank off a couple of shots, and then the subject switched to the skittishness of the rainfall this season and on to people in the village.

About that time, Cazadero's two grown sons returned from taking a load of baskets into Oaxaca on the bus. They accepted a shot and confirmed Amazon's story about the new market. They said they had walked over to see it before catching the last bus. Ernesto had added that, even late in the afternoon, there had been a big crowd of people standing across the street, staring at the rubble.

Amazon next asked the Fuentes how the old man in the mountains, called The Cockroach, was doing.

Cazadero laughed. The last time anyone had seen La Cucaracha was two weeks earlier when he had walked into Bernardo's *tienda* from the hills to listen to *The Scorpions of the Valley Show* on Bernardo's radio. After it was over, the old man had walked back up the ridge. Most of the village, the Fuenteses included, thought The Cockroach was a little weird. Twenty years earlier, when he was already an old man with two dead wives behind him, The Cockroach declared that he was tired of being poor and was going into the mountains to find Cresensio's treasure. Cresensio had been a bandit who robbed the silver trains to Mexico City in the middle of the last century. He was said to have buried his wealth in stashes throughout the hills near the village. From the time The Cockroach walked into the mountains, the villagers had begun seeing the old man digging holes here and there in the overgrown countryside. Arguments broke out periodically about whether The Cockroach had found anything yet but were never resolved to anyone's satisfaction. The one thing everyone knew for sure about the old man was that one of his highest aspirations was to go to *The Scorpions of the Valley Show* and sing "La Cucaracha" on the radio. Despite his having spoken of doing so to most everyone in the village, The Cockroach had never gotten around to making the journey into town to stand in line. The village rumor was that the old man was frightened of Garcia Garcia Garcia, although others said he just didn't want to leave all the treasure he'd found. No one knew of the old man's arrangement with Amazon.

After talking about The Cockroach, more shots were drunk around the table and followed by short splices of talk about corn, Texas, and the kind of clothes *gringas* wear under their dresses. Amazon, Cazadero, and his sons all had a pretty good *mescal* buzz going by the time Joaquina and the daughters-in-law came in with some cold *tamales*.

Darkness had fallen over the courtyard by then, and the bells from the Church of the Martyrs of the Cross rang out to signify the beginning of night. When they heard the sound, the Fuenteses all rose and greeted each other and Amazon with the phrase that means "hello when it's dark outside."

Soon afterward the family went to their room to sleep, and Henry Amazon rolled his bag out in the empty room used to store baskets. He fluffed his duffel up for a pillow and lay there listening as the Fuenteses' turkeys stumbled around the dark courtyard outside.

That night the city of Oaxaca continued its routine as though the new market had never been blown up. The old market was crowded with wares, and tourists strolled through the blocks of peddlers fingering merchandise and marking bargains until well after dark. There were more soldiers stationed on the corners, but their presence hadn't seemed to inhibit a concert at the bandstand by the Oaxaca State Band. Their repertoire was straight John Philip Sousa, and the sounds they made carried throughout the valley.

For a while Henry Amazon lay on his back at the Fuenteses' picking up the far-off strains of brass music. The marches made the animals restless at first, and several dogs barked around the village. The last tune Amazon heard as he drifted off into sleep was "The Stars and Stripes Forever!"

When he awoke, bright light was washing through the open doorway and the birds were busy in the courtyard. He pulled his boots on. It was time to meet Rascón.

The meeting with the Indian Rascón was critical to Henry Amazon's plans. If things with Rascón didn't work out, there was still Gomez Gordo, but Amazon wanted to stay away from him. Rascón was a better arrangement. The Indian and his friends had access to everything Amazon wanted: top-notch Kind and a dirt airstrip behind Chichicapan in the south foothills. It was Rascón's importance that had prompted Henry to leave Zorro in town, for Rascón was easily spooked.

The Indian's meeting place system was known only to a few, and constructed so that he could control things. After leaving the rocks behind the cactus, Amazon was supposed to show up twenty miles beyond the Fuenteses' in Tlacolula on its market day and proceed to a street on the other side of the marketplace. The *plaza* across from Tlacolula's church and the streets surrounding it were full of Indians.

Amazon parked, proceeded on foot down the main street for another block past the teeming market, and then turned right at a tiny hardware store. The street here had a slight grade to it and no sidewalks. Within five minutes he could see the edge of the village, where the *adobes* stopped and the fields began. The flat surface of walls facing the street along this stretch was broken only by a dead-end alley separating the Tlacolula Rotary Club from a doctor's office. Amazon stepped into the mouth of the alley, deep enough to be hidden from the street, and waited. The alley ran on behind him another twenty feet to a steel door that led into the doctor's courtyard. On the two occasions Amazon and Rascón had used this meeting spot before, the Indian had arrived by a different means each time. Once he had jumped off a passing truck; the other time he materialized out of a doorway a half block closer to the plaza and arrived on foot. Amazon lit a cigarette and leaned against a wall, waiting. Rascón showed up five minutes later. This time he stepped out of the steel door at the dead end of the alley and closed it softly behind him. Rascón accepted the cigarette Amazon offered and leaned against the other wall, facing the *gringo*. The Indian was wearing an old brown wool *serape* and straw hat that cast shade across most of his face. Rascón fidgeted and kept glancing at the mouth of the alley when the business discussion began.

As Amazon told him how much Kind he wanted, Rascón let out a low whistle.

He then added in quick and sloppy Spanish that his friends didn't have anything close to that much around now. "All we got is the last two boxes from the harvest before," he explained.

Amazon felt a sinking feeling in his stomach.

"But my friends," Rascón continued with another look out toward the street, "will go back in the mountains in three more days to get a new crop."

"How many days till they get back?"

"Dos, quizás, tres semanas."

Amazon said three weeks would suit him fine. He just wanted to make a down payment to hold the new crop for him.

Rascón said it was one hundred dollars a pound, American money, and to get five hundred pounds, Amazon had to leave twenty percent down before Rascón's friends went back into the Sierra Madre.

Amazon tried to bargain, but Rascón was unyielding. His eyes squirmed and wandered in their sockets. Worried about blowing the connection, Amazon eventually gave in, and they smoked another cigarette on the deal. The *gringo* was to be at the arranged spot on Tuesday night to pick up the remaining two boxes from Rascón's friends and make his deposit.

Amazon left the alley first and walked back up the street without looking behind him.

On his way through the market he stopped once to buy a dozen size-C batteries as a present for The Cockroach and one more time where a young boy was working his fortune-telling bird. When a peso was placed in front of the sparrow's cage, the bird hopped out to a box full of folded paper slips, picked one out, and hopped back again to the cage where the boy gave him a few seeds. Each slip had a different fortune.

Henry Amazon put his *peso* down but never got to read about his future. Twice the bird hopped out to pick his fortune but each time returned without choosing one. Despite the boy's coaxing, the bird refused even to leave the cage. Finally the boy gave Amazon's peso back and apologized. He said his bird couldn't help *gringos* with their future.

He was a Mexican bird.

After leaving Tlacolula, Amazon tried to pass through the Fuenteses' village with as little notice as possible. Soon the Sunday band concert would begin in the church, people would gather there, and he didn't want to be noticed. He wove through the village's outer streets and rejoined the main road on the other side.

He picked up a narrow dirt road leading along the slope outside of town and followed it to where it intersected a largely overgrown tract four miles beyond the village. Amazon parked behind some cypress trees and climbed a narrow dirt path farther up the hill. The trail rose to a wide thicket and then popped out the other side and onto a relatively flat and gently rolling meadow. The Cockroach's one-room *adobe* with a thatched roof was on the far side.

The old man's wife—his third—sat next to a smoldering fire by the front door, toasting a *tortilla*. She was a nineteen-year-old mountain Indian. In the five years she and the old man had been married, they'd had three children but The Cockroach still didn't understand all her highland dialect. Today he was on the hammock inside the hut, and at first he didn't pay any attention when she began jabbering. The word *gringo* changed all that, and The Cockroach shuffled quickly out the doorway. Henry Amazon was making his way across the open space, carrying a paper bag.

"*¿Quiubo, Cucaracha?*" he shouted.

The Cockroach had no teeth at all on his upper jaw, and when he smiled a greeting, all that showed was his brown gums.

Amazon extended the bag he was carrying. "I heard you had to go into the village to listen to The Scorpions," he explained, "so I figured you must need some of these."

When the old man saw the batteries, he got very excited. "It is true," he mumbled in loud and wet-sounding Spanish. "It is a month since the last ones went dead." Then, ignoring the *gringo,* the old man shuffled back into the room to get his portable Sony radio. Amazon had given it to him nearly a year before as partial payment for growing the *gringo*'s own crop of Kind. The Cockroach listened religiously to The Scorpions of the Valley whenever he could. Amazon helped him put the fresh batteries in his set. The old Indian was so excited he wanted to celebrate immediately with *mescal,* but Amazon said he'd rather do business first.

The Cockroach slipped on his battered straw *sombrero* and, after talking in Zapotec with his wife, led the way into the nearby treeline and onto a path leading farther uphill. The climb to the crest of the ridge was a steep one, and Henry Amazon struggled along behind the old man. By the time the path turned downhill and onto the opposite slope, Amazon had sweat through the back of his shirt. Here and there gnats swarmed up from the bushes growing out over the trail Finally the old man stopped and pointed off to the left.

"Look behind that bush with the blue flowers," he said, motioning at a seemingly solid ten-foot wall of undergrowth.

Amazon pushed through the screen of foliage and broke into a small hidden clearing. Fifteen eight-foot-tall female marijuana plants were arranged in a cultivated space. All of their lower branches had been trimmed back so each plant had assumed a manicured diamond shape. The plants were topped by thick *colas* of tightly bunched, tiny leaves poking up at the afternoon light. The Cockroach had planted twenty other small clearings just like this one and spaced them throughout the face of the ridge. Amazon pushed his nose up against one of the marijuana bushes. The smell was almost of pine, only sweeter.

"They're ready," The Cockroach said.

Amazon agreed. The leaves were laced with the red hairs, and there were no discernible seed pods.

After inspecting a few more plants, he sat down under a nearby cypress and propped his feet up on two ten-gallon cans The Cockroach used to haul water from the creek two hundred yards farther down the slope.

"You did real good," he said. "They're beauties."

The old man crouched across from Amazon and accepted the cigarette he offered. "Is best when an Indian grows it," he answered. "Indians know how to talk to a plant and make it feel welcome."

Amazon lit a cigarette for himself. Far away he heard the faint strains of music as the band in the Fuenteses' village on the other side of the ridge began its concert. The players always climbed to the roof of the church so that everyone on this end of the valley could hear.

They began to discuss how the plants should be cured and packaged. By the time they'd finished, the sweat on Amazon's back had dried, and he stood up for the climb back over the ridge.

That night Amazon slept at the Fuenteses'. First Cazadero nodded off in his chair as they were all sitting around the table talking. Rather than wake him up, the sons of the family and the visiting *gringo* whispered good night to Joaquina and each other and made their way across the courtyard to their separate huts. Henry Amazon walked out into the dark yard with Ernesto, Cazadero's oldest son, and Ernesto asked him how old he was.

"Thirty-two," he said.

"You know you aren't a boy anymore," Ernesto joked.

"I know," Henry Amazon grinned. He wanted to deflect the question. "I've noticed, believe me, I've noticed."

"So how come you don't have a woman and babies?" The Indian persisted. "Don't you like to fuck?" Ernesto was getting ready to go inside and lay his wife as he'd done almost every night since she was fifteen and he twenty.

Amazon reassured him that he liked fucking a lot but that a piece of ass was different from what Ernesto was talking about. "I got enough to carry around without having to carry a full-time woman, too."

Ernesto let out a long whistle. "Is that how *gringas* are? They must be strange women," the Zapotec offered in great seriousness. "You should get yourself an Indian woman. You wouldn't have to carry her. She would carry you."

Henry Amazon laughed self-consciously and walked on to the storage room. The conversation had stirred a pang of loneliness. He was rooted nowhere or with no one. That isolation translated into pain whenever he loosened his guard. His one great love affair had been with Wanda Lamar, and that had disintegrated so long ago he could barely remember it. He had invested nothing in any woman since. He explained it as a function of his business, always being on the move, and sought consolation by telling himself over and over he would be free soon. Maybe then there'd be a chance for a life larger than himself.

7

For the pilot Emil Grimes Monday began at four thirty A.M. on the runway at the airport. Operation Sunrise was scheduled to commence in an hour.

Two Huey helicopters were parked behind the barrier, and after Grimes and the Mexican pilot, Quadrafone, turned the engines over and ran a systems check, they turned the machines off again and joined the Federale navigation officer in the corrugated metal shack on the edge of the runway. An aerial map of the valley was spread out on the table under a hanging hundred-watt bulb.

The briefing officer first pointed out the village of Morelos Lapalapan where the warehouse was. By best guess there were no more than five hundred Indians living in the settlement. Lapalapan was connected to the San Dionisio Road by a one-lane tract that crossed a ridge, circled another, and then died in a small swarm of village streets halfway up the next slope. No road led out of Morelos Lapalapan's back side. The other Federales, Cruz, Fletcher, and a truckload of troops, would be waiting for them five kilometers outside of the village. As soon as the helicopters passed over Ocotlán, they would signal the group on the road, and the strike would begin.

The chopper's target was another mile up the ridge from the village itself. The Federale pointed to a circle penciled in on the slope. The marijuana field was here, he said. The choppers would have to spot it on their way in and find a place to land. After the cultivated hillside had been secured, the pilots would ferry their force to an open alfalfa patch on the south edge of the village and join with the others.

Soon after the briefing the rest of the Federales and Hog Wissle arrived at the airport. Hog was so pumped full of adrenaline he could hardly stand it. His hands were cold and wet and drawn like magnets to the thirty-eight on his hip. Mostly he just rubbed and checked to see that it was still there. This was the real thing for Hog's first time. "Poppin' your cherry," is the way Purd had described it. Ray Bob Wissle's stomach ached in anticipation.

After Cruz's number-two man, Garcia Huahilote, issued each man an M–16 and a hundred rounds from the trunk of his car, Hog and the others waited by the sandbags for zero hour. Some of the Mexicans were making jokes about what they were going to do and waving their weapons around to illustrate their stories. Wissle kept clicking his safety on and off and laughing a little more than any of the jokes deserved.

The pilot Grimes still hadn't figured out how he felt about Hog. The junior agent was a damned sight easier for Emil Grimes to take than Purd, but both of them were so deep into cops and robbers they made Grimes uncomfortable. Grimes didn't trust people who took themselves that seriously. They had a way of making everyone else, including their employees, expendable. Hog's passion for his work was decidedly adolescent, but Purd was a different case. From the first time they'd met in the Mexico City Embassy, Emil Grimes had sized up the aging cop as a load of shit with a badge in its pocket. He didn't go for the "Ole Purd" number or any of his other boss cop roles. In Mexico City Grimes had the first sinking feeling in his stomach. He'd gone and put himself in the hands of assholes again, something he'd sworn never to repeat when he walked out of the First Air Cavalry with his discharge papers in 1971.

On the runway by the Federales' choppers, Emil Grimes reminded himself his contract was just for three months and then he'd have enough money to hold him until he found another crop-dusting gig.

At 5:30 A.M. the pilots were told to saddle up, and when the engines were warm, the rest of the strike force divided themselves between the two birds. Hog rode with Grimes as second in command of this half of Operation Sunrise and manned the intercom in the belly of the ship.

When the first line of dawn light appeared on the far column of mountains, the choppers lifted off and flew side by side due south. Both were painted light blue and seemed to glow a bit in the still dark sky. When Grimes spotted Ocotlán, Garcia Huahilote got on the radio in Quadrafone's ship to notify his boss and the *gringo* Purd, who were down on the road to Morelos Lapalapan.

"*Azul Uno a Salido del Sol.*"

When the radio crackled, one of the two Federales in the front seat of Pizarro Cruz's black Ford four-door unhooked the microphone and handed it to his *jefe* in the backseat.

"*Jefe aquí,*" Cruz responded over the air.

"Ready," Garcia shouted over the clatter of helicopter blades.

As soon as the chopper force signed off, Cruz's driver signaled the rest of the caravan with his headlights, and the charge down the Lapalapan road began. A two-year-old Chevy carrying four Federales was in the lead, followed by Cruz's brand-new Ford, an unmarked Kombi with two Federales in the front seat, and a lumbering Dodge transport full of infantry. Recognizing the relative speed of the vehicles, Pizarro Cruz had divided his road force into two elements. The Kombi would stick with the slower army truck while Cruz followed the charge of the Chevy. Right away, it proved impossible to stay as close to each other as Cruz had planned.

Domingo Santa Fe was steering the Chevy, and he was famous among the Federales for driving like the devil. Purd and Cruz were thrown against each other as Cruz's car tilted and bounced over rocks and deep ruts in a frantic attempt to keep up. By the time the lead Chevy stormed into the outskirts of Morelos Lapalapan, it was a block and a half in front of the command car. The one-lane road dropped momentarily as it entered the village, and the Chevy sailed over the dip and slammed into the rise on the far side, shattering Santa Fe's front left shock absorber. The belly of the car touched bottom long enough to find a sharp and substantial rock poking out of the clay. The obstacle tore the Chevy's oil pan open but didn't stop the charge. Trailing a continuous spray of oil from the car's underside, Domingo Santa Fe kept accelerating up to where the road made a T and drifted through a hard right-hand turn.

The target was a house located a long block down this street on the next corner. Aside from the door leading into the street, the only exit was a pair of cane gates. The gates were the Chevy's objective. Cruz's plan called for the lead car to crash through them and into the courtyard of the house, while the Ford covered the door. As the gates came into view, the Chevy's now oilless engine was beginning to make high knocking sounds and hissed steam out of several hoses. Instead of echoing throughout the heretofore quiet village, the noises the car made were drowned by the roar of the choppers passing over Lapalapan on their way to the field on the other side. The helicopter racket set off a hundred dogs and twice as many donkeys. A woman starting out one of the passing *adobe* doorways saw the Chevy screaming down the street and ducked back inside to hide. A group of turkeys headed for the same door and were picked off by Domingo Santa Fe's bumper and splattered.

The cane gates at the warehouse proved to be as insubstantial as Cruz had expected and provided no barrier to the onrushing Chevy. Something Pizarro Cruz hadn't thought of proved a more significant problem.

One of the oxen tethered against the target house's courtyard wall went berserk in the terror inspired by the choppers and pulled loose from its nose ring. The two-thousand-pound beast was right behind the gate when Santa Fe crashed through it. The ox had just enough time to duck its head before the Chevy hit. The impact drove the beast's neck back into its shoulders and flung the carcass against one of the posts holding up the house's overhanging roof. The post shattered, and pieces of tile clattered down in swarms of plaster dust and wood splinters as a portion of the overhang collapsed. The Chevy's radiator was forced back into the fan as its front end crumpled against the ox and clouds of steam billowed over the hood when it screeched to a stop. Three Indians ran out of the doorway farthest to the right, hoping to get over the wall, but stopped when a warning burst from an M–16 stitched across the *adobe*. Immediately they put their hands over their heads. Three other suspects tried to hide in the house and were rounded up without resistance. One last man tried to sneak out the front door and walked straight into Purd's leveled thirty-eight.

"Don't even twitch, creep," the *gringo* said in English, "or Ole Purd'll blow the front of your head out the back."

The Indian didn't understand a word but sank to his knees anyway and lifted his arms up over his head. By the time the Army arrived, the warehouse was under wraps. Two of the rooms were packed to the ceiling with freshly cured *mota*.

The rest of the Indians' crop was still out on the hillside.

The field there ran up the slope in a scraggling acre-and-a-half patch, and the Operation Sunrise choppers spotted it on their first pass. The only place flat enough to set down was above the field, and it was only large enough for one chopper at a time. Garcia Huahilote said his force would land there and wanted the *gringo* pilot Grimes to drop his load below the field so they could sandwich anyone out working the hillside. Because of the steepness of the slope, Emil Grimes said he would have to hover and let his passengers jump out when he was as low as he could safely get.

The maneuver was a tricky one, and Grimes warned Hog over the intercom to be sure to jump out the front corner of the cargo hatch, facing uphill, so the fall would be the shortest possible distance. The warning was in vain. In his eagerness to get into action Hog had already stripped his earphones off and was poised in the back corner of the hatch with one foot on the skid. He jumped when the chopper was six feet over the hillside. As soon as he did, he realized he'd forgotten to calculate how much the angle of the slope was going to pull him off his planned drop. On the way down, he felt himself begin to tumble. The tumble accelerated when he reached the ground, and his M–16 went flying out of his arms. Hog hit with a resounding thump, cartwheeled over onto his face, and slid down the cultivated slope. To break himself, the junior agent had to seize onto a long stalk of marijuana with each hand and dig the toes of his boots into the soil. Ray Bob "Hog" Wissle came to a stop thirty yards lower than any of the Federales who jumped after him. The *gringo*'s hands were covered with *mota* resin.

At first Hog just lay there trying to get his senses back. He couldn't figure out where he was or where his rifle had gone. The thirty-eight was still strapped in its holster, and the first light of day was splashing over the upper reaches of Morelos Lapalapan's marijuana field.

The chopper force collected three Indians in its attack on the hillside. These Zapotecs fled downhill to escape Garcia Huahilote's men and ran right into the arms of the Federales with Hog. All three had their hands tied behind their backs and were thrown into Quadrafone's chopper waiting on the flat spot above the *mota* farm.

During all of this Grimes hovered at two hundred feet where the scene below was no more than stick figures scurrying about. Eventually the Huey on the ground revved up, and Garcia got on the wire. He, Hog Wissle, and two other Judicial Federales were taking the prisoners down to meet the force in the village. Grimes would land and wait for the remaining Mexicans to collect the "evidence." Then he would haul it and them down to Morelos Lapalapan.

While Grimes waited, on the ground the Judicial Federal moved from plant to plant with garden clippers, cutting off the best tops and tossing them into heavy-duty American-made garbage bags. It took two hours, and as they worked, the tide of advancing yellow sun spread across the valley floor, puddling in the open stretches. Waiting by his machine, Grimes could pick out the soft haze of cooking fires all along the San Dionisio Road. In Morelos Lapalapan he could see the pattern of the village itself and the other bird parked in the alfalfa field on the edge of town. Some Indians moved about on the opposite side of Lapalapan from the warehouse, but the closer streets were conspicuously empty. A lone Federale was lounging near the Huey with a rifle. The remaining elements of Operation Sunrise were all at the scene of the crime.

When Hog and Garcia had arrived at the village warehouse, Cruz's men had all their suspects kneeling in a line across the dirt courtyard on the other side of the wrecked Chevy. The Army was leaning up against the wall with their weapons on safety. The Federales stood close to their captives, sometimes nudging them with a rifle barrel, sometimes asking them if they were nervous. The Indians from Morelos Lapalapan believed that Federales have evil eyes, and they tried to avoid their gaze. The cops in the courtyard played with them, sometimes kicking them or spitting in their faces. The interrogations themselves were taking place inside the warehouse in an empty room. Cruz, Purd, and two others questioned each in turn. Mostly it was Cruz's show, and Purd did little but display his Big Ten pictures with no results. The waiting Indian suspects could hear the sounds from inside. A few winced visibly. The prisoners from the field were added to the line, and Hog sat on Domingo Santa Fe's Chevy. One prisoner tried beseeching the *gringo* in Spanish that he had nothing to do with no *mota* but had just stopped by the house on his way to the grocery. Wissle turned away and began making small talk with some of the Federales. One of them said the *Jefe* had called the State Police on the radio to send a wagon for the prisoners and a wrecker for Santa Fe's car.

From his vantage point on the ridge behind the village, Emil Grimes was the first to spot the approaching State Police column. In addition to the two vehicles they'd been expecting, there was a flatbed truck for hauling evidence, a Volkswagen bus for hauling prisoners and *Jefe* Cobraa's car in the lead. In the field below Grimes saw that the Judicial Federal had almost finished the last stage of their work with the evidence. They had waded through the field with *machetes* and toppled all the plants already stripped of their tops. These were stacked in a pyre in the middle of the field. Then they had doused them with aviation fuel and set it all on fire. The sooty smoke drifted straight up in a long column. Grimes noticed that there was almost no wind at all until he started the chopper and scattered the marijuana cloud in all directions.

Once he had deposited the Federales and their evidence at the alfalfa field, the pilot walked into the village with two of the Mexicans to see what was happening at the warehouse. It was 10 A.M.

The first thing Grimes saw up the street was the wrecker with Domingo Santa Fe's Chevy in tow. The ox carcass was piled up in the soldier's truck, ready for division amongst the soldiers' families at the barracks. Inside the splintered cane gates the *mota* confiscated at the warehouse had been piled in a giant mound, and beyond it the prisoners were kneeling in a row. Standing in another line behind them was a selection of Federales with their weapons. Cruz was on one end of the line, and *Jefe* Cobraa on the other. The *Jefe* had come out just to partake in this final ritual. He had also provided the photographer, a short brown man crouching twenty feet away from the posed cops and their captives, trying to capture it all in his camera's viewfinder. The Federales pulled their suspects' heads back so their faces stood out. Three of the pictures would run the next Wednesday morning in the *Carteles* along with a story about the nine narcotics traffickers and the six tons of *mota* that had been seized in Morelos Lapalapan. All the Federales' features were blacked out with heavy bars of ink.

Jefe Cobraa's would be the only police face that remained visible to the public. He had sunglasses on and a smile full of very white teeth shaped like lizard eggs.

When the picture taking was done, Operation Sunrise began getting itself together for the journey back to town. Finally all the cars were started and a layer of auto exhaust and *adobe* silt had been raised twelve feet in the air. Through it all Hog Wissle felt a deep sense of unease. He'd jacked himself up for all the action he'd expected, and when it happened, he was on his belly down the slope. His body was full of leftover adrenaline, and his mind obsessed with embarrassment. During the long wait Hog had overheard several Federales laughing at the story of the giant *gringo*'s leap from the helicopter. Several more had grinned at Hog in a knowing fashion. He felt desperate for some way to redeem himself and rescue his reputation before the operation was over.

The opportunity he was looking for presented itself almost immediately.

As the prisoners were being walked to the Kombi, the Federales overseeing them were bored and distracted. Assuming the captives had learned their place during interrogation, they expected no further trouble. But one seventeen-year-old Indian, thin as swamp grass, figured he might be able to get away. He bolted out of the line past the Federales and within seconds was in the open, sprinting barefoot up the mud street with his arms still handcuffed behind his back. Everyone was caught flatfooted except Hog.

Hog instinctively responded to the Indian's movement and became the middle linebacker intent on making the game-saving tackle. The fleeing suspect had a little lead on him, but the length of his stride soon made up for that. Within thirty yards Hog was pounding in the Indian's footsteps. As he prepared to leap onto the suspect's back and collapse him onto the ground, it looked for a moment like the *gringo* had made another serious miscalculation.

101

Just as Hog launched himself, the seventeen-year-old Indian stooped over and put on the brakes. The giant *gringo* flew over him, hitting empty air with his arms and only managing to touch the Indian with his feet on the way to his approaching belly flop in the dust. That was enough to flatten the suspect but not stop him altogether. With surprising quickness he got back on his feet and started running again. This time he got three strides and no farther. With even more surprising quickness Hog Wissle had sprung up swinging and caught the suspect with a right cross in the middle of his onrushing mouth. The blow knocked the suspect out, dislocated his jaw, and broke three teeth off level with the surrounding gums. Hog stood over the unconscious Indian for a moment, breathing hard with his hands on his hips.

The stunned crowd of police and soldiers down the block broke into a spontaneous cheer.

Dusting himself off, Hog made a grinning stage bow in their direction, and they cheered again.

From that time on Ray Bob Wissle began to feel much more at home.

Minutes later, when Purdee Fletcher approached him and said that he, Cruz, and the *Jefe* Cobraa were taking one of the choppers back to Oaxaca and invited Hog to come along, Hog declined. He said he would rather stay with his "men."

Hog's shirt and pants were dirty and torn. Smudges on his arms were mingled with crusts where blood had rushed in to cover missing skin, but the enormous *gringo* liked these signs of combat and the idea of parading back through "enemy territory," looking like he'd just weathered hand to hand battle.

As the caravan out of Morelos Lapalapan wound down to the San Dionisio intersection, Hog was in a state of quiet ecstasy. The Indian farmers beside the road didn't know what to think when the lead Ford passed with the giant, mean-looking *gringo* in the front seat, but after two more vehicles went by, they turned their heads away as though by not looking they would not be seen. By the time the infantry truck rattled past, last in line with its extra cargo of dead cow, the Indians had quietly slipped into the corn and disappeared.

It was the same in the village of Ocotlán. Children stared, but everyone else looked at walls or stepped back into open doorways. For the first time since he'd come to town, Ray Bob Wissle felt like he didn't have to worry about staying on top of whatever was going on.

"It was real good," he finally said to Garcia Huahilote in Spanish.

Garcia was in a fairly mellow mood himself. "It was good," he agreed. "We made those Indians piss and cry like women." The number two Federale guffawed several snorting sounds and slapped the *gringo* on the thigh.

"It's all part of what we get paid for," Hog answered with a studied nonchalance. Then, almost as an afterthought, he slapped the Mexican's thigh in turn.

Back in Oaxaca, the vehicles double-parked in front of the Federal Building, heading the wrong way on a one-way street, and drew a lot of attention. Hog stayed outside with the group of Federales watching the evidence while the prisoners were being booked inside. Marijuana tops poked out of the mouths of the sacks packed in the truckbed. Passing *turistas* gawked at the scene, especially when they noticed the massive *gringo* who'd obviously been in some kind of tussle.

Ray Bob Wissle met their looks with one of his own, full of hard-ass. Without thinking about it he flexed his arm so that the bicep rippled beneath his polyester shirt. He felt eyes on his shoulders and the side of his head, but he enjoyed hanging around where strangers could get a look at what a bad motherfucker he imagined himself to be.

From this time on Hog Wissle would become increasingly impressed with himself. He would hero-worship Purd less and less. More than a month later that change in Hog would isolate Purdee Fletcher completely.

Back in Oaxaca on that same Monday Henry Amazon felt his luck had begun to turn. The feeling was a vague one. Certainly nothing dramatic happened when he rejoined his partner at the Modesto. Fat Albert's money order hadn't yet arrived, but Amazon had figured Albert would be slow and didn't really expect the money until Tuesday. Still he was worried. The Fat Man's cash was essential, and some intuition kept telling him problems were going to arise. He decided to place a call to Jersey City through the hotel switchboard. But when the operator finally made the connections, a woman answered the phone and said Fat Albert wasn't there. Amazon rang off and continued to worry while wasting the morning around the swimming pool with Zorro.

At noon the two smugglers got dressed, and Amazon, in the Land Cruiser, followed Zorro down to the Hertz dealer to return the rent-a-car. They planned to drive back to the Modesto for lunch, then go to Chorizo's. The afternoon streets were full of diesel smells and hand-carts selling soda pop. On the return trip to the hotel Amazon stopped at the railway station to place another call, but Fat Albert still wasn't home. Amazon slammed the receiver down and trotted back across the street. Zorro CeAttle was watching his every move. The Mexican knew something was up.

Amazon himself was in a quandary. He wanted to tell his partner what he was feeling but didn't want that to be taken as an admission that any hitches were developing in the scam. That kind of confession would only invite scorn and inevitably provoke some comment about the shape of their partnership. For a moment the *gringo* said nothing, just climbed behind the wheel and stared straight out the windshield at the glare of the street in an attempt to avoid Zorro's eyes.

"What's going on?" Zorro finally asked. "You've been jumping around all day."

"Nothin'," Amazon answered. He didn't turn his head. "It's nothin'. Just a feeling I've been getting about that *dinero*."

Zorro rubbed the hair on his lip and stared at the side of his partner's head. "Didn't that *amigo* of yours say for sure he was gonna send it?"

"'For sure' is what he said all right," Amazon admitted, "but 'for sure' means a lot of different things to a lot of different *gringos*." Amazon finally turned to look through his shades at his partner. "*¿Sabe?*"

"*Yo sé,*" Zorro gestured at his chest with a certain amount of bitterness. "I know. For sure, I know." The Mexican looked straight at Amazon. The unease that had come over his partner made the Mexican feel perversely comfortable. He sensed a potential advantage in the situation and wanted to let him stew.

Amazon turned away. His voice now assumed its business tone. "It ain't nothin' to worry about now. We got other things to do." He started the Land Cruiser and quickly changed the subject. "This afternoon," he began, "we're . . ."

His words were drowned out by a passing caravan of dump trucks grinding their way out of town with several tons of rubble from the remains of the new market. All of them had straight pipes and made a noise roughly equivalent to that of a B–17. When they passed, Amazon started again.

"After we eat, we're goin' out to Chorizo's place and get the load car ready for tonight."

Zorro nodded in silent agreement.

"Then tomorrow night we're goin' out to meet with Rascón and his friends."

"Both of us?"

"Both of us."

The news pleased Zorro. He was tired of hanging around and wanted to make a connection with these mysterious people who sold the super dope. If the *gringo* really did go out of business when this scam was over, his partner wanted to be able to come back for more on his own.

Later, at Chorizo's, Amazon and his partner lined the Ford's trunk with a double thickness of green garbage bags. Then they left, telling El Chorizo they would be back to pick it up at ten thirty.

At ten thirty the blanket of gray clouds that had been hanging over the valley all day erupted in the darkness. Water was running every which way along Chorizo's street, and the air stank of wet sewage. Zorro ducked his head, pulled his poncho over it, and dashed for the garage doors. After swinging them open, the Mexican started the load car and drove it out into the storm. Amazon pulled the Toyota into the Ford's place, shut the garage, and hopped into Zorro's car on the passenger side. He was glad for the downpour. The headlight beams were full of slanting rain stripes and mud splashes. He was sure the Army wouldn't be running roadblocks on a night like this.

The Pan American was clear of obstacles, but the twenty-three miles of clay into Heronimo's village were covered with gobs of mushy red mud. It churned under the treads and clumped off the car's under-belly. The night outside was thick and seemingly empty. As soon as the headlights passed, the wall of blackness sealed up again.

Amazon checked the green numbers on his watch face. At midnight the road dipped through a small creek on the outskirts of the village and Zorro turned left onto Heronimo's street. The Indian heard them coming and opened his gate. Earlier in the day, when it had become obvious that heavy rain was on the way, he had moved the *mota* into his shed.

The three of them stood in the darkness until Heronimo lit his candle. Then they saw the weed. It was piled in one corner, and Heronimo had erected an old set of scales next to it. The *gringo*, his Mexican partner, and the Indian spent the next hour crouched over the scale, determining how much the load weighed and figuring up the price. Amazon then paid the Indian, pulling thousand-*peso* notes off the roll in his pocket.

Outside the rain was still falling steadily when Zorro backed the Ford up to the shed door for loading. They crammed the *mota* into the trunk and then sat together on the wet trunk lid to force it closed. Afterward Amazon and Zorro got in the front seat. The Indian stuck his head in the passenger window.

"*Qué le vaya bien,*" he smiled.

"*Adiós,*" the *gringo* responded.

Heronimo sloshed over to open the gate and watched the Ford until it disappeared through the storm.

The rain slowed to a drizzle, but by the time they reached El Chorizo's housing project, a fresh wave of thunderheads had rolled in. The men exchanged vehicles and, inside the house, Amazon paid a groggy Chorizo the next installment of the garage's rent.

But in the Land Cruiser Zorro lit a joint and took a deep drag before passing it to Amazon.

"One down, two to go," the *gringo* rasped as he exhaled a mouthful of smoke. They still had two other loads to pick up before they could head north. Amazon knocked on the dashboard for luck.

Despite his relief at having Heronimo's *mota* ready to travel, Henry Amazon continued to worry.

"What the fuck is Fat Albert up to?" he wondered as he headed back to the Modesto. "And why am I so goddamn antsy about it?"

On Tuesday Fat Albert's telegram hadn't arrived, and no one picked up his phone in Jersey City all day. That night the sky was a black sheet, pierced with pinholes of starlight.

At 10 P.M. the Toyota pulled out of the Modesto's courtyard and drove east on the Pan American. Amazon and his partner followed past the spot where Rascón's message had been left the day before and went farther on the dirt lane that wound steadily deeper into the mountains. The surface was still sloppy, and the *gringo* kicked the Toyota into four-wheel drive.

He was looking for three boulders clustered together on the right-hand side of the road. When they reached the landmark, Amazon parked the Land Cruiser behind some bushes, and they continued on foot. A path dipped through the undergrowth and led into a meadow where the grass was tall and gorged with rain. As the smugglers walked, fireflies swarmed out of their way, winking and making popping sounds. The trail led back into the underbrush and finally reached another meadow smaller and rockier than the first. An *adobe* hut was crouched on the far side with a dozen Indian shadows near it. "I'll do the talking," he whispered to his partner as they approached the hut.

The reminder rankled Zorro, but he said nothing.

An Indian stepped away from the rest of the shadows and greeted the two smugglers. *"Buenas noches,"* he said from under the brim of his hat. It was Rascón.

"Buenas noches," the *gringo* answered. *" 'Stá mi amigo Zorro,"* he added, motioning at his partner.

"Mucho gusto."

"Mucho gusto," Zorro smiled.

"We go inside," the Indian said in clipped Spanish.

The other men in the clearing kept their distance and watched. They were all dressed in twill pants, T-shirts, and *huaraches*, but none of their faces were visible in the dark. Rascón motioned for Amazon and Zorro to follow him into the hut.

The one room was lit by a single candle, stuck to a low wood table in the corner. Two men were waiting in its pale glow. Rascón introduced the first as Juan. He was obviously an Indian.

Rascón's second friend was introduced as *"Mi amigo, El Cubano,"* and although dressed like an Indian, he had a whole different set of features from Rascón and Juan. The Cuban had much paler skin that had only recently turned brown and thick-looking from the sun. His face had none of the sharp jawline or high cheekbones of Zapotecs—it was fleshy and much wider than the Indians', and his thick black mustache only accentuated the width.

Zorro was taken aback. Amazon had never mentioned there were Cubans in these hills.

"¿Cubano?" the Mexican blurted.

El Cubano looked Zorro over from head to toe several times. *"Si,"* he finally smiled. "It is a nickname."

Amazon himself had seen The Cuban twice before. The first time was while arranging a planeload for a Canadian through Rascón. Then this Cuban and several of his countrymen had been at the airstrip when they loaded out. The second time he had negotiated with El Cubano himself for another scam that had fizzled when Amazon had been unable to pull his end together. Amazon knew the band The Cuban was attached to controlled a big piece of turf deep in the Sierra Madre and produced fine *mota,* but that was all. The presence of Cubans usually meant politics, but Henry Amazon had no idea of what sort. They were in the business for the money, and Amazon didn't want to know the uses it was put to. On such questions ignorance was the safest stance. Amazon mostly thought of The Cuban as someone a long way from his native country and identified a little with him because of it.

El Cubano did most of the talking for the two Indians. His eyes watched everyone in the room. At first he was leery because of the difficulty he and the *gringo*'d had with their last business.

"What can I tell you I haven't told you before?" Amazon responded. "Some of 'em come together, and some don't. That's the way it works, like I told you at the time. I didn't leave you out on a limb, and I know you offed the *mota* real quick after I pulled out 'cause I sent you the dude that bought it. *¿Cierto?*"

"*Cierto,*" The Cuban agreed.

"Besides," Amazon promised, "this one is goin' to happen. My end's real straight."

The Cuban wanted one hundred dollars a pound in American cash and twenty percent down just like Rascón had said. There was little use trying to bargain, but Amazon did so, just in case The Cuban had changed his way of doing business. The Cuban hadn't.

Eventually Henry Amazon agreed and started to pull several rolls of hundred-dollar bills out from under his belt.

The Cuban watched and motioned to Rascón. Then the Indian went to the door, said something in Zapotec, and immediately two Indians brought the boxes inside and set them down on the wooden table.

The boxes were normally used for packing thirty dozen eggs. Now each was full of twenty small bundles of seedless *mota* tops, each bundle delicately tied in three places with twine. Henry Amazon spread a piece of Saran Wrap on the table near the candle, opened the first box, plucked out several tops, and laid them on the wrap. Carefully Amazon examined one. It was a deep, rich brown leaf with streaks of gold and forests of tiny red hairs that stood out when he held it up to the faint light. The leaf wadded up under the pressure of Amazon's fingertips and left them gummy and sweet smelling. Henry Amazon couldn't spot a seed in any of the samples.

"Is what I'm gonna be getting later this good?" he asked The Cuban.

"Better," The Cuban said. He smiled again.

Amazon wrapped the sample up and tucked it into his boot. They arranged for Amazon and Rascón to rendezvous in the Tlacolula alley once again in three weeks. If Amazon didn't show, Rascón would return the next week. If Amazon still hadn't returned from the north by then, his down payment was forfeited, and Rascón and his friends would sell the weed elsewhere.

Rascón and The Cuban went with the *gringo* and his partner to the door.

Amazon turned to look at them. He wondered when The Cuban would come out of the hills and, like himself, call it quits. The Cuban too must have something more that he wanted, Henry Amazon thought, and if he did, he would never find it here. Dreams didn't come true in Mexico; they just got unbearable.

"*Hasta luego,*" Amazon said.

The night outside was quiet. None of the armed shadows moved or said anything. Zorro led the way into the underbrush. Both he and the *gringo* were carrying a box of Kind.

After they reached the Land Cruiser and were churning along the dirt road toward the Pan American, Henry Amazon let out a deep breath to try and reduce some of the tight feeling across his chest.

"Well we're down to it now, partner," Amazon told Zorro, motioning at the wallet in the back pocket of his jeans. "We don't even have enough to pay Vincente all the way off, much less get north."

Zorro said nothing. The cab was dark, but the *gringo* was convinced he saw a smirk play across Zorro's cheeks.

Fat Albert's wire had better arrive by tomorrow. Henry Amazon could sense his control of the whole scam slipping. He felt like a man on the back pedal; all he could do was hope against hope his luck would hold.

Agent Purdee Fletcher was all the while feeling more and more like things were going his way. Purd had begun to adjust to his new circumstances and had hit his investigative stride. Operation Sunrise had left the senior agent in an optimistic mood as well. Condor Director Norton Longbeem had been very pleased when Purd called in to announce the Monday raid's success. The numbers would look good on the Condor scorecard, and although they would be credited to the Federal and Pizarro Cruz, credit would rebound indirectly to Purd as their chief American adviser and Condor liaison. Fletcher would rather have been at the head of the list, but at this point he had no choice but settling for reflected glory. He knew, though, that he would soon have to find a way to focus the spotlight on himself. Comebacks were not made in obscurity.

Pizarro Cruz could guess what Purd was thinking. The Mexican had clawed his way up the federal ladder with no family connections to speak of and was an experienced bureaucratic infighter. He did not want competition, and he had watched the *gringo* Purd long enough now to be sure the American was competition personified. Pizarro Cruz liked to operate in the removed position of his *jefe* role with all movement of information confined to a one-way ladder from himself down. Since Purd had settled in, that pattern had been increasingly disrupted by the *gringo's* meddling and suggestions. The more initiative he took, the more credit he would claim. Purdee Fletcher was always sure he knew the best way to do everything, and it irritated Cruz immensely.

On Tuesday evening Fletcher was continuing his behavior at a meeting between the head *gringo* and the Judicial Federal chief in Cruz's office. It was supposed to concern itself with the mechanics of transferring operational funds from the Mexico City Condor books to the Oaxaca task force, but Purd immediately pushed it into a series of nagging questions about the wisdom of Pizarro Cruz's troop deployment. If the discussion had been allowed to continue without interruption, there was every likelihood of an argument. Cruz was restraining himself in deference to Purd's pivotal role in channeling *gringo* money into his command, but his self-control was slipping fast. As always when he was angry, Pizarro Cruz lit a cigarette, took several puffs, and crushed it out.

Then one of Cruz's men rushed into the room. The Federal *jefe* bridled visibly at the absence of a knock on the part of his underling and only lessened that demeanor slightly when the agent said it was very important. El Tasajo had been found.

Purdee Fletcher's ears perked at Tasajo's name. El Tasajo was the missing suspect who had hired the three Indians Purd had inspected during his first night in town. It was Purd who had pushed Cruz from the beginning to chase down that lead, and it was Cruz who had resisted. Only after Operation Sunrise had been a raging success did Pizarro Cruz assign four of his men to press the search. On this, their first day at it, they had already scored. Although Cruz recognized that the capture did credit to the training of his men, it was also very much a strike in Purd's favor. It had been Purd's idea, and the *gringo* would tell exactly that to Mexico City. He would also want even more credit from whatever came out of it. The accuracy of Pizarro Cruz's assessment was apparent as soon as Purd got the drift of the Spanish report being given to Cruz.

"Where'd you find him?" the *gringo* interrupted.

The agent who was reporting spoke no English, was confused by the interruption, and lapsed into a silent questioning look at his *jefe* about how to respond to the *gringo*. Pizarro Cruz had been caught off guard by Purd's presumption and translated the question. In Pizarro Cruz's scheme of things that momentary reversal of roles was another score for the *gringo*.

The agent's answer was even another. As Purd had argued from the beginning, El Tasajo had been found by watching his woman.

When he walked into the arms of the Judicial Federal, Gabriel Penitente alias El Tasajo or The Piece of Meat was taking his girl friend to a job as a cocktail waitress at the Cozumel whorehouse. He was driving a battered Vokswagen sedan that burned oil badly. Tasajo parked his old car in the alley that dead-ended at the Cozumel under the broad tree with white flowers that Mexicans call Water of the Rain. The Mexican was up to his ears in domestic relations and had momentarily dropped his guard even though he knew from his mother that the Judicial Federal had been looking for him. The suspect and his woman were arguing about the icebox he had promised but so far failed to buy. El Tasajo kept excusing himself by saying that things hadn't been going well for him. When he said so, the small-time *mestizo* had no idea just how true his statement was about to prove to be.

The Federale in charge of the Condor stakeout awakened Tasajo to the fact by sticking a forty-four revolver in his ear.

"*Buenas noches, señor* Piece of Meat," the Federale said in Spanish. "We been looking to talk with you."

El Tasajo came within inches of fouling himself on the spot. He felt his stomach go cold and drop into his bowels but was able to cinch his asshole tight enough to keep it from going any farther. The fiber in his arms seemed to have dissolved as well. Tasajo wanted to say something but couldn't think clearly or group any words into a complete sentence. When the Federale told him to step out of the car real slow with his hands up, the small-time *mestizo* obliged silently and almost fainted when he reached his feet.

The agent laughed and slapped the handcuffs on after twisting the stunned suspect's arms behind his back. El Tasajo didn't come out of his shock until he saw the Federales handcuffing his woman too. "I thought you wanted to talk to me," the suspect blurted in Spanish. "She don't have nothin' to do with nothin'."

At the time Tasajo's woman was arguing with the Federale who'd grabbed her on the other side of the car. Another Federale was standing with the *mestizo* on the driver's side, watching the scene. When El Tasajo spoke up, this Federale stepped forward and brought the barrel of his own forty-five down on the bridge of El Tasajo's nose. The suspect immediately dropped to his knees. It felt like a fire had been lit inside his skull, between his eyes. Tears ran down his cheeks, and he tried somehow to suck his body over himself to cover the spot, like a turtle pulling into its shell, but couldn't. In a moment blood began dripping out of one nostril.

After spreading some newspapers in the backseat so this Piece of Meat creep wouldn't bleed all over the upholstery, two of the arresting Judicial Federal agents hauled the suspect to the funeral parlor where the Judicial Federal had its offices. Two others followed in Tasajo's VW with his handcuffed woman in the backseat. The cars parked in an alley behind the parlor.

On the building's plans the back entrance in the wall there led into a large high-ceilinged room with a slab floor identified as the mortuary's storage space. Tuesday night the room was lit by several one-hundred-watt bulbs and empty except for a fifty-gallon drum full of water. The only other door in the room led through a small office, big enough for two bare desks and chairs. Another door led from there into the back of the funeral parlor and on up a set of stairs to the Judicial Federal offices. Cruz, Purd, Hog Wissle, and several more Federales were waiting downstairs.

The stakeout cop made Gabriel Bolero Penitente alias El Tasajo kneel facing the back wall ten feet away, and for a moment left him to himself. The Federales, Cruz, and the two *gringos* huddled out of earshot. Tasajo's woman was brought in while he was still kneeling there. The suspect heard her call his name and tried to answer, but before he could, one of the Federales skipped back toward the wall and kicked Penitente in the side of his head. He should talk when the law said to talk and not before.

Tasajo's woman was taken into the little office. Three of the Federales who'd come downstairs with the *gringos* and Cruz followed the woman into the tiny, windowless space and closed the door.

Tasajo had a good idea what was coming his way and quickly postponed the question of his woman's fate. El Tasajo listened to the footsteps recede and continued to stare straight ahead at the wall, spitting pieces of his mouth out on the floor in front of him.

Cruz eventually decided to let his number two, Garcia Huahilote, handle the initial questioning. Garcia walked up and stood behind the small-time *mestizo*.

"What were you planning to do with all that *mota* you had out in San Rafael?" the Federale opened.

Tasajo replied in a high, jabbering voice that he didn't know about any *mota* in San Rafael, and they could straighten this all out. It was all some kind of misunderstanding. The cops really didn't want him. Somebody must have told them some lies. The cops didn't want him. He'd gone straight and did no more for cash than lay bricks with his uncle. They ought to let his woman go right away too because she had nothing to do with nothing. El Tasajo was busy talking at the wall and could see no one behind him. As a result he never even heard Garcia Huahilote's attack coming.

Garcia's first blow was struck with the heel of his cowboy boot against the nape of El Tasajo's neck, just as the suspect was getting to the part about laying bricks with his uncle again. It felt like a sledgehammer had landed flush on his brain. As he pitched forward onto his stomach, El Tasajo's skull seemed ready to explode.

Garcia Huahilote's next kick caught the suspect in the small of the back. The *mestizo* tried desperately to scramble away, but his arms were handcuffed behind him and useless, so the best he could muster was an awkward scuttle. When he made it as far as the wall, Garcia pounced, spinning the suspect around and lashing a right hand into the side of his nose.

It was at this point that Tasajo's head went into a major fog for the first time. Blood was gushing from his nostrils again, and the pain inside his skull was so intense El Tasajo let out a loud and wretched gargle sound. Somewhere far off he could feel more blows rain onto his head and shoulders. Each sent a fresh wave of needles washing over the top of his brain and into the middle of his face. El Tasajo wanted to pass out but was unable to.

When his focus returned, El Tasajo was being dragged over to a chair that had materialized out of the little office where the Federales were holding his woman. After sitting him down on it, Garcia Huahilote asked about the *mota* again.

"I don't know nothin' about *mota*," Tasajo pleaded. He was having trouble holding himself erect and kept rocking forward in the chair. "No shit. Is *cierto*. I been workin' with my uncle who's a bricklayer, and we—"

Garcia Huahilote cut the explanation short with a well-placed foot in the upper reaches of the suspect's chest. The Federale timed the kick so he caught the *mestizo* on the upswing, barely clearing his chin and landing full force on the lungs. Tasajo flew over backward, slammed his head on the concrete, and went foggy again. He wanted to breathe but could only manage little gasps and sucking noises.

While El Tasajo lay there trying to keep from choking, Garcia Huahilote's *jefe* Pizarro Cruz interrupted the interrogation.

"Maybe his throat is too dry to talk," Cruz suggested. "You ought to give the poor *hombre* a drink."

Garcia smiled and immediately jerked the suspect to his feet.

El Tasajo had both heard and seen the *Jefe* speak the words, but they made no sense. Why would he want Tasajo to quench his thirst? The suspect groped in his bleary mind for an explanation and for a moment landed on the conclusion that the cops had believed his story. That illusion disappeared quickly.

As Garcia pulled the stumbling Tasajo behind him toward the barrel of water in the far corner, the small-time *mestizo* flashed on what was about to happen and didn't want to believe it.

"No," he begged Garcia. "No, you don't understand." Two of the other Federales grabbed the suspect's shoulders and bent them down over the water. "Really. I've been layin' bricks. I was just taking my woman to—"

Garcia wrapped his hand around Tasajo's long hair and plunged the *mestizo*'s head into the barrel.

El Tasajo's legs kicked and kicked until Garcia pulled him up again. "Really," the suspect gasped, "I got no—"

This time Garcia held him under for a long while.

El Tasajo kicked his legs and felt his lungs convulsing. They were so hungry for air they seemed to be climbing into his throat. Tasajo could feel his eyes popping out of the front of his face but could see nothing. He struggled against the arms holding him, but Garcia only pushed him farther under. El Tasajo then felt his mind losing touch with his body and stopped kicking. As he went numb, the suspect felt his asshole opening and warm wet shit dribbling on the back of his legs. Tasajo used up the last of his willpower trying to stop it but was no longer able to control his sphincter or any other muscle.

Garcia seemed to sense Tasajo's imminent collapse and pulled him back into the air.

El Tasajo slumped onto the floor and was allowed to lay there in his own mess, gulping for breath and gagging. When the suspect finally spoke, he said he would tell Garcia about the *mota*.

The Federale was furious. "So you was lying to me before," he shouted. Garcia jerked El Tasajo back to his feet.

"I was lying," the groggy *mestizo* agreed.

Garcia immediately punched him in the middle of the face again. The suspect flew against the barrel and then fell over sideways.

"Please," Tasajo gasped. He was hacking up water between words and having trouble seeing. "I'll tell you all about it."

Everyone in the room heard El Tasajo say those words, and once he'd said them, there was obviously no going back for Gabriel Bolero Penitente. Garcia Huahilote left him lying there to catch his breath for a moment.

Hog, Purd, and the rest of the audience had followed the action over to the barrel. Purdee Fletcher nudged his junior partner with his elbow and offered an explanation of the procedure while Garcia paused.

"He's got him broke," the senior agent whispered.

Tasajo lay on the floor slowly digesting what he had just promised to do. El Tasajo didn't want this to be happening to him and for a while tried to pretend that he was somewhere else and none of this was actually going on. He wanted desperately to return to the beginning of the ride with his woman into the Cozumel and start over. El Tasajo succeeded in receding in time as far as when they were sitting outside the whorehouse arguing, but kept getting hung up on the gun sliding in the window and against his head. Gabriel Bolero Penitente was stuck right where he was with no place to run. To keep his pride, he decided to make a deal instead of just giving flat in.

"I'll tell you everything," he finally spoke at Garcia in Spanish, "only you got to let my woman loose. She didn't have nothing to do with it."

The Federale jerked Tasajo up by the scruff of the neck and started shouting again. "You worried about your woman, *señor* Piece of Dog Shit? I'll show you your woman."

With that Garcia Huahilote ran with Tasajo stumbling in tow to the door of the little office. Garcia jerked it open and thrust El Tasajo's head inside.

His woman was stretched on her stomach over one of the desks. Each of her wrists was anchored with handcuffs to the furniture's legs. Her skirt had been rolled up on to her back, exposing her fleshy hips and the greasy hair between her thighs. No one had bothered to unbuckle her platform shoes. One of the Federales who had come downstairs with Cruz and the *gringos* was mounted up back there and pumping her pussy for all he was worth. The Federale was holding a fold of the woman's hip flesh in each hand and was so busy trying to get his nut that he didn't even look up when the door popped open. Another of the Federales who'd arrested her had already had his turn between the woman's legs and was now on the other end of the desk with her hair wrapped around his hand, taking seconds in her mouth. When he saw Garcia Huahilote standing in the open doorway with the dripping suspect, the arresting officer pulled out so Tasajo could see the size of his hard-on. Erect like that, the head of the Federale's meat poked from under his heavy flap of brown foreskin like a pink mouse.

Garcia slammed the door shut and slung Tasajo backward onto the floor. "You don't tell nobody what's gonna happen, *sabe*?" Garcia yelled. "You don't tell nobody who's gotta be let go. You're just shit. You just talk real good and hope that maybe I'll like you."

When El Tasajo didn't answer him right away and just stared at the concrete, Garcia cocked his foot. The motion provoked an instant response.

Gabriel Bolero Penitente alias El Tasajo, small-time *mestizo* and would-be *mota* baron, spoke up and said that the arrangement would be fine with him.

* * *

119

Tasajo perched on the chair again and slowly told the Federales the details about his little warehouse operation they had busted two days before Purd reached town. When the time finally came to ask him about the *gringos* he'd dealt with, Purdee Fletcher took over.

Ole Purd had been feeling one step ahead all day long and was sure before he'd even asked his first question that this Piece of Meat fella was going to give him some *gringos* to chase.

"Just who were you planning to sell this dope to?" Purd began.

After waiting for Hog's translation into Spanish, El Tasajo admitted he had *gringos* in mind. On instinct Purd immediately whipped out his Big Ten photos and showed them to the suspect one by one. El Tasajo stopped him the third face in.

"I know this one," he said.

The picture in Purdee's hand showed a stubbly Caucasian male with straggling black hair, a hooked nose, and a County Jail booking number on his chest. "Hot damn," Purdee Fletcher blurted. His ticket back to the top had just shown up.

Fletcher turned the photo over and examined the summary on the back while Tasajo kept talking to Hog.

The suspect said that he had tried to sell this *gringo* some of the *mota* Cruz's second raid had busted in the south Valley, but the *gringo* hadn't been interested. The *gringo* said he had something else in mind and was coming back in a month and might have some driving work if Piece of Meat was interested. Tasajo said that he'd told the *gringo* he was. That was three weeks ago.

Cruz and his men crowded up close behind Purd to get a look at the picture Tasajo had identified. The summary on the back of the snapshot identified the man as Jerome Whitehurst, age thirty-two, five foot eight inches, 147 pounds, former Marine Corps corporal and squad leader, 1965–68, Vietnam. His only previous conviction was a Sale of Controlled Substances in late 1973. Whitehurst had been sentenced to three years' probation. The probation had been revoked by the United States Board of Parole in late 1976, but Whitehurst had fled, whereabouts unknown. He was also wanted for the 1976 killing of Grady

O'Grady, a drug enforcement agent stationed in Albuquerque, New Mexico. Intelligence identified Whitehurst as a shadowy figure whose aliases had popped up in a lot of other cases. Little of his actual operation was clear, but it was suspected he was a major leftover from Monroe Jessee's long-defunct gang of smugglers that had only now begun to gain some belated recognition in the Agency's intelligence estimates. Whitehurst was known to have used the names Morris Wilson, William Spence, Hector R. Cruz, and Ramón Ramón.

"What'd you call this guy?" Purd asked, looking up from the photo.

"Don Ramón," the suspect answered after a pause for the translation. El Tasajo added on his own that he'd heard some Indians refer to the *gringo* as El Liebre, short for The Jackrabbit, but he never did himself. "I just always called him *don Ramón,"* Tasajo said in Spanish. *"Solo don Ramón."*

Hog translated.

"This is big time," Purdee responded to his partner in English. "We got us a very large fish on the line."

Purd wanted to continue questioning but decided to restrain himself until he had a chance to convince Cruz of a strategy for using this creep. One of the Big Ten was a heavy case, and Purd wanted to move carefully. This Ramón Ramón character might very well be Ole Purd's ticket back to the big time if he played it right.

The senior *gringo* agent turned away from the suspect and took Pizarro Cruz off to the corner by the water barrel. He suggested breaking for now and talking the situation over in the morning. It was already late Tuesday night.

The head Federale agreed. After he and Purd finished talking, Cruz walked back to his men and told them to haul this garbage to City Prison for the night.

9

Fat Albert's wire reached Henry Amazon Wednesday morning.

    HENRY AMAZON
    HOTEL MODESTO
    OAXACA, OAXACA
    SORRY. TWO ALL I COULD GET TOGETHER. HAPPY TRAVELS.
      AL.
    END OF MESSAGE.

The form attached to the telegram indicated two thousand dollars was waiting for Amazon at the telegraph window at the downtown Correos instead of the five thousand dollars Fat Albert had promised. The shortfall was devastating.

"You lousy cocksucker," Amazon swore out loud.

The widow looked up from the hotel desk.

"*¿Qué?*"

"*Nada*," Amazon smiled, recapturing his temper, "just bad news."

On his way across the Modesto's wide courtyard Henry Amazon ran the finances through his head one more time. He still had 7,200 dollars left from his original stash and owed all that plus two thousand more to Vincente and his friend for the *mota* they were holding. That left exactly nothing to pay El Chorizo for hauling part of the load north, gas to get there with, or greasing their way across the line itself.

"Fat Albert stuck it to us," the *gringo* told his partner when they entered the bungalow sitting room. "We ain't got enough money."

The news struck Zorro CeAttle as Amazon's just comeuppance. The *gringo* had been saying all along that he had everything covered. Now they were halfway into a scam and stuck with their butts up in the air because the know-it-all Amazon didn't have his act together. To Zorro it felt like vindication, and he figured his partner deserved the bad news. He wouldn't be able to bullshit his way around this one. Zorro didn't say anything at first, just stared at Amazon with his purple eyes. For a moment Amazon stood there, caught in the open, feeling both flustered and embarrassed. Then he fought his paralysis and walked quickly over to the phone.

"What you gonna do now?" Zorro asked.

"Call this motherfucker and get it straight," the *gringo* snapped.

Amazon picked up the receiver and told the switchboard to place his call to Jersey City collect. Ten minutes later the Mexico City operator rang back with Fat Albert.

"Go ahead, *señor* Amazon," she said.

"You asshole," Amazon blurted. But by the time his voice reached Jersey City, it had lost most of its threatening tone and sounded like a small man shouting up a long drainpipe.

"Ain't that some kinda way to talk," Fat Albert answered in a flurry of buzzes and long scratchy sounds. "If it wasn't for me, you'd be nowhere."

"Well, as it is now," Amazon broke in, "you left me hanging with my balls over the saw blade, Fat Man. You said it was five you were sending for the girls."

"So I did, but it wasn't all that easy. Like I said in the wire, I'm sorry. Things are hard all over. My last favor for you stretched me too far, if you can dig that. I should never had told ya I'd send anything. I can't even pay for this fucking phone call, so don't give me a bunch of asshole talk."

For a moment neither end of the line spoke. Henry Amazon stared at the bare wall through the bungalow's bathroom door. It was painted the same flat gangrene color most mental hospitals use. The trim was an enamel version of the identical shade. When Amazon started talking again, his tone was more apologetic and pleading.

"Look, I'm sorry I got so hot, man, but I'm strapped. Can't you just get up off two more?"

"Listen to me carefully, Henry," Fat Albert repeated. "It don't make no difference how big that strap is. I ain't got it. *Nada*. You know? I'm past my limit and waiting for to get your slowpoke ass home to cover my bills. You said you wouldn't need more than what I gave you the first time. The rest's gravy. It ain't my problem you're in a bind. That's just the way it is."

Henry Amazon listened to the crackle on the line for a while, then said "Thanks a lot" and hung up.

"Did you get it all straight?" Zorro asked. One corner of the Mexican's mouth was turned up, ready to laugh at his partner.

"What do you think?" Amazon snapped. "You heard it."

"Since you got it covered, I figured it must have turned out all right," Zorro jabbed back.

"Why don't you stow that shit for a while, Zorro," he said in a much slower voice. "I got no use for it right now."

He proceeded to ignore CeAttle until the Mexican finally said he was going to get breakfast before the dining room closed, and left. Amazon then stood up and began pacing back and forth across the floor, trying to figure his way out of the corner. He thought of several people to call for last-minute financing, but he was doubtful about all of them. He figured he still had enough cash to pay some more to the two Indians he and Zorro were scheduled to meet later that night and that they'd just have to go on, hoping something would drop into place. Vincente would hold the load for a while, and Amazon was convinced that something would turn up. In the meantime he decided to cash in the wire before Fat Albert had second thoughts and reclaimed the money.

He found Zorro CeAttle sitting at a table by the window, sipping coffee and waiting for his eggs to be served. The Mexican was preoccupied, looking at the Frenchwoman two tables over, and didn't see Amazon come through the double doors separating the dining room from the lobby. He had just caught the French tourist's eye and slipped his Foster Grants off for maximum impact when Amazon grabbed his arm.

Zorro looked up with an annoyed expression.

"I'm gonna be gone for a while, but I'll be back," the *gringo* said.

"Where you goin'?"

"The Correos telegraph office. *Muy pronto.*"

When he returned, Amazon spent the afternoon sitting by the phone waiting to be connected to the international lines. Zorro lounged by the pool with the Frenchwoman. Everyone Amazon called either wasn't there, said he was broke, or wouldn't consider fronting money south of the border, whatever the circumstances.

By the time dark crept in and the two smugglers set out to meet Vincente out the Pan American, Amazon knew he wasn't having much luck finding relief north of the border and that maybe he should start looking in other directions. The only thing he could come up with was the loan shark who owned the grocery store on the *zocolo,* but something in him balked at doing business with the man. He just didn't trust the Mexican not to pass the word that a certain *gringo* needed cash in a hurry. That kind of information could prove deadly in the wrong hands. As he drove through the seemingly vacant night, waves of anxiety rushed over him. He debated the pros and cons of the loan shark's money over and over again. Mostly Amazon worked hard at suppressing a growing sense of desperation. When they were close to Vincente's village, he put his turmoil on hold and concentrated on the business at hand. He didn't want the Indians to pick up on his momentary disadvantage and get spooked.

Amazon parked his Toyota so it was hidden from the road by a ten-foot-tall pile of maguey hearts inside the open gates to the courtyard at Alejandro's *mescal* factory, where Vincente was waiting as arranged.

"You're late," Vincente said.

"Not by much. Where's the *mota*?"

"It's not here."

"What do you mean?" Amazon sounded quarrelsome and tense.

"I don't want to do business here," Vincente explained. "Is too close to home. The *mota*'s in the next village at my cousin's." Vincente said he had planned to meet them here and lead the *gringo*'s Land Cruiser in several miles to the next village but had decided against it. "Is too much *chivas* on this road now," he continued. "Is no good that they see a *gringo* driving out there. It would attract too much attention. You got to ride with me."

Henry Amazon couldn't help but agree that his driving into a poor *campesino* village this time of night would be a dead giveaway, but it pissed him off that Vincente hadn't brought any of this up before. "*Chinga, mano,*" he swore, "this is a bad way to do business. You shoulda told me about all these arrangements."

Vincente shrugged. "You don't want to do it?" he asked.

The thought had crossed Amazon's mind, but he was in too much of a hurry. "No, we're gonna go through with it," he told the Indian. "You just oughta know better than springing this shit on me at the last minute."

Vincente told them to hide in the bed of his truck. He had a load of barrels there, arranged with an empty, four-foot-square space in the middle. Amazon and the Mexican could crouch in there. With a tarpaulin lashed over the load, it would seem no more than an innocent cargo of barrels, a commonplace sight in the heart of *mescal* neighborhood. "It won't be no problem," Vincente said.

126

Henry Amazon wasn't sure. The *gringo* stood in the *mescal fábrica*'s muddy courtyard kicking at the sloppy ground with the toe of his boot. He was scared of being locked into such a tiny, dark space, with no means of escape.

"All right," he said finally. "Let's do it."

When Amazon and his partner were wedged between the barrels, Vincente spread the tarp over the back of the truck and lashed it down. The space was even worse than Henry Amazon had expected. Amazon had to fight back the impulse to try and push his way through the tarp and get back into the open air. He couldn't see a thing in the darkness, and the cramped space smelled of old canvas and barrel staves.

Henry Amazon gagged a little in the stifling air.

"What?" Zorro whispered.

"I'm keeping my heat ready," Amazon said, slipping the pistol out of his boot.

Amazon heard the sound of his partner's pant leg rustling as he did likewise.

The drive to Vincente's cousin's house was over exceedingly rough road, and the truck did little but pitch in one direction and then roll back in the other. It took half an hour and felt three times as long. On several occasions the load shifted, allowing the barrels to encroach even farther on the two smugglers' tiny black space. When Vincente's Ford flatbed finally came to a complete stop and the engine coughed into silence, Amazon clicked the gun's safety off and tensed his cramped muscles, ready for quick action.

But nothing happened. The only person outside when the tarpaulin was rolled back was Vincente himself.

" '*Stá seguro,*" he said. "Come out."

The truck was parked in an enclosed yard attached to a two-room house. Vincente's cousin's family was asleep in one room, and the other was half full of weed. Amazon and his partner tucked their guns away, climbed down, and followed the Indian into the *mota* room.

Flacco was waiting inside under the light bulb with a set of scales.

127

For the next two hours the four of them processed the load for shipment. Using duct tape and the plastic garbage bags they had brought along, Zorro CeAttle lined each of the empty barrels. Henry and Vincente weighed the burlap bags full of *mota* while Flacco stuffed each of the lined barrels with weed that had already been weighed. Then Vincente wedged the tops of the barrels in and cinched down the last hoop. When the Indian finally finished, ten half-sealed barrels of marijuana were lined up along the wall, and Amazon owed him a little more than nine thousand dollars American. The *gringo* tossed Vincente a bundle of twenty-dollar bills and waited while the Indian counted them.

"When I pick the *mota* up to go north, I'll pay you the rest," he said.

"How long do I have to wait?" Vincente asked suspiciously.

"It'll be soon," Amazon said. "Five days at the most."

As it turned out, it was less than five, less even than two, but Henry Amazon still had to struggle through Thursday to find that out himself.

Thursday quickly turned into a stew of high anxiety and irritable depression. Amazon called a dealer named Spider Man in El Paso and a dude in Duke City, but the dude in Duke City's number was disconnected, and Spider Man wasn't sure he could swing any kind of arrangement. He admitted he owed Amazon a favor but claimed things were tight and he'd have to talk to a few people first. He promised to call back before the day was out.

"I'll be waitin' right here," Amazon said.

Which is exactly what Thursday was all about.

Henry Amazon never left the Modesto. He just waited and worried and then waited and worried some more. He spent the morning pacing back and forth inside the bungalow, smoking cigarettes. Around 11 A.M. Zorro left to take the Frenchwoman sight-seeing, and Amazon was relieved not to have to deal with his partner's pressure along with everything else. His mood improved for a few hours but by two, when Spider Man still hadn't called, Amazon had lunch sent to the bungalow and continued his vigil. He ate too much and felt bloated and sleepy.

During the *siesta* hours Thursday came crashing down on him.

He rolled a reefer out of a small stash he'd kept from Rascón's boxes and smoked half of it. The day outside was as hot and muggy as any since he had first arrived in town, and Amazon opened all the doors and windows to try and scare up a breeze. After unbuttoning his shirt and slipping his boots off, he tuned his portable radio to some promising *mariachi* music and settled onto the couch to wait out the afternoon.

It was the light that first made Amazon think of Wanda. The hard afternoon glare, filtering through the leaves of the giant avocado trees in the Modesto's courtyard, produced a pale yellow glow inside the bungalow that didn't so much shine as hover. It seemed just like the *siesta* light in the one-room *adobe* Wanda Lamar had rented in Mitla during the summer eight years before. The trees outside then had been tamarinds. The house had tile floors and glass windows. It had been built for use by the students who visited the museum during the summer to study the ruins with Professor Glez. Wanda was one of those students then, and from their first meeting, Amazon had wanted her badly.

Stretched out on the couch, he thought of that first afternoon he'd spent with her in the house under the tamarind trees.

Amazon had been putting Ramón Ramón off about hauling another load north and instead was looking for excuses to run into Wanda. In those days she was still calling herself Judy Rosenberg. One afternoon he finally succeeded in getting her to show him the ruins by herself. Out there she asked what he did, and Amazon had hedged and tried to change the subject. Finally he had called it "import/export" and offered her a joint. Wanda had laughed, and the two of them got stoned together on the steps. But Amazon's capacity to stall Ramón Ramón had eventually run out before he'd been able to do more with Wanda than kiss her good night on the street that ran by her house. It was time to go north, and he couldn't put it off anymore. At midnight he and Ramón Ramón were going to run the gauntlet one more time, and he had no idea when he'd be back. To say good-bye, he had asked Wanda to cut her seminar and have one last lunch with him on his final day in town. They had eaten heavily that afternoon and in silence. When lunch was over, she had said she was sleepy. It was *siesta* time.

"Like some company?" Amazon had asked impulsively.

"Yes," Wanda answered. "I would."

They made love all afternoon in the pale yellow light hovering over Wanda's slat bed. In between they had lain on their backs next to each other, smoking and letting the sweat dry. She had been everything he had wanted at the time.

Lying there on the bungalow couch, Amazon enjoyed the memory immensely. As it began to fade, he strained to bring it back. He wanted to feel like that for a little while more. It'd been a long time since he'd had anything nearly so close. But his memory got away from him. He retrieved the picture of Wanda, but in a time that had changed drastically. It was a year later, and by then, Wanda had dropped out of school, decided "home" had nothing to offer, and was staying on in Mexico to get a little adventure into her life. She, Henry, and Ramón Ramón had been inseparable for that year. When she'd learned what they carried on their runs north, Wanda had wanted to come along, but Amazon wouldn't let her. She went barefoot now, and her dress had switched to wide Indian skirts. She had become brown enough to pass for Mexican if she wanted to, and by this time, she wanted to a lot. She was tired of being Judy Rosenberg and successively called herself Juanita, Rosalie, and then Wanda Lamar.

The trouble between Wanda and Henry Amazon had begun several months after the blowout at the airstrip ten miles outside Mitla that had destroyed the partnership between Amazon, Ramón Ramón, and The Patchoolie Kid. For a while Amazon and Ramón had tried to get their business back together again, but finally Ramón and he had agreed to go their separate ways. They had been at the end of a last smuggle with five hundred pounds of gold leaf into New Mexico at the time. After dissolving their partnership, Ramón Ramón had returned straight to Oaxaca, while Amazon had spent a couple of days buying new clothes in Albuquerque. He had planned to go south again to pick up Wanda and maybe drive on into Central America, but that hadn't worked out.

When he had arrived at her house in Mitla, her greeting had been perfunctory. Instead of inviting him inside, she had said they ought to go down to the Sorpresa for coffee. When they got there, Wanda got straight to the point.

"I've been making some decisions while you were gone," she had said.

"Yah?" Amazon had asked. He sensed something was coming, but he felt frightened, frozen in his tracks.

"Yah."

"You feel like telling me, Judy?" Using the old name made him feel closer to her.

"I'm not Judy anymore, I'm Wanda Lamar from now on."

"Okay, Wanda it is." He wanted to humor her.

"The second decision," she persisted in a harder voice, "is that I'm leaving here tomorrow and going to Huautla for mushroom season."

"What are you going to do by yourself in Huautla?" Amazon sounded argumentative. He started to add that he'd go to Huautla.

"I'm not going to be by myself," she snapped.

From the tone of her voice Amazon had known what was coming and looked around the panic in his mind for a place to hide. "Who are you going with?" he asked mechanically, not really wanting to hear.

"Ramón."

Amazon didn't say anything.

"It's time you and I called it quits for a while," she continued. "I want to move on." Wanda stood up. The waiter hadn't even taken their order yet, but she turned toward the door.

"Take care of yourself," she had added over her shoulder.

With that, she walked out of his life. Amazon heard later that she and Ramón parted company in a year, but when he finally saw her again in the Oaxaca market after it was over with Ramón too, Wanda had gone totally native, and he hardly recognized her and felt nothing.

Now, lying on the couch in the Modesto, he felt as humiliated and worthless as when she'd first left. He bolted up off the couch, but the sense of disgust wouldn't let go. He kicked a chair across the room and wanted to break something. Finally he took a shower, but it didn't help.

He was sick of this silly snake game, the wounds, and falling on his face. He was sick of everything that was under way. Get out and be poor but alive and not yet crazy.

At nightfall Spider Man called.

"What's up?" Amazon asked.

"Well," the El Paso dealer began, "I'm real sorry, man, I know I owe you and all, but . . ."

"But what?"

"But I can't get nothing together. Maybe when you get home. Right now I'm having trouble raisin' bread."

The news didn't surprise Henry Amazon. It fit right in with everything else.

After he hung up, Amazon kicked the chair across the room for the second time that day. "Son of a bitch," he cursed. "Son of a bitch." Then he knocked the lamp over and listened to it shatter on the floor. The bulb itself continued to shine until he walked over and stomped the room into darkness.

The dark felt soothing, and after a while Amazon began to chuckle. He seemed to have sprung some safety valve in his mind. He fetched his bottle of *mescal*. The radio was tuned to a San Antone Country and Western station that was audible all the way to Gautemala late at night. Jessi Colter sang about how crazy she was back then. The light from the Modesto's front office across the way shimmered up off of the tiles. Amazon was drunk in twenty minutes and numb twenty minutes after that.

When Zorro came back from an evening on the town, Emmylou

Harris was on the radio, singing about her daddy. Henry Amazon focused on his partner with difficulty.

"What're you doing?" Zorro asked.

"Getting drunker than you," Amazon answered, extending the *mescal*.

They finished the bottle. Henry Amazon wanted to stay outside and listen to his radio, and the Mexican went inside after a brief stop at the flower bed to puke.

Finally Amazon rose to go to bed and bury Thursday in his mattress. Falling asleep, he remembered the loan shark. "Maybe I will see that son of a bitch," he thought. "What the fuck. It beats another day like this."

He had not forgotten about the loan shark when he woke late Friday morning with a cast-iron head and a mouth full of wool. He did his best to shake off the effects of the night before in a cold shower and then drove to the *zocolo*. He had every intention of stopping at the shark's grocery to discuss a loan, but the closer he came to acting on it, the more hesitant he became. The man still felt wrong.

Yet he knew that without the shark he had no options at all. He procrastinated over a cup of coffee and the South American edition of *Time* in the Hotel Monte Alban dining room. It was past noon when he finished reading, and the question of the loan shark was right back in his lap.

This time he ducked it by telling himself that the shark always took an early lunch break and wouldn't be back at the store until six in the evening. There was no use going by there now. Instead he decided to walk to the Fontana for a big lunch: fighting back worry was making him ravenous.

Amazon took a seat in the rear corner with his back to the entrance and ordered *ceviche* and *camarónes diablo* with a Tres Equis beer *muy helado* and right away. He gulped down the first beer and half of another in silent reflection before the *ceviche* arrived.

He had been coming into this place off and on for the last eight years. When he and Ramón Ramón had still been partners, the Fontana was almost their second home. Wanda had loved coming here too. That had all been during the heyday of Monroe Jessee, when *traficantes* could still safely hold public court in the spots that now had long since been given over to tourists. Then all the waiters had known the two *gringos* on sight and saved them the best tables, even at the most crowded hours, but time, the Judicial Federal, and the growth of the tourist industry had changed all that. Henry Amazon had receded to the status of one more *gringo* face, and that suited him fine. On this Friday he just wanted to eat in peace.

Then Ramón Ramón walked in. Still short, dark, and hooknosed, this Friday Ramón was clean-shaven, except for a well-trimmed mustache. His once straggly hair was styled and curly. He was wearing a shiny yellow shirt decorated with red flowers, corduroy bell bottoms, and expensive cowboy boots with a mirror polish on the toes. Ramón looked like an aspiring young Texas car dealer, which was exactly what he was pretending to be. He moved up the Fontana's front steps quickly, with a smooth-gliding stride.

Ramón Ramón was expecting to do not more than grab a quick bite, but he did an immediate double take when he saw Amazon hunched over the back table. He changed his plans immediately. Ramón Ramón had business of his own in which his former partner might be very helpful. He advanced on Amazon's table, formulating a spontaneous plan for milking the coincidence to his maximum advantage. They hadn't seen each other since Ramón passed on the news about The Patchoolie Kid the year before. Right away Henry Amazon recognized the look of business on the dark, hooknosed face.

"Well, if it isn't the great Double R himself," he said.

"In person," Ramón grinned. He slipped into the chair across the table with the same quick motion and easy grace his body exhibited in all its movements. There seemed to be no deadweight to Ramón at all.

For several minutes the two of them exchanged small talk until Ramón nudged the conversation toward his true intentions.

"You just checking the scenery out, or you got business in town?" Ramón asked.

"You know how it is," Amazon answered. "A little of this, some of that, and a little more of the other thing."

"I know that list myself."

"I figured you might. You still on the run?"

Ramón Ramón looked around the restaurant. Most of the tables were empty, but the lunch rush would begin soon. Ramón leaned forward in a confidential manner and lowered his voice. "I ain't goin' north much anymore is all. Got myself a California partner to off the shit." Then he leaned back and resumed his usual voice. There was a jesting edge on it. "How about yourself? I woulda figured you'd been retired by now."

"I got to admit that my time in the business is just about up," Amazon answered. He was looking off at the fountain. "It's all too much."

"Shit, Enrique, it was too much for you a long time ago."

"Whatever," he shrugged. He didn't want to fall into Ramón's acid tone. "I'm hung up looking for money to escape with at the moment."

He had mentioned his financial jam to see how Ramón might respond. It occurred to him that his former partner might have some financing available.

Nor was Amazon's reference lost on Ramón.

"That's too bad," he responded. For a moment he played with the edge of his mustache. "You know," he said, "I might be able to help you out." The shift of the muscles in Amazon's face told Ramón that he was interested. "How'd you like to make five grand for nothing more than putting me in touch with some folks you know?"

"Who?"

Ramón Ramón looked around the Fontana again before answering. A party of eight French tourists were standing in the restaurant doorway, waiting for their table to be set. When his eyes returned to Amazon, they sought the middle of Henry's face. "My California partner and me are looking to invest in a little hash," he continued in his whispering voice. "I been looking for a connection but keep comin' up empty. Seeing you, I remembered you once told me about that *indio* who makes fine blond cake."

Amazon didn't respond.

"You know the stuff," Ramón pressed. "It comes in those small, round patties."

Amazon still held his peace, trying to act like he was thinking it over.

In fact, he had no doubts about whether to take the offer. As soon as the five-thousand-dollar figure entered the conversation, Amazon had been ninety-five percent convinced. If he got on the road right away, the sum would be just enough to cover the remainder of his first load all the way to Colorado, with a margin for emergencies.

"It'll have to be soon," he said warily.

"It's up to you," Ramón grinned. "As soon as you say yes, the ball's in your court. The quicker you hook me up, the quicker you get paid."

Before actually coming out with an agreement, Henry Amazon retreated into his head one more time. The offer had all the feel of the opportunity for which he'd been waiting the last two days. He didn't allow himself even a premonition of trouble. Friday over lunch it felt to Amazon that he'd found a door leading out of his corner and nothing more.

"Grab the money and run," he told himself. "You'll be across the Rio Grande three days after it's done."

10

Lots of dope and money had slipped through Ramón Ramón's hands during the last decade. He'd had seven different partners since Amazon and had always seemed to end up one big score short. After he'd killed the narc in Albuquerque, it had been even worse. The present partnership with the Californian was Ramón's comeback from fugitive status, and he was set on riding it all the way to a fortune sizable enough to put him into the big time and keep him there indefinitely. It was evidence of the shift in Ramón's fortunes that the comeback was as flawed as it was.

Ramón Ramón's California partner was the same Bruno Sawyer, alias Beef Stew, that Hog had photographed driving a camper with two unidentified companions the week before on the San Dionisio Road. Neither Ramón nor his partner had any inkling of it, but an hour before Ramón Ramón chanced on Henry Amazon at the Fontana, positive identification of Beef as a suspected violator had reached the Oaxaca Station from Condor Central along with instructions to treat his case with high priority.

Ramón and Beef's plan was to order a half ton of hashish, pick up a ton of prime virgin seedless *mota* that Ramón had been arranging in the south Valley over the last three months, and drive it north with the assistance of an Indian Ramón knew, El Tasajo. Once the *mota* had been offed, they had planned to return for their load of hash, off that, and be on Easy Street. The profits were to be split forty percent for Ramón, forty for Beef, and the other twenty for an investor Beef had found. If it had worked out, Ramón's share of the business alone would have cleared two million dollars. At the time of his meeting Amazon at the Fontana, Ramón had no idea that Tasajo had turned snitch when questioned by the Judicial Federal on Wednesday night.

Perhaps if he had been a little more frightened, he would have trod lightly enough to hear the end coming, but by then Ramón Ramón had been getting away with fearlessness for so long he had begun to take his own survival for granted. Ramón had a much higher estimation of himself than of anyone else. Sitting across from Henry Amazon at the Fontana, Ramón exuded nonchalance.

It was an attitude that irritated Amazon once again. Lapsing into silence to think the offer over, he could tell by the look on his face that Ramón was sure he would take it. Amazon disliked being treated as so easy a mark and kept silent, holding off minute by minute from accepting the offer.

He would have liked Ramón at least to put on a show of entreating him for assistance, but Ramón wouldn't. Ramón made a point of never letting on how much he wanted anything. Finally Amazon broke the silence himself.

"So you'll pay me on the spot when I make the introduction?"

"My partner's the paymaster," Ramón answered.

"I'm not introducing anybody else but you," Amazon said.

Ramón Ramón laughed. "Come on, Enrique. I been around long enough that I ain't gonna float some cop in on you."

"You want a connection, you make it my way. I don't want to get tied up with somebody I don't know on this kind of short notice."

"However you want to do it," he shrugged. "If you don't want to bring my partner along, you don't have to, but that means you can't get your bread on the spot either," Ramón Ramón grinned.

"How soon would I get it?"

"That all depends on the time of day we do what we have to do, but I guarantee it'll be quick."

"How quick is quick?"

"Twelve hours max."

"You mean if I take you out to meet the hash man tonight, you'll have the bread in the morning."

"Exactly."

Amazon fell silent again to continue the impression of thinking it over, but Ramón had tired of the game. "You in or not?" he demanded.

Amazon took a last hit on his beer. "I'm in," he said.

He led the way back out into the afternoon sunlight. When they had reached a spot past the vendors in the park, Amazon stopped. A little breeze was rubbing against the trees, and black clouds were beginning to build up to the southwest.

"Where can I find you later?" he asked Ramón.

"Set a time and place."

"The Gallo Más Plumado at half past five."

That afternoon he spent chasing down his old acquaintance The Hash Indian, on the side of the valley where clouds were gathering. After crossing the Río Atoyac and driving through Santa Cruz Xoxocotlan, he encountered a ten-minute pocket of rain, but on the whole the storm looked a lot meaner than it actually was. Amazon's mood had shifted one hundred and eighty degrees. His former lethargy and doubt had dissolved.

He was back in the goddamn saddle again.

After Amazon left him, Ramón Ramón retraced his steps to the Fontana and continued another two blocks north to the Hotel San

Cristóbal where Beef Stew was staying with his nineteen-year-old girl friend, Stella Ranch—the unidentified "female suspect" mentioned in the Oaxaca Station's report to Condor Central. They were registered there under the names Gordon and Betty Stern.

Besides being Beef's old lady, Stella Ranch alias Betty Stern was also the anonymous "investor" Beef had lined up when the deal was first being put together. Ramón Ramón had already been in the Oaxaca Valley for more than two months arranging for their load of *mota*, but he hadn't learned anything from his partner about Stella's involvement until Beef had showed up with her just two weeks earlier on the flight from Mexico City.

"You got to be shitting me," Ramón had screamed at Beef in the middle of the terminal. "What the fuck is the broad doin' here?" The two partners had spent the better part of the next two days arguing about her presence. Beef Stew had been around the business for a long time and had done three years in San Quentin along the way, so Ramón Ramón had no qualms about Beef's ability to hold up his end of a smuggle, but Stella Ranch was another question. She didn't know the first thing about scamming. As far as Ramón was concerned, she was a danger to both of them and herself. Ramón admitted he could understand Beef wanting to have steady pussy—he was the same way himself—but it made more sense to buy some woman or even hand-job it than it did to go into the bush with a nineteen-year-old chick who'd never been south of San Diego before.

Beef Stew was normally pretty easygoing, but about Stella's presence he had been uncharacteristically stubborn and insistent. It wasn't until Ramón Ramón had taunted him with being "pussy-whipped" that Beef had admitted that Stella was the heretofore anonymous investor. Old man Ranch had been a rich son of a bitch, and Stella had hardly dented her personal stock portfolio to finance this run. One of the conditions the adventure-hungry Stella Ranch attached to her money was that she get to come along.

In the old days Ramón Ramón would have stopped right there and started over. On the face of it the arrangement spelled *hassle*, but now he wasn't about to let it stand in the way of his comeback. Ramón thought Stella Ranch was just slumming and playing Beef for a chump, but he figured his own skills were strong enough to smooth over whatever problems her presence might add.

At the San Cristóbal he found Beef and Stella down by the pool. Stella was rubbing suntan oil on her arms. Beef was laid out in the lounge chair next to her with his eyes closed.

Despite his distaste for her Ramón had to admit he could see what Beef Stew saw in Stella Ranch. She didn't have much but a couple of bumps in the way of a chest, but her legs were long and topped with a high and tight-looking ass. Stella gave the impression of being very fresh meat and seemed to know it. What she saw in Beef was a little harder for Ramón to evaluate.

Bruno Sawyer alias Beef Stew was halfway through his thirties, a surfer type who'd learned the business with the old Orange County Brotherhood of Love in the late sixties and spread out on his own as the years went on. Aside from the tattoo on his arm, Beef's only other mark was a long purple scar snaking across his rib cage. It was obvious Beef Stew had been around the block more than a few times. Ramón figured it wouldn't be long before Stella dumped Beef and moved on to greener pastures, but he didn't really give a shit one way or the other. By then Ramón expected to be rich and didn't plan to need any partners at all.

"Hey, *hombre*," Ramón said, nudging Beef's arm. Stella looked over at Ramón for the first time.

"How ya doin', Stella?"

"Worse than I was," she answered. Stella knew what he had said to Beef about her, and she didn't like him. She always seemed to talk with a whine, and the style pushed all of Ramón Ramón's buttons.

"You should try sitting on your thumb," he offered. "It might help."

"Kiss my ass, Ramón," she said, flustered. Barely out of. high school, Stella didn't have a lot of experience dealing with people like Ramón. "Just kiss my ass."

141

"In a hot minute, Mama," Ramón jived. "Just say it's all right to use my tongue."

By this time Beef Stew was awake.

"Hey, cut that shit, will ya, Stella" the California dealer interrupted. "Just cut it out. This man and I got to do business."

Stella Ranch looked hurt and went back to rubbing oil on her arms. Beef Stew and Ramón Ramón walked over to one of the poolside tables and signaled the dark brown waiter for two cold beers.

"I got a line out on that crumbly blond stuff," Ramón opened.

"All right," Beef Stew beamed. "All fucking right. I was about to give up hope."

The hashish had proved to be the most difficult part of their plans. For three weeks Ramón had been unable to come up with a good connection.

"I told you it would happen," Ramón boasted. "I've been around this place too long to come up empty."

"All right," Beef Stew repeated. "All fucking right." His head was already full of dollar signs. "We're gonna end up so rich we'll shit quarters and piss dimes."

El Gallo Más Plumado was located on the southern edge of downtown in one of the oldest buildings in the city. The drinking establishment inside was dark and fairly lowlife. The bar's name meant "the cock with the most feathers," but it implied a lot more than that. El Gallo Más Plumado is also the boss cock, the one who wins, and is among *machismo*'s highest rankings. The bar El Gallo Más Plumado was nasty and rough, and the drinkers who spent their nights there were in the habit of making open displays of their manhood. It wasn't unusual for the establishment to report between four and seven knifings a week.

When Ramón arrived for his rendezvous with Henry Amazon, *siesta* was barely finished, and the only drinkers inside were two scruffy-looking *mestizos* at the end of the bar. Ramón sat at a table with his back to the wall, ordered two shots of *mescal*, and saved them for Amazon's arrival.

Walking at a crisp clip, Henry Amazon came through the door at a quarter to six.

"It's on," he said as soon as he sat down at the table, facing Ramón and the wall behind him. "You and me will meet The Hash Indian tonight. I'll pick you up at ten o'clock."

"*Qué bueno,*" Ramón grinned. "*Qué bueno.*" Shoving one of the *mescals* toward his ex-partner, Ramón Ramón raised his own in a toast. "Just like the old days," he saluted.

He drained his glass in a quick motion. Henry Amazon did the same.

But it wasn't like the old days. Sitting across from him at El Gallo, Amazon felt remote and estranged, turned off by Ramón Ramón's pushiness and his mean streak.

"Speaking of old times," Ramón continued after a long exhale to cool the sting left in his throat by the *mescal*'s passage, "you'll never guess who I saw in Veracruz six months ago."

"Who?" Amazon asked reluctantly.

"Wanda Lamar."

"How's she doing?"

"Didn't do much more than say hello," Ramón answered. "But she looked all right. Said she was living with some Frenchman."

"What'd her kid look like?" Amazon asked. The memory of Wanda's frantic mating with El Chorizo three years earlier flashed across his brain. The last time he had seen or heard of Wanda she had claimed to be pregnant and headed for the Yucatán to give birth.

"Didn't see any kid," Ramón answered, "and she didn't mention nothin' about one. But then she wasn't all that friendly." He grinned; obviously her attitude hadn't bothered him much. "You know how she could be," he added.

Henry Amazon stood up to go. He had better things to do than sit around with Ramón Ramón, examining the ghosts of their past.

"Be in Juarez Park at ten o'clock," Henry Amazon said as he

turned toward the street. "I'll pick you up." He nudged his way through El Gallo's crowd of empty chairs and disappeared.

They reached the outskirts of The Hash Indian's village on the other side of Cuilápan near midnight. Hurry was Henry Amazon's whole world now. He wanted to get this done and be an the way. Spending time with Ramón again was making him edgy.

The afternoon storm on the southwest side of the Valley had long since blown on toward Mexico City. A graceful slice of moon covered the countryside with splatters of white glow. Henry Amazon drove the last mile with the Land Cruiser's lights off.

"It's on foot from here," he told Ramón when they parked behind several trees. "You ready?"

Ramón Ramón was in paratrooper boots, black Frisko Jeens and a navy blue T-shirt. His automatic was strapped into the top of one of his boots.

Before leading him off into the darkness, Henry Amazon had one more question. "Who do you want me to tell this guy you are?"

"Your friend," the short *gringo* answered without hesitation. *"Don Ramón."*

Don Ramón. Sure. It was just like Ramón Ramón to insist on dealing with Zapotecs from one step up the ladder. Only the oldest and wisest Indians were accorded *don* in front of their names, and Ramón had just reached out and claimed the distinction. *"Qué macho,"* Amazon said to himself. As far as Ramón was concerned, everything was just there for the taking, no questions asked.

Amazon led the way down a gully and across several fields to a creek. The Hash Indian's village began another five hundred yards upstream, but the wide, dry skirt of the streambed made easy walking. The creek was only two feet across and no more than six inches deep. Just before they reached the first block of village houses, the two smugglers hid for several minutes while a sleepy Indian woman squatted up ahead, taking what seemed to Amazon to be a very long piss. When she disappeared back up the bank, Amazon and Ramón continued up the creek at a quiet dogtrot.

At the point where a village dead-ended above a six-foot drop, Henry Amazon clambered up the bank with Ramón gliding effortlessly behind him. The Hash Indian's house was the second on the left.

A puffy-looking Indian with salt-and-pepper hair and whiskers answered Amazon's knock.

"Buenas noches," he whispered, motioning the two *gringos* into the courtyard.

After the door had closed behind them, Amazon made the introductions.

"Hash Indian," he said in Spanish, motioning first at the Zapotec and then toward the short *gringo* next to him, "this is my friend, Ramón."

Ramón Ramón noticed that Amazon had left off the *don,* but he knew better than to open his meeting with the Indian by disagreeing with the man who had brought him here.

"Mucho gusto," he smiled at the old Indian.

"My friend Ramón," Henry Amazon continued, consciously repeating his own version of Ramón's name, "wants to do some business with you."

It took twenty minutes. Ramón Ramón bought a small sample outright and arranged to return the next night with his partner and put a down payment on a load.

As he and Amazon drove back to town afterward, the two former partners agreed to handle payment the next morning in a corner of the municipal market, but Amazon was still anxious about collecting his money. For most of their conversation on the way back that night, Ramón Ramón was trying to reassure his ex-partner.

"There's no problem," he said again when the Land Cruiser reached the Río Atoyac and crossed into Oaxaca proper. "Nobody's gonna rip you off. I'll just show my man this sample and bring the cash tomorrow morning. Don't be so freaked out."

Ramón was feeling little sympathy for the rush his former partner seemed to be in. "Fuck him," Ramón was thinking. "He don't like my name, I don't like his problem."

Henry Amazon was tired, and his tension caught up with him shortly after he dropped Ramón off and proceeded to the Modesto. The bungalow was dark. He unlocked the door to the bedroom and stepped quietly inside. The first thing he saw, etched in the moonlight, was Zorro CeAttle mounted on the naked Frenchwoman and frozen midstroke by the intrusion.

"*Yo lo siento mucho,*" he apologized. He stepped back outside, closed the door, and went around to the sitting room.

Ten minutes later he heard the bedroom door open and the sound of the Frenchwoman running along the Modesto's tile walkway toward her own room. Seconds afterward Zorro came through the bathroom with a towel wrapped around his waist.

"You shoulda knocked first," he complained.

"I'm paying for the room. Why should I have to knock? Besides, you need your sleep. We're taking off tomorrow night."

"You've got the money?"

"Picking it up in the morning." The trace of a smirk began lifting up one side of the *mestizo*'s mouth. Amazon saw it. "No bullshit, *compadre,*" he said, motioning with his finger at Zorro's chest. "This is for sure. The train north leaves tomorrow night, and your stuff better be together."

Leaving Zorro standing there in the sitting room, Henry Amazon walked on toward his bed. He felt like all the fiber had gone out of his body, and it took most of his remaining strength just to get all his clothes off and climb under the covers. Once he was there, the bedroom quickly faded into a haze. The Frenchwoman had left behind a thick scent.

Like most scams this last one was starting to feel sleazy before it was halfway done.

11

At 9 A.M. Saturday the Judicial Federal and its American helpers set the bait in their trap for Jerome Whitehurst alias Ramón Ramón.

During the two days since the capture and interrogation of El Tasajo on Wednesday night, Purdee Fletcher had argued that the best use for their new snitch was snaring the big-time *gringo* he'd identified. Others said El Tasajo might be lying, but Purd finally won the argument by reminding Pizarro Cruz how much importance the Mexico City *gringos* placed on this Big Ten of theirs. To nab one of these creeps might well end up being worth a lot down the line when Condor's operational funding was divided up. Cruz resented being talked to that way but agreed with the logic.

When Tasajo was released from the City Prison on Saturday morning, he left in the company of a young Federale dressed like a city Indian. Tasajo was instructed that this man was to be identified as his friend Jaime from Tehuacán. The two of them would wait for Ramón Ramón at Tasajo's house. Both had been put under firm or-

147

ders to make sure they became part of whatever deal the *gringo* was working on.

Purdee Fletcher and Pizarro Cruz stood in the prison courtyard to see Tasajo off. Cruz just stared at the *chiva* and said nothing, but that was more than enough. El Tasajo got the message.

The *gringo* standing next to Cruz was friendlier. "Good hunting," Purd called in English.

After El Tasajo and Jaime had driven past the guards at the gate, Purd leaned his head toward Cruz. "That *gringo* creep's gonna bite," the American senior agent predicted. "You watch and see, Pizarro, that sucker's gonna walk right into Ole Purd's hands."

Cruz responded with a square grin that hid his fury. If they were caught, it would be by Cruz's hand, not Purd's. The *Jefe* puffed twice on a fresh cigarette and then ground it into the pavement.

Ray Bob Wissle was back on the *zocolo* working the photo stakeout again. At first glance Hog had figured that this day would be a repeat of the one before. Signs of approaching rain were everywhere, but only a few sprinkles were actually falling here and there around the valley.

It was market day downtown, and both Indians and *turistas* were out in force.

Hog's only special instructions concerned the violator Condor Central had identified as one Bruno Sawyer alias Beef Stew. Purd had told Hog to cruise the downtown the same as always, but to drop it all if he spotted the suspect Beef or the blond woman who'd been with him in the pictures. He was to tail them from a distance and report back.

Ray Bob Wissle spent the first hour of the morning meandering around the park catty-corner from the *zocolo* and drinking coffee at the Hotel Monte Alban. At ten he switched to the *zocolo* itself and concentrated on the outdoor cafés along the side of the square known as Gringo Corners. The usual assortment of tourists were there along with several full-time American expatriates. None of them struck Hog as suspicious, but he watched them anyway, snapping several surreptitious photos of the ones he hadn't seen before. The street and side-walks were crowded, and most of the flood of people were headed south toward the old market. Drivers and pedestrians alike ignored the traffic signals, and amidst a fusillade of horns, the snarl of vehicles, and angry shouts, Hog wove in and out, watching. Then he stumbled onto the biggest coup of his career.

It was just a momentary flash of an unusual straw color between cars. Hog immediately connected it to the blond woman in the photo of Beef Stew and looked closer through his telephoto lens. The view lasted only for three seconds, but it was enough for Hog to be sure he'd seen a *gringo* with a heavy tan leading a blond-haired woman wearing a pair of round decorator shades. The couple had then vanished into the flow of shoppers toward the market.

Afraid that running would be too obvious, Ray Bob Wissle trotted across the *plaza,* dodged through the traffic, and started down the street that led south, skirting one edge of the huge building housing the municipal market. Both the sidewalks were overflowing with knick-knacks, cloth, *tortillas,* blankets, and chilies. As a result, most of the pedestrians were making their way along the middle of the street in a sea of bobbing heads and backs. The fleeting patch of straw color was not among them.

Hog's best guess was that the couple was headed into the market itself, and he made his way toward the sprawling two-square-block building as fast as he was able.

He entered on the edge of the meat section. Slabs of pig and goat were mounted on hooks next to several butchers waiting patiently to slice off any part the customer was willing to pay for. The floor was sticky with the drying blood of dead animals. Hog slowed himself and began to move steadily along the wide row of stalls leading to the heart of the building. "Be systematic," he said inside his head. "Be systematic and don't panic. They're in here somewhere, and they don't know you're after them." Hog shook his hands to try and ease his nerves and calm himself. A Zapotec woman with only three teeth showing stepped out of a crowd of Indians and waved a handful of *tortillas*

149

at the passing *gringo,* but Hog strode by with quick steps and a look of preoccupation welded to his face.

Beef Stew and Stella Ranch knew exactly where they were going, and they were late. They were headed for a corner on the far side of the giant market near the opposite doorway from the one they had entered, where several tables were arranged into a little café. The proprietor there served beer, soda pop, and thin strips of meat cooked on charcoal and wrapped in one of his wife's *tortillas.* Stella could have given the money to Ramón, but instead she had insisted that both she and Beef came along to meet Henry Amazon. It was her first opportunity to be in on a payoff, and she didn't want to miss it.

Ramón and Amazon were already there. Amazon was annoyed. He had been the first to arrive and had positioned himself at the table so he could watch the doorway leading into the milling, babble-filled street. Five minutes later, Ramón came and sat down beside him.

"Where's my money?" Amazon asked immediately.

"It's on its way," Ramón explained. "As soon as my partner gets here."

"Your partner? What's this partner bullshit? You were supposed to meet me with the bread. Nobody said nothin' about this other dude."

"Hey," Ramón snapped, "I told you my partner was the paymaster. Nothin' since has changed that." Henry Amazon was rapidly becoming a pain in the ass as far as Ramón was concerned. "Lighten up. No one's trying to slip one by you."

Amazon retreated into silence.

When Ramón Ramón started up again, he said, "Beef's all right, you'll see. He's a class-A smuggler. Did some time in Quentin and holds his mud real good. And with my connections down here, the partnership's a natural. I mean a real natural. I guarantee you it's one meal ticket this grunt's gonna get fat on."

Amazon said nothing.

Ramón was the first to spot Beef and Stella.

"Here he comes," he said.

Henry Amazon swiveled around to look. Stella was dressed in jeans that were rolled up to right below her knee and high silver lamé boots. She carried a matching silver lamé jacket over her shoulder, wore a clinging aqua-colored T-shirt with no bra, and her nipples showed through the tight material.

"Who's the broad?"

"Name's Stella," Ramón explained. "Beef's old lady."

Despite his irritation, Amazon smiled. "Some class-A smugglers," he thought.

"She's richer 'n shit," Ramón added lamely.

Amazon's smile grew into a chuckle.

The laughter bothered Ramón Ramón: he knew exactly what Henry Amazon was laughing at. Dressed the way she was, Stella might as well have been a neon sign. Most of the Indians she passed stopped what they were doing to watch her little tits bounce by, and a swarm of stage whispers in Zapotec and pidgin Spanish rose like dust in her wake.

Henry Amazon turned back to the table.

After catching Beef's eye, Ramón Ramón did likewise.

For the first time this morning Amazon looked straight into his former partner's face. "With that for a meal ticket," he drawled with a suppressed grin, "you're gonna eat your lunch."

When Beef and Stella sat down, Henry Amazon got right to the point. This was the last time Amazon would ever see Ramón, and he wanted to leave him toppled off his high horse, the way he was at that moment. The picture of Ramón on the defensive was the one he wanted to keep.

"You got my money?" he asked.

"You don't waste no time, do you?" Beef joked. The California dealer was trying to make friends, but the effort was lost on Amazon.

"I figure it's the best way to do my business."

"Pay the man, Stella," Beef said with a motion of his head in his woman's direction.

Stella pulled an envelope out of her matching lamé purse and extended it to the tall blondish *gringo*.

Henry Amazon hunched over with the package in his lap and checked its contents. Without counting every bill, it was obvious that there were somewhere in the neighborhood of fifty one-hundred-dollar U.S. Treasury notes inside.

Stella lit a Benson and Hedges and sat there in a cloud of tobacco smoke.

"All right," Amazon said, standing up. "It's a pleasure doing business with you." As the tall *gringo* circled toward the nearest exit, he swiveled his head back to the still silent Ramón Ramón. "Have a good one, Double R," Amazon grinned at his former partner.

Then he headed for the door.

Ramón Ramón smoldered for a moment before coming out with a voice that had blades on its edges. "Goddamn it," he snapped in Beef's direction, "how can you let this dumb cunt walk down here looking like that? You ought to have brought a fuckin' flag and a marching band as long as you were gonna bring a blond *gringa* dressed like a thousand-*peso* whore into a crowd of Indians on market day. You got shit for brains or somethin'?"

Stella immediately started babbling at Beef that he ought to make Ramón take that back, and when that didn't work, she began demanding to leave.

"Just shut up, Stella," Beef growled. "Just shut up. We'll leave in a second. What about tonight?" He then turned and asked Ramón.

"Meet me at the corner north of your hotel at ten sharp." Ramón bit his words off with a violent motion of his jaw. He ignored Stella and with a short "later" in Beef's direction, headed for the door. When he reached the street, Henry Amazon had long since vanished.

Hog Wissle had caught up with the patch of blond hair just as Stella was taking the money out of her purse. He made a quick halt by a banana stand, fifty feet from the group at the table, and went for his camera. His first picture was of Stella with her hand extending an envelope to one of the two shapes with their backs to the camera. The second was part Stella, part Beef, and the hunched back of one figure on the left bending over something in his lap. The third was Beef, Stella, and the two shapes again. This time Stella was lighting a cigarette.

By then the Indians in that part of the market had noticed the camera pointed in their direction and had started quite a commotion in their efforts to get out of its view. When Hog noticed their panic, he was forced to stop shooting for fear of revealing his presence. As he continued to watch the transaction, the junior agent only went back to his camera for two more shots. The next-to-last one was of the tall man who had taken the envelope from Stella Ranch. He was leaving, and he had turned back for one last comment. Hog snapped just as the unidentified American was turning away again. The picture that came out was mostly the back of the man's head. It showed his ear and the shape of his skull, but only the faintest outline of a cheekbone and a jaw.

Nevertheless, it would turn out to be the only photograph of the *mota* smuggler eventually identified as Henry Amazon ever to make its way into police files on either side of the border. After examining it for hours, both Hog and his boss Purd would later swear they could detect the hint of a smile in the man's face, even though none of his features were distinguishable.

Junior Agent Ray Bob Wissle followed the suspect already known to the authorities as Bruno Sawyer alias Beef Stew and his woman, later to be identified as one Stella Ranch, to the hotel San Cristóbal. He stayed a good fifty feet behind them, too far away to hear their conversation, but it was obvious that they were arguing. The couple disappeared inside the hotel and didn't come out again all afternoon. After an hour of watching the San Cristóbal's front door, Hog Wissle went to find Purd.

Purdee Fletcher was at his desk in the offices over the funeral parlor, filling out the weekly accounting of the station's business for the finance officer in Mexico City. He was beginning to think about lunch and was surprised to see Hog.

"Run out of film?" he asked.

"Something a whole lot better than that," Hog beamed. "I found that Beef Stew creep...."

Purd started to interrupt but Hog blurted on.

"And his woman," he added, holding up his hand to keep Purd quiet for a few seconds more, "and the rest of his gang."

"The rest of his gang?"

"That's what I said."

"What gang?"

"Beef Stew's gang."

Purdee didn't say anything.

"I spotted him and his woman going to the market about ten," Hog continued. "When I caught up to where I could see him, they met two others and—"

"Two other what?"

"Two other American males. Maybe in their early thirties. One was as tall as me, only skinny, and the other was short, maybe five foot seven or eight."

"Did you get them on film?"

"Hope so," Hog said, patting his Nikon camera. "We'll have to see."

Purdee wanted to know what made his partner so goddamn sure they were all a gang.

"They were all sitting at the same table," he explained. "The broad gave one of the guys what I think was money."

Purd rubbed the side of his face. If that was so, Hog's theory made a lot of sense.

"All right, Hog, my man, you're doing all right," Purd drawled. "I may make you a narc yet."

Hog Wissle was insulted by the statement but hid his feelings. He considered himself a first-class narc already.

Purdee Fletcher didn't dwell on the subject. "Git that film out and haul it over to Pastilla's, lickety-split," he continued. "Tell him I'll pay double to get it all back today."

After walking to the photo lab and arranging for Purd to pick up the prints at 10 P.M., Ray Bob Wissle returned to his watch at the San Cristóbal. To make sure the suspects were still there, Hog walked through the lobby and out into the courtyard until he located Beef and Stella sprawled near the pool. Reassured, he returned to a spot in the shade across the street from the hotel doorway, but neither suspect came out all afternoon.

At six Hog walked back to the office and told Purdee that he needed some relief. Purd in turn said to get Garcia Huahilote to send someone to keep an eye on the *gringos*. Garcia said he would send one of his men and did, but the Mexican didn't stay long. No one saw Beef Stew slip out the front door at 10 P.M. and return two and a half hours later, having successfully made the down payment on a large load of hashish.

By ten o'clock Saturday night just about the only narc in the Oaxaca Condor Station still working was Ole Purd himself. Until 11 P.M. he was waiting in Pastilla's tiny office for the Mexican to complete the developing job. When it was finally finished, Purd headed back across the *zocolo* for the Judicial Federal headquarters to have a first look at the "gang." A light and grainy mist was beginning to fall on the long arms of the square's tamarinds and the exposed surface of the asphalt. Purd bent the collar on his sport coat up and broke into a jog. The Indians selling gum and pumpkin seeds out of baskets near the bandstand had all long since packed up and split for home.

As Henry Amazon, Zorro, and El Chorizo waited along the Pan American for Vincente, the *gringo* felt his luck was on the upswing. This meeting along the Pan American was the last rendezvous before heading north with the goods. Rain provided the best camouflage he could imagine.

North and west of the city the mist gently drifting on to the downtown *zocolo* was a wall of water falling in drops the size of sparrow eggs. The smugglers were fifteen miles north of town. Henry Amazon had parked his Toyota Land Cruiser and El Chorizo his Dina in a wide dirt area off the road, behind a row of cypress trees. Zorro and his Ford with the trunk full of *mota* was stationed as a lookout on the main road with lights out but engine running. The rain cascaded down in a clatter on the roofs of all three vehicles, and each of the drivers waited alone, cut off from the others. The dark outside was total, broken occasionally by a set of headlamps passing on the nearby highway.

Henry Amazon was as nervous as a cat with its back up. In his mind each passing car was supposed to be Vincente and his load of *mota*. As each rolled on toward Mexico City, his nerves tightened. "Come on, *indio*," he said to himself. "Get here."

The rain was a blessing, and Amazon wanted to take maximum advantage of it. He smoked steadily and flipped each cigarette out into the storm before it was halfway burned. The stand of cypress hiding them from the highway was bending in the gusty wind. His windows were fogged over, and he rolled one down to get some air. A blast of rain slammed into his face. Then Zorro's voice crackled on the CB.

"He's here," Zorro said.

"*Bueno,*" Amazon answered into his microphone. In his side mirror he could see the lights of Vincente's truck driving up behind the trees. Henry Amazon pulled the hood of his poncho over his hair and stepped out into the storm. The wind immediately grabbed at the garment's loose skirts, and the *gringo* had to use one hand to hold it down. Vincente's Ford flatbed splashed through several puddles before coming to a halt. Amazon sloshed up to the driver's window and mounted the running board. Vincente's face was worried.

"Who's that car out there?" he said, motioning in the direction of Zorro's Ford. The *gringo* could barely hear him because of the roar of the weather.

"It's the Mexican," Amazon shouted back over the wind. "Keeping lookout."

Vincente appeared relieved.

"You're late," the *gringo* said.

"It's a bad night," the Indian explained, motioning at the avalanche of rain around them. The Indian leaned halfway out the window so Amazon could hear him.

"No, *compadre*," Amazon grinned. "It's a very good night. Couldn't be better." The smuggler paused a moment to look back at Chorizo's truck and then returned to business. "Can you back around and butt your ass-end up against his?" he asked. Vincente took one look at the maneuver and said it was no problem at all. Amazon jumped down off the running board, and Vincente turned his truck around, backed its bed up to the lip of Chorizo's, and then killed the engine and lights. For several moments there was no sound except the rain and several men sloshing around in it, untying Vincente's tarpaulin. Once the load was undone, Amazon, Vincente, and El Chorizo shifted the barrels from one truck to the other. The Amazon's Indian driver lashed his cover over them while the *gringo* and Vincente sat in Vincente's cab and counted Amazon's final payment. Henry Amazon then stepped back into the rain again. Water ricocheted off his head and shoulders. With a wave out his window, Vincente headed back toward his village.

Amazon checked to make sure Chorizo had tied the *mota* barrels down right, returned to his Land Cruiser, and started the engine.

Eventually, Amazon wiped his face with a rag he kept under the seat and got on the CB.

" 'Stá listo," he called to Zorro. " 'Sta listo."

"About time," the Mexican growled. His headlights clicked on. Then those on the Land Cruiser and finally the Dina's followed suit.

The caravan sloshed onto the Pan American and pointed north with Amazon in the lead. His Land Cruiser was clean, and the *gringo* could ride as much as three or four miles in front of the other two, free to encounter any obstacles in the road with relative safety while giving the others warning in time to run. El Chorizo and his Dina with the barrels of *mota* came next, equipped with two walkie-talkies, and Zorro and his Ford brought up the rear. It was a hard position for the

Mexican to fill. His car was the fastest, and he wanted to cruise at eighty-five.

"Breaker One Nine," Amazon called. "This is Turtle Leader. Give me a sound check. Over."

"Sausage here," El Chorizo crackled in Spanish.

"*Zorro también*," the Mexican added.

"Over and out," Amazon said.

The storm was assaulting the first ridge that loomed over the flat stretch where they'd been parked, and Henry Amazon hunched down in his seat. Outside the wind was blowing so hard it smeared blotches of standing water across the face of the safety glass and tugged at the nose of the Toyota. Amazon had to wrestle with the wheel simply in order to stay on the pavement.

At midnight Agent Purdee Fletcher was just about to call it quits. Purd was tired of looking at the goddamn pictures and a little disgusted at himself for putting in a sixteen-hour day when no one else did. At the same time Purd knew it was his own fault. He'd volunteered to stay late and pick up the pictures because he'd wanted very badly to see them. They were potentially extremely important to his comeback. If Wissle's idea about a gang was accurate, it would mean Ole Purd had two major smuggling cases cooking at once, this one and Ramón. Mexico City would notice that kind of production. Purd knew it. His midnight sense of disappointment centered around the pictures themselves.

Purd had come to expect more than was actually there. For starters, out of the pile of photos, there were only a total of six separate snapshots of Beef Stew and his friends. Purd had imagined there would be at least half a roll.

In addition the photographs were far from good. The first was a long shot with a zoom lens of a woman's blond head in the middle of a sea of pedestrians. The next were of Beef and his woman friend at a table with two anonymous shapes between themselves and the camera.

This sequence did tend to confirm Hog's statement about money being exchanged, but that was all. It gave Purd no new information about who the two shapes were, which is what he needed to know in order to take the junior agent's theory any further. The last two shots Hog had taken were the only progress the investigation had made.

The first framed the shape Purd guessed was the larger of the *gringos*. Without even using his magnifying glass, Purd knew the minute he laid eyes on the picture that it would tell them nothing more than the suspect's general configuration and coloring.

The sixth and final shot, while not the best angle, showed the shorter *gringo* had a well-trimmed mustache and hair styled so it curled onto his ears. His nose was somewhat hooked and his complexion close to that of a Mexican. Purdee Fletcher didn't even think to check it against the one of Ramón Ramón on the wall ten feet away, in the County Jail photograph from five years earlier that was Ramón's Big Ten identification. His hair had been long and stringy then, and he had been skinnier, but the hook in his nose hadn't changed. Nonetheless, the senior agent had filed the two cases separately in his mind and continued to do so.

Purd stared at the face for a long time. Something about it felt very familiar, but he couldn't quite put his finger on it. The harder he looked, the less Purd seemed to see. The senior agent's energy was flagging. Finally he pushed away from the desk and told himself it was time to hit the sack. He would go over the pictures again in the morning when he was fresh.

Just as Purd switched his desk lamp off, the radio behind him crackled to life.

"Breaker One Nine," it sputtered. The words had a heavy overlay of static, but at least the first few were clear. "This is Turtle Leader. Give me . . ." The rest of the statement was lost in the rising garble as were the message's two quick responses. Only the final "over and out" was faintly audible.

When no other transmission followed, Purd seized his radio's microphone and tried to locate the voice.

"Breaker One Nine," he drawled. "This is the ole Mongoose calling that Turtle Leader I just heard. Read me. Over." Purdee was doing his best to sound like an Alabama teamster. No one answered.

"Breaker One Nine," the agent called again. "Mongoose callin' Turtle Leader. Over."

The radio remained silent.

"Breaker One Nine, Turtle Leader, pull my handle. This is the ole Mongoose. I'm a *gringo,* too, and you're the first one I heard all day. Give me some *gringo* talk. No bullshit. I'm lonesome. Over."

There was still no response. Purd started to go back on the air to try again but thought better of it.

Out on the Pan American, none of the three radios in Amazon's caravan had picked up the agent's attempt to make contact. The storm was too fierce. Lightning flashed several times as the highway snaked up the first ridge. A small rock slide had already been washed over one lane near the crest. The wind was unusually cold and had teeth.

12

Agent Purdee Fletcher didn't put the two pictures together until late Sunday morning. By then it was once again clear and sunny outside his window.

Purd was standing in the shower with his chin on his chest, letting the tepid water roll over his back and down the length of his lumpy and larded-over body. Sunday morning sat real heavy on Purd, and it was taking him a longer time than usual to wake up. As he slowly came around, the agent found himself studying the patterns the water made on its way to the drain. In one of them he recognized the puzzling profile from the night before. That led to a reassuring thought about how he had two cases going and brief glimpses of the Big Ten Ramón Ramón. At that point Purdee Fletcher clicked.

"Well, fuck me," he blurted out loud. He closed his eyes, and with his memory flashed the recent pictures from the market and the old County Jail mug shot next to each other. They fit. He turned the water off and hopped out onto the tile floor. Without slowing down he grabbed a towel and proceeded into his adjoining hotel room where he had the photos themselves.

161

He laid them out next to each other, and they indeed did fit. All the window dressing was different, but the hooked face of Jerome Whitehurst alias Ramón Ramón was obvious in both of them. It wasn't Beef Stew's gang at all. That was what had slowed Purd down. The *gringo* was in town and using this Beef Stew character and his woman in some kind of deal. Instead of two cases Purd only had a crossfire on one, but it was much bigger than he'd thought and obviously well on its way to coming to a head. If money was changing hands now, the deal must be close.

He picked up the phone. Pizarro Cruz should be told right away. They were onto something, it was hot, and his men better be ready. He called Cruz's private home number. It rang eight times without an answer. He was about to hang up when the connection was made on the other end of the line.

"*Bueno.*"

It was Cruz's voice, but Purdee Fletcher checked to make sure. "Pissaro?"

"*Sí.*"

"This is Ole Purd."

Cruz let out a deep breath.

"I'm real sorry to bother you on Sunday and all, but I'm afraid we got some information late last night that just won't wait."

"Tell me," Cruz said.

"Well," Purd answered, "I'm afraid I need to show it to you. It involves some pictures my partner Hog took yesterday, and you ought to see them to understand what I'm talking about. The gist of it is that the *gringo* that creep identified is in the neighborhood."

"It is important?" It was obvious from Cruz's voice that he didn't relish seeing the *gringo* on his Sunday off.

"Very," Purdee insisted. "We're real close to them now and need to stay right on top of things. You should see these pictures before tomorrow. I know it's a hassle, but the law's business just won't wait."

Pizarro Cruz did not want to be lectured about the obligations of the law by a *gringo* who didn't know his place. At the same time he wanted to know what Purd was so excited about. He told Purdee Fletcher to stop by in an hour.

Hanging up, Cruz was irritated. His intention had been to spend Sunday watching the soccer matches on the television.

Back at the Trocadero, Purdee Fletcher dried himself off. The Big Ten aspect of the whole thing excited him. Catch one of those, and Ole Purd was on his way.

The house where the taxi delivered Purdee Fletcher at half past noon was in a residential neighborhood built along the rising slope between the *zocolo* and the observatory on the hill that anchors the city's northwest corner. The house was down a dead-end, one-lane mud alley that intersected the paved street at a small *tienda* on the corner. Turkeys were wandering among the puddles when the taxi arrived. Purd stepped gingerly through the mud and scattered clumps of bird shit. He was wearing a turquoise leisure suit and white patent leather loafers.

Cruz led the *gringo* into his tiled kitchen. An open doorway connected it to another room with several couches and a television set.

Pizarro Cruz poured Purd a cup of coffee, and they sat at the table to conduct their business. Cruz was in his shirt-sleeves. Even though it was Sunday and he was in his own home, the Federale was wearing a revolver in his shoulder holster. He was also wearing sunglasses. Behind them, his eyes bored in on the *gringo*. This Poord would have to be put in his place, but so far Pizarro Cruz hadn't found the right way to do it.

"You'll excuse me if I seem rushed," Cruz began, "but it's Sunday, and I have other things to do." The Federale smiled his square smile in Purd's general direction.

"Of course, Pissaro," Purdee smiled back. "You don't got to apologize for a thing. I understand completely. With your permission I'll just lay out what's cooking."

163

The head Federale continued to smile and motioned for Purd to proceed.

"The best place to start," Purd began, "is with a quick review. At the moment we have two active *gringo* suspects going. Am I right?" The question was rhetorical. "The first of those is this creep." Purdee threw the mug shot on the table. "Jerome Whitehurst alias Ramón Ramón. In violation of parole and suspected of murder. One of Condor's Big Ten."

"The other," Fletcher went on, "is this ex-convict, Bruno Sawyer alias Beef Stew, identified by Condor Central as an active suspect in L.A." The American senior agent slapped down the surveillance photograph Hog had taken on the San Dionisio Road the week before. "It's three suspects if we count his woman."

So far Purdee Fletcher had told Pizarro Cruz nothing he hadn't known before. The information was hardly worth a piece out of the middle of his Sunday, and the Mexican was thinking about getting openly irritated.

"Yesterday," Purd pushed on, slapping down six more photographs, "Hog was watching the zoke and picked up this Beef Stew asshole's trail downtown, followed him into the market, and took these." Purdee spread the photos out in a line and began to describe them one by one. He could see Cruz's attention had been captured. "Forget this first one," he said, "it's just where he picked up their trail. These next three are the first important part. You see this Stew character there?" Purd pointed at one of the shapes.

"Yes," Cruz answered.

"And this," Purdee went on, shifting his finger, "is his woman. Right yet we don't know who this guy is," Purd admitted, pointing next to the left-hand shape in the foreground. "But we can sure as hell tell what's going on. Look at that thing the broad is passin' to him. Take a close look at it."

Cruz held the print up to the light.

"If they're not passing an envelope of cash, my name ain't Ole Purdee Fletcher, and I never seen hide nor hair of Manila or any niggers in L.A."

All Purd's references to his personal history were lost on Pizarro Cruz, but the detail the *gringo* pointed out was not. It was an envelope, thick enough with bills so that the unsupported half of the shape in the woman's hand flopped over toward the table.

"How much you think that is?" Cruz asked.

Purd shrugged. "Who knows? What is clear is that if they're paying people for things, they're getting real close to doing the deed."

"Maybe," Pizarro Cruz allowed, "and maybe not. Who is this she's giving it to?" The Federale pointed to the left-hand shape, ignoring Purd's previous statement that the suspect was unidentified.

Purdee answered by pointing at the next photo in line. "Him," he said. The photo showed parts of a shoulder, ear, and the faint outlines of a jaw on an otherwise indistinguishable *gringo* head.

"Who is him?"

Purd shrugged again. "Who knows? He's a *gringo* with some kind of brown- or blond-colored hair and tall. What we do know is the identity of the guy sitting next to him."

"Who is he?"

"This one . . . ," Purd said, pushing the last photo in front of the Federale. He let Cruz's eye come to rest on this hooked profile from yesterday at the market for a few moments before slapping the original Ramón Ramón mug shot down over one of the last photo's corners, like he was playing a trump card. "Jerome Whitehurst alias Ramón Ramón."

Pizarro Cruz compared the pictures and could quickly see what Purd meant.

"Don't you see, Pissaro? The two cases are one. The two cases are one."

Cruz didn't like being pushed. "I see," he said, dropping the square smile for a moment. "What do you think it means?"

Purdee didn't hesitate. "I think it means that this Big Ten creep is putting together some kind of scam down here. I mean, look. We know he's hooked up with this Beef Stew character, and this other dude they were paying in the picture, and our Piece of Meat friend he told he wanted to drive. That's a maximum of three *gringos,* a woman, and a driver. There must be at least two, most likely three, maybe even four vehicles involved. We know at least one of those is a camper. I look at that and say this Whitehurst alias Ramón Ramón is getting ready to load up. With that much wheel strength we're talking over a ton, maybe even two or four. Which, as you know, ain't all that chicken shit, especially if they're buying quality."

Cruz knew full well it wasn't and also knew the *gringos* would need a goodly sum of money to pay for it. "How much you think they're carrying?" he asked.

"Maybe eighty or even a hundred G.'s."

"Maybe more."

"You're right," Purd said.

Silence descended for a moment while the numbers sank in.

"It's my guess," Purd continued, "that our number one *gringo* is going to get in touch with the snitch and his friend Jaime from Tehuacán. I think you should get a car out watching the snitch's house right now. If they see the number one come by, maybe try to put a real loose tail on him. Find out where he stashes himself. Someone should be on duty down at the office too."

Pizarro Cruz said he would see about it and stood up.

"No," Purd pressed, "you don't seem to understand. There can't be no 'see about it' on this one. This is more important than that. You've got to get some men out there, Sunday or not. Goddamn, Pissaro, that's elementary police basics."

The remark broke the surface of Cruz's heretofore hidden hostility.

"It is you that don't understand," the Federale snapped at Purd. "I am the *jefe* here. You are my assistant. You don't tell me what has to happen. You don't tell me where to send my men. All you do is what I decide. You are working on Mexican soil by Mexican permission. You make suggestions; you don't give no orders. When I say I'll see about it, I'll see about it. That's all."

Pizarro Cruz stopped to light a cigarette and puffed on it several times before crumbling it into the ashtray.

Purd wanted to tell him to take all that goddamn Mexican soil and stick it up his ass. He didn't. "Whatever you say, *Jefe,*" he said.

"We will meet on this at ten tomorrow in the office," the Federale announced without expression. "If something happens in the meantime, I will let you know."

"Certainly," Purd mumbled.

Pizarro Cruz then flashed his square smile until Purd reached the gate.

Alone again, the *jefe* of Oaxaca Station retreated back into the room with the TV. After several minutes of soccer Cruz returned to the kitchen for a beer. He knew the *gringo* was right. Pizarro Cruz did not want to give Purd reason to complain to Condor Central or let pride get in the way of sound maneuvering. Coupled with the hopeless soccer effort he'd been watching, they were reasons enough to drive the resentful Cruz to the phone. He reached Garcia Huahilote at his home and told him to get someone out watching El Tasajo's street. There was new information from the *gringos*. The head *traficante* was about to come by. When his deputy answered that it would be hard to get people away from the game, Cruz's voice landed like an ax.

"Then go yourself, Garcia. And go now."

As it turned out Purd's guess was pretty much on the mark. At the same time the narcotics agent had relayed his suggestions to Cruz, Ramón Ramón was on his way to find El Tasajo, The Piece of Meat.

Tasajo lived south of the Periférico, down a six-block-long dirt street that was one of two dozen identical roadways in the neighborhood. Ramón was in a rented Ford LTD. The car drove like a boat. Ramón Ramón was dressed in his tourist polyesters and shades. After he'd parked in front of Tasajo's house, he sat in the Ford and checked the street in both directions. When he was satisfied that everything was calm outside, Ramón knocked on the *mestizo*'s solid wood door.

The door was opened by a stranger. "*Buenas tardes,*" the man greeted.

"Is Tasajo here?" Ramón asked in Spanish, wishing he'd picked a time to stop by when the Mexican didn't have guests.

"Yes he is," the stranger smiled, gesturing for the *gringo* to step inside. "Come in. He's playing ball."

The courtyard of the *mestizo*'s house was tiny and narrow, and the two rooms themselves weren't a lot larger. One ran the length of the left-hand wall, and the other the length of the right, with the yard in between. Tasajo slept in the left room and used the right to play a game called "ball" that amounted to batting a tennis ball around an empty room with bare hands. Although Ramón would have preferred to catch El Tasajo alone, the presence of others didn't seem unusual. It wasn't the first time the *gringo* had come by and found a small crowd inside, smoking *mota* and taking turns on the court. The twenty-four-year-old Tasajo liked to entertain.

At the moment of Ramón's arrival he was playing with an eighteen-year-old kid named Domingo. Ramón had seen Domingo before. The *gringo* stuck his head in the doorway. "*Quiubole, señor* Meat?" he shouted. El Tasajo stopped the game immediately and seemed flustered. Ramón passed it off as surprise.

"*Don* Ramón," El Tasajo said. "What a pleasure." His eyes shifted quickly to the strange Mexican standing behind Ramón and then back to the *gringo*.

"*Don Ramón*," Tasajo continued with a motion to the man behind him, "this is my friend Jaime from Tehuacán."

Ramón turned for a moment to the man who had answered the door. "*Mucho gusto*," he said.

The Mexican had a line of hair running along his upper lip and was about the same height as Ramón. The hair moved little when the disguised Federale Jaime answered, "*Mucho gusto, Don Ramón*." The Mexican didn't smile until Ramón had turned back to Piece of Meat. Then he smiled across the width of his face.

"You know Domingo," El Tasajo continued.

Ramón tipped his hand toward the eighteen-year-old and got the same motion in return. All three Mexicans were dressed alike, in bright colored twill pants, T-shirts, and *huaraches*.

"Have you gotten any better?" the *gringo* joked at Domingo. The last time Ramón had seen this Mexican, Ramón had trounced him in a game of ball.

"Not a bit," Tasajo replied.

Domingo took joking exception. "What you talking, *pinche chinga?*"

"What's the score? *Chinga madre?*" El Tasajo laughed back. "Three games in a row."

Then the *mestizo* turned back to Ramón Ramón. *"Don Ramón,"* he suggested, "you ought to play Jaime here."

"Is he the champ of the day?" Ramón asked, looking at the Mexican and sizing him up. Jaime looked quick.

"I can't beat him," El Tasajo admitted.

"I'd like to," Ramón said, taking one last look at the Mexican who'd answered the door. "But I'm too much busy at the moment." Ramón turned back to Tasajo. "I got to talk a little quick business with you."

"Just ten points," Jaime interrupted.

Ramón Ramón turned back to the strange Mexican with a little irritation. "I can't," he said. "I have to go soon."

"Just up to five."

"Some other time," Ramón answered him, with a tone that left no doubt about the outcome of Jaime's attempted persuasion. Ramón then motioned to Tasajo to come outside and began walking the four steps across to the bedroom doorway.

"Some other time," Jaime grinned at the departing *gringo*. "For sure."

As El Tasajo walked out of the court and past his friend Jaime from Techuacán, the undercover Federale's eyes bored into the *chiva*'s. Tasajo tried to make a hidden motion with his brows to indicate he understood what Jaime was worried about and that he had it covered.

When Tasajo and Ramón Ramón reached the far corner of Tasajo's bedroom, Ramón got right down to business. "We got this Tuesday night," he said in his usual flat, cold style. "You still game?"

"The pay the same as you said before?"

"The same."

"I'm going," the *mestizo* answered.

"Bueno," Ramón continued. "You know where the basket part of the market is?"

"Yes."

"Be at the southwest corner of it at nine o'clock Tuesday night."

"Then what?"

"Then we'll go pick up the load and head north," Ramón answered. "You'll be driving a camper with American plates."

"How many of us is there?"

Up until this point Ramón had not been looking at the *mestizo* but was watching the empty doorway over his shoulder. "You don't need to know that yet," he snapped, looking up and down Tasajo's face for a moment. "You just get ready to drive, *compadre.*"

"Where we drivin' to?" El Tasajo persisted. "I got a right to know that."

"North."

"How?"

"By the Tehuacán cutoff."

"And the load?"

"It's on the San Dionisio Road, maybe twenty-five miles in from the Angel side." Ramón answered the question as he moved to the door. He had said enough for now. "You just be where I told you on time and don't worry about nothin' else."

"Don Ramón," the *mestizo* called out, trying to hold him here for a few more moments.

Ramón stopped and looked back at Tasajo.

"My friend Jaime," the *mestizo* said in a soft voice, "the one you met in there?"

"Yah?"

"You got any work for him?"

"If I'd wanted two drivers, I would have found 'em."

"He's a good man," El Tasajo pressed, "and he could use the money."

"Look, Meat, you just stop worrying about your friend Jaime's shit and concentrate on getting your own together. Tuesday night. Nine o'clock. The southwest corner of the market."

With that the *gringo* went quickly out of the house. His rented Ford started with the first touch of the key, and Ramón Ramón took a left and made his way in a pattern of zigs and zags through the neighborhood and back to the asphalt Periférico.

Five minutes later Garcia Huahilote arrived to begin his stakeout.

The first sign of activity he saw was when Domingo left the house several minutes later and disappeared down a cross street. In another five minutes Jaime led Tasajo outside, in search of a pay phone to call headquarters. Garcia Huahilote watched for a bit as they walked off in the opposite direction and then pulled up in his car and rolled down the window.

"What are you doing?" he barked.

"He came, he came," the undercover Federale blurted out. "The *gringo*."

Garcia motioned the two of them into his car. When he had learned the whole story, he dropped the *chiva* and his keeper off at a *burrito* stand and headed for his office.

Then he called the *Jefe*. The *gringo* had taken the bait, he said.

Word of Ramón reached Purdee Fletcher two hours after it reached Pizarro Cruz. By that time the American agent had parked himself on a lawn chair down by the Trocadero pool next to his partner Hog. Hog was busy getting brown, and Purd was slowly working his way through a succession of *cuba libres*. The senior agent had changed into a pair of flowered boxer trunks that were a size too small and gave him the look of a mattress stuffed into a carpetbag. At the time he was called to the phone in the hotel lobby, he had been discoursing to Hog about how these Mexicans were too fucking lazy to catch crooks. He had next to no faith the Federales could stay on top of things. Those feelings disappeared in a tide of satisfaction when Cruz told him the Ramón *gringo* had made contact. Ole Purd had been right on the money.

Fletcher then went back to his room. He had another, more private, phone there.

Purd had the hotel operator put through a call to a number in the Distrito Federal.

It was eventually answered after three rings. "Condor Central," the unidentified male voice said.

"Give me Longbeem." Operation Condor had a uniform set of operational codes, and the one covering the Big Ten program required that the Mexico City Station Chief and Operation Condor Supervisor, Norton Longbeem, be notified personally as soon as the presence of one of these suspects had been confirmed.

"Director Longbeem isn't on duty. Who's this?"

"This is Fletcher down in Oaxaca," Purd said, "I've got to talk to him. It's a Code Four."

"Code Four?"

"Code Four."

"Hold on."

After five minutes of silence, the voice returned to the other end of the line and gave Purdee another Mexico City number to call. Purdee hung up.

Norton Longbeem answered Purd's next call.

"Hello."

"Nort?" Purdee didn't know where the number was, but from the sound of the TV in the background and the fact it was Sunday, he guessed it was Longbeem's home. "This is Ole Purd."

"I know."

"Sorry to bother you on Sunday, but—"

"What's this Code Four business?" Longbeem interrupted.

"That's what I called about. Condor instructions call for immediate notification in the Big Ten program."

"You got one of those?"

"Coming and going," Purdee bragged. Fletcher knew the news would sound especially sweet to his old friend. Norton Longbeem had

172

designed the Big Ten program and had pushed it through all the channels between the inception of the idea and the operation itself.

"Which one?"

"Number eight by my set of photos. Jerome Whitehurst alias Ramón Ramón. Wanted in New Mexico, Federal Parole warrant, and suspicion of murder. Known violator. Referenced in the Monroe Jessee material."

There was silence on the other end of the wire for a moment while Longbeem pulled out his own set of photos and consulted the old County Jail mug shot.

"So you got that one, huh? Ramón Ramón. That's a mean sucker. Did you ever know old Bud O'Grady?"

"You mean the guy that was running training school when you and I first joined up?"

"That's him."

"What's he got to do with this?"

"Bud had a kid, Grady, second generation narc and good at it. With the Agency in Albuquerque. That's who this character killed. Happened when Grady was undercover. What we figured is that somehow this Ramón got wind he was a cop and iced him. The last time we can place Grady O'Grady alive is when he left his house riding in Ramón's car. Next time we saw Grady, he was laying with his brains blown out on some godforsaken mesa. That's mostly how this son of a bitch got to be Big Ten. I probably don't need to tell you how some of us feel about this. Bud O'Grady was a damn fine man, and so was his kid."

That personal connection only made it better as far as Purd was concerned. A lot of men over him would feel like they owed him a favor if he gave them Ramón Ramón.

"I also probably don't need to tell you," Longbeem continued, "that this Ramón Ramón customer is one slippery son of a bitch."

"He's gonna have to be," Purd bragged. "We're already into his hen house." Fletcher went on to lay out for his boss the crossfire they had set up for the suspect Jerome Whitehurst alias Ramón Ramón.

"When's the deal coming down?" Longbeem asked.

"Tuesday night at nine o'clock," Purd answered. We even know his planned route."

"What is it?"

"North through Tehuacán."

There was another pause as Longbeem left his receiver to fetch a pad and pencil. When he returned to the line, his voice sounded as though he were writing a note to himself.

"We'll have the Tehuacán office put a block at the state line," Longbeem said, "just in case you miss them." After another pause, Fletcher's old friend and boss continued in his normal voice. "Where do you plan to take him?"

"That's Cruz's business," Purd answered. "We're meeting on it tomorrow morning. My guess is he'll want to jump them when the whole gang is in one place out south of town here."

Longbeem was pleased with Purd's answer. "You're right about it being the Mexicans' business. The Drug Enforcement Administration is here to assist the Mexican government. Our only policy is that we want these suspects out of business."

"Gotcha," Purd answered. He was somewhat annoyed that Longbeem kept treating him like some kind of dummy who didn't know how the game was played. "I haven't forgot," Purd reminded his boss. "Ole Purd won't let you down."

"You're really tearing up the old pea patch down there, aren't ya?" The Mexico City Condor chief seemed genuinely pleased.

"Nothin' I haven't done before," Purd bragged again.

"Well, pull this one off, and I guarantee you'll have a lot of friends upstairs."

"It's in the bag," Agent Purdee Fletcher said.

Late that night, just as Sunday was turning into Monday and two days before Ramón Ramón was planning to travel the same route north, Henry Amazon's caravan took its first break for sleep. They were twenty miles past Zacatecas, Zacatecas, almost a thousand miles from Oaxaca, and the three vehicles had already passed through the states of Puebla, Mexico, Querétaro, León, and Aguasclientes, stopping only for gas. The endless road had left Amazon numb and slow, and he figured they should sleep now, before they started making mistakes. When they spotted a deserted tourist rest stop ahead on the right, he called on the CB and told the vehicles behind him to turn in.

The rest stop was a picnic table with a tin roof mounted over it on nine-foot poles. Amazon said each of them could sleep for four hours. They would alternate standing guard in two-hour shifts. He took the first turn, sitting on the picnic table in the dark. After a while Amazon lit a cigarette to keep him company. There was no traffic at all on the nearby highway. For the first hour the only sound was a series of coyotes calling out from the sharp spine of rocks breaking through the alkaline and mesquite-covered plain several miles away. Later a double trailer truck charged by. Then a train whistled on the far side of the ridge. It scattered a pack of wild dogs and set off a ferocious howling that lasted most of the night.

13

Except for the gummy black highway the countryside Henry Amazon's caravan drove through on Monday morning between Zacatecas and Torreon was universally brown: a landscape of alkali flats between ridges of acned rock and sprinklings of cactus. Every thirty miles or so an *adobe* hut with several emaciated cows clustered around it broke the monotony. Amazon paid them no attention. He was looking for signs of the Judicial Federal and little else. More than two miles behind his clean and legal Land Cruiser, masked by the shimmer and warp of the heat lifting off the Pan American, El Chorizo followed in his barrel-laden truck. Last in line, Zorro lagged impatiently behind in his Ford Galaxie. Slightly before noon Amazon crossed the Río Aguanaval on the outskirts of Torreon. On either shore of the river the cottonwoods were enormous.

This leg of the smuggle encountered its first and only trouble when Amazon announced his intention to stop for gas in Torreon.

"Breaker One Nine, this is Turtle Leader," he opened. "Let's gas up in the city. Over."

The outskirts of Torreon were visible ahead, and the Río Aguanaval was running parallel to the Pan American now. Its banks were cased-in concrete.

El Chorizo quickly agreed with the *gringo*'s directions, but Zorro didn't. The Mexican made no response at all until Amazon hailed him again.

"This is Turtle Leader; do you read me, Zorro?"

"I still got half a tank," the Mexican's voice finally crackled over the radio. "Over."

"Top off," Amazon answered.

Again there was a pause. "Zorro to Turtle Leader," Zorro called after a minute of silence. "Why waste time? I got enough to get to Jimenez. There's gas there. I'll go ahead and wait for you. Over."

Amazon was on a four-lane street in Torreon itself when his partner's message came through. There was a Pemex with vacant pumps a block ahead. "Read me, Zorro," he called. "I've got to get off the wire. No way, you should not go ahead. I'm at the first Pemex on the right. If you pass me, stop in the next block, repeat, stop in the next block. Over."

Chorizo broke in and agreed, but once again Zorro didn't answer. When Amazon had to switch the CB off as he pulled into the station, he still hadn't heard any response from his partner. The silence worried him. He knew full well Zorro could be an impetuous son of a bitch when he got stewed up, and he had little doubt the Mexican was agitated. All trip long Zorro CeAttle had complained about having to keep pace with the Land Cruiser and the truck: he was much too conscious of position to drive fifteen hundred miles as the last man in line. Henry Amazon figured there was a strong chance that his junior partner would break formation, get out on his own with the accelerator to the floor, and make a little speed. Breaking formation was the last thing Amazon wanted. He figured Zorro CeAttle knew it; but if anything, that would make him go right on by and not look back. Amazon felt frantic and worried about the load but was careful to hide his agitation from the young *mestizo* manning the Pemex's pump.

177

"Lleno con extra," he told the boy.

Amazon paced back and forth next to the Land Cruiser's driver's side while the tank was being filled. Without making a show of it, he was watching the approaching street for signs of the rest of the caravan. After what seemed like several minutes, Amazon spotted El Chorizo's Dina grinding toward him in the right-hand lane and preparing to turn into the Pemex where the Toyota was parked. Zorro CeAttle came into the picture shortly thereafter when his dark green Galaxie whipped around Chorizo in the fast lane and passed the gas station at fifty miles an hour.

Amazon gave no sign of recognition and casually stared off in the direction of the northbound city streets. The Dina, loaded with barrels, was being filled at the other service island, but once again Amazon made no signs of recognition.

After the boy returned with his change, Amazon got back in the Land Cruiser and pulled on to the street. Half a block north and out of sight of the Pemex, he snaked over to the curb and switched his radio on.

"Breaker One Nine, this is Turtle Leader. Come in Zorro. Over."

The Land Cruiser's speaker was full of crackles but little else. Amazon called four more times without luck. When he was about to start his fifth, Zorro answered.

The signal was faint and swarming with flocks of static and interference.

"Zorro," was one of the intelligible words. The others were "ahead . . . road . . ." and "Sierra de Hueso."

The last place name amounted to the worst of Amazon's fears. The Sierra de Hueso were the mountains near the Rio Grande where Zorro had a cousin with a twelve-acre ranch. According to the plan the caravan was to stop there, bypassing the checkpoint on Highway Sixteen outside of Ojinaga, and shift the load in preparation for a border crossing. El Chorizo would be paid off in the Sierra de Hueso and sent back to Oaxaca. The fact that Zorro mentioned the spot at all convinced Amazon that the dumb Mexican son of a bitch was going to make the rest of the run there solo. If there were any roadblocks ahead, he'd be blind, naked, and on his own. Amazon switched his radio to broadcast.

"Breaker," he said. "This is Turtle Leader for Zorro. Repeat transmission. Repeat transmission."

Henry Amazon repeated his own transmission ten times at ten-second intervals but raised nothing but grainy air. By then Chorizo was pulling out of the Pemex, and Amazon nosed back into traffic and raised the Indian on the radio. "The Mexican seems to have decided to make his own pace," he told El Chorizo. "Keep me in sight."

If Zorro had been there, Amazon would have punched him out.

When the last signs of city traffic had been left behind, Highway Forty-nine north for Chihuahua stretched ahead of them in a straight, black line across a mesquite plain that looked endless. At this point Amazon stopped mumbling to himself and broke into shouts. His window was rolled down, and a warm wind was roaring by his face. "You dumb Mexican son of a bitch," he shouted at the empty road ahead.

When he reached the turnoff for Zorro's cousin's ranch north of Chihuahua on Highway Sixteen, Henry Amazon knew that Zorro had had a clear run. There had been no evidence of a wreck or roadblock. The turnoff was some forty miles southwest of the village of San Juan, branching away from Highway 16, due north into the badlands and barren Sierra de Hueso. He pulled ahead onto the track with Chorizo one hundred yards back. The *mescal* truck rapidly disappeared from sight in a swarm of dirt. Amazon got on the CB and told the Indian to run with his headlamps lit so he could find him in the rearview mirror.

Henry Amazon had gone numb again. The solid day at the wheel had left a dull pain in the shoulder blade where the Huavis had once stabbed him. There was a buzz in his arms and face. Most of Amazon's attention went to keeping track of El Chorizo and repeating the directions he had memorized the month before. North over four ridges and into a valley. The road forks twice, and each time take the right fork. The *rancho* is reached by turning right one more time at the only crossroads in the valley four ridges over. Four miles along it, a sign on the left will say *Rancho Lobo*. Turn left on the dirt track and drive one more mile to the compound of *adobe* buildings with the alfalfa bales stacked next to it.

When he crossed the last ridge and descended into a sunburned valley, the end of day had turned purple and cast a soft, shadowless light throughout the jagged hollow ahead. Amazon found the crossroads and led the *mescal* truck to the right for four miles until he saw a piece of board stuck in the ground with *Rancho Lobo* lettered on it. When the caravan reached the compound of buildings listed in his directions, Amazon recognized the pile of alfalfa with Zorro's Galaxie parked in the yard.

His first reaction was relief for having put the bulk of the scam's mileage behind them.

He parked next to the Ford, turned the engine off, and stepped out. His ears tingled with the sudden quiet. Amazon motioned El Chorizo to park by the windmill and then noticed a *mestizo* standing outside the largest building's front door.

"*¿'Stá Zorro aquí?*" Amazon asked.

"*Allá,*" the Mexican motioned at the door. "I'm his cousin."

Zorro's cousin then walked across the yard to the *mescal* truck and began helping El Chorizo unload the barrels full of weed.

Amazon took a deep breath and stared across the valley, trying to center himself. Then he walked into the house. Zorro was sitting at a plank table in the first room, eating beans and *tortillas*. His head snapped up when his partner entered. "What took you so long?" Zorro CeAttle grinned.

Amazon stopped in his tracks.

Zorro kept grinning.

"I don't believe you said that," the *gringo* finally burst out. "I don't fucking believe it. *Chinga, mano, es como pinche hue.* You run off and leave me with no one to cover the truck, and then you say 'What took you so long?' What if *los Federales* had been out? Your smart-ass trip would have blown everything we got. I don't fucking believe it."

After swallowing a forkful of beans, Zorro smiled again. "You worry too much, *gringo*," he laughed. "I know what I'm doin'. I just stopped in Camargo and called my friend who has a trucking company in Chihuahua. He said the whole road was clear. So why wait? I know what to do."

"Sure," Amazon shot back. "Like last time."

With that reference to the lost Chrysler Zorro's smile disappeared. "This ain't no last time, Enrique." The Mexican said the words with a motion that made him look like he was biting the air in front of his face. "There ain't no more last times. *Todo*."

Henry Amazon said nothing and struggled to get his anger under control.

Zorro took a drink from the bottle of warm beer on the table and then smiled again. "Whatever you say; we made it, didn't we?"

The Mexican took another swing. "Maybe you just too nervous," he said. "I know this road better than you. It's probably a good thing you're getting out of the business. Maybe you too scared to think right."

Amazon wanted to grab his partner by the throat and call him forty-six kinds of asshole, but he didn't have the energy. Instead he looked at the floor. "Right," he said with a heavy flavor of disgust, "that must be it." Then he turned and walked outside and across the yard.

El Chorizo and Zorro's cousin had unloaded all the barrels by then, and the Indian was washing the dust and sweat off himself at the water trough under the windmill. Henry Amazon went over next to Chorizo and began throwing handfuls on his face and neck.

"I told you about him," the Indian said, nodding toward the house.

"Es cierto," Amazon responded between splashes, "you did." The water was running down his back and along his arms. He seemed to lose himself in the sudden cool sensation.

"What you gonna do now?"

Amazon didn't answer. After throwing more water over his face, he stood for a moment, looking across the desert and blowing air to shake the water off his mouth. "Make do," he finally said with a soft resigned voice in English that seemed directed as much at himself as the Indian. "Making do is all there is, *muchacho. Es todo el mundo*."

Amazon leaned into the trough and immersed his entire head so the green liquid wrapped completely around his skull. He could hear or see nothing under there. He rubbed at the *adobe* silt baked into his pores and momentarily felt a welcome isolation inside his skull. It felt easy and calm and as close to someplace else as he could get right then.

One more day, and the first half of Henry Amazon's last scam would be over.

They were in a stage of the game in which Amazon would have to rely on the Mexican the most and he himself would be at the largest disadvantage. Crossing the Rio Grande was the reason for Zorro's share in the partnership, and Amazon had no choice but to take a back seat.

Zorro's plan was simple. With money the *gringo* had supplied, his cousin had been buying alfalfa bales in the irrigated farm country to the west, stockpiling them, and then, starting three weeks earlier, he had carted a load of bales across the international border at Presidio every Tuesday and Thursday morning with a bill of lading for their delivery at a feed lot in Valentine, Texas. By now he was a familiar figure at the checkpoint when he arrived sometime between 4 and 5 A.M. This Tuesday morning would be no different except that the pile of hay strapped to his flatbed truck would be hollow and stuffed with prime Oaxacan marijuana cuttings.

After eating dinner and paying El Chorizo, the two partners set about getting the load ready for the border crossing. By the light of a lantern in the cousin's front room, each of the barrels packed by the Zapotec Vincente in the south Valley was emptied, and the cuttings repacked in a double thickness of plastic garbage bags. The loose leaves and shake left in the bottom were extracted by carefully stripping the barrel's lining free, lifting it out whole, and pouring the contents into a separate double bag. When that was done, the operation was repeated outside with the load in the trunk of Zorro's Galaxie. Henry Amazon and Zorro CeAttle packed without a lot of talk in a sort of unspoken agreement to concentrate on the business at hand.

When all the weed was repacked in bags, Zorro's cousin pulled his flatbed truck next to the hay pile and the construction of the load's camouflage began. Sweating and grunting in the moonlight, they laid a solid three-bale layer on the bed and then began creating compartments. The next layer was laid so that it appeared solid from the outside but had a roughly four-by-six-foot space in the center. That space was stuffed with bags. When the hollow was full, Zorro's cousin brought out a sheet of half-inch plywood and covered the opening for structural strength. The plywood sheet came to within a foot of the surface edge of the bales, and Amazon camouflaged it further by running a layer of glue on the wood's outside length and attaching handfuls of loose alfalfa around the entire shape. That process was repeated for three additional layers, and the last of the marijuana was stashed. Then two more solid levels of hay bales were added, the load topped off with a tarpaulin, and all of it cinched as tight as possible with heavy rope. Amazon inspected the arrangement with a flashlight: it looked like a truck loaded with hay.

Satisfied with what he saw, he took his sleeping bag out to the alfalfa pile to grab what rest he could. His watch read 11 P.M. To reach the border at the cousin's usual time, they would have to leave in three hours.

Zorro woke him with a flashlight at one thirty. He pointed the beam of light in Amazon's face and shook his arm.

"*Nos vamos,*" the Mexican whispered.

"*Bueno,*" Amazon answered. " *'Stá listo.*"

Zorro walked back across the yard to the main house, where a lantern was burning, and Amazon followed, shaking and stretching himself awake. Inside, the two partners sipped instant coffee for a few minutes before leaving to thread themselves through the eye of the needle one more time.

The jumping-off point for their run at the international boundary was a vacant lot on the outskirts of the Mexican town of Ojinaga. Zorro's cousin was behind the wheel of the alfalfa truck with Zorro himself riding shotgun. At the vacant lot he walked back to Amazon's Land Cruiser and climbed inside.

"He will come a half hour after we leave," he explained with a motion at the cousin's truck. "Don't worry. It's not good for us to cross any closer to him, but he will be all right. He knows what to do."

As they accelerated down the street toward Ojinaga and the border checkpoint in Presidio, Texas, Amazon took a last look at the load in his rearview mirror. Zorro's cousin was sitting outside on the hay truck's running board, smoking a cigarette. It was dark, and all he could see was a pinprick of orange light.

Fifteen minutes later the Land Cruiser approached the end of Mexico. The U.S. Customs shack on the other side of the Rio Grande stood out in a splatter of phosphorescent light and polished cement. The only vehicle in line ahead of Amazon and CeAttle was a truck full of tomatoes bound for San Antone. When it was waved through, Amazon steered up to the officer in the pale blue suit and came to a stop. He rolled down the window.

"How you gentlemen doin' this morning?" the customs official asked, bending even with the window and looking across the American at CeAttle.

"Just fine," Amazon smiled, passing him their passports. "Yourself?"

"Gettin' ready to go home," Customs answered. For a few moments he examined their documents and then passed them back. "Where are you coming from?"

"Chihuahua."

"On business?"

"No," Amazon grinned sheepishly, "just a little vacation. Got partying last night and almost forgot we had to be in Pecos by ten."

"Anything to declare?"

Amazon declared a half-empty bottle of *mescal*, an ashtray shaped like a *sombrero* with *Chihuahua, Chihuahua* lettered around its brim, and a carton of Delecados. Zorro declared another carton of cigarettes and a key chain with an image of The Virgin of Gaudalupe imprinted in plastic. On the officer's request Amazon got out and opened up the Land Cruiser's back doors. After examining their luggage, the officer crossed to the rear end and inspected the Land Cruiser's undercarriage. The two smugglers were rolling into the United States within five minutes.

Their temporary destination was Lurkee's Truck Ranch, a diner two blocks into the United States of America and one block to the right. Lurkee's had plastic tables, an immense asphalt parking lot, and picture windows. Unobscured, its view looked through several layers of Cyclone wire and out onto the customs shack and border checkpoint. When they parked, half of the windows were blocked by a Peterbilt loaded with concrete pipe, but Amazon and CeAttle managed to secure a table where they could watch for the cousin's crossing. The *gringo* ordered steak and eggs, and Zorro a waffle. There was nothing to do now but eat and wait.

Amazon had to force himself to chew slowly. Even so, the food seemed to sit just past his windpipe and go no farther. His stomach felt as though it had a giant bubble in it. He bought a copy of the San Antonio *Light* from the rack by the door and tried to read it while finishing off breakfast. Both of them wanted to talk about the approach of Zorro's cousin, but those kinds of conversations were unwise two blocks in from the Mexico line. At four twenty-eight Zorro motioned with his eyes at the window. Amazon followed them and saw what he meant.

Down at the customs shack, the hay truck was next in line. Cautioning himself to move slowly, Amazon took one last hit on his coffee and stood up to pay the bill. He paused again for some toothpicks from the glass next to the Lurkee's Truck Ranch cash register. Outside he and Zorro walked at a leisurely pace to the Land Cruiser. Both of them had their eyes glued on the border crossing. The hay truck was even with the customs shack window now, and Zorro's cousin was showing his green card to the officer. When they reached the Toyota, Henry and Zorro got in and let the engine idle. On the other side of the Truck Ranch's fence, the customs officer was under the hay truck, looking at the gas tank and the axles. When he returned to the driver's window, the officer made conversation with Zorro's cousin and examined the bill of lading for the feed lot in Valentine. Henry Amazon saw the cop laugh at something Zorro's cousin said and hand the paper back. The cousin waved at the cop and pulled forward into the United States.

"All right," Amazon said in a stage whisper. "All fucking right."

Zorro extended his hand, palm up, toward his partner. "What'd I tell you, *compadre?*"

Amazon slapped his palm on the Mexican's. "No lie, Jack," he exclaimed. "You didn't tell me no lie at all."

After that brief celebration they got back to business. The Land Cruiser pulled in front of the cousin's truck while it was still in Presidio and led the load along at a steady fifty-five miles per hour. Out on the empty Texas highway north of town, they stopped for gas in Fort Davis. From there on Zorro rode in the truck with his cousin, and they continued pushing north across the Pecos River and into New Mexico. When they passed Roswell at eleven thirty, Amazon began thinking they were in the clear.

At half past five in a Standard station outside of Albuquerque, he was sure of it. Tuesday had been hot and without mishaps. The hay truck was at the other island, but the American acted as though he had never seen it before. He walked over to the phone booth on the east side of the station and placed a call to Jersey City collect. Fat Albert answered after three rings and accepted charges.

"*Coma 'stá,* Fat Man?" Amazon joked.

186

"I'm all right, *amigo.* Sounds like you're callin' from close to home."

"Close and getting closer," Amazon grinned into the receiver. He was watching the attendant top off his tank and screw the cap on. "You ought to come visit me now that I'm back."

"I was thinking about that," Albert answered. "I got a little time on my hands right now. How soon would you like to see me?"

"Sooner the better."

"Done," Fat Albert said. "Look for me in a couple of days max."

The pump jockey was waiting to be paid, and Zorro's cousin had started his engine. Amazon was in a hurry. "I got to boogie now, Fat Man," he said, "but I'll see you soon."

Henry Amazon got back on the road with the load truck close behind. He was grinning ear to ear. Not long after Albuquerque disappeared behind him, he lit up the joint he'd carried across the border in his sock and held a one-man celebration.

While Henry Amazon was driving north through New Mexico, Ramón Ramón was fifteen hundred miles south of the border, in Oaxaca, waking up from a Tuesday afternoon nap. That morning he had checked out of his hotel and, after wasting several hours with Beef and Stella at the Presidente, ended up at the house of the widow Lara Bernal Rodrigon Shafter, just in time for *siesta.*

Lara Bernal Rodrigon had added the Shafter onto the end of her name after two years of keeping house with a Texas scammer listed as Casper Shafter on his papers but known as Ghost to his friends. Their house sat north of the city, on a bluff overlooking the Río Atoyac. The late Casper had owned fourteen acres there. After Ghost left home one night three years ago to make a score in the Sierra Madre, he was never seen again, and Lara had inherited the place as the Texan's common-law wife. Ramón Ramón had known both of them in the course of business but got to know Lara a lot better when Casper Shafter was dead. He rarely stayed longer than one night, and often, as on Tuesday, it was just for an afternoon stopover when he was horny.

When he arrived at one thirty, Lara knew what Ramón wanted. He liked sex in any circumstance, and the prospect of danger only increased his appetite. They had spent from two to three thirty balling and sucking on each other before sprawling out for some rest.

When he woke up late in the afternoon, Ramón's first thoughts were to get outside and take a look at the weather he would have to deal with after dark. Lara was asleep next to him, and he rose stealthily to keep from waking her.

He left the bedroom barefoot and stepped out on the patio. The building surrounded the space on two sides and an eight-foot wall on the two others. The tree outside the wall gate was blooming with white flowers, and their sticky fragrance hung suspended in the dead air. A solid gray blanket had covered the Valley for almost three days since the storm the night that Henry Amazon had left with his load. No rain had fallen since. Clouds came in every day but were blown on deep into the Sierra Madres. In the Oaxaca Valley it had been sultry and unseasonably hot.

Ramón climbed a ladder to the house's flat roof.

From up there he could see across the Río Atoyac and into the village on the other side. The river bed, running between dirt dikes thrown up ten years ago by the state government, was almost a hundred yards wide, but the water itself was no more than a foot deep and thirty feet across. A *fiesta* was starting somewhere in the village on the far bank, and Ramón could hear scraps of electric guitar and conga drums drifting his way. Beyond that village the last sloping edge of Monte Alban's wide skirt of hills was noticeably less green than after the last rain. Ramón tested for wind and felt the temperature of the air on his bare chest.

It wouldn't rain tonight either, he told himself. They would run dry, and the moon would be hidden.

It never occurred to him, as he stood on Lara's rooftop, that the journey out the San Dionisio Road that evening might turn into a disaster. Ramón was far too sure of himself even to imagine it.

14

Purdee Fletcher, Hog Wissle, and the Federales spent most of Tuesday waiting.

The law's plans had been finalized Monday afternoon at a meeting of the Oaxaca Condor steering committee in Cruz's office and repeated again at a briefing on Tuesday morning. A dozen Judicial Federal were scheduled to take part, and the Army had agreed to provide some thirty soldiers and three trucks. The entire force was to be called Task Force Rat Trap. The principal feature of Cruz's plan was its provisions to take Ramón's gang before they reached their destination on the San Dionisio Road. From the information the snitch El Tasajo had provided, Cruz's guess at the Monday Condor meeting had been that the *traficantes* were headed for the village of San Dionisio itself. In any case the Judicial Federal knew Ramón intended to drive at least twenty miles up the road and therefore any ambush along the way would suffice. A spot some twelve miles in from where the asphalt ended at Ocotlán had been selected for the interception. Along this stretch of road the dirt one-lane climbed through a pair of switchbacks

189

and over a rise. The slope on the other side was a straight one-hundred-yard grade with a hook in its low end. In that hook the road circled behind a large rock and several trees and then dropped into a dry streambed. Most of the Army and the Federal would be stationed in this wash. Their roadblock would be invisible until the *traficantes* were right on top of it. A smaller portion of the detachment would be hidden in the bushes on either side of the rise's peak one hundred yards away. Their assignment would be to cut off any retreat. Another car with two Federales would be stationed off the pavement in Ocotlán to wait for the smugglers to pass and act as the last cork in the bottle. The possibility of anyone escaping seemed remote, but just in case, Purd had reminded everyone that Condor Central in Mexico City had arranged for a block at the Tehuacán state line.

Cruz planned to capture the *gringos* and then extract whatever he needed to know about their destination. With that information in hand, Task Force Rat Trap would divide its forces; half would go up the road to bust the stash while the other half stayed with the prisoners at the site of the ambush. The only change in the *Jefe*'s original plan came on the advice of Cervantes, a young Mexico City political officer who had been dispatched to Oaxaca in the wake of the terrorists' destruction of the new market.

The political officer pointed out that the San Dionisio area was a place of "highly questionable security." His intelligence labeled the deeper reaches of the road as home of the mysterious FDP, the group claiming credit for the recent bombing. There were armed Indians in the mountains on that edge of the valley. According to the political officer's estimate these Indians had linked with dissident students to make up the heretofore unheard-of Fuerza del Pueblo. Dividing an already "streamlined" force in such a situation left both halves extremely vulnerable.

The ranking Army officer responded by saying that General Cortez de Corriente would gladly double his manpower contribution, and the plan was set.

Tuesday morning Pizarro Cruz relayed the plan to the rest of his men. Each was assigned a position, and then Cruz closed the briefing, saying the task force would leave for the San Dionisio Road, thirty-five miles away, in time to get there by twilight.

Purd spent the rest of the day at his hotel, trying to sleep. By the time Ramón Ramón woke on the north side of town, Purdee Fletcher stood under the shower, letting water slide along his back. Outside his bathroom window the last hours of daylight were stuffy and gray. He was exceedingly anxious for the evening to begin. This Ramón Ramón creep was Purdee's ticket out of the minor leagues. The sooner the law had him in hand, the better Ole Purd would feel.

At eight thirty Ramón Ramón was at a corner one block south and east of Oaxaca's ancient central marketplace.

El Tasajo got right down to business as Ramón Ramón drove off. "What's the plan?" he asked.

Ramón made a right-hand turn onto the Periférico and picked up speed. El Tasajo sat silently and watched the outline of the *gringo*'s hooked face in the pale glow cast by the passing streetlamps. Finally Ramón Ramón answered. "Right now," he said, "you and me are going to get the truck you'll drive. It's got a camper on the back and a CB. I've got this," Ramón continued, pointing to a walkie-talkie next to him on the seat, "and the other load truck has a CB like yours. When we get your wheels, you'll follow me out the highway past the airport. Out there we'll meet my partner and the other truck. Then we'll fetch the load and head north, *a la norte*. You get paid off in Mexicali and sent home."

"Where do we go out the San Dionisio?"

Ramón Ramón turned left, passed the train station, and stopped in front of a warehouse. Then he looked straight at the *mestizo*. "You'll find out later," he snapped. "Right now you just follow me."

The *gringo* opened one of the doors of the warehouse and motioned Tasajo inside. A 1977 GMC pickup with camper top, fat tires, and Arizona plates was parked next to several crates of pottery. Ramón tossed a set of keys to Tasajo.

"The tank's full," he said.

Ramón and his driver waited for the other truck outside of town on the edge of the highway. As usual Beef and Stella were late.

Tired of waiting, Ramón Ramón went ahead and briefed his driver on the details. Dark had swallowed the countryside around them, and the other's features were invisible to each. Occasionally the scurry of a lizard or field mouse erupted in the dry shadows, but otherwise the *gringo*'s voice was the only sound. Ramón explained that the caravan out of the San Dionisio would be led by his partner, Beef, in the other truck. El Tasajo would follow Beef, and then Ramón would bring up the rear. Before they got the load, Ramón was more worried about being tailed than anything else and had assigned himself the rear guard task accordingly. On the way out with the *mota* the order would be reversed, with Ramón's sure nose in the lead all the way north. El Tasajo was to keep his radio on at all times, respond quickly when called, and not initiate any radio traffic unless his vehicle was in trouble or he was lost.

To avoid the possibility of the vehicles becoming separated in the village of San Dionisio itself, Ramón Ramón said he had drawn a map of the location of the *mota*.

The *gringo* brought the drawing out of his pocket and began explaining the penciled lines under the flame cast by his cigarette lighter. The caravan was to drive along the village's main street to the crossroads past the church and turn right. At the third cross street in that direction the *tienda* on the far right-hand corner had a backyard enclosed by a cane fence and reachable through a gate on the east side. There Ramón had drawn a simple *X*.

El Tasajo pocketed the drawing and asked no more questions.

When Beef and Stella's truck finally arrived, the three vehicles got back on the highway. Beef knew the road on the other side of Ocotlán well, and Stella was his only worry. Her hunger for adventure had melted the closer the adventure got. Her skin had taken on a pasty color, and her hands were sweating uncontrollably.

192

"Ain't nothin' to worry about," Beef tried to reassure her.

Stella smiled weakly and stared out the windshield. Soon they were into the foothills, and she was rapidly edging over the borderline of terror.

El Tasajo's following highbeams still remained visible in the rear-view mirror, but Ramón Ramón's lights had disappeared. The trucks threw up a heavy wall of dust on the parched road, and the *gringo* in the trailing rent-a-car slowed to avoid it. By the time the caravan was six miles past Ocotlán, Ramón's Ford was running a full two hundred yards behind the others with the *gringo* glancing regularly at the seemingly empty road to his rear. On the edge of one of those glances Ramón thought he saw headlights and immediately slammed on his brakes to take a better look.

By the time the dust settled so that he could see clearly, the road toward Ocotlán showed no lights at all. He waited several minutes to see if they reappeared and then decided it must have been some reflection from his own car and not another vehicle.

He could not have been more wrong.

What he'd seen was the cork in the Federale bottle attempting to slip into place. It was a five-year-old Plymouth Valiant manned by two Judicial Federal agents.

When this Valiant climbed out of a gully and on top of a flat stretch, the driver spotted taillights ahead and responded instantly, killing the lights, turning off his engine, and slamming on his brakes. Then the Federales sat there in darkness until the taillights ahead finally disappeared. The driver didn't start his engine again until his ears made out the sound of Ramón's rent-a-car pulling ahead in the distance. Even then, he ran for a while without headlights just to be sure the *gringo* didn't get spooked.

Eventually that decision on the part of the Judicial Federal tail car to drive with his lights off became one more chapter in Ramón Ramón's legend of invincibility.

193

The Federale driver failed to see the edge of a sharp left-hand curve half a mile later, and the Valiant sailed twenty yards through the air and landed headfirst in a ten-foot-deep gully. The driver was killed outright, and his partner had both legs broken in four places and was unconscious for more than an hour.

In the meantime everything between the ambush and the Ocotlán pavement was open and clear.

When Beef Stew's truck stumbled into the Federales at 11:47 P.M. in a dry wash where the road hooked, the prize *gringo* Ramón Ramón was still outside the trap's back door in the second of two switchbacks on the other side of the rise and the hundred-yard straight slope immediately preceding the roadblock.

Ramón Ramón had his walkie-talkie on and thus far had heard nothing but crackles and blank pops. There was no expression on his hooked-nosed face and no thinking in his head. He was a step beyond thought. His mind had moved out along his skin, and he kept track of the situation by sensation alone. Had he been the slightest bit slower, he would never have survived the ambush.

The only warning he had was the same word, repeated twice, on the radio. It was Beef Stew's voice. The transmission took no more than three seconds. Ramón's Ford had just cleared the second loop of the road's ascent up the rise, thirty yards short of the trap's back door, when the voice came on. The word he heard was *Scorpion*, their prearranged signal to cut and run. It was the last communication between Beef Stew and Ramón Ramón. Beef barely had time to repeat it once more before a dozen soldiers with automatic weapons caused him to slam on the brakes. Behind the soldiers was a sudden solid wall of headlights. Stella Ranch opened up with a scream, and the hysteria rising out of her throat clogged the airwaves. Ramón immediately slammed on his brakes and threw the Ford into reverse. The wheels spun for a second before grabbing, and then Ramón Ramón careened his car backward around the curve.

194

A plainclothes Federale and two uniformed soldiers leapt out of the bush along the crest of the rise and ran into the glare of Ramón's high beams. He pushed the accelerator down even harder. The Federale cut loose with a thirty-eight, and the two soldiers blasted with their M–16's on rock 'n' roll, but Ramón had a second's edge on them. The fusillade of gunfire shot out the right half of the windshield, but then, suddenly, the Ford was once again protected by the intervening rock wall of the cut. Accelerating even more, Ramón rattled down to the elbow of the first switchback, still hidden from the weapons at the crest of the rise. He whipped the car into the wide spot inside the elbow and pointed its nose in the direction of Ocotlán. Driving with his left hand, he slipped the pistol out of his boot with his right, and as soon as he churned out of the last switchback and was briefly in view of the marksmen on the rise, he cut loose with six wild rounds in their direction.

Slugs ricocheted harmlessly off the rocks; by then the Ford had dropped out of sight again. When it pulled back into the open, Ramón was more than six hundred yards away from the posse and accelerating through a fifty-yard gap between two cornfields. The soldiers tried their luck again, but only one of their rounds even came close. It entered the rear window at an angle, tore through the front on the passenger's side, and buried itself harmlessly in the glove compartment.

There was sweat rolling down from his hairline, but Ramón Ramón's face was still expressionless. With his free hand, he reloaded his thirty-eight.

Back at the main roadblock, Purdee Fletcher heard the gunfire and immediately tried to raise the detail there on the radio.

"Breaker," he called. "This is Rat Trap One. Come in Rat Trap Two. Over." They didn't answer.

Meanwhile, Beef Stew and Stella had been ordered out of the cab of their truck by an Army lieutenant and lined up in the glare of the roadblock's high beams. Beef tried to give someone his story about

195

being the owner of a string of southern California import stores, but was told to shut up and stand in front of his truck. Stella was sobbing and holding onto Beef's arm.

Purd tried the radio again. "This is Rat Trap One," he called. "Come in Rat Trap Two."

Cruz was up the road with Garcia Huahilote and the snitch Tasajo who'd driven the second truck.

"This is Rat Trap One," Purd repeated. "Come in Rat—"

"The last car got away," the detail at the ambush's back door interrupted.

"What?"

"The last car got away."

"Goddamn," Purd screamed. He kicked at the pebbles covering the dry creekbed with his wing tips.

"Rat Trap One to Rat Trap Two. Did you hit him? Over."

"Maybe," the radio answered. "But it didn't make no difference."

"Shit," Purdee exploded.

Without bothering to sign off, the desperate *gringo* agent immediately began trying to raise Rat Trap Three, totaled at the bottom of the wash.

Standing in the blinding light, the prisoner Beef Stew could hear the far-off sound of English radio jargon being spoken, but he couldn't see beyond the glare surrounding him. A soldier prodded Beef with the barrel of his rifle, and he gritted his teeth. He tried to ignore the sounds of Stella next to him gagging on her fright.

"Son of a bitch," he heard the English voice say. "The fucking greasers blew the big one."

Purdee was panicking. The collapse of the trap had brought the roof of Purd's mind down with it. Spasms of anger were welling up in him, and he ran out of the wash at a half trot, skirted the cage of lights around the two captive suspects, and headed around the hook and up the slope to Cruz.

The head Federale and his number two man Garcia Huahilote had just finished receiving El Tasajo's report, and Cruz was even more pleased than El Tasajo had expected. It was the map that had done it. Pizarro Cruz immediately instructed Huahilote to take The Piece of Meat and half of Task Force Rat Trap into San Dionisio eleven miles away and seize the marijuana.

"Rat Trap Two blew it," Purd blurted out. "The big *gringo* got away."

Cruz stopped in the dark road. "What about Rat Trap Three?" he asked.

"They don't answer," the *gringo* snapped.

"Is most likely the radio," the head Federale answered reassuringly. He did not want to think about failure and reacted to Purd's announcement as an imposition. "Just the radio," he repeated.

"It is not just the radio," Purd pressed. "It ain't here yet," he went on, motioning to the surrounding darkness and the absence of the Valiant. "The plan says it would arrive by now." Cruz said nothing, shifting his feet uncomfortably in the dark.

"We got to go after the *gringo*," Purd continued, getting angrier. *"Muy pronto."*

Cruz made no response.

"Goddamn it, Pissaro. That fucker hasn't got that much of a lead. We could still nail his ass if you'd get off yours."

Cruz stiffened and finally spoke. "We will trust the plan," he said. Then the head Federale started back down the road to meet up with the rest of his men.

At that point Purdee Fletcher made one of the larger mistakes of his checkered career. He grabbed hold of Cruz's arm and twisted him around. Out of control, he shoved his face up close to the Mexican's. "You can't let him just go, goddamn it," he shouted. "It's bad enough your *tortilla* brains missed him. Don't make it worse. That *gringo*'s high priority. The rest of this operation is just shit compared to him."

The mistake was immediately obvious.

A chilly silence spread from the cement-faced Cruz. Purd sensed it and fell down another set of stairs in his head. Now he'd fucked up double and blown it with the Mexicans too.

Without changing a muscle in his face, Pizarro Cruz stared at the black air until Purd took his hand off his arm. Then Purd gave an embarrassed chuckle which only irritated Cruz further. Purd had violated every possible rule. To question his orders at all was disrespectful, but to do so in front of his lieutenant and a lowly *chiva* was an insult of the worst kind. Pizarro Cruz spit into the night and then, leaving the *gringo* to stand alone in the silence of the pitch-black slope, he walked back toward the main Federal party.

Whatever status Purd had built up was irretrievably squandered: he was back to ground zero.

When Pizarro Cruz and his lieutenant were within sight of the roadblock, Huahilote offered that the *gringo* didn't know his place. Cruz joked about the big shot Poord and how he had just lost his head in the heat of battle. The head Federale then laughed, and Garcia Huahilote joined in.

At the roadblock Huahilote rounded up his raiding party and headed off for San Dionisio. Cruz turned to the prisoners. The *traficante* Beef Stew and his woman were pinned in the bank of headlights up ahead like bugs on a board.

While the approaching Cruz was still out of earshot, Beef heard the sounds of Garcia Huahilote's trucks starting and loading up somewhere behind the soldiers and the wall of light. When the guard nearest the *gringo* seemed distracted by the activity, Cruz saw the smuggler dip his head toward the now deathly silent Stella Ranch next to him. He seemed to be saying something, but only Stella heard it.

"Get your shit together Stella," Beef whispered. "We can still bluff our way out of this."

Beef's voice sounded like it was a thousand miles away. Vaguely, Stella remembered she was supposed to be Mrs. Gordon Stern, co-owner of Stern's Furnishings with outlets in Pasadena, Garden Grove, Malibu, and El Cajon.

The bank of lights shining in his face unnerved him, but Beef Stew tried to hold on to himself. He had to stick to his cover story whatever happened. Beef felt a momentary sense of relief when another figure finally entered the glare in front of him. From the way the soldiers made room for this man, it was obvious he was the one they had been waiting for. In the shadows Beef could see little of the *Jefe*'s face. The head man said nothing. Stella continued to whimper.

Eventually Beef began to talk. His face assumed his best Southern California smile, and his voice took on a reasonable, dignified tone.

"There must be some kind of mistake, *señor*," he said. "You see, my wife and I have a chain of stores in *los Estados Unidos,* and we were out here looking for Coyotepec, the pottery village, and lost our—"

Beef's monologue was interrupted by a Mexican noncom who rushed forward and planted the butt of his rifle on the *gringo*'s chest. The Mexican stepped back, and Beef fell to his knees, sucking wind and trying to recover the use of his lungs.

"Espera por el Jefe Cruz por hablar," the soldier shouted at the suspect. *"Usted no habla primero."*

Stella began to sob uncontrollably.

Bruno Sawyer alias Beef Stew struggled back to his feet, and the *Jefe* stepped forward so the *gringo* could see more of his shaded face. It seemed almost rectangular, with right angles at the jawline. Adrenaline was pumping in Beef's glands, and he felt light-headed.

"What did you say your name was?" Cruz asked.

Beef cleared his throat. "Gordon Stern of Garden Grove, California, and this is my wife, Betty." The smuggler motioned at Stella. "We're American citizens," he added.

"Could I see your papers?" Cruz asked.

Beef and Stella produced their tourist permits and handed them over. Cruz looked at the papers for a few moments and then wadded them into his breast pocket.

"And you, young lady," he asked at Stella, "you are Mrs. Gordon Stern?"

Stella gasped for breath and stopped crying. When she finally found her voice, it came out squeaky. *"Si,"* she said. The sound evoked laughter in Cruz and the soldiers near him.

199

Flustered, Stella squeaked again. "My father is a very important man in the United States," she said.

The Mexicans only laughed.

"Does this look like the United States?" Pizarro Cruz asked.

Another wave of laughter rose out of the glare and the darkness behind it.

Stella didn't say anything. Instead Beef spoke up again. "You see, *señor*," he began, "we import handicrafts. We had heard about the wonderful pottery in Coyotepec and wanted to buy as much as we could. I'm afraid we must have become lost somewhere along the way and ended up here."

Cruz interrupted with a wave of his hand. "I think something else," he offered. "I think maybe you came up here to buy as much marijuana as you could and you're lying to me."

Beef Stew did his best to act indignant. "You're mistaken, we just—"

Cruz interrupted again and said the same thing to Stella.

Stella's voice hadn't changed. "No," she said, "we're just looking . . ."

Laughter drowned out the rest of her answer.

"Very well," Cruz said. He stepped back behind the soldiers and in rapid Spanish barked out several orders. Immediately the three infantrymen near Stella grabbed her arms and began pulling her back up the road toward the spot where the second smugglers' truck was parked.

As soon as the soldiers touched her, Stella got hysterical. "Beef," she screamed, "Beeeeeef."

"Hold on just a minute," Beef shouted at Cruz. "What do you think you're doing?" He moved in Stella's direction, but then someone jammed a rifle butt in his chest and another against his jaw. Unconscious, Bruno Sawyer a.k.a. Beef Stew dropped like a sack of flour in the dirt.

Stella continued screaming all the way up the road, but it made no difference. All the enlisted men who had been at the ambush site crowded around her as she was dragged up the road. One of them then tore off her underpants and gagged her with them.

Down the hill Beef Stew regained consciousness in a different situation from the one he'd left. The glare was gone, and he discovered that each of his arms was tied to the bumper of his truck. There was a glowing campfire about ten feet away, and he realized that the truck had been turned sideways so it blocked the road. He could make out a number of plainclothes shapes near the fire, but he had trouble focusing. When his head finally cleared, Beef saw the *Jefe* standing about four feet away.

"Can you hear me, *gringo?*" the Mexican asked.

Beef nodded.

"I already know who you are," Cruz told him in smooth English. "You are Bruno Sawyer from Malibu, California. I know your mother's name and where you were in prison."

The information stunned Beef. Then Cruz held a copy of the American's San Quentin mug shots up to his face.

"*No, señor,*" Beef mumbled, even more surprised. What had happened, he wondered. How had they found out? How much did they know? "It's a mistake. Really. My name is Gordon Stern."

Cruz laughed. "It doesn't matter, *gringo*. I know who you are." Beef saw that the other figures near the campfire had fanned out around him to watch. "Nor do I care if you tell me about the marijuana you were going to buy," the head Federale continued. "I already know about that, too."

Beef Stew started to object, but when he did so, the nearest Federale stepped up and clouted him in the ear with his boot. Beef's head banged back against the bumper. Cruz then took another step forward and crouched close to the *gringo*, at eye level. "What I care about, *Señor* Stern," he said with a sneer, "is that you tell me right now where the money is you were going to use to pay for that marijuana."

"There is no money," Beef answered. "There is no marijuana. All I have is the cash in my wallet."

Cruz, who had already searched the wallet and the truck, slapped the *gringo* across the face. "I am serious, *señor*," he muttered.

"Really," Beef pleaded. "Honest. There is no marijuana. Just pottery for our stores."

Cruz stood up suddenly and issued more orders in Spanish.

Beef didn't understand until a Federale grabbed each of his legs. Cruz walked back to the fire and, using a leather glove, pulled a soldier's bayonet out of the hot flames. When Beef saw what he was doing, his heart raced, and he began to stutter.

"Come on now. Really . . . this is all a mistake. Check with my embassy. My name is Stern. I own import stores."

The words made no difference to Cruz. Making no noise at all, he touched the glowing bayonet to his prisoner's rib cage.

Beef Stew bellowed and bit at his lip. He could smell his flesh burning.

"As I said, we are serious," Cruz said. "Perhaps now you will tell me where your money is."

Beef made motions to repeat his fabricated story, and Cruz touched his ribs again with the red-hot steel. Afterward Beef tried to claim innocence one more time. He figured they'd kill him if they got the money but that if he stood enough of this, they'd have to believe him.

It was a serious misunderstanding of Pizarro Cruz.

Without asking again, the head Federale held the bayonet in his right hand, and with his free left hand he opened the zipper on the *gringo*'s jeans. Then he reached inside and pulled out Beef's pecker.

"No. Come on," Beef shouted. He tried to struggle but the Judicial Federal had him securely under control.

Cruz stretched Beef's meat up over his belly, so the long underside was showing. He applied the blade to the point where the scrotum joined the shaft, and Bruno Sawyer alias Beef Stew screamed like a wounded pig. Stew thrashed against his bonds, shit in his pants, and eventually passed out.

Purdee Fletcher stood at the back of the crowd watching Cruz work on the *gringo*. Ramón's escape and his own fuck up with Cruz had left Purd feeling one down, and he couldn't bring himself to feel altogether a part of what was going on. Hog had departed with the raiding party, so during the interrogation Purd was the only *gringo* present to watch. Word of his earlier insulting scene with the *Jefe* had already made its way around the Federal, and the senior American felt trapped in a hostile sea of greasers. He tried to be friendly, but his efforts only came across as obsequious. Purd kept remembering Norton Long-beem's remonstrances against cutting across the Mexicans' path. Trying to hide his anxiety in an official function, he walked back to the command radio and began another series of attempts to locate the missing Rat Trap Three.

When he returned briefly to the interrogation, Beef Stew had come to and told Cruz where to look for the cash in the wall of the camper. A crew of Federales found the money, and more than one hundred thousand dollars was counted and locked up in Cruz's car.

Then Cruz had more questions about smuggling, Oaxaca, and Ramón Ramón. After every question that Beef didn't give an immediate answer to, Cruz worked the blade. The *gringo*'s nipples were burnt, then the skin around one of his eyes, and when Beef tried to conceal the identity of Ramón Ramón, the hot bayonet was stabbed into his chest, hooked under his broad pectoral muscle and twisted.

Beef passed out then, and he passed out one more time after that. Then he blubbered out everything he knew about Ramón Ramón, their deal, and the route north.

Sometimes Cruz paused to let the smuggler sit in silence and suffer. Beef could no longer see out of one eye, and vision in the other was blurred. Sometimes he heard the same far-off voice, calling in English on the radio for Rat Trap Three.

After he had told Cruz everything he knew, Beef began to fix on the American voice in the background. There was an American out there with these bastards, and he was watching all this happen. "You lousy son of a bitch," he screamed. "Where are you? I'm American, too," he said. "Why don't you help me? Whose side are you on?"

The outburst took Pizarro Cruz by surprise. The Federal *Jefe* was standing with his back to the suspect, joking with his men, and like everyone else, he looked at Beef and then looked at the *gringo* agent Purd over by the command radio.

Cruz laughed. "Good idea, *gringo*," he shouted. "You need help. Poord," he called. "Come here."

Purd approached the Mexicans warily. "What's up, *Jefe*?" he asked.

"Your fellow *gringo* wants you to help him."

Purd guessed this was some kind of joke and grinned. "Shit," he drawled.

"No, no," Cruz interrupted "is true. He thinks you should help him, and I do, too," the Federale added. "Don't you?" He asked the assembled Mexican agents.

They responded with several yeses and yells. One called out that the *Jefe* was right. *Gringos* should look out for each other.

"I want you to let him go, Poord," Cruz continued. He took a cold knife from one of his men and gave it to the American agent. "Go ahead: let him go."

Purd knew he was being made fun of but had no choice. Gingerly he walked up to the mutilated Bruno Sawyer and cut the rope holding his arms to the bumper. Beef Stew sagged to the ground.

"Go," Cruz said. "Your countryman has helped you. We are going to let you escape."

Slowly Beef got to his feet.

"You better run before I change my mind," Cruz goaded.

Beef looked up the road. It was dark there. He could hide. After a deep breath, the smuggler lurched away from the truck and made his staggering break.

A round from Pizarro Cruz's thirty-eight caught up with Beef Stew after two steps. The bullet exploded in his lungs and he pitched forward on his face in the wash. Several more shots were fired into his corpse, but he was dead after the first.

Inside El Tasajo's camper Stella Ranch heard the gunfire echo off the surrounding ridges, but the sounds had no significance. She was numb and delirious. The shots in the wash sounded like firecrackers and made her think briefly of the Fourth of July. She didn't notice much else until she heard the sounds of the entire task force pulling alongside the truck where she was.

Then an Army lieutenant poked his head in the camper door and ordered the enlisted men out. After a moment's hesitation he fired his forty-five into the back of her brain and closed the door.

Like her boyfriend Beef Stew, Stella Ranch died instantly.

As Task Force Rat Trap pulled away toward Ocotlán and then Oaxaca, the lieutenant pulled the pin on an incendiary grenade. He tossed it in through a window next to the dead woman and jumped on the back of the last retreating truck. By the time the caravan passed over the rise, smoke was billowing from the camper's windows, and flames were crackling out the undercarriage and into the surrounding dark.

Six miles down the road Task Force Rat Trap came upon the badly injured survivor of Rat Trap Three. The Federale had pulled himself back to the road with his arms. When the caravan stopped, the burning vehicle behind was no more than a flare of light on the slate-colored horizon.

It was obvious to everyone that the last hope for catching Ramón Ramón was the Condor roadblock on the Tehuacán state line. At best Purd considered it a slim possibility.

Ramón Ramón was too slippery to catch once you'd given him three hours lead and a chance to run.

Purdee Fletcher was right.

Ramón made his way out the San Dionisio Road and decided to head for the Gulf Coast to hide out, but he knew enough to wait at the last ridge before hitting the Tehuacán line. By his watch it was 2:45 A.M. Eventually a Cristóbal Colon first-class bus blared past, and Ramón followed the passage of its lights down into the next valley where the state of Tehuacán began. Halfway across, a sudden eruption of headlamps blocked the bus's path.

That was enough for Ramón Ramón, and he pointed the rented

Ford back the way he'd come. A ferocious wind was blowing through the missing pieces of his windshield, and the air was decidedly cooler here than in Oaxaca. The *gringo* was two more valleys to the east now, where the clouds that had missed Oaxaca throughout the week had been dumping their soggy load at regular intervals. Although no rain was falling now, the pavement was still wet from the last downpour.

Ramón finally pulled off the road again when he reached a ravine twenty winding minutes' drive down from the crest. The gorge was spanned by a two-lane cantilevered steel bridge, and he parked in the wide turnout immediately preceding the foot of the span. On one edge of the shoulder, the ground dropped away into a *barranca*. Moving quickly, he went to the trunk of the Ford, opened the duffel bag there, and changed from the up-and-coming-used-car-dealer outfit into his night-creeping clothes of jeans, T-shirt, and combat boots. He topped these off with a brown wool *serape* and wide-brimmed hat made of straw.

Ramón had quickly developed a plan to cover his tracks. The first step after changing was to ditch the car. Using a cord to bind the steering wheel so that the car pointed straight ahead at the gorge, he started the Ford in neutral, placed a rock on the accelerator, and stepped out, closing the door behind him. When he reached back in and knocked the automatic transmission into gear, the car squealed up to the edge and sailed over. Ramón listened to the metal fall apart on the way down. Then he hoisted his duffel and set out across the bridge.

A mile farther along the highway, he turned off on a single dirt road that wound through low hills and ridges. He humped along at a good clip, his destination the village of Teotitlan del Camino, eight miles off the asphalt. There he planned to catch the third-class bus headed for Huautla de Jiménez nine hours farther into the mountains. Ramón figured that since the Federales blocked his way to the Gulf, Huautla would be the next best place to shake them and regroup.

Ramón reached Teotitlan del Camino shortly after dawn and the bus stop was swarming with Indians. Ramón pulled the brim of his hat down over his face and joined the crowd. He felt angry yet safe, as if there were nothing but dime store mannequins around him.

Eventually he said to a man that there were *mucho* folks waiting for the bus.

The Indian answered it was the weather. Because of the rain the road into the mountains had been impassable beyond the first ridge for four days.

Ramón Ramón said he was headed for Huautla de Jiménez.

The Indian said no buses had gotten that far in a week, but today Oscar Gomez was going to try. He had a fourteen-year-old Dina, *la Máquina de Jesus,* the Indian said, and he was scheduled to stop at Teotitlan in fifteen minutes.

When *la Máquina de Jesus* arrived, caked in dried *adobe* slop all the way up to the windows, it was clear Oscar Gomez had been over the road before.

The bus was already crowded when it reached Teotitlan, and after Ramón and the others got aboard, passengers were stacked in the aisles with the baggage on the roof and wedged into the open loading door. Ramón himself ended up standing right by the driver Oscar Gomez. Gomez had garlic on his breath and pieces of *cilentro* between his teeth.

The bus farted its way up and over the eighty-five-hundred-foot crest of the first ridge for two hours, and finally there was a clear view of the mountains ahead. The sky was sunny blue as far as the eye could see, and the Dina charged along the sloppy one-lane, scattering puddles in the switchbacks where the mud was axle deep. The road wound around one ridge after another with a four-thousand-foot drop on either side. Gomez honked his horn through the blind corners and ground back and forth among his gears. Most of the bus's steadily dwindling load of passengers was dropped off at seemingly empty spots where just a narrow footpath could sometimes be seen cut into the surrounding highland rain forest. Six hours out of Teotitlan Gomez stopped briefly at a roadside *tienda* to clean one of his spark plugs, and then he drove straight on through to Huautla de Jiménez, elevation eight thousand feet.

The main street of town had been turned into a quagmire by a long succession of storms. After dropping Ramón Ramón and the last of the passengers in front of a concrete shoebox called the Hotel Olympic, Oscar Gomez gassed up and headed back for Teotitlan with *la Máquina de Jesus* full to the gills.

By 9 P.M. that evening the rain rattled through the Sierra Madre Occidental in sheets.

,

15

The next bus reached Huautla two days later. Its driver delivered the latest editions of *Carteles* to the café where Ramón Ramón was eating dinner. When he looked at the issue from Thursday, Ramón stopped in midbite.

The entire lower half of the *Carteles*'s front page and top half of the back were devoted to a story about the mutilated bodies of two *gringo* tourists that had been found in the south part of the Oaxaca Valley beyond Ocotlán. As near as the State Police could piece the story together, the two tourists had taken a wrong turn out this road and had been attacked by one of the gangs of bandits and revolutionaries known to inhabit that section of Sierra Madre. The victims had been tentatively identified as Mr. and Mrs. Gordon Stern of Garden Grove, California. Their vehicle, a camper with Arizona plates, was burned by the attackers along with the body identified as that of Mrs. Stern. Mr. Stern was found down the road a ways shot to death after having obviously been tortured. Since no money was found on his body, the police theorized robbery was the motive. In a statement *Jefe* Jorge

Palomino Cobraa buttressed his analysis by pointing out that Mexico City intelligence sources had long recognized the presence of illegal bandits and revolutionaries around the San Dionisio Road. As evidence he mentioned that the State Police Task Force sent to investigate the scene of the crime on Wednesday afternoon had been watched by a group of armed Indians, visible on the crest of the ridge dominating that section of the San Dionisio Road. A picture on the back page showed a line of about forty stick figures standing among the rocks. Rifle barrels could be discerned in the glare of the sun behind them.

A picture on the front showed what remained of the bodies. Despite the disfigurement and signs of torture on the face of the unburned corpse, Ramón Ramón recognized Beef Stew. The smuggler's body was bent at the armpits, but, the caption explained, that was the result of someone having driven a truck over the corpse after it was dead. A picture of the late Stella Ranch was next to Beef's. She amounted to a charred hunk of torso running from her tailbone to the stub of her neck.

The final photo accompanying the *Carteles*'s account featured the destroyed hulk of a pickup camper. Ramón noticed the story never mentioned either the other camper, the one with California plates driven by Beef, or El Tasajo, the *mestizo* driver of the vehicle that had been burned. Their absence ran like sandpaper over ·Ramón's brain. He understood he'd been had.

Rising abruptly, Ramón Ramón took the paper with him, followed the street uphill until he reached the schoolyard steps, climbed them, and crossed the yard itself at a quick pace. The ground was sloppy, the mud stuck to his combat boots like gum. He felt soggy, stale, and mean. His hands were clenched into fists. Two stray dogs tried to approach him but ran off when he flailed out with his foot. At the far end of the schoolyard he climbed another set of steps that led to the marketplace and the street running in front of it. The marketplace, no more than a long thin slab of concrete with a tin roof, was closed down for the night. Ramón attracted no attention. It was mushroom season in this part of the Sierra Madre, and several dozen scruffy *gringos* were in town to eat *ongos*. Three were sitting on the market slab when Ramón passed. Their hair hung in greasy ropes; their eyes were pink and wired.

In the distance church bells were ringing, and Ramón picked up the sounds of an approaching brass band. Soon a wedding procession came into view, making its way through the mud. The bride wore a white lace wedding gown, rented for the occasion, and her Indian groom a rented black suit, white shirt, and black tie. The bride wore no shoes at all, the groom his regular *huaraches*. The attendants were busy keeping the bride's gown out of the muck and walked gingerly, trying to pick their way around the puddles. The eight-piece brass band following behind them had no such caution. They were too busy playing and kept their heads erect and eyes forward. Occasionally one of the musicians would drop up to one knee in a soft spot, and the band would halt, continuing to play and march in place until the man who was trapped had pulled himself free. Ramón stood and watched until the procession had rounded the corner toward the church. Then he continued his route to the hotel. The Olympic was up the way the wedding party had come from, and after five minutes of climbing the street's mushy incline, he was home.

Ramón got his key at the manager's room and climbed the stairs to number twenty-three on the second floor. Like all the Olympic's rooms, it was locked with a padlock on a hinge. Ramón undid his and carried it inside with him. It was dark enough so that he had to switch on the bare overhead bulb. The only furniture inside was a single steel bed with a mattress. The air was dank. The walls and the floor were made of unfinished concrete. If the window was left open, water dripped from the ceiling. If it was closed, the room was just a little bit damp. Ramón shut the solid steel door behind him and attached the lock to the inside hinge.

His duffel was under the bed. He went straight for it and extracted a package wrapped in a greasy cloth. His Smith & Wesson thirty-eight revolver was inside. The wet up here would erode the barrel if it wasn't cared for right. Each night since he'd been here he'd taken the thirty-eight apart, cleaned and oiled it, and stuffed it back in the duffel. Tonight he sat on the bed holding the gun in his hand. The *Carteles* was spread out next to him.

As Ramón saw it, he had no choice but to go back and kill the son of a bitch who'd snitched on him. Otherwise it would be said *don Ramón* let a *chiva* off his partner and steal his money without answering back. Word would get around. He couldn't work with that being said about him. No one backpedals in the jungle without taking it in the ass sooner or later. Ramón pointed his weapon at the *Carteles*'s picture of the incinerated truck.

"You're a dead motherfucker," he said. "I'm gonna do your ass, El Tasajo, just like you tried to do mine."

Then Ramón pulled the trigger and listened to the hammer slam down on an empty cylinder.

It would be late Sunday before another bus made its way through the slosh to Huautla, but when Nostaro Nostromos showed up in his "Pantera de Papilsocho," Ramón Ramón would ride out with him. From that Friday night on, revenge became Ramón Ramón's principal agenda. "Unfinished business" was how he described it to himself. Betray *don Ramón* and you get greased: there could be no exceptions. He knew he was still hot in the Valley, but the risk didn't faze him. Oaxaca was a big place, and he had learned how to hide in it. He figured the cops wouldn't think to look for him on their doorstep. Ramón planned to splatter Tasajo's head like a fucking egg.

Saturday morning Henry Amazon arrived back in Oaxaca on the nine o'clock jet from Mexico City. He could have stayed in the States longer but instead had headed south again as soon as the first load was sold. It was better that way, he told himself. Less time to think about it. Less temptation to take what money he had and run. Amazon wanted to see this through, and a lot of trepidation stood in his way. Like a man lost in the Arctic, he felt he had to keep moving or freeze in his tracks.

212

Henry Amazon was one of twenty-seven passengers, twelve of them *gringos*. He was wearing clean jeans, a polyester shirt, and polished cowboy boots. His papers identified him as a businessman from Colorado on vacation. He was distinguishable from the rest of the tourists only in the fluency of his Spanish and the way his fingers dug into the arms of his seat throughout the forty-minute flight. Airplane rides frightened Amazon. The one from Mexico City to Oaxaca had been full of particularly vicious updrafts, and his forehead was covered with sweat. After the plane finally touched down, with a sharp rubber slap and a bounce, he fumbled a handkerchief out and wiped his face. While taxiing back to the terminal building, Amazon noticed a compound on the runway edge with two helicopters in it. Three soldiers were leaning lazily against a nearby pile of sandbags. Another was waving at the passing airplane. When it reached the gate, Henry Amazon was one of the first passengers down the ramp.

He rented a Kombi in the terminal, then drove to the Modesto and rented one of the bungalows. From there, he telephoned Chorizo's house. The Zapotec's wife said Chorizo had been back from his trip for a couple of days but wasn't around right then. She didn't have any idea where he was. Amazon thought he might know where to look.

From the Modesto the *gringo* headed for the whore street, a long, one-way block off the Periférico, south of the *zocolo*. The stalls and the whores were on the west side of the street. The men looked them over from the opposite sidewalk. At eleven on a Tuesday morning there were few customers. Less than half the booths were working. El Chorizo's pickup truck was parked near the Periférico intersection. He had his eye on a woman in a tight green dress, sitting barefoot on a folding chair across the way.

Amazon parked behind him and walked up to his truck before being noticed.

"*¡Tortuga!*" the Indian exclaimed. "I was wondering about when you was going to show up. Get in." The Indian grinned his silver smile and motioned with his arm. He was drinking beer and opened a fresh bottle for Amazon.

"Whatchyou thinks about the *puta* over there, *compadre?*" he motioned with his beer.

"Which one?"

"With the green dress."

The woman knew the Indian and the *gringo* were talking about her and stood up. Facing them squarely, she lifted the front edge of her dress and showed a thick patch of hair between her legs. After offering them a glimpse, she covered the snatch up again and did several humping strokes with her hips in their direction.

El Chorizo let out an appreciative yell, and Amazon joined in. Both toasted her with their warm beers.

"I don't know, Sausage," Amazon joked, "she may be too much for you."

The Indian blushed. "I can handle anything that walks," he bragged back.

"On two or four legs?"

El Chorizo laughed.

"One thing I do know, *compadre:* you can damn well afford her."

"How do you know that?"

"I brought you a bonus." Amazon produced a thousand dollars American out of his shirt pocket and tossed it on the seat between them.

Chorizo ran his eye over the bills. "You're all right, *gringo. Es más bueno.*"

"I also know you haven't got time to mess with her yet," Amazon added, motioning at the woman across the street. "You got a little business to do first."

El Chorizo turned serious.

"You're moving again right away, huh?"

"It's the way it has to be," Amazon explained. "Real quick, in and out. You told me you knew a man who sells gas for airplanes."

"It's true."

"I need enough for two engines."

"No problem. We can see him whenever you want."

"I want to now."

"Like I said," the Indian answered after a sip of beer, *"no problema."*

Amazon said they could take his wheels and leave the pickup here. El Chorizo said that was fine. Then he had a question: "Is this going to be the last one? Like you talked about?"

"The last one," Amazon said. *"Es todo. Finito."*

He didn't wait for a response, turning on his heel and walking back to the Kombi. Chorizo locked up his truck and followed. As the two of them pulled away from the curb, the Zapotec rolled his window down and stuck his head out toward the whore in green.

"I'll be back," he shouted. "Don't go nowhere else."

After waving a ten-dollar bill, Chorizo pulled his head inside and gave Henry Amazon directions that led to the outskirts of town.

Henry Amazon's intention to "retire" fascinated Chorizo.

"You really goin' to do it, huh?" he asked again as the van sped toward the edge of Oaxaca.

"Really goin' to do it."

"¿Porqué, compadre? You makin' good money."

"It's a long story. I'm burnt out on it all. Too much hassle, too much fear, too much bullshit."

El Chorizo thought about the *gringo*'s response, but it still didn't make much sense to him. Among other things, the English phrase "burnt out" confused him. His face assumed a quizzical expression.

Amazon noticed and was a little irritated. "You can understand that, *mano*. People have been trying to kill me or lock me up for nine years. I'm tired of it. I don't want no more. There's other things to do in life besides this. I'd like to live with nothing over my shoulder for a while."

"You know how long it's been since I slept without a gun close by?" Amazon went on. "Twelve fucking years. An even goddamn dozen. Know how many people I know who have died since I first came

215

here?" Again he answered his own question. "Twenty-four. Two dozen on the nose. I've counted them, over and over. Don't you see? I've used up all the battle I was born with. Now it's past my time."

This rush of emotion startled Chorizo. He stayed silent, thinking. Finally he asked, "What will you do when you're not smuggling no more?"

"*¿Quién sabe?*" Amazon shrugged. His voice was subdued now and sounded tired.

"What'd you do before?"

"Not a whole lot. I was a Marine." The paucity of his own skills bothered him when he repeated them out loud.

El Chorizo motioned to him to turn down an *adobe* road. It led past several warehouses and dead-ended at a storage yard bordered by Cyclone fence. Rainy season and the passage of trucks had churned the yard's entrance into a thick, soupy paste. Chorizo told Amazon to park outside the gate and wait. He would go inside and find his friend.

As Chorizo made his way through the mucky yard, Amazon sat in the rent-a-car. The fact that he was in Oaxaca for the last time hovered in his mind. He was tired from the plane ride and trying to adjust to being south of the border again. In a couple of weeks he would begin being someone else. He wondered how easy that would be, but his mind moved quickly to suppress the insecurity. This was no time to get antsy. He had to let the future take care of itself. He wasn't through being a smuggler yet.

Chorizo trotted back to the Kombi and hopped in the passenger seat. "He's here," he said. The Zapotec pointed to a loading dock. "Over there."

Amazon could see a solitary *mestizo* loading fifty-five-gallon drums with a dolly. Chorizo introduced him as Gonsolvo. Gonsolvo was extremely fat.

"*Mucho gusto,*" Amazon said.

"*Mucho gusto.*"

"Chorizo says you got airplane fuel."

"Is true. *Mucho* gasoline." The fat man motioned at the dock covered with drums and laughed.

"You cut it with diesel?"

Gonsolvo acted outraged. "Cut it? What kinda *hombre* you take me for, *gringo*? I don't never do nothin' like that. This is good gas." To prove his point, he unscrewed a cap off one of the drums and ladled out a cupful. He then thrust the cup at Amazon. "You see? Ain't nothin' brown about that gas. No diesel been near it."

"This the same gas I'm gonna get when I pick it up?"

"No different."

"How much you want for it?"

"Three hundred dollars American."

"For each?"

"For each," Gonsolvo echoed, kicking the drum next to him to emphasize the point.

Amazon and Gonsolvo then launched into five minutes of dickering that reduced the price to 290 dollars but no farther. Finally Amazon backed off.

"I'll pay that," he said, "even though it's too much."

Gonsolvo shrugged.

"But when I pay it, I don't wanta have to worry about your end anymore, *sabe*? I'm payin' that too-much price because you got good gas and you're gonna have it for me when I want it. If you don't, you're robbin' me."

Gonsolvo nodded.

"I'm gonna come back on Monday to see my gas. I'll pay you twenty percent now, twenty percent then, and the rest when I pick it up."

"When's that?"

"Maybe a week."

" *'Stá bien*," Gonsolvo agreed.

Back on the Periférico, Chorizo was jubilant. He made Amazon stop so he could buy two cold beers from a roadside stand.

"You know, Tortuga," Chorizo told him, "you don't need to get out of the business. You just need to dump that Mexican and be partners with me. My way, there's no problems."

From the Indian's ambiguous tone of voice, Amazon knew he had the option of treating the remark seriously or as a joke. He laughed and lit a cigarette. Chorizo laughed too. So be it: it was a joke.

While Henry Amazon was arranging for his airplane fuel, Purdee Fletcher was waiting outside a conference room on the seventh floor of Operation Condor's Mexico City headquarters. Whenever a Big Ten Code Four was invoked, someone had to give an oral report on the outcome to Condor's Intelligence Evaluation Committee. In the case of Ramón Ramón, Purd was the someone. Normally it would have been Cruz's responsibility, but Cruz had no interest in explaining Rat Trap's one failure. He had, he said, more pressing matters. The interrogation of the prisoners they had taken along with the *gringo*'s dope in the village of San Dionisio had yielded the location of an airstrip and warehouse even farther south, in the mountains behind Chichicapan. Cruz planned to hit it right away and was spending Saturday making final preparations for a Sunday morning raid.

Purd was nervous, dressed in his best white leisure suit, white patent leather shoes, blue shirt, and a green tie with a sparkling pheasant on it. Sweat was already leaking around his collar. He knew Longbeem would be uptight about Purd's letting Ramón slip through their fingers. The program had been the Director's idea, and he had a lot riding on Big Ten's success. Ramón would have been his first score. Worse than that, Purd had assured him of the capture before the fact. And Purd had his own problems with Cruz going against him as well. His mind had been scrabbling around for a strategy all day.

Purd sat at one end of the table. When he was finally ushered into the room where the Intelligence Evaluation Committee was meeting, Norton Longbeem, the Director, was at the other end. The remaining six members of the committee were spread on either side between them: three Mexicans and three Americans. Purdee cleared his throat and began by describing the ambush itself. He said flat out that it was Cruz's mistake. The Federale underestimated the length of the column they had to trap, and as a consequence, Ramón, the trail man, was out of reach when the ambush was sprung. Under hostile questioning from the Mexicans, Purd had to admit that he had sat in on all the planning sessions himself, and in his role as Oaxaca Condor's American liaison he had approved the arrangements. Purd tried to explain that it was a formality to do so, a gesture of respect to Cruz's final authority and nothing more. That set off a round of squabbling amongst the committee members as to who had authority over what.

When the discussion got back to him, Purdee Fletcher made his move. "In any case I say there's not a lot of sense in crying over spilt milk, if you know what Ole Purd means." He paused to lick his lips. "I haven't given this Ramón creep up for lost myself."

The statement drew stares.

"What are you talking about?" Longbeem asked.

Purd leaned on the table with his elbows. "Yesterday," he answered, "the State Police found the car Ramón was drivin' that night at the bottom of a canyon next to the Tehuacán Highway."

"Was he in it?"

"No."

"So what's the point?"

"The point is the way that all fits together with everything else. Up to findin' this car Ole Purd had figured like everybody else that Ramón had just flew the coop. I mean, he didn't hit any of our roadblocks, and you all know both Puebla and Tehuacán stayed out there for two days. But there are three other ways outa Oaxaca, and his car coulda handled two of 'em. And then we find the car, and this whole ball game looks different. He either had another car waiting, or he went to ground near there somewhere. This son of a bitch knows the country, and he's cool, if you know what Ole Purd means. Twenty years on the job says he ain't left yet."

"Preposterous," one of the Mexicans interjected.

"Maybe so," Fletcher answered, "but ain't the real point that we got no way of finding out whether it is or it isn't? This Ramón and his kind got to be chased if you want to catch 'em. The fact is pure and simple that we got nothin' to chase with." Purd was in the heart of his

219

strategy now, and he kept his words close enough together to make sure nobody interrupted him. "I mean Ole Pissaro Cruise has demonstrated Oaxaca Condor can cut up an operation real good," Purd continued with a nod of credit toward the Mexicans. "But a son of a bitch like this Ramón fella ain't easy to catch in the same place as his goods. He's like a cat. You gotta stalk him. Ain't no possibility for Condor to do that the way things stand now. All of us are pointed at jumpin' on pieces of the traffic. That'll getcha dope and lotsa violators, but it won't getcha anybody slick enough to land on no Big Ten, take Ole Purd's word on it. We only even got close to him by accident this time."

One of the Mexicans started to assault the idea, but Longbeem quieted him with a glance. Purd had guessed the Director would be anxious to find an explanation for how little success the Big Ten'd had, and he was right. "I think Fletcher may have a point," Longbeem interjected. "Just what exactly are you suggesting?"

"I'm suggesting that we just flat-ass go after this Ramón. It's the only way to make Big Ten really work. Put a half dozen men on his trail while it's still warm. I call it a Hunter Squad. Give me that, and I'll bag him, same way I got those spades in L.A."

"You're talking about your own command?"

It was an audacious request, and Purdee knew it. "The Hunter Squad: it'd be an experiment, of course. My idea'd have it work right outa this committee. I mean, you all figure out who the Big Ten is; the Hunter Squad'll just chase 'em for ya."

Longbeem seemed to think about that.

Purd then gave him what he hoped would be the kicker. "Not only will I find the ones ya know about that way, but I'll find their replacements, too." Purdee had brought a briefcase with him, and he now extracted several photographs from it. "This Ramón chase is an example of what Ole Purd is talkin' about. Once we got on his trail, we started findin' out who he was connected to. I mean a man in the Big Ten's got to associate with someone who's even a higher level than him sometime. Am I right?" Purd did not pause for an answer. "You see, in trackin' him we get to penetrate, if you know what I mean. With this here Ramón, that's already happened."

Purd now turned his attention to the photos he'd brought along, began identifying them one by one, and passing them down the table. "You can see in this first one what situation we got here. There's Ramón on this side. Across the table is the guy he was runnin' with and his old lady. Next to him with his back square at ya is a fourth violator. At this point I'm callin' that fella 'Mystery Man.' In this next one you can see that the broad is givin' Mystery Man money. Now it ain't but two days after these pictures got took that Ramón heads out to get his dope. Maybe what we see right there is the down payment being given to the principal in the operation himself. Could be that Mystery Man is the wholesaler in all this. We grab Ramón and then grab him. Work our way up the chain a command, so to speak."

Purd could tell he'd hooked Longbeen with the notion. The Director wanted to know more about this Mystery Man.

"Well, we got a picture," Purd answered, "but it ain't much good." He slid it down the table. "As you can see, ain't much you can tell from it 'cept about how big he is and maybe the hair color. The only thing else I can tell ya is I'll get the rest as soon as Ramón's in the bag."

"It makes no sense," one of the Mexicans said.

"Let's not be too hasty," Longbeem interrupted. "We ought to talk this over some." The Director then looked at Purd. "We won't need you for that, Fletcher. Why don't you wait for me down in my office while the committee talks."

A secretary then came in and led Purd down the hall and around a corner to Longbeem's office. One wall was solid glass, tinted brown. Purd spent all afternoon waiting there, looking out of the window and smoking cigarettes.

Henry Amazon spent the first part of his afternoon driving to Rascón's message place and back. Then he returned to the Modesto where he tried unsuccessfully to sleep. Lying there with the shades drawn, he kept thinking about his decision to quit. Now that he was carrying it out, its finality gnawed at him. Other than the money he would have, he had no idea what he'd do when he was done. The money made the prospect more comfortable. To further bolster himself, he thought about the day he'd first begun deciding to get out. That made him think of The Patchoolie Kid, broiled next to the road, and the obnoxious way Ramón had broken the news. There was no future in all this ducking and dodging, Amazon reminded himself. Much longer, and he'd end up like Ramón, hooked to it with no place else to go. Better just to get his plane in quick and be done.

The subject of airplanes took him back to Patchoolie and The Kid's colossal fuck up at the airstrip outside of Mitla, eight years ago. Amazon had been living with Wanda then. Ramón had arranged for the plane. The pilot had been someone Ramón knew named Seymore Block. The three partners had all been at the strip, waiting in the dark.

The most immediate danger once the plane had landed was the possibility that it had been tailed. If so, the pursuers would land behind it and bust them all. To prevent that possibility, The Patchoolie Kid had been stationed on the edge of the runway in the flatbed truck used to haul the load. The load itself was sitting under a tarp next to the gas for refueling. As soon as the plane passed Patchoolie, he was supposed to drive his truck across the runway to the middle, park it, and block any planes trying to follow. The Kid had wanted very badly to perform well.

Perhaps that intensity explained why he'd jumped the gun. When Block's Cessna twin-engine touched down, its trailing elevator clipped against the onrushing truck's front end. The plane immediately fell off to its left, and when the wing tip touched the ground, the aircraft began to slide sideways. Then it flipped onto its back and continued sliding straight for where Ramón and Amazon were standing with the gas and the load. The two had to run for their lives. Block's Cessna carried the marijuana and the airplane fuel into a ditch and exploded in flames.

Within fifteen seconds, it was obvious that Seymore Block, his Cessna twin-engine, and the load were all fried.

Amazon had been momentarily unable to grasp that Patchoolie had been that dumb.

Ramón Ramón was much quicker on the draw. He ran down the airstrip to where The Patchoolie Kid was cowering next to the truck, watching the forty-foot-tall bursts of flame. Ramón had tackled The Kid and held him flat on his back. With a quick reach of his free hand, Ramón Ramón pulled a forty-five out of his boot and was going to execute Patchoolie on the spot. Only Amazon's arrival had stopped him.

"Ramón," Amazon had screamed. "What the fuck are you doing? We got to get out of here. Let's sort this out in the village where we can hide."

"Bullshit," Ramón had snapped. "We sort it out now, and this chump pays. The sucker just ripped us off and killed our pilot. Ripoff artists die. That's the rule."

"You can't be serious. He saved your ass last time out. He's your partner. You don't think the cops aren't comin' straight for us when they find his body?"

Fortunately for The Patchoolie Kid, the argument moved Ramón.

"All right," Ramón Ramón said, keeping The Kid pinned. "I don't off him, but there ain't no more partners anymore. Between me and you, yes, but he's out, and I don't have to see him again. Starting now."

With that Ramón let The Kid up. Amazon then persuaded Ramón to let him give Patchoolie a ride as far as Mitla, and they had all fled back to the village in the truck. The Kid had been dropped without a word at the Motel Mitla, Amazon at Wanda's house, and Ramón had driven on to Salina Cruz, to hide near the Pacific until the heat from the wreck finally lifted. The Kid had left Mitla the next day, saying he was going north to find money and get in the business for himself.

Maybe I should have quit then, Amazon told himself. Nothing much had changed since. Everybody's only got either older or dead.

223

"Snap out of it," he suddenly warned himself out loud. He swung his legs off the bed and sat up. Thinking about wrecks would jinx the scam, sure as shit.

Longbeem finally came through the office door at half past six. Purd had been waiting more than five hours. Longbeem went to the sideboard and began pouring a glass of Scotch for each of them.

Purd couldn't contain himself. "Well?" he asked.

The Director looked up and handed him his drink. He took a hit on his own before answering. "You're gonna get the Hunter Squad," he said. "You, Wissle, and three Mexicans."

Purd was jubilant. "I swear, Nort, you're not gonna regret trustin' Ole Purd like this."

Longbeem walked over and sat at his desk. "Look, Purd," he said, "let's get this straight from the beginning. I didn't go for this scheme out of trust for you. Quite frankly, if all I had was your theory, I'd never have gone for it at all."

"What d'ya mean?"

"I mean we came across something up here that just might make a plan like that work. Without it I couldn't have let you near any Hunter Squad with a ten-foot pole."

Purd swallowed. "What is it?" he asked.

"A woman. Says she knows Ramón. We picked her up in a sweep at the airport here. Just fell into our hands." The Director slid a manila file over to Purd.

The report inside identified the person in question as female suspect 8/14, coded D.A./Big Ten for Director's Attention. As part of the airport detail's routine random search of young Americans at Mexico City International, a small amount of cocaine had been found hidden in this woman's purse. Subject to standard Condor procedure, 8/14, like all suspects, was shown the Big Ten photos during her interrogation.

The female suspect had picked out Jerome Whitehurst alias Ramón

Ramón, and as soon as she did, 8/14 was transferred immediately to the holding cells at Condor Central where she'd been debriefed steadily for two days. According to her, she had lived in Oaxaca for six years before moving to the Gulf of Mexico three years ago. Some of those years had been spent with the suspect himself. She said she'd last seen Ramón in passing, six months before, in Veracruz. According to this preliminary report, female suspect 8/14 showed "remarkable knowledge about Whitehurst alias Ramón's personal habits and patterns of activity." It was the report's conclusion that she could be put to effective use.

Purd looked up when he was finished reading. "Just exactly what do you have in mind?"

Norton Longbeem seemed a little annoyed that Purd had to ask. "Come on, Purd," he snapped. "The broad's gonna bird-dog for your Hunter Squad. She knows where this guy hangs out and what he likes to do. Get her out on the streets to make contact. Once she does, our man's in the bag."

"Will she do that for us?"

Condor Director Norton Longbeem chuckled. "The bitch is so scared she'd give us her own grandmother."

Purdee Fletcher smiled. "When do I get a look at her?"

"Right now."

Longbeem led Purd back into the hall, and in three minutes they were leaving the elevator in the second floor of the building's basement. They were stopped immediately by two uniformed Mexicans who checked their passes and then let them through. Their first stop was the office of the Duty Officer, a young American in a short-sleeved shirt who jumped to his feet when the Director walked in.

"Good evening, Mr. Longbeem," he opened.

Longbeem acknowledged the greeting with a touch of his finger to his forehead. "Where you keeping 8/14?" he asked.

"In the fishbowl," the duty officer explained, reaching for the key ring in his desk. "Just like your office instructed."

The fishbowl was a windowless cell, like all the others in the basement. Its principal difference was the giant rectangular piece of one-way glass on one wall. The caged suspect got the shiny side, and the cops got to watch without being seen. When Purd and his director reached the cell, the woman inside was sitting restlessly on her cot. She had a heavy tan and wound her long black hair around her head.

The cops watched for a while in silence. The woman stood up, went to the sink, and splashed some water on her face before sitting down again with her head in her hands.

"What's this broad's name?" Purd asked.

"Rosenberg," the Director replied offhandedly. "But she goes by Lamar, Wanda Lamar."

It must be something incredibly ugly in her karma, Wanda Lamar told herself. The consequences of some transgression darker than anything she could remember, maybe even in a previous life.

When Wanda Lamar had been arrested at Mexico City International, she was on her way back to the United States for good. Nine years south of the border had become more than enough. The madness of her life here had become steadily more apparent over the last two years. Three days ago she had reached the end and decided to leave. She had even seriously considered changing her name back to Rosenberg and reenrolling in Barnard. Now she felt like she was being forced backward over the ledge she'd just crawled up. She was almost hysterical.

The thought of Oaxaca again was suffocating. It had been the scene of her worst craziness. Worst of all was her departure three years ago from the Valley pregnant. She had been knocked up by an Indian and was intent on having her baby in the Yucatán. The subsequent bus trip had turned into a nightmare. She was bleeding by the time she'd reached the Veracruz station and gave birth to a three-month-old, lifeless fetus in the emergency ward. Then she contracted hepatitis and almost died. After a year's recuperation Wanda had become bored with Veracruz and departed for the Yucatán.

There she imagined herself Gauguin, endlessly sketching the native fishermen and cane cutters. On one of those artistic expeditions she had met a French painter and cocaine user named Lucien Denard and had soon fallen under his spell. His paintings were giant splashes of orange and green, laced with all varieties of abstract symbols, a style he considered an offshoot of Miró's.

After living together in the Yucatán for a few more months, the two of them had made their way back to Veracruz where Denard rented a studio. For Wanda, it was the beginning of her "late artistic period." During it she sketched less and less and spent more and more time swallowed in battles with Lucien. The Frenchman's paintings had by now turned into shades of black and thin strips of phosphorescent orange. His nose habit had turned him into a stark paranoid.

All of that had come to a head two months earlier when Denard beat her up for the way she looked at another man on the beach. From then on Wanda had just waited for the bruise over her eye to heal and made secret plans to leave for good. She had known that the Frenchman would try and stop her if she told him, so the day Wanda left Veracruz she carried only a purse. On her way out the door she shouted to Denard that she was headed for the market. That had been three days ago. Wanda Lamar had planned to carry her little bit of cocaine into the airplane lavatory and take one final noseful in toast to the life she was leaving behind. Needless to say, she never got a chance to indulge.

Between flights at Mexico City International the four Mexicans in civilian clothes came up to her, and suddenly Wanda Lamar's trip home was over.

The Americans who questioned her during the next three days kept saying things about giving her back to the Mexicans. She knew what that meant, and when Ramón's picture came up, she grabbed at it like a drowning person grabs a life jacket.

"I know him," she said, pointing. She was in shock over the loss of her future, and she saw her options as this or prison. The Americans had hinted they might be able to save her from five years in Santa Marta if she went along.

227

On Saturday night Wanda Lamar frequently broke into sobs. Her face was puffy and her dress bedraggled. She threw water on her cheeks, and a few minutes later she heard a key slide into the door latch.

The solid door opened, and two Americans she had never seen before came in. One was tall, thin, and somewhat imperious. The other was shorter, looped with suet, and wearing an enormous pair of white patent leather loafers. The fat one smiled a big smile and came on in a friendly voice.

"Glad to know ya, Wanda," he said, extending his hand. "Whole name's Purdee Fletcher, but it's just Purd to you."

Wanda made no response to the offered hand.

Purd saw a quizzical expression in her face. "You and me are gonna find your friend Ramón Ramón together, honey," he explained.

Wanda Lamar cringed. She felt a cold cloud cross over her life as soon as the narc said Ramón's name.

16

Pizarro Cruz's Sunday morning raid left the Oaxaca Airport at 5:00 A.M. He called it Operation Buzzard's Nest. The operation was by far the biggest yet conducted by Oaxaca Station, involving ten helicopters, mostly borrowed from the Army, and a combined force of more than a hundred Judicial Federal, soldiers, and State Police. The target was a ridge beyond Chichicapan. On Friday Emil Grimes, the *gringo* pilot, had flown over and taken pictures of the place.

The first was a shot almost straight down on a broad ridge. Although lines of brush had been placed across its surface, the outline of a dirt airstrip suitable for small twin engines was clearly visible. At one end of it there were two faint huts. The second photo was a blowup of the western slope of the hill. Close to its base stood three much larger huts. The third photo captured another two buildings even farther to the west along the foot trail that eventually wound up to the strip itself. According to what the prisoner from San Dionisio said, all of the structures were used to store *mota* for the *gringos* who flew in to load up.

229

The way Cruz had planned things, the raiding force would split into three groups once it reached the target. The first and largest would land on the commanding ground of the airstrip itself. This element would include the operation leadership and a demolition squad who would rig mines on the runway. The second element would attack the three large huts at the bottom of the slope. The third would drop down on the last two buildings, two or three miles to the west on the edge of the trail. When all the evidence and suspects had been collected and ferried back to the city, Operation Buzzard's Nest would withdraw, exploding the mines and crippling the strip.

Grimes was flying the lead ship. Since Purd Fletcher was in Mexico City, Hog Wissle was in the seat next to him, manning the intercom. Cruz, an Army captain, and a combined force of soldiers and Federales rode in the back. Emil Grimes lifted off on Hog's signal and headed south with the others stringing out in a line behind. The racket of their passage echoed along the washes and could be heard for miles. Twenty minutes outside of Oaxaca the pilot warned Hog the target was up ahead and Hog passed the word on to the rest of the caravan. Ten minutes later he punched Wissle on the arm and pointed at the far side of an approaching ridge where a finger of rock jutted out into the surrounding hollow.

"That's it," he shouted.

Hog checked to make sure his pistol was in its holster before answering. Then he shouted back to "get it on." The big *gringo* was grinning, and the rotor noise was everywhere.

Now came the part Grimes was worried about most.

His assignment, once the primary target was in sight, was to swoop, lay a flare down, and then get out of the way while two of the Army gunships worked the marked landing zone over and pronounced it secure for occupation. Emil Grimes made the run with all the speed he could muster from his Huey. When he was on top of the strip, Grimes backed off, loosed his marker, and then jammed the chopper straight up like it was in an elevator shaft. The Army was close behind on full automatic. Thirty-caliber tracers were spewed out of their side doors as the choppers wove a saturation pattern over the flat top of the ridge.

The other Federale chopper, loaded with explosives and sappers to mine the strip, was hovering at the same altitude as the command ship, waiting for the landing zone to be pronounced secure. Two other Army helicopters had passed the primary target and were beginning to give the same treatment to the second target, a group of huts at the base of the ridge. This element was composed of both soldiers and Judicial Federal agents led by Garcia Huahilote. The third part of Operation Buzzard's Nest was a joint Army and State Police force being ferried in the three slowest birds. Those ships were only just then passing the primary target on their way along the winding trail to the west in search of the third set of buildings identified in the aerial photographs.

The Army had formed a perimeter and seized the warehouse at the end of the camouflaged runway when Grimes touched down. Cruz and his men rushed out into the dust storm whipped up by the whirling blades and headed for the building.

Hog was slower to leave. His assignment was to set up an overall operational command post on the edge of the strip and act as radio officer, coordinating the operation's three parts. It was the most responsibility the junior agent had ever been given thus far in his career. Just before he stepped out of the helicopter, he turned and thumped the pilot on the arm.

"What'd I tell you," he shouted over the roar of the machine, "a fucking piece of cake."

Emil Grimes smiled and switched his engine off.

Hog ran over to the edge of the packed dirt runway to select a command post site overlooking both the secondary target immediately below and the third group of buildings another two or so miles west on the trail. After setting the radio up, his first call was to Cruz and the force at the warehouse. The Federale had little to report. They'd found only four boxes of *mota,* several empty beer bottles, and that was all. At the secondary target Garcia Huahilote reported even less success

231

than Cruz. Both huts, one on fire from the rain of gunship tracers, were completely empty.

When Wissle called the third and last element of the Operation, bad news turned to worse. His post looked out at their target, and the choppers were nowhere in sight.

At first, their signal weak, Hog had trouble even making radio contact. When he finally did pick them up, the element's command reported they still hadn't been able to find the buildings they were supposed to attack.

"Shit," Hog stormed. Then he used the authority Pizarro Cruz had invested in him and ordered a response.

"Grimes," he shouted into the radio.

"I hear ya, boss." The pilot had been sitting in his cockpit with the earphones on.

"Those fuckin' last choppers are lost up there somewhere. I want you to go find them and then lead them where they're supposed to be."

"Ah, come on, Hog, that's—"

"Pronto," the junior agent interrupted.

Then Cruz came on the air and announced they'd found nothing along the slope. He was returning to the command post.

Grimes was well on the other side of the next ridge before he made contact with the errant task force and told them to climb up and join him. He hovered while the three squat Hueys slowly rose into formation.

"Follow me," he told the lead Mexican, "and watch for my smoke."

As soon as his ship crossed back over the ridge, Emil Grimes descended rapidly and then swooped toward a clearing where the *barranca* widened into a sparse meadow with a long shed on one edge. As he crossed this wide space, Grimes let loose another marker of phosphorescent orange smoke and then climbed out in a steep sweeping left-hand turn. Behind him, two of the three choppers pounced and disgorged their occupants. The third hovered high in case anything ran out along the trail and had to be chased. Here they also found nothing

232

and no one. Operation Buzzard's Nest would probably have had no suspects at all during their raid into the mountains outside Chichicapan if Emil Grimes hadn't finally found them by accident.

He was in the middle of reporting to Hog when a flash of movement on the ground appeared in the corner of his eye. "Hold on," he radioed as he nosed over for a better look.

All Grimes got was a brief glimpse of a short line of men and loaded burros moving along the path at a dogtrot. Then they disappeared in the cypress and tamarinds in the *barranca* bottom.

"I see something," he informed Hog. "Proceeding to take a look."

Those were the last words anyone ever heard from the hired pilot Emil Grimes.

At that point Operation Buzzard's Nest was just a large, expensive failure. Within ten minutes the Sunday morning raid would tumble into outright disaster.

It took a while for Grimes to again find what he'd seen. He followed along the *barranca* bottom and swooped lower. At the lowest point of his descent along the almost invisible path, he spotted the caravan again. It was under the cover of a high, broad tree. This time the pilot counted not a dozen beasts, as he'd first thought, but only six, accompanied by what looked like an equal number of armed men.

Immediately after they came into view, he heard the ground fire open up. To his ear, it had a tinny ring. He attempted to climb away, but at three hundred feet, two thirty-eight-caliber rounds tore hunks out of the cable connecting the front and tail rotors. A hundred feet later the cable snapped. Emil Grimes knew exactly what had happened when he felt the tail begin to whip sideways. The chopper wound into a ferocious spin four hundred feet straight down. Grimes was dead on impact. Moments later the Huey's fuel tanks exploded with a sound that was heard for miles around.

Just seconds before the gunfire began, Hog Wissle stopped watching the far-off speck of Grimes's airborne chopper to look at Pizarro Cruz come out across the airstrip from his futile search of the slope below. Then the sudden sound down the *barranca* turned his head around, and Hog spotted the orange fireball as soon as it lit.

"What happened?" he screamed into the radio. "Grimes? You read me?"

The reaction force hovering over the third target answered. "The *gringo* is crashed," the pilot gasped. "We are on our way."

So was Hog. He dropped the microphone and sprinted to the approaching Cruz.

Like everyone else, Cruz had been frozen in his tracks by the explosion. At first, he didn't quite hear what Hog jabbered at him.

"Grimes is down, *Jefe*," the *gringo* repeated. "Let me take a reaction force."

The news stunned the head Federale, and at first a look of indecision and nakedness passed over his usually composed face. Then he stiffened. "Go," he ordered.

Hog shouted for six of the Federales around the *Jefe* to follow him and sprinted toward the parked choppers, shouting and making an eggbeater motion over his head. The nearest chopper was revving up when the *gringo* and the others piled in. Several seconds later the bird lifted off, and the *mestizo* machine gunner strapped himself into the door behind his weapon.

"Head for the fire," Hog ordered the pilot.

The third target's reaction force reached the wreckage ahead of them, and one pass over the flames was enough to determine there was no helping Grimes. Then the combined force of State Police detectives and infantrymen began to search along the rail, hovering at two hundred feet, looking for action below.

Like Grimes, they were taken unawares by the sudden eruption of carbine fire. The first slug drove through the underside of a State Police detective's jaw and blew the lid of his head off on the way out. The second hit the box full of ammunition belts for the machine gun in the door. The resulting series of explosions doubled the size of the Huey's hatch. Both the pilot and copilot were killed by flying frag-

234

ments of the fuselage, and the khaki helicopter pancaked into the ground and exploded just like Grimes's had half a mile away.

When Hog reached the site of the second crash, he didn't even slow down to take a closer look. Instead he yelled at his pilot to work up the trail and warned the gunner to stand ready. A mile and a half later they came upon the remnants of the caravan first sighted by Emil Grimes.

By now it had dwindled to one loaded burro led by three men moving at a trot. As the chopper approached, two of the men stopped in their tracks, and one, armed with an M–1 carbine, got off two rounds before the door gunner cut him in half with his first burst. The second, armed with a thirty-eight revolver, fired aimlessly three times and then fell in another string of tracers from the helicopter door.

The gunner then turned his sights up the trail and caught the third suspect ahead with the burro just as the Indian wheeled to try and get off a volley with his shotgun. Three rounds hit within inches of each other in the middle of his lungs.

After the chopper landed up the trail, Hog made his way back to check the bodies on foot. The Indian with the thirty-eight was still breathing. Half his face was shot off, but he still sucked air through the side of his head.

Hog looked away. The smell of burned men was carrying along the *barranca* from the site of the second crash. Turning back to the gurgling suspect, Hog paused for a moment and then finished the Indian off with a round in his one remaining temple.

Operation Buzzard's Nest reassembled on the airstrip to assess its losses. Two helicopters were down, thirteen men dead, and Cruz had nothing to show for it but nine thirty-pound boxes of *mota*. Most of the Federales stared silently at the corpses recovered from the trail while Cruz called General Cortez de Corriente's headquarters to inform them of what had gone on.

Two of the bodies were obviously Indians, but the third was more of a mystery. He was the one who'd been carrying the carbine, and while he was dressed like an Indian, his features didn't match the disguise. His face had wide, almost Negroid, lips and nose, café au lait skin, and silky, dark, black Latin hair. He began to stink in the sun before the others and drew more flies as well.

Twenty minutes later the Operation mounted up. When the last ship was off, three giant dynamite charges set in the runway were exploded. Shock waves from the explosion rocked the waiting choppers, and after the smoke and dust cleared below, two craters thirty-five feet deep by forty feet across were now dead center in the runway.

Cruz then ordered the caravan to fly over the scene of the disaster one more time. Smoke was still lifting off the wreckage. Next he set off toward Batista Laredo, a small village six miles farther west of the second crash. There, as the caravan hovered, the bird hauling the three bodies dumped them on the thatched roofs almost a thousand feet below.

This was those bandits' territory, Cruz said. Let them know Pizarro Cruz would be back to avenge himself.

The two Indians were thrown out first. They tumbled like sacks of rock. The strange, light-colored *traficante* seemed to fall more slowly, end over end. One of his feet was gone, sawed away by machine-gun bullets, and on the way down an arm fell off as well.

Cruz then turned Operation Buzzard's Nest back for town.

General Cortez de Corriente was waiting at the airport when they landed. The General was furious. The news had hit him like a rock slapping into a hornet's nest. Cruz started to explain, but Corriente was in no mood to listen. Clearly, Corriente shouted, the Federal was not capable of handling the south Valley. He would have to do that himself. These *guerrilleros* had to be crushed. After that pronouncement, the General sped back to military headquarters in a blaze of sirens.

The Oaxaca Station Duty Officer then delivered a wire from Condor Central addressed to Cruz. It informed him that Fletcher and Wissle, the two *gringos,* plus three of his own men were being stripped from

236

his command and assigned to the new Big Ten Hunter Squad. The duty officer also had a wire for Hog Wissle. It told him to pick Purd up when he arrived on the noon flight from Mexico City.

Henry Amazon waited for Rascón in the Tlacolula alley from ten to almost half past eleven. Finally a fourteen-year-old boy showed up with a message. He said Rascón couldn't come this morning. The *gringo* should return at seven that night. Amazon then walked back across the teeming Sunday market to his rent-a-car and headed for The Cockroach's place to check on that half of the load.

The Cockroach wasn't at his house, but his wife led Amazon to where he was. Amazon and the woman climbed a short ridge east of the meadow. At the top the trail dipped down with a steep pitch. Halfway to the bottom of the *barranca*, on the other side, the woman showed him the mouth of a cave that had remained hidden from view by the surrounding brush until they were right on top of it. Cucaracha was inside. He was crouched on the ground, listening to The Scorpions of the Valley and Garcia Garcia Garcia on the radio.

"Tortuga!" the Old Indian grinned through the gap in his front gums.

"*¿Quiubo, don Cucaracha?*" the *gringo* laughed back, bending slightly at the waist. "What's going on?"

"Garcia," he lisped, pointing at the radio. The old man was on a cane mat, clipping marijuana tops and packing them in cardboard boxes with HUEVOS DE CONSUELO and a bright blue chicken printed on the sides. Behind him the cave branched into two equal-sized forks, each twenty feet deep with about twelve feet between the floor and the roof. Both were full of cured and dried female plants waiting to be packed.

Since the old man was preoccupied with his radio, Amazon decided to look the cave over by himself. He walked deeper into the space and inspected the storage area with the Indian's Coleman lantern. Each plant was suspended head down from a frame by means of a stick tied across the cave roof. The plants were tall enough that their tips touched the floor. Amazon broke a bud off and took it with him back to the entrance to examine in sunlight. The shriveled leaves were the color of spinach and crusty as hell.

Sitting down across from the old man, Henry Amazon rolled a little of it up into a joint to see if it smoked as good as it looked. He took a lungful of the sweet-tasting fumes and then passed the *mota* stick to the Indian.

Cockroach gummed it and passed it back.

When Garcia Garcia signed off, the Indian spoke up. "You know, Tortuga," he said, "some day I'm gonna be on that show."

"Garcia's?"

"Of course. Is the only show for Indians to be on."

The old man's expression made it apparent he expected to be questioned on the subject, so Amazon obliged. "What're you gonna sing?"

"My name song," Cucaracha exclaimed. Then he launched into his squeaky singing voice.

> *La Cucaracha,*
> *la cucaracha,*
> *ya no quiere caminar.*
> *Porque no tiene,*
> *porque le falta,*
> *marijuana que fumar.*

The old man paused long enough to cackle like a chicken and then went on.

> The Cockroach,
> the cockroach,
> it doesn't want to walk anymore.
> Because it doesn't have,

because it needs,
marijuana to smoke.

His voice echoed in the *barranca* and made Henry Amazon nervous.

Amazon was back in Tlacolula at seven. Half an hour later, a Ford flatbed churned by in the street, and the same fourteen-year-old boy jumped off. "Rascón," the boy told Amazon, "he says for you to follow me."

"Lead the way."

"We should not walk together."

Amazon nodded.

He kept twenty yards behind as they climbed back to the main street and then turned right and deeper into the village. Soon they were zigzagging on side streets. After fifteen minutes the boy stopped at a wooden gate in a solid *adobe* wall. Making a motion for the *gringo* to follow, he disappeared inside.

Henry Amazon knew something was wrong as soon as he crossed the threshold into a tiny courtyard. An Indian carrying an M–1 carbine shut the gate behind him.

"*Buenos días,*" Amazon said.

The Indian said nothing and just motioned with his rifle barrel for the smuggler to go into the hut across the yard.

Another armed Indian opened the door there. Behind him was a table with a candle burning on it. Rascón and El Cubano were sitting on either side of the glow.

"We got trouble," Cubano opened.

Amazon sat down on the bench across from him. "What kinda trouble?"

"Airplane trouble."

"Airplane trouble?"

The Cuban shifted nervously on the bench. "The Federales took our airstrip this morning. They blew it up. Is no more."

"Goddamn. God fucking damn. Did you lose the load too?"

The Cuban lit a Farito cigarette. "We lost some," he said through a cloud of low-grade tobacco smoke, "but we still got enough to make our deal."

"Our deal was for dope and a place to fly it out of, *compadre*." The remark was pointed, and Amazon meant it to be.

El Cubano was clearly in no mood to argue. "That's the game, *mano*. You know the risks," he snapped. "We don't got no control of the cops."

"What a kettle of shit," Amazon muttered.

"*¿Qué?*"

"I said what a kettle of shit."

"Things is bad all over," The Cuban answered. He evinced no sympathy at all. "We lost three mens."

Amazon looked up. "Busted?"

"No," The Cuban answered, leaning forward. "Dead."

"Jesus."

For a moment, things went silent as Amazon's mind turned to making the best of the situation.

"You gonna give me a break on the price?" he finally continued, "since you can't deliver the strip like you promised?"

"No," The Cuban answered.

"No?"

"No."

"*Chinga*. That's a too much ripoff and you know it."

The Cuban's face was stiff. "Is a new game now. Our losses already more than make up the difference. We'll deliver the goods any place you want."

"How much warning you need before delivery?"

The Cuban talked to Rascón. "Forty-eight hours," he said when they were done.

"It's still a deal that smells," Amazon complained.

"You want out?"

Henry Amazon lit a cigarette before answering. "No," he said. "I don't."

240

He knew he had no choice but to agree. It would be hard enough to find another place for the plane to land without having to find more Kind to fill it as well. "We still got a deal," he continued. "I just need you to sit tight while I figure something else out."

The Cuban seemed to ease up some now that an agreement had been reached. "Rascón here," he said with a motion of his hand toward the silent Indian, "will stay in this house until you come back with word of where you want delivery. Come any time, night or day."

"Bueno," Amazon said as he stood up. He was in a hurry.

The boy led the *gringo* back to the main road, and then he was alone again. It was dark and rain had begun falling in a thin mist.

At ten minutes before midnight Ramón Ramón was awakened from a light sleep by the sounds of the bus pulling up in front of Huautla's Hotel Olympic. He pulled his shoes on and went downstairs. When Ramón found Nostaro Nostromos, the driver said he was going to sleep for a few hours. His bus would leave at 5 A.M. from the market.

Ramón was there an hour early, just to be sure he got a seat.

17

General Fernando Vega Cortez de Corriente went after the south Valley on Monday morning. The early edition of *Carteles* described the move as "Surprise War Games Commence in Oaxaca."

At roughly 6 A.M. elements of a Federal paratrooper division from Mexico City descended on the fields around Oaxaca International scattering south and east in the wind. The paratroopers were the spearhead of a military maneuver that would bring an additional thirteen thousand soldiers into the state of Oaxaca during the next twenty-four hours, quadrupling Cortez de Corriente's garrison. Of the more than four hundred men who jumped that morning, eight died when their parachutes failed to open. Another twenty-one experienced major injuries to their limbs. One of the dead was pictured on the *Carteles*'s front page, skewered on a lamppost in Coyotepec after free-falling more than one thousand feet.

In a statement to *Carteles* General Cortez de Corriente's office insisted on calling the operation a standard, regularly scheduled Army test of preparedness and made no reference to the loss of helicopters Sunday morning behind Chichicapan. The assumption of the "reaction exercise," as explained by the General's office, was that the security of the state capital was being threatened by an "imaginary" hostile force based in the Sierra Madres to the South. After the paratroopers succeeded in throwing up a perimeter around the airport, transport planes began landing at the rate of one every half hour, disgorging troops and supplies. At 10 A.M. a twelve-mile-long armored column that had left Mexico City on the Pan American the day before would arrive at the city's northern outskirts. This element's responsibilities were to secure the railroad station with a small detachment and move on to link up with the airport force. Together, the first two elements would then proceed farther south to a field bivouac several miles outside of Ocotlán. There they would spend the afternoon taking weapons practice on the surrounding foothills. The south Valley echoed with howitzer fire all afternoon. A third element was scheduled to begin arriving by train at eleven but wouldn't finish unloading until nine thirty that night. When it finally joined the other two, some eight thousand men would proceed out the San Dionisio Road and into the foothills behind Chichicapan where they were to seize their fictional enemy's "headquarters" and accomplish the object of the exercise. The General's office gave little indication of the games' schedule and left all eventual departure dates up in the air.

The impact of the surprise Army action in the Valley was immediate. In addition to those roadblocks already being maintained by the General's normal garrison, the new troops cut the Pan American toward Mexico City at the suburb of Pueblo Nuevo, the Pan American on the other side of town toward Tehuantepec, and the due south state highway connecting Oaxaca and Ocotlán, at four separate locations. A shortage of trucks plagued the Operation's logistics from the beginning, and when the elements moved initially by train began arriving, they had to be ferried in shuttles. As a result, for the next several days the city would be constantly full of large clusters of soldiers waiting to be picked up or dropped off. Lines of buses were backed up for hours at checkpoints while the Army searched each for contraband. Military traffic had the right of way, and long columns that included tanks made their way south toward the San Dionisio. More than a thousand soldiers were posted on corners throughout the downtown.

Henry Amazon saw the *Carteles* in the dining room of the Modesto. Zorro was due in this morning, and Amazon was just drinking coffee and waiting. He groaned when he read the headline. The news couldn't have been worse. There would be roadblocks everywhere, and he didn't even have an airstrip yet.

Purdee Fletcher figured the General's move couldn't but help the five-man Hunter Squad. The more Ramón was forced to maneuver around obstacles, the more likely he'd have to pop out in the open. First thing Monday morning Purd sent Hog to Pastilla's to get a couple dozen glossies of Ramón's mug shot done up for distribution to the Army roadblocks. Those wouldn't be ready until Tuesday. In the meantime he dispatched two of his three Mexicans out to where Ramón's car had been found to begin questioning people in the vicinity. Hog and Garcia Huahilote, the other Mexican assigned to Purd's new command, were to begin working Wanda. Purd himself manned command central in his office.

Wanda was being kept under guard in a suite at the Trocadero. She didn't think she could find Ramón just by asking around town. It had always been next to impossible to find him if he didn't want to be found. Purd had told her he didn't care what she thought. She was just supposed to work her butt off or get kicked in it. If she didn't produce, she would be sent back to the Mexicans and Santa Marta Prison. The prospect terrified her. Sunday night, Purd had her list every place she'd ever seen Ramón and everyone in town who might know him. Monday she started checking each one out personally.

First on the list was Tonebar's Veracruz Café, a place where she and Ramón had eaten breakfast. She walked there from the Trocadero.

Wanda was wearing a loose skirt, an Indian blouse, and *huaraches*. Men stared at her body even though little of it showed. Hog followed ten yards back with a two-way radio hidden in the flight bag over his arm. Huahilote stayed even with her on the other side of the street. Wanda paid scant attention to all the Army around town. To her, it fit right in with everything else that was happening.

The Veracruz Café had six tables and a counter. Four of the tables were occupied. The room was full of hot lard smells and chili peppers. Wanda went straight to the counter where a man's back was visible, bending over the stove.

"Tonebar?" she asked at the figure working at the collection of frying pans behind the counter.

A *mestizo* wearing a pair of horn-rimmed glasses that were spattered with grease turned around. He wore no shirt and a dirty apron inscribed *Tonebar's Veracruz Café*. His hairless chest seeped out from under the straps. The *mestizo* adjusted his glasses but still didn't seem to recognize the *gringa* across the counter from him.

"*Sí*," he said. "*Me llamo Tonebar.*"

"You don't remember me?"

The *mestizo* shuffled his face, wiped his glasses, and squinted again.

"All those times you made me breakfast, and you don't remember?"

The *mestizo* broke into a laugh. "*¡Qué milagro!*" he exclaimed. "*¿Es Wanda?*"

"*Es Wanda*," she laughed.

"Is long time."

"Three years."

"I thought you were gone for good, Wanda Lamar. *¿Qué pasa?*"

"Things change," she explained, mysteriously. The *mestizo* didn't pursue the question.

"Let me make you some *huevos* Veracruz with bananas," he offered. "Celebrate your coming back."

Wanda was polite but declined. "I have many things to do today and can't stay but a minute," she said. "I'm back in town on a sort of

245

sentimental visit, you understand. I wanted to see the old sights one more time before I go back to the States."

"So have *huevos*. Is all the more reason."

"No, really, I can't."

Tonebar looked disappointed.

"I will before I leave. I promise."

"Qué bueno," he answered. "Then I'll make you something special. Maybe some *huachitengo* or baby crabs."

"Right now," Wanda continued, "I'm looking for Ramón Ramón. You remember him?"

"Of course," the *mestizo* laughed. Then his mouth settled into a leer. "You interested in Ramón again, huh? For old times' sake, I bet."

The response dated from seven years ago when Ramón and Wanda had been a hot item running around town behind Henry Amazon's back. It was so long ago Wanda felt like telling the *mestizo* to keep his fucking leer to himself. Instead she just blushed.

"I ain't seen him for two, maybe, three weeks," Tonebar explained. "At least that long. But if he's in town, he'll be by. You know how he loves my cooking."

"Will you tell him I'm looking for him?"

"Sure thing."

"I'm at the Trocadero," Wanda added. Tonebar had already turned back to the stove to tend to a fish smoking on the second burner. "Tell him to call after ten at night."

Back on the street Wanda walked north until Hog caught up with her.

"Any luck?" he asked.

"The owner hasn't seen him in almost a month. I left a message."

Hog checked his notebook and then looked back at her appreciatively. He had been thinking about getting in Wanda's pants ever since Purd had introduced him the day before.

"Next stop the organ player at the Luna Doble Restaurant on Tinoco y Palacios," he grinned.

Wanda would work until nine thirty that night. No one had seen Ramón Ramón since two weeks before.

Zorro CeAttle, driving his Ford, reached the Modesto at ten Monday morning. In the bungalow Amazon told him what had happened to their strip.

"I thought you said there was no problems with that place?" Zorro complained.

"Can I control the Federales?"

"You said it was safe."

"It was until Sunday."

"*Chinga, mano.* You losin' your touch. You useta be smooth." Zorro's voice was mocking.

It set Amazon off. "You want out, motherfucker? I've about had it with your whinin' shit. I'm not gonna start back up where we left off. You can take your split of what we got and get out right now. This is my last one, Zorro, and I ain't in any mood to do it with you bitchin' at me. *Sabe?*"

"I jest don't want it to be my last one too."

"Don't worry, Zorro," Amazon snapped, "a pushy son of a bitch like you'll never see your last one comin'."

Zorro sputtered.

With his partner momentarily backed off Amazon called the question. "You want out?"

Zorro took a long time answering. "No," he said.

"Then shut up."

Henry Amazon paced back and forth in the sitting room to cool himself off. Zorro smoked a cigarette. Finally, the *mestizo* spoke.

"So what you gonna do now, *mi jefe?*"

Amazon ignored the sarcasm. "Find another place to land the plane."

"That ain't gonna be all that easy. You seen the Army crawlin' over this place? Everything's gonna be shut down."

"Everything's never all shut down."

"So who's gonna have an airstrip now?"

"Gomez Gordo," Amazon answered. There was more certainty in his voice than he actually felt.

Zorro had never heard of Gordo.

"We're goin' out to his place this morning," Amazon continued. "Unless you want to stay here."

Zorro didn't.

The two of them headed out the Pan American almost immediately toward Mitla and Tehuantepec in Amazon's rent-a-car. They passed through two roadblocks before intersecting with the highway leading into the mountains to Ixtlán. When they turned up it, they soon hit another. Amazon noted that the block was located before the road off to the Fuenteses'. Gordo's restaurant was another twenty minutes beyond that.

Gomez Gordo's restaurant, The Fat Man's, perched on the side of a ravine halfway to Ixtlán. It was a regular stopover for the tourist buses headed up to the cathedrals there. Two Cristóbal Colón first-class specials were parked in Gordo's lot when Amazon stopped. He and Zorro reached the dining area by walking across a wide porch that opened into an even wider room with a long counter along one wall. That room in turn opened onto a veranda that afforded an uninterrupted view downhill to the east end of the valley itself. Most of the tourists took tables out there and chattered in French and German while they were waiting for the kitchen to whip up Fat Man's Special Flaming Meat Brunches. The only person behind the counter was a young Mexican woman at the cash register. She was Gomez Gordo's daughter, Dolores. After taking a table inside and leaving Zorro at it, Henry Amazon approached her by himself.

Dolores was eighteen years old and managed to look sleek, sultry, and virginal at the same time. All of which was further complicated by her tendency to flirt. She was Gordo's pride and joy, and the fat man made no secret of the fact he planned to marry her off to someone in Mexico City with influence. In the meantime he spoiled her considerably. Dolores didn't recognize the lanky *gringo* who approached, but liked his looks.

"*¿Sí?*" she asked.

"Is your father here?"

"You're a friend of his?"

"I am. Is he around?"

"He's gone."

"Is he coming back soon?"

"Not until late tomorrow. You should come back again Wednesday. He'll be here all day."

Amazon thought for a moment, clearly agitated. "I'll do that," he said. "In the meantime will you tell him Tortuga came by with something important to discuss?"

"Tortuga?"

"He'll know who you mean."

Amazon retraced his path to his table as Dolores watched him. Then she looked at the Mexican with him. Zorro, noticing, lifted his sunglasses at the *señorita* and made a doffing motion with them, as though they were a top hat.

Dolores started to smile back at Zorro but was interrupted by yells from the kitchen to come and help. When Gordo's daughter returned to the dining room, the *gringo* Tortuga and his Mexican friend were gone.

By twelve thirty, the two smugglers were back at the Modesto. Zorro stayed next to the pool all afternoon while Amazon checked on the airplane gas and then stopped at a pay phone to call his pilot R.W. in Texas. Amazon told R.W. to hang tight and claimed he would have it all worked out by Wednesday night. He'd call him again then.

At two Nostaro Nostromos's "Pantera de Papilsocho" dropped Ramón next to the Tehuacán Highway, where he waited for another bus bound for Oaxaca. The one that stopped was painted with orange and black stripes. Ramón handed his pack up to the Indian on the

249

baggage rack and found a seat next to a Mixtec woman on her way to market. The two goats the woman planned to sell there were tied to the arm of the seat and stood in the aisle. Farther back Ramón heard chickens. The bus was crowded, and no one paid the new passenger, dressed in a motley *serape*, much notice. He leaned against the window and thought about his plan.

The first thing was to secure some more money. He had about four grand American in his pocket, but the sum was insufficient to get Ramón back in business. Fortunately, obtaining more cash would be relatively simple. Following his standard operating procedure for any scam, Ramón had prepared getaway provisions for his venture with Beef Stew. Before their trip out the San Dionisio, Ramón had left a large manila envelope in the safe at the Hotel del Campo in downtown Oaxaca where he knew the night clerk. In it were forged papers under new names for Beef, Stella, and Ramón, five thousand dollars cash, and a stash of credit cards. He had been in too much of a hurry to get it the night he'd left Oaxaca, but he was sure it was still there.

With that in his pocket Ramón Ramón planned to turn his attention to El Tasajo, his most pressing business. The gun he intended to use was in his duffel on the bus roof. Once the snitch had been killed, Ramón was going to put a quick load together and hustle it north. He and the late Beef had already put money down on a quantity of south Valley hash, and it would be ready in two more months. If Ramón could sell five hundred pounds of Grade-A tops in the meantime, he would be able to make the final payment and proceed with his and Beef's original plan. By Christmas he'd be rich.

At seven thirty, the Oaxaca third-class express reached the Pan American, thirty miles outside of town, and turned left. A light mist was falling, and the driver's windshield wipers did little more than smear it.

Fifteen minutes later Ramón got his first glimpse of what General Cortez de Corriente had done. A military roadblock was dead ahead near the village of Pueblo Nuevo. An officer there signaled the bus off onto the shoulder. Seven trucks, two cars, and three other buses were ahead of them. They would have to wait their turn. A private with a machine gun was posted on the step by the driver, and an announcement was made that all persons and baggage would be searched when the bus reached the front of the line.

Ramón Ramón's first thoughts were about his duffel on the roof. The gun inside was enough to send him away for five years. Ramón was nervous but knew better than to show it. For the moment he was cornered, and it was too late to do anything but wait for an opening.

Ramón Ramón shifted in his seat and pulled the window up to try and get some air. The crowded bus smelled of Indian sweat and the piss of goats.

Ramón's bus waited another thirty minutes by the side of the road before a search team led by a lieutenant walked up to where it was parked. The lieutenant climbed inside.

"You will all file out one at a time," he instructed, "and show me your identity papers."

After a long murmur in several Indian dialects the passengers disembarked as ordered. Many had no form of identification at all to show the lieutenant, and some were arrested. Since Ramón Ramón was sitting about halfway back, it was another fifteen minutes before it was his turn to file out the door. The Mixtec woman and her goats were in front of him. She got in a ferocious argument with the soldier about the goats and despite her protestations, the animals were taken from her and tied to the front bumper of the bus. She was told to go stand between the two soldiers on the edge of the shoulder along with everyone else. Then it was Ramón's turn.

"*Buenas tardes,*" the officer said curtly. "Your papers?"

Ramón Ramón produced a tourist permit.

The lieutenant read it over twice before speaking up.

"A *gringo,* huh?"

"*Sí,* your honor," Ramón answered. "Just traveling around on my vacation."

The lieutenant then looked Ramón over. "You don't look like a *gringo.*"

"What can I say?" Ramón answered with a smile and a shrug.

"You can say, 'Yes, your excellency, I don't look like a *gringo,'*" the Army officer said menacingly.

"Yes, your excellency," Ramón agreed, "I don't."

The lieutenant then thrust the tourist permit back at Ramón Ramón and directed him to a sergeant five paces away. Like all of the men on the bus, Ramón was then frisked. When the *gringo* came up clean in that search, he was directed on to join the other passengers. Most were huddled under a tamarind tree there. Behind the cover cast by the tamarind the roadway dropped off in a fifteen-foot embankment that led down to several thick clumps of bushes. The first houses of the suburb Pueblo Nuevo were another fifty yards across a cornfield beyond that. Darkness was just beginning to fall, and the lieutenant at the doorway identity check stopped briefly to fetch a flashlight. Out of the corner of his eye Ramón watched the two soldiers guarding the passengers but turned his head whenever they began to watch back.

The rest of the search team unloaded the luggage rack on the bus's roof. When everyone's identity had been checked, the lieutenant would then begin going through each of the packages and bundles in turn. Ramón saw his own duffel come down and wiped his hands on his pants. He would have to go soon, the *gringo* told himself. Just slip down the bank when the soldiers weren't watching and make his way into town on foot. Under his *serape,* Ramón Ramón was poised like a cat while he waited for the right opportunity.

That opportunity came suddenly when one of the Army trucks backfired nearby and the goats tied to the front bumper of the bus freaked. Bucking fiercely, they pulled themselves loose of their moorings, romping past the officer and out into the highway. Seeing her property scattering, the Mixtec woman screamed, ran out from the crowd under the tree with several of her friends and tried to catch them. The soldiers on guard were distracted by their movement, and Ramón immediately headed down the bank. He crawled under the bushes at the bottom and sat still for a moment. He heard no noises except those of the goat chase from up above, so he sprinted away into the field. The corn came up over his head, and Ramón made barely a ripple as he moved through it. When he reached the muddy streets of Pueblo Nuevo fifty yards away, he stopped for a moment to get his bearings in the dark. Ramón had no sense of fear from his close brush with the soldiers. Eventually the sounds of yelling back at the roadblock drifted his way. Figuring they'd found the pistol in his bag, he broke into a dogtrot through the mist toward the river.

It took him an hour along the Río Atoyac levee before he reached the bridge that connected the road to Zaachila with the Periférico. The levee there was dotted with the cardboard and sheet tin lean-tos of the squatter village. Most of the squatters were women from the whore street. One of them was washing her clothes in the river when Ramón walked by; she paid him no attention. At the bridge he climbed up onto the Periférico, and just as he crossed the four-lane street, a caravan ferrying troops from the railroad station to the Ocotlán bivouac rolled by. The soldiers were hunched over against the weather, and the truck lights were skipping along the slick pavement.

When he reached the Hotel del Campo, it was almost ten o'clock. Ramón's friend, Luis, the night clerk, was the only one in the lobby.

"*Qué pasa, don Ramón,*" the night clerk said. "Looks like you been on the move." He pointed at the mud on Ramón's pants and boots.

"It's wet outside."

"Must be," the Mexican laughed.

"Say, *amigo,* you still got that envelope I left with you?"

"The envelope?"

"The envelope," Ramón snapped.

"Oh, *sí,* the envelope." Luis stepped over to the safe and then returned with a lumpy manila package. A smile spread across Ramón's face. "You got a room too?"

"No," Luis apologized, "I'm sorry. All the rooms is full."

Eight blocks away Ramón Ramón checked into the San Marcos and took a room for a week at three dollars a night. Once he'd looked the place over, Ramón Ramón walked to Bandito's Roast Chicken Take-out down the block, bought a bird to go, and returned to the San Marcos to eat. Before going to bed, he took the forged papers that were originally intended for the now-dead Beef and Stella and burned them in the bathroom sink. Then he sat under the covers and thought about the revenge he had planned. First he had to get another gun.

18

Having nothing to do but await Gordo's return, Henry Amazon decided to spend Tuesday visiting the Fuenteses. It was a moment he had been anticipating since he first decided to get out. Amazon had few ties left to break, but his with Cazadero Fuentes was one of them. The man was like a family to him. Saying good-bye to Fuentes would be a landmark in Amazon's exit. Now was as good a time as any to do it. As Amazon imagined it, he and the old man would drink several *mescals* to his new life, and then it would be over. He expected his years in Oaxaca to feel resolved afterward. The good-bye would seal his scam even further in finality. Afterward there would be nothing left but business.

Amazon heard the bells when he was still a mile from the village. At first they confused him. It was too late for mass, and they were being rung in a pattern that was unfamiliar. Spotting a young boy tending goats near the roadside, Amazon stopped to ask him what they meant.

The boy listened for a moment and then answered. "They mean someone has died," he said.

Amazon's stomach went cold immediately. He sped toward the Fuenteses' house, slinging slush out from under his back wheels. There, the truth to his premonition was obvious. A crowd of Zapotecs was already gathering to pay their respects. Inside Cazadero Fuentes was laid out on the table.

Cazadero had risen late that morning and complained of stomach pains. About nine he had gone outside in the rain to check his livestock. Standing in the open doorway, the old Indian had taken a deep breath and then pitched over face down in the mud. He was dead of heart failure before he hit the ground.

Henry Amazon felt cheated. He resisted going in to look at the dead Indian and stood in the Fuenteses' courtyard for more than an hour. A drizzle began to fall, but he still didn't move. He wanted Cazadero to be sitting up drinking their last *mescal* together. He hadn't wanted to end on this note. Now the old man would never know he'd changed his life. It couldn't ever be completely over this way. Amazon eventually figured he should have known better than to expect different. Everything down here was unfinished like that. When he finally went inside to the wake, his pant legs were soaked through to the skin, but he didn't really notice.

Cazadero Fuentes was dressed in clean clothes and laid out with his hands folded over his paunch. Candles stuck to the planks beyond his head cast shadows along his features. Just three hours of death seemed to have been enough to sag the flesh so the cheek bones were much more prominent than they had ever been when Cazadero was alive. His skin was as close to gray as it was to brown. Henry Amazon took a seat on one of the benches pushed back against the wall along with the other mourners. Twice he checked his watch but didn't move. Periodically one or another among the Indians around him got up and approached the corpse. There they crouched over the body and whispered things in its ear the way Zapotecs did with their dead, seeing them off. At three in the afternoon Henry Amazon finally stood up and followed suit.

He spoke to Cazadero in a voice so soft and close to the Indian's ear that no one else in the room could hear him. "I'm not coming back," Amazon said. "My life here's almost done with." Only the scam remained.

Straightening up, Amazon turned on his heel and walked back into the weather. With the exception of Cockroach on the ridge outside of town, no one in the Fuenteses' village would ever see him again. He drove back to Oaxaca and the Hotel Modesto, glad that Zorro wasn't there when he arrived.

Purdee Fletcher left his Hunter Squad Command post that afternoon when Palomino Cobraa, the State Police Chief, called. Cobraa said he'd found a little something that Purd might be interested in.

State Police headquarters was doing a land-office business in the wake of the General's roadblocks. One entire corner of the courtyard there was full of suspects being guarded by *mestizo* detectives in raincoats and automatic weapons. The crowd was awaiting questioning, and some had been there twenty-four hours. Purd found the *Jefe* inside at his desk, enjoying a break for coffee between interrogations. The police chief had his sleeves rolled up over his chubby arms and was pleased to see the *gringo*. Cobraa liked *gringos* in general and had a new respect for Purd in particular. Cutting off part of Cruz's authority for himself had been no mean maneuver on the *gringo*'s part, and, familiar with the treacherous currents of Mexico City influence, *Jefe* Cobraa gave Purd maximum credit.

"Poord," he grinned, "come in."

"How ya doin', *Jefe*?" Purd asked as he slipped into a chair across the desk.

"Is *mucho* work," Cobraa grinned. It was obvious he was pleased with the crowd of prisoners he could now take credit for.

"I'll bet it is. I'll bet it is." Purd had an expectant expression on his face.

"You want to look at what we got goin' on here?"

"Well I'd love to, *Jefe,* but I'm a little rushed, if you know what Ole

257

Purd means. What about that little somethin' you called me about?"

"Is not much," the *Jefe* cautioned, "but it made me think of you."

"I appreciate it. I sure do. Just what was it you found?"

Cobraa called out for his assistant *jefe* and sent the man off. He eventually returned with a cup of coffee for Purd and a manila envelope. Cobraa opened the envelope, extracted a Smith & Wesson thirty-eight revolver wrapped in an oil cloth, and plunked it on the desk. Then he pulled out an old newspaper.

"Last night, out at the Pueblo Nuevo *aduana,* this was found in a bag on a third-class bus," Cobraa began, motioning at the pistol on the desk. "The Army officer in charge says he thinks it belonged to a *gringo.*"

"This," the *Jefe* continued, unfolding an old issue of the *Carteles,* "was what made me think of you. It was also found in the bag." The front page featured pictures of the *gringo* remains "found" out on the San Dionisio a week ago. The photo of the torched camper had been heavily circled with a ball-point pen. Scrawled next to it was the statement, "*Chivas* die."

"What happened to the *gringo* who owned the bag?"

"He disappeared before he could be questioned."

"Disappeared?"

Cobraa just shrugged his shoulders.

"You still got the bag?" Fletcher pressed.

The *Jefe* allowed as how they probably did and sent the assistant chief looking for it. He didn't return for fifteen minutes. By then Cobraa had been called to the interrogation room. The assistant *jefe* dropped a khaki-colored duffel bag on the desk and then left the *gringo* to himself.

Purd examined each of the articles in the bag carefully. None gave any indication of who the owner was. It wasn't until he rechecked the bag itself that he learned anything more. This time he noticed a small pocket sewn on the inside of the panel covering the duffel's deep end. Opening it, he found a bag of loose marijuana, rolling papers, and a strip of plastic with pockets in it, full of snapshots.

The first snapshot showed the fugitive Jerome Whitehurst alias

Ramón Ramón standing in front of an *adobe* wall. He had a full beard and looked younger around the eyes than in Purd's pictures. A woman with dark hair tied up on top of her head was standing next to him. She looked like a younger version of his snitch Wanda Lamar.

The next few snapshots were basically the same as the first, except of Ramón alone. Then another series started. Judging from their creases and frayed edges, these were much older. Once again the central character was Ramón. He was wearing Marine fatigues. In each of the pictures the hooknosed Marine was crouching next to at least one corpse. In the first five he was holding the dead man by the hair and smiling. In the sixth he was standing with three bodies at his feet and a grenade in each hand.

Ramón Ramón stayed holed up in the San Marcos until 10:30 P.M. Tuesday. Outside the night air smelled brand new. The rain was gone, but the back streets south of the *zocolo* were slick and shiny.

After twenty minutes' walking, Ramón turned into the courtyard of a small apartment house and climbed the outside stairs to the second floor where Dumbo Nuñez lived. Standing on the threshold, he could hear the sound of several laughing voices inside and smelled a faint trace of *mota* smoke leaking under the door.

A *mestizo* harelip answered his knock. "*¡Don Ramón!*" he gasped. "I heard you was dead!"

Ramón Ramón flashed his teeth. "I'm a hard motherfucker to kill, Dumbo. You know that."

"Come in. You'll be the first ghost I ever had visit me."

Ramón laughed, but turned the invitation down. "I got to talk to you in private."

"You got business?"

"If you got guns."

"Then you got business," the harelip said, stepping out onto the outside walkway and closing the door behind him. "What kinda piece do you want?"

"What kind you got?"

259

"Thirty-eights and forty-fives."

"How much will one of those little ones and a hundred rounds run me?"

"Two hundred dollars American."

"Jesus, Dumbo."

Nuñez shrugged. "The guns are good," he explained, "and times are bad."

"One hundred and seventy-five," Ramón countered.

"Sold," the harelip quickly agreed. "Wait here."

Dumbo Nuñez slipped back inside and then returned with a large paper sack which he deposited at the *gringo*'s feet. Inside was a thirty-eight automatic and a box of ammunition. Ramón stuck his hand into the bag and hefted the weapon. It had good balance, and the action seemed smooth.

"You still got that Dina flatbed?" Ramón Ramón asked.

"*Sí.*"

"How'd you like some of that kinda business too?"

"Like what?"

"Like driving a ton north."

"*¡Chinga, don Ramón!* Is too much soldiers around to move *mota.*"

Ramón Ramón laughed and scolded the harelip. "You're too worried, Dumbo. You know *don* Ramón knows his business."

"Is true, but—"

"Then don't worry," Ramón pushed. "We'll take the load on the Mitla side and run the other direction, toward the Pacific. The money's good, and we won't even see any Army, I guarantee you."

"I don't know, *don* Ramón," Dumbo hedged. "I got to think that over."

"That's all right by me," Ramón answered. "I got something else to take care of now. I'll come back in a couple days."

All his preparations were complete. Only the killing itself remained undone.

* * *

260

Wanda Lamar was back on the street looking for Ramón again Wednesday morning. So far she'd found no traces whatsoever. Ramón had disappeared two weeks before, and no one she knew had seen him since. Wanda was sure that the longer this lasted, the worse she was going to feel about it. She wanted it over quick and woke up frantic that morning. Her first stop was the Hotel Monte Alban for coffee, more to get herself together than in any hopes of crossing Ramón's trail. Ramón never had gone to the Monte Alban much.

Just inside the doorway she ran into Henry Amazon.

Wanda saw him before he saw her. Amazon was with a Mexican she had never met, counting money out on the table to pay their bill. When he turned around, she was five feet away.

"Hello, Henry."

He was a little taken aback. "Hello, Wanda," he finally said. "What the hell are you doin' back in town? I thought you left for good a long time ago."

Wanda shrugged her eyebrows and pursed her mouth. "I thought so, too. Just had to get a little more of the place for old times' sake. Couldn't stay away."

"For old times' sake."

"I guess so."

Hog Wissle was watching the conversation from the lobby but was too far away to hear.

"Well," Amazon said, "there's damn sure plenty of old times around here."

"I remember." Wanda hesitated and then continued. "You ever see Ramón anymore?" she asked.

"You're gonna ask me about Ramón? You're a cold lady, Wanda, sure as shit."

"Come on, Henry. That's all ancient history."

"It sure is. I don't run with Ramón no more. You're gonna have to find him on your own."

Wanda just looked awkward. Amazon looked at his watch.

"Good luck," he said. "I got to take care of business."

With that Amazon and the Mexican headed out the door. The Mexican nodded and smiled at Wanda as he passed. He had violet eyes.

When Wanda finished her coffee and went back to the street, Hog Wissle came up and touched her waist.

"Who was that you talked to?"

Wanda pulled away from his hand. "Someone who used to know Ramón," she said. "He hasn't seen him."

Hog put his hand on her back. "You sure?"

Wanda pulled away with a violent motion. "I'm sure, goddamn it, and keep your fuckin' hands to yourself."

Hog's anger flashed up out of his beefy neck. "You know, woman, if I was in your spot, I'd be lookin' to make friends. You're gonna need 'em," he growled. "You're gonna need 'em in spades."

Wanda winced.

Henry Amazon and Zorro CeAttle drove from the Monte Alban out to Gordo's. His encounter with Wanda stuck in Amazon's head. He had wanted to tell her he was getting out, but his own touchiness had gotten in the way. Amazon shrugged it off: nothing with Wanda mattered much anymore. The fact that he'd seen her at all was surprising. Amazon took the coincidence as proof he was indeed getting out. The way things were going, he should have guessed he would have seen Wanda one last time.

Amazon and Zorro reached Gomez Gordo's about 11 A.M. Gordo's brand-new Chrysler was parked against the building in full view. Two small boys with water buckets were cleaning off all traces of road from its fenders. Amazon and his partner walked past them and on inside.

Dolores Gordo was behind the register. She greeted the two men with a flash of her lashes. "You're back."

"We're back," Amazon responded, "just like I said. How about your *padre*?"

"He's back too. In the office." The young woman motioned at a door in the restaurant's far wall.

Leaving Zorro to wait at a table, Henry Amazon went on into the fat man's office. Gomez Gordo was sitting behind a giant antique desk with a telephone on it. The office itself had deep red wall-to-wall carpet. The Fat Man stood up and flashed a wide Teddy Roosevelt grin when Amazon entered. Gomez Gordo was only five foot three inches tall and had very small, almost doll-like, feet. Several of his teeth had gold caps, and he wore conspicuous diamonds on two of his pudgy fingers. That morning Gordo was dressed in a three-piece gray silk suit, but the coat was off, the tie undone, and the vest unbuttoned. Suet surged out through the opening in folds.

"Tortuga, my old friend. *Es más bueno. Más bueno,* indeed."

"For me too," Amazon lied. He was still uneasy about The Fat Man and was very careful not to let it show. With the perfunctory greetings over, he pulled up a chair and sat down. Gomez Gordo settled back behind the desk and spoke first. "My daughter tells me you got something very important to talk about."

"I do," Amazon said. "It's a business problem I thought you could maybe help me with."

Gordo proceeded to make a display of jolly familiarity that belied some of his inner viciousness. "I am always prepared to help an old friend like the Turtle," he said. "We been around together for a long time."

"A long time," Amazon agreed. "What I need is a place to land a *mota* plane."

Before answering, Gomez Gordo stripped the wrapper off a long, thin, black cigar and began sucking on it. "Is a hard time to do such things," he said. The harder the task seemed, the more it was worth, and Gordo moved quickly to establish his position. "You seen for yourself how much Army there is." When mentioning Army, he made a sweeping gesture with his unlit cigar that indicated the general presence in the Valley itself.

"I can see," Amazon grinned and adopted his own air of familiarity.

"At the same time I've been around this place long enough to know that if anyone can do it, the man is *señor* Gordo up on the hill. You're the *jefe* of us all."

Gomez Gordo seemed to find the remark intensely amusing and laughed with a great quivering of belly and chest. The Fat Man expected to have his ass kissed, and such compliments were sufficiently respectful to please him. "You still know Gordo," he admitted.

No, Gordo, Henry Amazon wanted to say, I don't. I think you may just take my money and give my ass up to the law when you've got it. Instead, Henry Amazon maintained a respectful silence.

"Is true I've got a strip," The Fat Man continued, "and it's still working. Whose *mota* you goin' to use?"

"My own."

"Where'd you get it?" Gomez Gordo pressed.

"Around."

Gordo laughed. "You are still the same Tortuga, crawling back in your shell just like Jessee used to say." Again chuckles rippled off the fat man's front and slapped into the desk like waves against a breakwater.

"The same one," Henry Amazon answered.

"Is all right. I like you anyway. You do business real safe. Of course," he went on with a waggle of the long tobacco stick in his hand, "it will cost you more since I'm not loading you with my goods."

"Give me the bad news."

"Five thousand dollars American today, five thousand dollars when we set a final landing date, and twenty thousand dollars when you're loaded and ready to fly."

Gordo's response had been immediate and well prepared, all of which told Amazon that there wasn't a whole lot of negotiating room.

"That's real expensive."

"I got a lot of people to pay."

"It must be an awful lot for that much."

"Times are hard," Gordo grinned, "as you can see." Once again,

264

The Fat Man made a sweeping motion with his hand. "Of course," he added, "you could always shop around."

The fact that Gordo said he could was ample evidence to Amazon that he in fact couldn't and most every other option was no doubt shut down. "No, Gordo," he answered in something of a lie, "I'd rather do business with my friends."

Henry Amazon immediately began counting American money out on the desk. "I want to bring my pilot out here real soon," he continued while Gordo confirmed the count. "He needs to look it over and set up our landing arrangements."

The Mexican looked up from his money. "You movin' quick?"

"Quick as I can. We may be ready to load out within the week."

Gordo chuckled again for no apparent reason. "You got to give me at least twenty-four hours notice is all. Just call me on the phone," The Fat Man indicated with a wave at his desk, "tell me your friend's coming to town and give me a date."

"How about the inspection? Can I just come out here after I pick my flyer up at the airport?"

"*Bueno*," Gomez Gordo answered. "Whatever you like. I ain't goin' nowhere."

With business settled The Fat Man had some coffee sent in and insisted on another ten minutes of conversation with the *gringo* about the old days. Afterward they walked out into the restaurant together. No tourist buses had stopped at The Fat Man's place yet today, and the dining room was mostly empty. Henry Amazon looked for his partner and found him leaning against the counter next to the cash register where Dolores stood. At first glance it was obvious to Henry Amazon that Zorro was putting the hard rush on Gordo's daughter. She wasn't telling him either yes or no but enjoying the act of stringing him along. Zorro CeAttle had his shades off and was staring at her with his eyes on full purple.

Gomez Gordo appraised what was going on every bit as quickly as Amazon.

"You know that *hombre?*" The Fat Man asked. Gordo's jocularity had disappeared along with the gold-capped smile.

Henry Amazon knew immediately that Zorro's pass was an extreme miscue and secretly cursed himself for not warning his partner to stay clear of Dolores. "He works with me," Amazon admitted.

"I want to talk to him," Gordo scowled. Immediately The Fat Man shuffled across the dining room. Henry Amazon had no choice but to follow. As Gomez Gordo's approach reached Dolores's attention, she dropped the teasing smile she'd been wearing and scurried into the kitchen. Zorro looked over at what had apparently run the girl off, and his partner and a very fat Mexican were some five feet away. His partner spoke first.

"Zorro CeAttle," he said, motioning first at the border *mestizo,* "meet *señor* Gomez Gordo, Dolores's father."

"*Mucho gusto,*" Zorro smiled in his friendliest manner. CeAttle knew that Gomez Gordo was a very important man.

The Fat Man didn't bother to say *mucho gusto* back. "Tortuga says you're here with him," Gordo snapped. His tone was not familiar. It was hard and to the point.

Zorro nodded.

"We're doing business," The Fat Man continued, "and I got rules about doin' it. The first one is that you don't mess with Dolores. She's spoken for. You're going nowhere, and she isn't. So you don't even talk to her. *Comprende?*"

Zorro CeAttle wanted to act insulted by The Fat Man's scolding, but one look at his partner's eyes told him how dumb that would be. Instead he cowered somewhat and acted subordinate. "Of course, *don* Gordo," he apologized. "No offense intended."

"I only explain the rules once," Gomez Gordo added with a look in Amazon's direction as well. "After that you can take your business somewhere else."

Gomez Gordo then turned and went into the kitchen after his daughter.

Amazon and Zorro left quickly. Zorro resented Amazon for not warning him about Gordo's daughter. He felt set up. Amazon paid no attention. Back at the Modesto he spent the afternoon trying to get hold of the pilot, R.W., back in the States. When he finally did, it was too late to catch any connecting flights in time for the next morning's Mexico City-Oaxaca planes. That meant R.W. couldn't get to town until Friday.

"Another day lost," Amazon thought, but there was nothing he could do about it.

19

Ramón Ramón spent the middle of Wednesday staking out El Tasajo. For a while he watched the snitch's house from an alley up the block. Then he moved to a lounging position in a doorway. Four or five young *mestizos* came and went during the first several hours. Those who left were usually sweaty. Ramón guessed Piece of Meat was having a series of ball games. By three thirty in the afternoon, Ramón Ramón had yet to see Tasajo himself, but by his count only one visitor remained inside. That changed shortly after Ramón moved back to the alley.

At three forty-five a new Chevrolet sedan with Federal plates pulled over to the curb across from El Tasajo's door. The driver was a Mexican in a polyester shirt; Ramón Ramón had never seen him before. But the man who climbed out the passenger side was dressed city-Indian style and had a familiar look. Ramón placed him as the Mexican who had been introduced to him as El Tasajo's friend Jaime from Tehuacán. After Jaime got out, the Chevrolet started up and pulled away around the corner. Fifteen minutes after that El Tasajo

268

and his friend, Jaime from Tehuacán, headed up the street in Ramón's direction, only on the opposite sidewalk. Ramón Ramón pressed himself against the alley wall and studied them as they passed.

It was clear El Tasajo's fortunes had changed for the better. The *mestizo* was wearing a new pair of alligator cowboy boots, a bright pink disco shirt, and a brand-new pair of tight-fitting jeans. Neither he nor the disguised Federale with him looked across at the alley. Ramón continued watching them as they moved farther up the street. At the *burrito* stand a block away the Chevrolet with Federal plates was waiting. As soon as the two men were inside, it squealed off in the direction of downtown.

Ramón Ramón waited another ten minutes in the alley to make sure the Chevy wasn't coming back right away and then crossed the street. Tasajo's outside door was locked. Moving with seeming nonchalance, the *gringo* then turned the corner to the wall facing the side of the street. No one was in sight in either direction. The lower edge of the house's tile roof was eight feet above the sidewalk, and Ramón jumped up and gripped one of its support beams easily. With a smooth motion he then chinned himself, kicked his leg up onto the roof, and rolled over on the tiles. They tinkled softly, but none moved. Ramón lay there for a moment while he checked to make sure no one had been watching. Then he moved quietly across the edge of the roof overlooking Tasajo's narrow courtyard.

Ramón jumped down into the empty space and landed like a cat. The door to the room on his left where El Tasajo held his ball games was open, and no one was inside. The door to the room on the other side, where Tasajo slept, was closed but not locked. With the exception of the Mexican's bed and clothes chest, it too was empty. Ramón made a brief search, careful to leave no signs of his presence. He found the snitch's forty-five automatic under the goose-feather pillow. It had a full clip and a round in the chamber. Ramón emptied it and put the weapon back under the pillow the way it had been before he came. Then he laughed out loud. The sound echoed.

269

Ramón Ramón left the way he had entered. He planned to spend the afternoon in his hotel room laying low and getting ready.

Tasajo felt somewhat smug when Jaime had told him that Cruz wanted to talk. It was no secret to Tasajo that the head Federale was hungry for busts in the wake of the latest south Valley disaster. The situation gave El Tasajo leverage, and on Monday he was enjoying it.

For his part Pizarro Cruz was honest with himself about the disadvantage of his own position. He knew he needed to produce enough to make Mexico City forget the airstrip debacle. Purd's successful power seizure was a bad sign that would require lots of numbers to reverse. Cruz's intensity had immediately fastened on tracking down the same *traficantes* he'd missed in Operation Buzzard's Nest. Tasajo was his best bet. Pizarro Cruz had rejected the idea of seizing the snitch's girl friend again. This *chiva* Piece of Meat didn't need to be jammed or extorted. He was greedy now.

Pizarro Cruz greeted his *chiva* with something that sounded like camaraderie. "Here's the man," he chortled. "What's the good word?" The Federale had risen from behind the desk when Jaime brought Tasajo in and motioned the informant to sit.

"¿Como 'stá, Jefe?" El Tasajo opened.

"Good. And you?"

"I'm real good." The snitch's voice had something of a swagger to it. He crossed his legs in the chair where he was sitting and then continued. "I think I may have a name you'd be real interested to know."

"What's that?" Cruz grinned his square smile from under his dark glasses.

Tasajo didn't respond right away. First he hemmed as though embarrassed. "Well, *mi jefe,* you see, I'm running a little short . . ."

Cruz continued smiling and extracted a wad of twenty-dollar bills from his desk drawer. "Cash American all right?"

Tasajo nodded greedily and stared at the roll of money.

Cruz counted out five twenties on his desk and then returned the bank roll to the drawer it came from. Tasajo reached for the bills, but Cruz snatched his arm. The Federale's fingers were stubby, but his grip was like a vice. After a hard squeeze Cruz released the snitch and maintained his grin. "You forgot to tell me that name," he reminded Tasajo in a friendly tone.

"Of course, *Jefe*," he apologized. "Pardon my rudeness." After pausing to wipe some of the sweat off his forehead, Tasajo divulged his information. "Like I told you last time," he said in an earnest voice, "I've been trying to locate the guy who told me about that strip out the other side of Chichicapan. He's been gone, but I finally saw him last night. I told him I'd been thinking about what he'd told me, and did he think I could make a connection with those guys for some big *mota*. He said he couldn't help me since he'd never done business with them himself. The only other thing he knew about them, he said, was the name of the *hombre* who fronted for them. He is called Rascón, and he's an Indian."

Tasajo paused, but Pizarro Cruz said nothing. He was clearly waiting for more.

"This Rascón, he's a hard man to find, but this guy said he knew someone who knew how. The other guy's name is Lazero Cardonez, and I know him too. Lazero is gone now, but his wife said he will be back tomorrow."

Since that was all the information he had, El Tasajo stopped talking.

Cruz's only immediate response was a long silence. It was designed to let the snitch know that he considered the information somewhat insufficient. The technique succeeded. Tasajo squirmed in his chair, sweat more, and looked at the twenty-dollar bills. Finally Cruz pushed the money toward him.

"I will consider the money as payment for whatever information this Cardonez tells you as well."

"Of course," the nervous Tasajo agreed. "Of course."

Pizarro Cruz then turned the conversation to a more general vein. "You know," he said, "it is very important to your *jefe* that we arrest this Rascón and his friends as soon as possible."

Tasajo nodded.

271

"You also know that I am prepared to be extremely generous in the cause."

"More than generous, *Jefe*."

Pizarro Cruz smiled at the obsequious compliment. "Perhaps," he suggested, "you would be interested in knowing what I might be willing to reward the man who finally gives them to me."

"Of course, *Jefe*. I'm very interested."

"Do you have a minute?"

There was no real question about whether the snitch had time for Cruz, so the Federale didn't pause for an answer. He just stood up and silently led Tasajo and the Federale Jaime out of the office and down the stairs to the street.

After four and a half blocks Cruz turned into the open doors of a parking garage. The Chevy sedan Tasajo had ridden over in was parked just inside. Cruz walked past the sedan and headed deeper into the mass of parked cars. The head Federale finally stopped at the front bumper of a Chevrolet pickup with a camper on the back. El Tasajo recognized the vehicle by its California plates. It was the same one *don* Ramón's dead partner had driven out the San Dionisio.

"You like it?" Cruz asked.

At first Tasajo didn't understand.

"Do you like it?" Cruz repeated.

By that time the snitch had realized that the truck was the reward. "Is wonderful, *mi jefe*," he said intensely.

"Maybe you would like to try it out for a couple of days?" Cruz suggested, dangling the keys. "You could tell this fellow you're going to see that it belongs to your *gringo* partner. It would maybe help convince him."

El Tasajo accepted the offer without hesitation, and Cruz walked with Jaime back to the Chevrolet. The *Jefe* had a lot of confidence that the potential reward would push the *chiva* in the hardest possible way. When the two Federales started the sedan out the garage's gate, El Tasajo followed in the pickup he already thought of as his own. Cruz congratulated himself with a cigarette. His thoughts then turned to the threat posed by Purd's Hunter Squad command and how the *gringo* could be undercut if Tasajo produced.

Ramón Ramón, on his way back to the Hotel San Marcos on foot, recognized the Chevy as soon as it came out of the parking garage and cleared the sidewalk. His first response was to duck into the doorway of the fish market up the block. The man called Jaime was driving, but the Mexican with him was different from the one who'd accompanied Jaime to El Tasajo's earlier.

Ramón wondered where Tasajo had gone.

The next vehicle out of the parking garage was a pickup truck. When he saw California plates, Ramón Ramón recognized it as Beef's. He also recognized the *mestizo* driver in the pink shirt.

At 2:30 A.M. Thursday Ramón Ramón passed the darkened and shuttered *burrito* stand a block and a half from Tasajo's. Nothing was moving on the street. There were no lights, but Ramón's eyes were good enough in the dark so that he wasn't worried. In five minutes he passed the snitch's locked front gate and went around the corner of the house. He stopped and listened. After five minutes he mounted the outside wall and swung up onto the roof. The only difference in the courtyard below—from what he had seen earlier—was Beef's truck. El Tasajo had parked it inside the gates for safekeeping, and the vehicle consumed most of the open space between the two rooms. Ramón jumped onto the camper's roof and then off onto the ground. A hollow tin thunk sounded along the way.

On his feet in the courtyard he paused again, waiting in a crouch by one of the pickup's wheels to see if his noise had been heard. When he was sure it hadn't, Ramón Ramón drew his gun out of his boot, eased over to the bedroom door, and swung it open with his foot. Tasajo was inside on his bed asleep. He was lying on his back and snoring like a chain saw. After watching him for a moment, Ramón moved over to

273

the clothes chest. He remembered a candle had been placed there during the afternoon and hunted for it in the darkness. When he found the beeswax shaft, the *gringo* lit its wick with a match and stepped away from the light. The candle cast a thin film of yellow across the room. Ramón stood by the door and waited for the light to register on El Tasajo and draw him out of sleep.

In about five minutes the snitch's eyes seemed to blink and look at the light fuzzily. For a moment Tasajo had difficulty comprehending. Finally he pushed himself up on his elbow.

"Who's here?" he called out.

At that point Ramón spoke up.

"*Qué pasa*, Piece of Meat?" he asked softly. Immediately, Tasajo recognized Ramón's voice and went for the pistol under his pillow. Whipping it back in the direction of the intruder, El Tasajo squeezed the trigger three times in succession. Each produced a metallic click and nothing more.

Ramón Ramón began to laugh. It was a grating, unrestrained cackle.

Then Tasajo's world ended for good.

The first and only bullet Ramón fired tore into his forehead just above the eyebrow. He fell back onto the mattress, the contents of his head dripping down onto the dirt floor. The clap of sound from the thirty-eight had been followed by a few dogs cutting loose and nothing else.

Working quickly, Ramón Ramón lifted the five-gallon jerry can off the back of the camper and doused the truck's insides with gasoline. Taking one last look around, he tossed a match in and went out by the courtyard gate as flames began licking around the camper's back door. Once in the street, Ramón took off at a sprint, only stopping to look back when he was at least six blocks away. Behind him orange fingers were clawing up out of the heart of the ramshackle *adobe* and sheet tin neighborhood where Tasajo once lived. When the truck's gas tank finally exploded in a shower of metal, people in the streets nearby began running out of their houses to see what was going on. No one paid much attention to the short *gringo* six blocks from the turmoil. He was wearing a *serape* and looking very satisfied with himself.

Purdee Fletcher learned of Tasajo's execution at 7:30 A.M. Purd knew it was the work of Ramón Ramón as soon as he heard the part about the truck being burned. The duplication of fates with the fugitive's dead partner Beef Stew fit with the newspaper clipping in the duffel. It fit with Purd's estimation of Ramón as well.

Even though Purdee Fletcher and Pizarro Cruz had hardly spoken since the creation of Purd's independent command, Fletcher decided to approach Cruz with his theory right away. If his hunch was correct and Ramón Ramón was indeed around town, Ole Purd knew a city-wide sweep stood a good chance of picking him up. His own force was too small for the job. Purdee figured he could convince the head Federale that in joint action they would both get something they wanted. It was an extremely shortsighted estimation.

None of what seemed obvious to the *gringo* was anything near the way with Cruz. The Mexican assumed that Tasajo's death was connected to the recent inquiries the *chiva* had been making into the workings of the Indian, Rascón. Before Purd found Pizarro Cruz at the city morgue, the Federale had already dispatched agents to try and track down Lazero Cardonez, one of the two names the snitch had sold his *jefe* the day before. Cruz figured his only option was to sweat Cardonez, and he was anxious to get about it.

The head Federale was more than surprised to see Purd. Pizarro Cruz considered the *gringo*'s unannounced presence on Thursday morning an act of insolence itself.

When Purd walked into the room, the *Jefe* and four of his agents were clustered around the table where El Tasajo's remains were stretched out. Their Spanish chatter stopped immediately, and Cruz's underlings pulled back sullenly to make way for the approaching *gringo*.

"How ya doin', Pissaro?" Fletcher opened.

Cruz's arms were folded across his chest, and his cement face was locked into place. At first he said nothing.

"Well," Purd continued awkwardly, "you think there's some place we could talk for a second?" Purd motioned with his head at the other Judicial Federal in the room.

Cruz was brusque. "Here is fine," he said.

"Okay, Pissaro. Whatever you say." He shifted his wing tips on the concrete floor and motioned over his shoulder at El Tasajo's corpse on the table. "I came to talk about him."

"What about him?" Cruz asked tightly.

"My man Ramón is the one who offed him."

Pizarro Cruz snorted through his nose at the notion, and his underlings laughed openly.

"Oh come on," Purd bridled. "Can't you see it? He just did to your man what you did to his. What goes down comes around. It's the first rule a hard-assed son of a bitch like Ramón would follow. If we join forces and sweep for him, we can have him in a matter of hours."

Cruz pointed a stubby finger straight at Purd.

"Look, Poord," he said with knives on his tongue. "You and I should know something between us. We don't mix. You may get someone in Mexico City to buy your *chinga madre* chickenshit stories, but me, Pizarro Cruz, I know better. What you want is what I got. Already you have more than you deserve. Mexico City says I have to give you three men, and you got them. You get nothing more. All the rest of my agents are busy with things that are real."

"Oh get up off it, Pissaro. We don't got to butt heads. You can get your snitch's killer, and I can get my target at the same time. We both win."

The head Federale was deaf to the *gringo*'s words. If Purd was in over his head, then Cruz wanted to help him drown. If not, it was still warfare as usual. Pizarro Cruz didn't bother to answer. With a hand signal to his men, he started to leave. "We must go now," Cruz explained. "It is a long day ahead."

After they left, Purd returned to the Trocadero suite where Wanda Lamar was being held. When he walked in, Hog and Garcia Huahilote were lounging in the outer room drinking coffee. Wanda's door was still closed. Purd made his irritation obvious with his first words.

"Get the broad working," the pear-shaped agent snapped. "That Ramón son of a bitch is out there right now, feeling like he's got the fucking world by the short hairs."

Wanda had been awake for more than an hour, sitting in bed, listening to the male voices in the next room and thinking. What she was doing was getting to her. For the first time she'd admitted to herself that she'd become a *chiva*. Wanda remembered the first time she'd ever heard the term. Henry Amazon had used it when they lived together. "A *chiva*," he'd explained, "is a snitch, and a snitch is the bottom of the barrel. They don't come no lower. A cop don't make any pretentions about where he's at. A snitch pretends to be one of you. *Chivas* die. You just step on 'em like a slug." All of Wanda's instincts made her want to hate herself.

The door opened without a knock, and Hog Wissle stuck his head in.

Wanda pulled the sheet up to cover herself. "Knock first, goddamn it," she screamed.

Hog leered at one of her breasts poking around the sheet.

Wanda threw a nearby ashtray at him as he backed out of the room.

Two hours later she ran into the night clerk from the Hotel del Campo on the *zocolo*. He said Ramón had been in looking for a room two nights ago.

When Purd got the news, he called Condor Central, Director's Office, immediately.

"The son of a bitch is in town," he told Longbeem, "guaranteed." Purd went on to ask the Director to force Cruz to cooperate but got nowhere. Until he produced something, Longbeem admonished, Ole Purd had all the forces he was going to get.

* * *

Ramón Ramón spent Thursday following what he called "battlefield discipline." That meant no movement except for business, and no business during the light of day unless unavoidable. His only trip out was to a nearby appliance store to buy a radio. Listening to it was his day's only recreation.

At 10:30 P.M. Ramón Ramón finally got back on the street and headed for Dumbo's. The air was pleasant and sweet-smelling. For a while, the sounds of the evening marimba players at the *zocolo* drifted in his direction, and he drummed his fingers against his leg in an attempt to follow their beat. Since the roadblocks continued to tie up much of the south Valley's bus traffic for hours, many Indians from out there had taken to staying in the city until all their goods were sold. Most of those slept in doorways and along the curbs at night. Ramón passed several such huddled forms on his way.

Out at Dumbo's the far-off music faded and was replaced with the sounds of crickets, passing trucks, and night bugs. A small army of gnats was swarming at the light bulb burning over the harelip's door when Ramón knocked. No answer came right away, so he knocked again, only louder. The pounding was finally answered by a red-eyed *mestizo* whom Ramón had never seen before. The air from inside smelled of both chili peppers and smoldering *mota*. The stranger said that Dumbo Nuñez wouldn't be back until tomorrow. When Ramón identified himself, the *mestizo* said that Dumbo had left a message. He said to say he would do it but needed to talk in more detail about a price.

"*Qué bueno,*" Ramón grinned. With his teeth flashing in the half light, the *gringo* took on something of a wolfish look. Everything was rolling on according to plan. "You tell Dumbo I'll be back tomorrow night," he said. "Same place, same time."

Across town Hog Wissle was relaxing at the Luna Verde, a bar several blocks north of the *zocolo*. He and Garcia Huahilote were drinking with four other Federales, all of whom had been in the morgue that morning and witnessed Purd's encounter with Cruz. At first, they just talked about that. Wissle had become more and more open with his resentments of Purd Fletcher since the senior agent had returned from Mexico City and started up the Hunter Squad. Tuesday night his disparagements of "Turd," as some of the Mexicans had taken to calling the *gringo* boss, were indistinguishable from anyone else's at the table. Eventually that bitching turned to a discussion of the Hunter Squad. The Mexicans' immediate interest was in the foxy-looking *gringa* they'd all heard about.

"Is it true, Garcia?" one of them asked. "I hear she has real water-melons." The Mexican agent made a pantomime gesture with his hands cupped under two enormous imaginary breasts. Anticipatory laughter broke out among his countrymen.

Garcia Huahilote joined in. "You should ask Hog," he joked. "He's the one who looks at them all day long."

The laughter intensified, and attention shifted to the enormous *gringo*. Hog blushed as though he'd been caught with his pants down. Garcia Huahilote's joke was so accurate it was embarrassing.

"What about that, *compadre?*" the Mexican who started the discussion pressed. "You must have played with them by now. Are they the mushy kind, or do they stick straight out?"

One of the other agents began laughing so hard his forehead bounced on the table. The anticipation among the men was feeding on itself. It made Hog uncomfortable.

"Shit," Ray Bob Wissle countered with an exaggerated drawl. The remark was meant to deflect the subject as somehow undiscussable, but there was too much embarrassment in his voice to quite pull it off.

"What's the matter?" one of the other Mexicans spoke up. "She's your snitch, isn't she? You got rights, after all."

Another voice immediately followed the first. "Maybe the man don't like girls with big tits no more. Is that it, Hog?"

Laughter was rising from their corner of the bar in loud hoots now.

Hog swirled the ice cubes around in his drink for a moment while he searched through his head for something to say. The only way out of the present situation was to brag on the subject.

"The hot ones take a while," Wissle boasted. "Don't you *hombres* worry. Hog'll be in her shorts when the time's ripe."

The hooting magnified, shouts of *"¡Qué macho!"* broke out, and everyone drank a toast to Hog's success and "ripeness" in general.

All that talking about sex had got the Mexicans horny, and the next suggestion was a visit to the whorehouse. Despite everyone's protestations, Hog Wissle declined and headed back to the Trocadero. There he relieved the Mexican on duty in the outside room of Wanda's suite and covered the graveyard shift himself. When he was sure she was asleep, Hog silently opened her bedroom door and stood watching Wanda's body under the sheet.

20

Amazon and Zorro picked the pilot R.W. up at the air terminal first thing Friday morning. On the way out to Gordo's, Amazon ran down the airstrip arrangements. Assuming everything checked out today, R.W. would take the first flight back to Mexico City Saturday. He should be back in Texas that night, spend Sunday getting things ready on that end, and fly his Cessna south on Monday, arriving in Oaxaca after dark. Amazon and Zorro would load him out, and Zorro would ride back with him. Amazon would take commercial flights up and meet the dope the next evening. His old friend Monroe Jessee would handle the off-loading at the Texas strip.

R.W. was surprised that Amazon, the majority partner, wasn't riding along with the load.

"You couldn't get me into one of those little bouncing sons of bitches you fly," Amazon explained. "Mexicana is as much as I can take."

When they reached Gordo's restaurant, Amazon left Zorro and the pilot outside and fetched The Fat Man by himself. Gordo was in his office, dressed in a maroon Hawaiian-style shirt covered with giant marigolds. He led Henry Amazon through a private exit onto the parking lot. "You ride with me," he instructed.

Gordo's shining Chrysler led the way up the hill, and the rented VW Kombi followed. The Chrysler's seats were soft and plush, and Gordo kept the air-conditioning turned up full blast, so it was almost cold inside. As the two lanes of asphalt climbed, they passed through several deep cuts in the surrounding mountain. The sound of running water rose out of the *barranca* bottom, but Henry Amazon couldn't hear it. Gordo kept his window rolled up to complement the air-conditioning. He also kept the front seat as close as possible to the dash so his stumpy legs could reach the pedals. As a result Amazon rode with his knees bunched against his chest. After a while The Fat Man began to talk about the old days. He was apparently in a good mood.

Henry Amazon wasn't. He answered most of Gomez Gordo's attempts at conversation with short collections of syllables sufficient for politeness but little else. Working with Gordo made him tight inside.

That tightness jumped into his throat when Gordo finally turned off the highway. Some fifteen Mexican infantrymen were lined up across the mouth of the bare country road where Gordo had turned. Amazon's first response was to look nervously back at the following VW.

The Fat Man sensed his fear and broke into full-scale laughter that threatened to pop several buttons on his Hawaiian shirt. "Is all right, Tortuga. I own these ones. Come back out of your shell."

Henry Amazon was pissed at himself for showing his response so openly.

Gordo stopped his Chrysler next to where the lieutenant was standing and rolled the window down.

"*Buenas tardes, señor Gordo,*" the officer opened.

"*Buenas tardes,*" Gomez Gordo grinned in return. "How are you today?"

"Is boring," the soldier confessed in Spanish. "Very much boring."

"This should help you stay awake." The Fat Man slipped two folded hundred-dollar bills out of his shirt pocket and into the lieutenant's Sam Browne belt. "My friends and I," he went on, with a motion of his hand at the Kombi behind him, "have a little business to do this afternoon. I trust you'll see we aren't disturbed."

With that the troops made way for the Chrysler and the rent-a-car following it.

Henry Amazon was open in his admiration of Gordo's maneuver. "That's some arrangement you got there," he told The Fat Man as they pulled away from the roadblock. The *gringo*'s hands had been sweating, and he wiped them on his jeans.

Gomez Gordo took the compliment in stride. "I figured since there were so many soldiers around," he explained, "I might as well rent some for myself. You know?"

Henry Amazon laughed along with The Fat Man this time. "Doesn't look like they're costing you all that much either."

"That's just him," Gordo said, meaning the lieutenant. "Don't be fooled. His bosses, they cost me a lot more."

"How much is that?"

The Fat Man brushed the question aside. "A lot," he answered. He had nothing more to say on the subject of his own expenses and unsheathed a cigar and began chewing on it. Henry Amazon lit up a cigarette and accepted the silence willingly.

The road they were now driving along was dry with the exception of an occasional puddle. It dropped at a slight angle, ran out a finger of ridge, climbed again, and continued along the ridge's back side. At the point where this ridge intersected the next, the road switched directions and climbed suddenly up a steep incline to the crest. In a meadow there the road diminished to two well-worn tire ruts that disappeared into a thick row of cypress and tamarinds. The gap where the tracks passed through the windbreak was guarded by three *mestizos* carrying M–16s. One was drinking a Coors beer, and the other two just waved as the vehicles passed. The strip was on the other side of the trees.

283

As soon as they parked, Henry Amazon went over to the Kombi to talk with his pilot. "Check it out, R.W.," Amazon said. "Let me know what you think."

In the meantime Gomez Gordo took Amazon and his Mexican partner over to a large cane lean-to. Inside were a kerosene lantern, four chairs, and a table. Half the table was covered with a brand-new shortwave radio transmitter hooked up to an automobile battery. One of The Fat Man's guards brought over a cold six-pack, and each of them had a beer.

R.W. joined them in ten minutes. He paced the landing field and determined that it was workable. He had been especially impressed with the banks of lights Gordo had rigged on each of the airstrip's edges. Most landings at night in Mexico were lit by little more than a few cars with their high beams on.

After they drove back to the fat man's place, Henry Amazon sat with Gordo in the parked Chrysler for several minutes and counted another five thousand dollars out on the seat. Gomez Gordo recounted it himself and Henry Amazon set the embarkation date for the final act in his last scam.

"Today's Friday," he told The Fat Man. "We'll do it Monday night. I'll give you a call to confirm twenty-four hours earlier."

Ramón spent Friday at the San Marcos. The walls of his room were painted turquoise. The only furniture was a sagging spring bed. Ramón had bought an extension cord to go with his radio, and it dangled from the side of the overhead light socket. Most of the day he lay on his back listening to a *gringo* station broadcasting out of Pecos, Texas. Time passed in varying shades of light filtering through the room's one high window. For a while, in the grainy yellow patch cast in the floor after lunch, Ramón managed to sleep. When he woke, the rectangle of glass on the San Marcos wall had gone black. Ramón Ramón felt stir crazy and horny. The last woman he'd had was an Indian whore in the Huautla de Jiménez. He considered heading out the Pan American to Lara Shafter's in the suburbs but rejected it. Crossing town meant lots more roadblocks than it made sense to risk. He thought of the whore street as another option but eventually decided it too entailed an excessive public display of his face. The law would be hot after losing their snitch, and it was better to stay low and next to the ground. For a while he just stood at the window and watched the evening street below. The air lifting off the asphalt was heavily laced with diesel fuel. Indians with baskets of seeds and sticks of gum passed occasionally on their way to the *zocolo*. One hot-looking Mexican woman walked by on the far sidewalk, but she had a man on each side. Stymied, Ramón's sexual energy eventually found its way into an enormous appetite. At nine thirty he left his room to walk down the block to Bandito's Roast Chicken Takeout and bring a bird or two back to eat before heading to Dumbo's.

Wanda Lamar was headed in the same direction. Friday had been the most frustrating day so far for Wanda. Hog had been pushing her hard, and she'd turned up nothing. Her list was getting short, and Wanda was full of trepidation about what would happen to her when she'd covered it all. Purd had made it clear that he expected results and had hinted more than once that without them she just might very well end up back in the hands of the Mexicans at Santa Marta. Wanda had wanted to quit a lot earlier than nine thirty, but Hog wouldn't allow it.

Finally he relented when she continued to complain about how hungry she was. Wanda proposed the Fontana for a sit-down meal, but Hog Wissle wouldn't go that far. Purd expected to debrief her at 10 P.M. just like always. She'd have to get something quicker than that. Wanda then remembered the Bandito's Roast Chicken stand. From where Wanda and Hog had been talking it was just up the block and around the corner to the left.

As Wanda turned that corner, her feet suddenly rooted themselves to the pavement. Ramón Ramón was passing under the light in the Bandito's doorway not ten yards away. He moved inside without once

285

looking in Wanda's direction. She continued to stand right where she was. Hog bumped into her several seconds later.

"Now what the fuck's the matter?" he groused.

Wanda Lamar's voice came out in a bleating half whisper. "It's him," she said.

"Who?"

"Ramón."

For a moment, the junior agent was just as shocked as Wanda. Neither of them had ever really believed Purdee Fletcher's plan would work.

As soon as Hog positioned himself across from the Bandito's Roast Chicken Takeout's only door, Wanda Lamar made her way inside. If she'd had more time to think, it would have been much more difficult. As it was, she was impelled along by her fears and frustrations of the moment The only consequence she could imagine for what she was about to do was her own escape from Mexico. Ramón Ramón was her ticket north, and she couldn't lose him now. Whatever that took wouldn't be too much.

Ramón was standing with his back to her, leaning against the counter. Along with several Mexicans in folding chairs, he was watching the TV mounted on the back wall. The long, narrow room was hot and smelled of rendered chicken fat. The program they were watching was a dubbed-over rerun of *I Love Lucy*. The Mexicans were laughing a lot, and their sounds mingled with those of the meat cleavers at work getting Ramón's order ready to go.

Wanda stopped five feet behind him. "Ramón?" she opened.

He whirled as soon as he heard his name. At first the sound was threatening, but as soon as he saw who it was behind him, a smile crept across the width of his face. "I'll be goddamned," he said. Wanda was the answer to his fantasies. Far from suspicious, he felt more confident than ever with the knowledge of her presence. He remembered her as having the best body he'd ever gotten into, and he intended having her again as soon as possible.

Wanda tried to make nervous small talk. She had no strategy. Her only objective was to stay with Ramón until the cops finally jumped him. "What's up?" she asked.

"This and that," Ramón deflected the question vaguely. "How 'bout yourself? I thought you were in Veracruz?"

The comment evoked memories of when Wanda and the fugitive had last seen each other six months before. Then Wanda Lamar had treated Ramón Ramón like some form of lowlife. "I was just in a bad mood then," she explained. "Now I've left Veracruz for good and thought I'd stop by here for old times' sake, you know?"

"Sure," Ramón grinned. "Just how old-time you gonna get?" His eyes roamed over Wanda's clothes.

"What'd you have in mind?" Wanda teased.

Ramón went straight for the opening. "I'll tell you what, Wanda," he grinned. "Bandito here's doin' up a couple chickens for me right now. Why don't we take 'em back to my room and explore a little of that history you're talking about, up close and under the covers." Ramón Ramón was a blunt son of a bitch when it came to sex. "What d'ya say?" he pushed.

Wanda swallowed. The thought of Ramón touching her was revolting. At the same time the thought of him taking off was even worse. She knew he wouldn't wait around for the trap to spring if she turned him down. "Sure, Ramón," she answered, forcing a smile. "That sounds real nice. Only why don't you meet me at my hotel, a little later. I got a few things I got to do first." She was trying to maneuver a little so that the trap could be set without having to get that close to him.

"That won't work, Mama," Ramón replied. "I got some business cooking later. I'm staying real low, you know? It's now or not at all." The flicker of curiosity in Ramón Ramón's eyes frightened Wanda. She knew he was trying to figure out what her game was and called the question accordingly. "You up for that?"

Wanda hurried to defuse his questions. "If you are," she answered.

The chickens were ready in three minutes, and the two of them left Bandito's in a beeline for the San Marcos down the block. On the street Ramón grabbed a fistful of Wanda's ass through her skirt, but she brushed his hand away and told him not on the street. But Ramón only laughed and kept it up. He had no idea Hog Wissle and Garcia Huahilote were only a dozen or so steps behind, weaving through the evening foot traffic.

In cases where the target was encountered while "in motion," Hunter Squad operational procedures called for following at a distance until the suspect had gone to ground somewhere he could be cornered. Hog behaved accordingly.

When he'd ascertained that Ramón and Wanda had gone into room number eight, he left Garcia in the San Marcos lobby and went into a nearby alley to use his radio as inconspicuously as possible.

"Command," he called, "this is Hunter One. Do you read me? Over."

In a matter of seconds the voice of Senior Agent Purdee Fletcher was on the air. "This is Hunter One. Loud and clear. Over."

"I got a Code Zero," Hog announced. Code Zero signified a target both located and at rest.

The news hit Purd like a jolt of electricity. He had been sleeping uneasily or not at all for the last several days and up until that moment had been rapidly flagging. That exhaustion immediately fell away like water off a duck's back. His ticket back to the big time was almost a reality.

"Is he going to leave there soon?" Purd asked.

"I doubt it," Hog answered. "He's shacked up with Wanda right now."

Purd laughed and clapped his hands. After finding out where Hog was, Fletcher instructed him to cover all the exits and wait until he got there with the rest of the squad. Then they would pounce in force.

Back in room number eight Wanda Lamar wished that it all hadn't gone this far. She knew nothing of standard Hunter Squad procedure and had been expecting the cops to grab Ramón Ramón as soon as the two of them were back on the street. She had wanted to look around to see where Hog was but had been too frightened that Ramón would notice and catch on to what was going on. When he finally let her into his room, she felt trapped. She was going to have to give in if the cops didn't arrive soon. Wanda recoiled from the thought.

Ramón grabbed her by the hips and pulled her toward his belly. She pressed her hands against his chest to hold him off.

"The chicken'll get cold," she said with a motion of her head at the greasy bag Ramón had carried back down the block.

"It's better that way. First we ought to work up a little appetite."

When Wanda continued to resist, Ramón's tone changed sharply, and he stepped back. "What are you up to, bitch?" Ramón snapped. "You knew what I had in mind when you said you wanted to come up here. You gonna act like some *pinche* virgin on me now?"

"No, Ramón," Wanda said as she sat down on the edge of the bed. "I want you. It's just been a long time, you know, and you always want to go so fast."

Ramón Ramón broke into heavy laughter. "Need some mood, huh?" he chuckled sarcastically. With two quick steps, he reached the radio and turned it on to the Pecos station. Linda Ronstadt was singing about someone named Carmelita who was strung out on heroin on the outskirts of town. "How's that?" Ramón grinned in the darkened room. The only light was drifting in from the street below.

He didn't bother to wait for an answer. While Wanda lay down on the bed with all her clothes on, Ramón stripped his shirt and shoes off. The pistol he kept in his boot was stashed next to the radio several feet away. When he was back on the bed, Ramón pressed himself against Wanda and began chewing her neck.

She made sounds as though she liked it, but Ramón Ramón stank of several days' sweat, and he pawed at her roughly. She alternated between wishing the cops would come and being afraid that Ramón would notice how she felt. The bouncing back and forth soon frothed her head into a latent hysteria. By the time the song on the radio had switched to an old Johnny Cash number, Ramón had stripped her blouse off. Wanda just lay there, outwardly still, and let him play with her.

After a minute of that he ran his hand up onto her panties. Ramón noticed none of Wanda's reluctance or fear. She began to squeeze her legs together, but when she did, Ramón grabbed the underwear and jerked them down her thighs in a single violent motion.

Then he stood up and undid his pants. "I'll let you take the rest off," he said somewhat menacingly.

Wanda did so slowly. After standing up, she folded her skirt carefully and laid it on the floor at the foot of the bed. Ramón shoved his stuff against her leg as soon as she'd stretched out beside him. Then his mouth slid along her stomach. At the belly button, he silently switched positions and plugged his face into the hair between her legs. She could feel his tongue snaking in and out down there, but it only made her even more cold and frantic.

At that moment the thin wood door to room number eight splintered, and Hog Wissle charged inside with a phalanx composed of Purd and three Mexicans behind him.

Wanda screamed as though she'd been attacked by bats and at first instinct clamped her legs around Ramón's head.

By the time the fugitive had untangled himself, it was too late. Ramón Ramón leaped across the prostrate Wanda for his gun, but Hog Wissle intercepted his reach along the way. Swinging him by the arm, Hog flung Ramón against the wall on the other side of the room. Before his head had cleared, the other American agent who'd crashed in right behind the first one planted a giant wing tip on the fugitive's chest. This narc was older and pear-shaped. His thirty-eight was pointed at the middle of Ramón Ramón's head.

"You're busted, meatball," Purdee Fletcher chortled down at his prize. "The jig's up."

Wanda was sitting on the bed, holding the sheet in front of herself and sobbing hysterically. Now that the deed was done, she felt like day-old puke.

* * *

Purd, on the other hand, felt like all his dreams had come true.

He had the fugitive handcuffed, standing with his arms behind him, and then dressed in his pants. Ramón Ramón could do little more than glare helplessly. Wanda Lamar was putting her clothes on with her back to the men in the room and still sobbing. When she was finally clothed again, Purd ordered one of the Mexicans to take her back to the Trocadero and wait for instructions. She followed him numbly. As Wanda approached the door, Ramón Ramón lunged against the grip of the Mexicans holding him by either arm and shouted at her.

"You're dead," he growled at Wanda. "You hear me, cunt? You're dead."

With that comment Purdee Fletcher's wing tip whipped up and planted itself along Ramón's ribs. He flew against the wall and crumpled up at its base.

"You ain't in no position to threaten anybody, creep," Purd warned Ramón. "Your string ran out as soon as they put Ole Purd on your trail."

Ramón Ramón lay where he'd fallen and said nothing more. He knew perfectly well what was in store for him. He belonged to the fat sucker who'd kicked him now. That could only mean bad things. Just how bad Ramón knew depended on the way he played it. He felt something close to fear for one of the few times in his life and ransacked his mind desperately for a way out.

The voluptuous Wanda Lamar looked catatonic and just stumbled back to her hotel.

21

When Purdee Fletcher had his men move the captive Ramón to the storeroom behind the funeral parlor in the Judicial Federal building, he had expected to question him at length, privately, and without interruption. Instead Pizarro Cruz and eight of his Federales were already there awaiting the Hunter Squad's arrival. Purd never did learn just how the Judicial Federal *Jefe* had found out about the capture. His best guess was that Cruz was monitoring the radios. If not, one of the Mexicans assigned to Purd had informed him. Either way, the Federale's intentions were obviously to make things difficult.

The impact of the Hunter Squad's success was not lost on Pizarro Cruz. The capture of Ramón would be seen as a vindication of his enemy Purd and, by inference, a further reduction in status for Cruz himself. There was nothing the Federale could do to abort that success itself, but he could make taking advantage of it a lot more hassle than Purd wanted. Cruz had such an opportunity, thanks to the operating agreements between the United States and Mexico that allowed Americans to work Mexican turf. According to those arrangements Ramón was technically the Federal's prisoner. Pizarro Cruz had come to the storeroom to invoke that technicality in a purely vindictive gesture.

As soon as Ramón Ramón was in the door, Cruz ordered his men to take custody of the suspect from Purd's Hunter Squad and move him over against the far wall. The maneuver had already been carried out before Purd, last in line, had come inside. He immediately freaked.

"What the fuck do you think you're doing?" Purd bellowed.

Pizarro Cruz looked over at him with something of a smirk. "Taking possession of the prisoner, Poord."

"He's mine."

"No," the Mexican snapped, "he's not. You have no legal power in Mexico. The prisoner belongs to the Judicial Federal."

"According to the Hunter Squad directives," Purd sputtered, "the prisoner—"

Cruz interrupted with a voice so cold the agents across the room could feel it. He knew the directives Purd was attempting to cite, backward and forward. "According to Hunter Squad directives," Pizarro Cruz broke in, "the prisoner is to be processed by the local authorities before the Hunter Squad chief exercises his rights of first interrogation. This is that processing."

Cruz turned away from the *gringo* and made a wave of his hand to the group of Federals standing around Ramón Ramón by the far wall. The fugitive's hands were still bound behind him. One of the Mexicans stepped forward when the signal was given and lashed a right hand into the middle of the face of the helpless Ramón. The "processing" proceeded from there in a welter of kicks and left hooks with Purd continuing to fume at the cement-faced Cruz on the sidelines. In Pizarro Cruz's mind he was shaming Purd by being the first to extract Ramón's pain. Much as if he had been first of the two to take the same woman. It was a reminder that Cruz was in charge and Purdee Fletcher would have to wait his turn and be satisfied with seconds. Since the Mexicans weren't interested in information, they didn't ask Ramón a single question while they were beating him.

Had they asked, they would have received answers. Ramón Ramón had no illusions about his position. He had no choice but to maneuver whatever way he could in trying to make space enough to get away. He was willing to tell them whatever he needed to in the process. That willingness was soon well hidden in an onslaught of pain. All there was immediately for Ramón Ramón was the burning in his face and the immense sting that seemed to cover his entire rib cage. The barrage only intensified as it proceeded. After several minutes the agent doing the processing stopped to fetch a baseball bat.

Purd grabbed Cruz's arm at that point and whirled him around so they stood face to face. Several veins in the *gringo*'s neck were so swollen they looked as though they might pop. "Goddamn it, Cruz," Purd growled through clenched teeth, "if you kill that sucker before I get a chance to talk to him I'll have your ass in so much Mexico City hot water you'll feel like a pinto bean."

"You think so?" Cruz pulled his arm away. "Mexico City is my capital, not yours."

"It won't feel that way when Ole Purd gets done. I'll guarantee you that much. That *hombre*'s been targeted by the Condor Director himself. You murder him, and you're gonna be one big greaseball liability come budget time."

Behind them the Mexican agent had returned with his baseball bat. Ramón managed to see the first swing coming through the fog in his head and turned so that the bat only struck a glancing blow. Even so, the tip of it broke two of Ramón's teeth off at the gum, and his mouth filled up with blood.

The second swing would have landed flush on Ramón Ramón's ear if Cruz hadn't spoken up while his man was still on the back swing.

"Enough," he shouted at the agent. Then Cruz turned to look at Purd. "Your prisoner is ready," he said with a grin like razors.

Purdee Fletcher ignored the comment and pushed his way through the Mexicans to where Ramón was waiting on his knees. His head was bent over waiting for the next blow, teetering on the edge of unconsciousness until he felt someone jerking him to his feet. He concentrated on trying to see who it was, and finally the fat *gringo* who'd put his foot in Ramón's chest at the San Marcos came into focus. The narc was leading him to a chair. Before being pushed into the seat, Ramón felt the handcuffs being released from his wrists. He was dizzy for a moment and slumped forward, looking at the spinning floor.

Then Purd's meaty hand cupped under his chin and forced it up until it faced his. The pear-shaped *gringo* spoke paternally and as though the two of them were old friends.

"Name's Purd, son," he said. "I got a few questions I want to ask."

Purd didn't get to his questions immediately.

After Ramón was in the chair, Purdee provided a clean handkerchief and told him to bite on it to stem the bleeding in his mouth. When the dribbling from his broken teeth had finally stopped, Purd offered a Camel cigarette and lit it for him. Ramón Ramón smoked in silence while Purdee busied himself getting things ready for his interrogation. He had Hog bring in the tape recorder and string an extension cord through the surrounding Mexicans and over to the plug on the far wall. The recorder was set up on a chair across from Ramón, who used the break to clear his head and assess the situation. His eyes moved around the room in quick flinches, like a snake's. The first things he looked for were doors. Aside from the one he'd come in through, there were two. One was off to his right, beyond where Purd was standing. This door was open and led into a small office. From where Ramón sat, he could see a second door leading out the other side of the office. It looked slightly ajar as well.

Purd interrupted Ramón's observations by turning the tape recorder on. "You ready to give me some answers?"

"Depends," Ramón hedged. "What you want to know?"

Purd was not interested in general intelligence. He figured Mexico City could handle that when they got their turn with the suspect. Purdee was interested in doubling his own personal score. He wanted another target for his Hunter Squad and focused immediately on the identity of the Mystery Man he had introduced in his memo weeks before. Purd had brought a copy of the one unidentified photo from the market last June and shoved that at Ramón. "I wanta know who this character is."

At first Ramón examined it uncomprehendingly. The snapshot showed the side of some indistinguishable *gringo*'s head and shoulder.

"You and your dead partner met with him in the market," Purd added, "before you went out the San Dionisio. You paid him money."

Ramón Ramón knew immediately who Purd meant and looked up at his interrogator. With a quick reading of the narc's flushed face, it was obvious to him that Purd was hungry. Why that hunger had settled on Ramón's former partner Henry Amazon was at first a mystery. Ramón Ramón answered slowly again. "Henry Amazon," he said at the microphone.

"Spell that."

"H–e–n–r–y A–m–a–z–o–n."

Purd revealed his presumption right away. "Is this Amazon still the wholesaler around here?" he asked. The *gringo* agent was hunched over Ramón in anticipation of a positive response.

"The what?"

"The wholesaler," Purdee Fletcher blurted. "The big man."

Ramón quickly decided to tell the narc what he wanted to hear. "Sure," he lied. "I'm surprised the broad didn't tell you. She knows him real good." It was Ramón's idea to string Purd along with fabrications about Henry Amazon until a way out of this trap appeared.

Ramón hadn't planned it, but that opportunity appeared almost immediately.

Before Purd could ask another question, the tape recorder went dead. One of the milling Mexicans behind him had stumbled over the extension cord and dislodged it from the wall. The interruption turned Purdee Fletcher furious again. He whirled away from the suspect and advanced on the spectators in huge Florsheim strides. "Will you *tortilla* brains watch your goddamn step," he shouted.

296

When Purd abandoned the spot where he had been standing, he uncovered a clear path between Ramón and the open office door. Ramón needed no more invitation. He was on his feet and running immediately. The sudden move caught the cops by surprise, and Ramón was all the way through the first door before Purd bolted after him.

The second office door was as open as it had looked. Ramón slammed through it and plunged into the mortuary's darkened ground-floor sales-and-display room. In the shadows he made out the shapes of empty sample caskets erected on stands and scattered about the room. The only light came through the plate-glass windows looking out on the street sixty feet away. Ramón dashed toward them. He calculated that he could crash through without major injury. Once outside, he would be as good as gone.

He never made it that far. Two steps from the window, as Ramón was coiling his body in preparation for breaking through the glass, his plan ended abruptly and forever.

Purdee Fletcher braced his thirty-eight and snapped off two quick rounds at the shape silhouetted in the faint streetlight. The first was enough. It tore through Ramón Ramón's hunched back at a forty-five-degree angle and blew the fleeing *gringo*'s throat out. Ramón was halfway choked to death on his own blood by the time his momentum carried him through the mortuary window. As he fell toward the sidewalk, everything around him went terribly grainy and far away.

When Purdee Fletcher picked his way through the debris from the demolished window and reached Jerome Whitehurst alias Ramón Ramón, the body had already started to go cold.

Killing Ramón Ramón had not been part of Purd's plan, but there had been little choice. It was either fire or let the Big Ten fugitive get away again, and Purdee Fletcher found that last option impossible to tolerate. At least Mystery Man had a name now. Purd would have to take that much and run with it.

The first step was to call Longbeem in Mexico City and tell him the news. Then Purd would have to sweat as much as he could about this Henry Amazon character out of Wanda Lamar. When everyone from the storeroom was outside standing around the body, Fletcher informed Pizarro Cruz in a brusque voice that since Ramón was the Federal's prisoner, Cruz would have to handle the body and invent a suitable cover story to explain the death by gunfire of an American national. Purd himself was going upstairs to call Condor Central.

It was past midnight, extremely late by Mexican phone company standards, and it took Purd close to fifteen minutes to raise an Oaxaca operator. Another half hour passed before that operator was able to make contact with her counterpart in Mexico City. Once he was connected to the Condor Central number, the night desk answered the call after two rings.

"Central," a voice said.

"This is Ole Purd Fletcher down in Oaxaca. Give me the Director. I'm on a Hunter Squad Code Seven."

The night desk said they'd put him through. A long series of clicks followed. Purd guessed they had some arrangement to cross connect calls to Norton Longbeem's home and waited patiently. When ringing finally replaced the sounds of lines switching, it lasted for half a minute before being answered.

"Yah?" Longbeem's voice answered groggily. He'd clearly been asleep when Purd called.

"Nort? This is Purd."

After a pause the Director's voice sharpened. "What's up?"

"We got him."

"Ramón?"

"That's right."

Longbeem chuckled in groggy satisfaction. "In custody?" he asked. The Director now sounded wide awake.

Purd paused to swallow before answering. "I'm afraid not," he explained. "The sucker's dead as a doornail."

"Who greased him?"

"Me," Fletcher answered. "I had no choice. He was making a break for it." The silence on Longbeem's end reflected disappointment and doubt, so Purd continued. "For real, Nort. He did make a break for it. I wanted him alive, too, you know. If the fucking Mexicans hadn't got in my way, I wouldn't have had to do it."

Norton Longbeem dropped his disappointment relatively quickly and didn't bother to ask Purd what he meant about the Mexicans. Capturing Ramón, even dead, was the program's biggest success thus far. "Did you get any intelligence out of him at all?"

"Enough," Purdee tried to reassure his boss. "I got a name for my Mystery Man and a confirmation of his status." Purd spoke with as much confidence in his information as he could muster. Longbeem would have to designate a Big Ten replacement for Ramón Ramón, and if it was Henry Amazon, Purd stood to be the primary beneficiary.

"What's Mystery Man's name?"

"Amazon. Henry Amazon."

"Never heard of him."

"Me neither," Purd agreed, "but Ramón said the dude is the principal wholesaler down here. We goin' after him?"

Longbeem answered the question with one of his own. "You got some leads on where he is?"

"The woman Lamar knows him too. I figure we can keep playing her the same way we did for Ramón."

"You talked to her?"

"Not yet. I had to tell you first."

Longbeem seemed to think about the information for a while. "Well," he finally hedged, "we'll have to see. You get everything you can together on your Mystery Man by tomorrow morning. I'll be bringing a crew down by agency plane at 8 A.M. to confirm the body's identification. I'll want a detailed rundown then. If it looks like you got a real shot at this character, I may go for it."

"You're the boss," Purd said. "Ole Purd'll have it ready when you get here."

Purd leaned back behind his desk when the conversation was over

299

and lit a cigarette. His exhaustion was beginning to tell, but he fought it off.

Purd's night continued in Wanda's suite. Hog Wissle was waiting in the outside room as Purd had instructed him. Hog was dozing in an armchair. The senior agent kicked Hog's boot and brought him roughly back to life.

"Get your shit together," Purd stormed, "we got to question this broad."

Wissle checked his watch. "Jesus," he objected, "it's two thirty in the morning."

Purd snorted through his nose. "You know, Hog," he snapped, "you work more and more like a Mexican every day." Without further comment Purdee strode into the bedroom door and flipped the overhead light on.

Until then Wanda Lamar had been sleeping in fits and starts. She had done little but sob and sleep since returning from the capture of Ramón Ramón. Her only consolation had been that at least it was over.

That illusion disappeared along with her sleep when Purd stormed in.

Wanda bolted upright and clutched the sheet around her neck. Her voice was fuzzy, and from the look in her eyes it was obvious she was not all there yet.

"Where's Ramón?" Wanda asked immediately.

"You don't got to worry about him no more, little lady," Purd answered. Hog entered the bedroom as the pear-shaped agent spoke. "You better start worryin' about yourself."

"What do you mean?" she asked.

"I mean they're loadin' your friend Ramón in a sack right now. You got some more questions to answer."

"Jesus," Wanda blurted. Her head fell down against her chest, and she started sobbing again.

Purdee noted her devastation and moved immediately to prey upon it. "You been holdin' out, Wanda," he growled, "and Ole Purd don't like that kinda shit at all."

Wanda looked up at the narc's lardy shape. "What are you talking about?"

"I'm talking about Henry Amazon, that's what."

At the sound of Amazon's name, Wanda Lamar thought this was all a nightmare.

"What does he have to do with any of this? I saw him Tuesday. You never even mentioned him before now." Wanda's tone was desperate.

Purd grinned. "He's the next one you're gonna hunt."

Wanda exploded immediately. "Next one?" she screamed. "There's no next one. In Mexico City you said once Ramón was caught, I was free to go."

"That was Mexico City," Purd answered, "before I knew you'd been withholding information. You never even hinted this Amazon character was big-time."

"I never withheld a goddamn thing, and you know it. You chicken-shit motherfucker. You got no right to do this. You—"

Purdee interrupted by lunging forward and swinging his open hand into the side of Wanda's jabbering head. She immediately commenced whimpering loudly. "Watch your mouth," Purd warned in a cold voice. He had to be ready for Longbeem in the morning and was in no mood to waste time taking shit off a snitch. "You're in no position to tell anybody what they can do. Ole Purd's callin' the shots here."

Wanda responded with wide eyes and sobs that passed down her arms in shudders.

"I'm goin' down the hall and get us a pot of coffee. I'll be back in ten minutes and want you dressed and out there ready to tell me everything you know about this Henry Amazon fella." With that, he walked out.

Hog was still standing near the door, so Wanda turned on him with her pain.

301

"How can you do this to me? What kind of people are you? You made a deal."

"It's your own fault," Hog said. He looked at her body outlined under the sheet. "If you'd been friendly, then you'd have friends to help you out in this kind of situation."

"You asshole," Wanda shouted.

Fifteen minutes later, she was slouching in the suite's sitting room, telling Purdee Fletcher everything she could remember about Henry Amazon. Her syllables emerged one at a time and were clipped off like her teeth were scissors. The unthinkable was happening for the second time in as many weeks, and she could not bear the thought of it.

By the time Director Norton Longbeem's plane landed at Oaxaca International on Saturday morning, Purd had everything Wanda told him about the freshly identified Henry Amazon arranged in his head for presentation. Even though he had questioned her over and over again for three hours, the information he'd gleaned about Mystery Man was not in fact that much.

According to Wanda Henry Amazon was tall, maybe six foot one or two, trim with a tendency to hump his shoulders. Blondish hair, cautious, shy, and altogether a different type from Ramón, even though the two had served in the Marines together. Henry Amazon was much more low-key and outwardly friendly. Where Ramón was mean, Henry Amazon was indecisive and always trying to get along. Where Ramón was quick to act, Amazon was slow and ambivalent. The Indians apparently knew him under the name "Tortuga," The Turtle. This Amazon had been partners with Ramón Ramón years ago. After the two of them split, Wanda had left with Ramón and had only seen Amazon in passing since. She knew nothing about his recent smuggling activities; she was even surprised that Henry Amazon was still in the business at all. According to her, he wasn't really cut out for it.

Purd knew that Wanda's information would not be much with which to impress Longbeem, but he was counting on the Director's own ambitions to provide an added impetus. As Fletcher figured it, this Ramón success had to make Nort hungry for another one just like it.

Longbeem brought his assistant and two lab men with him. They would have to confirm Ramón's identity before his capture could be officially claimed. Longbeem was all business when Purd greeted him, and they drove immediately to the morgue.

Purdee Fletcher and Norton Longbeem got down to talking about Mystery Man in the examination room while the lab men lifted fingerprints from the corpse of Ramón Ramón and took photos. It would take them fifteen minutes to confirm the identification. Purdee started by giving the Director Wanda's rundown on Amazon, skipping the snitch's doubts, and then recounted Ramón's interrogation and the circumstances of his death. He placed heavy weight on Ramón's claims just before the escape attempt.

Norton Longbeem responded skeptically, but Purd thought he could detect a sympathy behind it. "You think just trolling with the woman will work twice in a row?" the Director asked.

"Not many folks thought it'd work with him," Fletcher answered with a motion at the dead Ramón behind them, "but Ole Purd scored anyway."

Ramón Ramón was stretched out full-length and naked on the table. His beating at the hands of Cruz's men had disfigured his face, but the hook in the nose was still obvious. His dead skin had an almost blue tinge that made the wiry clusters of hair all over his body look even darker than usual. The remnants of an Adam's apple were visible inside the wound in his throat.

Norton Longbeem shifted on his feet and lit a cigarette. "What's Cruz say about your Mystery Man?"

"What'd Cruz say about Ramón? He doesn't know shit, Nort."

A look of consternation flickered on the Director's face. "I thought I told you to get along with them."

"It's difficult," Purd mumbled. He was getting worried by Longbeem's seeming reluctance even to discuss Henry Amazon, much less add him to the Big Ten.

Norton Longbeem's own annoyance changed after the lab men interrupted to announce that the corpse was the same Ramón Ramón Condor had targeted two months before. The final confirmation seemed to lift a lot of the Director's pressure, and he broke out in a smile. "You did good work," he congratulated Purd.

"What about Amazon?" Fletcher pressed. "Now that I've shown you I can still do it, are you gonna give Ole Purd another shot at bringing home the bacon? I want outa this place, Nort, and the only way I can is to work my way up."

"You sure this Amazon is worth being listed in the Top Ten? Nobody in Intelligence Evaluation has ever heard of him."

"As sure as that creep on the table ain't gonna smoke no Mary Jane ever again."

Longbeem dropped his cigarette on the floor and crushed it with his shoe. "Then go at it," he said, "and don't fuck up."

"It's as good as done," Purd grinned.

The Director then added a few words Purd had been waiting to hear. "Nail this one and keep the Mexicans off your back," he went on, "and who knows? You just might get that job you want."

Purd had imagined he would be given even stronger assurances than that, but no such guarantees were forthcoming.

After returning his boss to the airport, Purd headed straight for the Trocadero. His original jubilation over Ramón's capture was now hopelessly muddled in new developments. He hadn't slept in almost forty-eight hours, and he felt numb around his face and cramped in the chest. The Saturday morning air was full of the faint smell of approaching rain.

22

After R.W. took a taxi to the airport in the morning, Henry Amazon finally got around to running down the rest of this load's arrangements to Zorro. He had to in order to work out Saturday's logistics. Amazon illustrated his explanation by drawing a map with a ball-point pen on some Plumbing Supply Company stationery he found in one of the bungalow's nightstands. The two smugglers were sitting next to the coffee table in the sitting room.

Amazon's first blue-ink line extended east out of the large square he'd drawn to represent Oaxaca and stopped at a smaller square he marked with *T* for Tlacolula.

"We drive out the Tehuantepec road to Tlacolula," he explained, "in separate cars." At the approximate location of each of the two roadblocks along the way, he drew perpendicular lines across the road. "Out there, you'll follow me to a house where we'll pick up the Indian Rascón you met last trip down." Amazon next scratched a line running out one side of Tlacolula past the Fuenteses' village. It was drawn

305

with a few wiggles to it. "This road will go around one village and through the *plaza* of another." He drew even smaller squares to represent those locations. "You'll follow me along it." Just past the second square he made an *X* and stopped drawing for the moment. "We'll take Rascón to a place out the road I'll lead you to. That's where we're gonna have him and his friends bring their *mota* tomorrow night. After we show it to him, you'll take Rascón back to Tlacolula and then come back here to buy some things we'll need." Amazon's shopping list included sheets of thick plastic, wide heating duct tape, two large-mouthed funnels, and several other smaller items.

"What about you?" Zorro asked. "What you gonna do?"

"I'm going to meet the other half of the load and make sure it's ready." As almost a second thought Henry Amazon added "by myself" to his statement to make sure his partner understood that the same rules as always still applied.

Zorro made no comment on the addition. "Where is it?" he asked. The *mestizo* was toying with the earpiece of his sunglasses while they talked.

"Nearby," Amazon answered vaguely. "It'll be ready to pick up tomorrow night, too."

At that point Henry Amazon returned to the stationery. He extended a perpendicular line of almost equal length to that connecting Oaxaca and Tlacolula out of his representation of the Pan American leading to Tehuantepec. This was the Ixtlán Road. At Gordo's restaurant he drew a circle. Shortly after it he drew another line intersecting that one from the right, gave it a few wiggles, and ended it with another *X*. Amazon's pen then returned to a spot below Gordo's restaurant and drew another wiggle connecting the Ixtlán Road to his first *X*, the two small squares, and the larger square marked *T* for Tlacolula. When he was finished, it all looked like a rough right triangle with two relatively straight sides connected by a wavy crosspiece.

"Clean the whole way," Amazon pointed out as he pushed the sheet across the coffee table for Zorro's inspection. "Except," he added in an afterthought, "for the ones who are bought." With that addition he

306

leaned across to the paper and made one more cross-hatch to represent the soldiers Gordo owned along the top wiggle leading to the airstrip marked X.

Zorro CeAttle fingered the paper nervously.

On Plumbing Supply stationery the arrangement looked smooth as silk.

Henry Amazon's rented Kombi led a two-car caravan out through the countryside to the spot he indicated on his map with the first X. Rascón rode with the *gringo,* and the Mexican was alone behind them in his Ford. The spot they headed for began as just a stretch in the road where a broad but shallow wash crossed through a culvert under the steeply elevated one lane of dirt. Henry Amazon slowed and turned right down the sloped side onto the wash.

The farther they drove along it, the higher its sides got, but its breadth didn't shrink accordingly. When the gully walls were a good twelve-feet high on either edge and covered with large bushes, Henry Amazon stopped. The gray sky had begun to drizzle.

Rascón got out and walked around, taking in everything. He finally declared that he knew this spot and that it was a good one. Almost immediately Amazon dispatched the Indian back to Tlacolula with Zorro. He watched the Ford pull out of the wash, climb up onto the road bed, and speed off. The drizzle was turning steadily thicker, and the air was full of the sound of birds fluttering for cover in the foliage overhead. By the time Amazon had returned to the road, the drizzle had become rain, large drops falling at a steady but still relatively sleepy pace.

His next destination was Cucaracha's place back over the ridge toward the Fuenteses' village, but for a moment he paused atop the culvert. To his right the foothills sloped off gently to the floor of the Valley. Down there the storm was a shiny curtain that seemed to be advancing along the far wall of mountains, obscuring everything behind it. Accompanied by winds strong enough to bend trees, the tailing end of the curtain was just now beginning to swing around in a cart-wheeling motion. Henry Amazon was directly in the storm's path.

Water was falling in sheets when he reached Cucaracha's. Despite the slashing weather the old man's wife and their three small children were standing outside under the flimsy awning. Cucaracha's woman ran out to him and began jabbering in dialect. He couldn't understand a word she was saying.

"¿Dónde Cucaracha?" he shouted.

She pointed at the door of the hut and began another hysterical monologue in unintelligible Zapotec. Amazon tried the plank door, but it was fastened tight.

"Cucaracha?" he shouted at it.

Finally the old man spoke on the other side of the door. His voice was tentative. "¿Tortuga?"

"That's right," Amazon said with a great deal of irritation. "¿Qué pasa? Goddamn, Indian, your woman and kids are out here getting soaked. Open the fucking door."

There was a long pause on the other side. "I can't," the old Indian finally said.

"What do you mean, you can't?"

"I can't."

Henry Amazon scuffed the ground with his cowboy boot. He did not need Cockroach to get crazy on him at this point. Everything had been planned assuming that the old man's part of the load was ready. Amazon tried to calm himself. "Why can't you?" he finally asked.

"It might get out."

"What might get out?"

Again the old Indian hesitated. When he spoke, it was in an unintelligible whisper.

"Speak up," Amazon shouted at the planks. "I can't hear you."

"I said it will get out."

"I heard that part. What'll get out, *compadre*?" Amazon tried to make his voice sound soothing in the odd hope that it might calm the old man down.

"The death that's in here with me," Cucaracha answered.

At first, the statement made no sense. "The death?"

"*Sí.*"

"What the fuck are you talking about, old man?"

"You know the black butterfly? It came in here." Cucaracha's voice sounded breathless. "On the day Cazadero Fuentes died."

Henry Amazon didn't answer right away. He knew the Zapotecs believed that if a black butterfly enters your house on the day someone dies, you will be the next to die if it flies out of the house. The old man thought he had his own death trapped in there with him. "Just what I fucking need," Amazon cursed. "This is crazy."

"What?" Cockroach asked on the other side of the door.

"Nothin'." Amazon felt like kicking the door off its hinges. "What has happened to our *mota* during all this?"

"It's still in the cave," the old man reassured him.

"It is packed?"

Cucaracha's answer was slow in coming.

"Is it?" Amazon demanded.

"Almost."

"Almost?" Henry Amazon's foot exploded in a rattle against the door. "Almost? *Chinga, indio,* I've got to have that load tomorrow night. You told me it would be ready right now. What do I pay you for anyway?"

Cucaracha remained silent.

After a few moments Amazon got hold of himself. This had to be dealt with speedily, absurd or not.

"Okay, old man," he spoke up. "You don't have to worry. I won't let the butterfly out. Maybe we can catch it together. How do you know the butterfly's still inside?"

"I have my lantern. I can see it on the ceiling."

"Well, you just keep an eye on it. I'll be right back."

Amazon loped into the storm. When he returned, he had a flashlight he'd fetched from his rent-a-car. He knew what he was going to do and was just pissed off enough to do it. Again he pounded the door. "Cucaracha?"

"*¿Sí?*"

"I'm back. Let me in."

"I can't."

"Where's the butterfly?"

"On the wall."

"Close by?"

"No."

"Well then, it's no problem, old man. You just crack it open, I'll slip in, and you shut it again. Simple."

"I can't."

At this point Henry Amazon's voice got its hardest. "Look, Cockroach: Either you open it or I'll kick it down. One or the other." To emphasize the point Amazon rattled the door with his foot.

"No, no. Don't," the old man shouted desperately.

"Then let me in."

Cucaracha's response was silence, followed by some foot shuffling and the noise of his hand on the latch. "You got to be fast," the Indian said with great trepidation.

"I will be," Amazon answered. "I will be."

As soon as the first crack appeared, Amazon eased through the doorway. Cucaracha immediately slammed the door behind him.

The hut was dingy inside and full of shadows. There was a moment of hysteria after the smuggler's entrance when the old man couldn't find the butterfly again, but that was quickly solved with Amazon's flashlight. The insect was perched on the bottom face of one of the roof beams, three quarters of the way to the back wall. It was four inches across, wing tip to wing tip, and pitch black. Henry Amazon approached part of the way, keeping his light on the insect, and then stopped. Water was still dribbling off his poncho. "It sure is black," he said.

The Indian spoke up behind him. "That's from the death in it," he explained.

310

Amazon ignored the comment. "You still got that *pistola* I gave you last year?"

When the old man had first agreed to grow Amazon's crop, the *gringo* had given him a forty-five automatic to guard his investment.

"It's in my trunk."

"Fetch it for me."

"Why?"

"Just fetch it."

The old man hesitated and then did as he was told. The gun was wrapped in a cloth and loaded. When the Indian handed it over, he asked, "Why?" again.

"Don't worry," Amazon reassured him. "Hold this." He handed his light to the Indian and checked the action on the forty-five. Then the smuggler took the flashlight back and advanced on the butterfly.

"What you gonna do?"

Amazon walked slowly until he stopped some ten feet from the insect's perch.

"Tortuga," the Indian shouted. "You can't shoot him. No, don't. If you miss . . . the hole . . . he'll fly out. Please—"

The Indian's voice was drowned by the explosion of the pistol.

Henry Amazon was standing with his feet spread and the forty-five extended upward.

As soon as the gun went off, the old man's wife commenced screaming and banging on the latched door. Cucaracha was afraid to look at what had happened, so Amazon fetched a chair and stood on it to inspect the target. He found part of a wing and some meat from the butterfly's shoulder plastered along the edge of the chunk he'd blown out of the beam and brought them back to where the Cockroach was standing with his head bent toward his feet.

"There's your butterfly," he said, wiping the remains onto the old man's palm. "Cucaracha one, death zero."

The Indian began shouting in Zapotec and making motions like he was jumping up and down. Then he opened the door to his family, and they did the same thing. Amazon sat on the chair, still not quite able to believe that all this had really happened. The Indians yelped around

311

him in a half-dance while the ferocious weather off the Pacific threatened to lift the roof and break it into matchsticks.

Finally, The Cockroach calmed down and wanted to drink *mescal* with the *gringo* to show his appreciation for saving his life. Amazon declined and stood up.

"We still got business to do," he said. *"Muy pronto."*

Within three minutes the two of them were back out in the storm on their way over the ridge to the shelter of the *mota* cave. They would stay there until seven in the evening when the last box was packed.

Wanda Lamar spent her Saturday sleeping when she could. Purd had given his Hunter Squad the day off. What she'd done to Ramón made her feel ugly. She woke up in a state of panic. Wanda could see no end to her dilemma. She tried desperately to remember who she had been going to be before the narcs busted her in the Mexico City airport. It composed her. She had left Denard because of the same claustrophobia she now felt. Leaving Denard, she told herself, had been a strong act, an act of survival. Now she had to do the same thing again. She couldn't afford to snivel about Ramón. What happened to Ramón was what was bound to happen to him sooner or later. That was his karma. What mattered was that Wanda was still afloat. It was Wanda she had to look out for: she must develop a strategy and stop feeling sorry for herself. Whatever it took was the only rule. The game would have to be one of maneuver with her police keepers, and she had only a captive's tools. Those, she told herself, were the facts of life in this moment.

Wanda thought about her plan of attack for an hour after that. Her hysteria dissolved. No more soul-searching and hand-wringing for Wanda Lamar. Her resolve was to save herself from life south of the border once and for all, by whatever means necessary. The plan began taking concrete form when the shift changed outside her door and a somewhat burned-out Hog Wissle came onto the nine-to-midnight watch. Wanda put her tight blouse and her best skirt on and then went out into the suite's sitting room. She greeted Hog with a gentle smile that lifted her cheeks up and made her look younger than she was. "I've been thinking about what you said about being friends and all," Wanda said with a touch of a blush. "I'd like to take you up on it."

When Wissle recognized the note of invitation in her voice, his eyes bugged out like a lizard's.

About that same time Henry Amazon returned to the Modesto. Zorro CeAttle was in the bungalow. Since the Mexican had already eaten, Amazon hurried on by himself to get a table in the dining room before it closed. He found a copy of that morning's *Carteles* on one of the other tables and read while he was waiting to be served.

Most of the front page was filled with a story about the termination of General Cortez de Corriente's war games, "Army Exercises Successful, To Be Phased Out." According to the story, the maneuvers had reached their goal a day ahead of schedule. The General's press release called it "an admirable demonstration of military preparedness and efficiency." Troops would begin being withdrawn the next day, and all but five thousand would be gone within the next seventy-two hours. This last contingent would remain as an adjunct of the General's garrison for an undetermined period of time. They would be bivouacked outside Ocotlán at the mouth of the San Dionisio Road in extended "field training" exercises.

Two pictures accompanied the story. The smaller of them showed a tank, turned over on its back like an upended beetle. It had driven off a forty-foot drop, killing six soldiers who were sleeping below. The other photo was of the General himself. Cortez de Corriente was standing up in the back of his command jeep, addressing his officers. The General wore starched fatigues, a silk ascot, and a helmet with four gold stars across the front. He also had a chromed forty-five automatic strapped to each of his considerable hips. The caption noted that, like Villa and Zapata before him, the General was loved by his troops.

313

DAVID HARRIS

Henry Amazon considered the Army's plans very good news. Over the next two days, the military would be occupied in moving itself. Now if only this storm would let up. He was ravenous and gulped his first course quickly. Afterward he returned to examining the paper.

His confidence diminished considerably when he reached the second inside page. The headline read "Berserk American Shot by Traffic Police."

His eye moved immediately to the small snapshot accompanying the account. It was obviously a morgue photo. After a cursory examination of it, sweat broke out in Amazon's palms. The line of the corpse's jaw was swollen as though it had been beaten, but the rest of the face was clearly Ramón Ramón.

The accompanying story was only three paragraphs long. It said that an American carrying papers identifying him as Stephen Smith was shot several blocks from the *Zocolo* when he apparently went berserk from the effects of some undetermined narcotic. According to officers of the Oaxaca Traffic Patrol a detachment encountered the American at 1 A.M. He was weaving around in the street with a pistol in his hand. He had already shot out a mortuary's plate-glass window. Upon sighting the officers, the man reportedly fired several shots in their direction. He was killed when the traffic patrol returned fire. There were no police casualties.

Henry Amazon didn't believe the account: Ramón wouldn't have gone that easy. He sat for several minutes examining the grainy head shot of his former partner and Marine Corps foxhole buddy. The photo was cropped right at the chin. Amazon was looking for some kind of clue, but there was none. The eyelids were shut, the face devoid of expression. Amazon abandoned the remainder of his meal, paid the bill, and returned to the bungalow.

As soon as he came into the sitting room, the Mexican jumped up, announced that he wanted to go have a few drinks at a whorehouse, and invited Amazon to come along. He declined and warned his partner not to get too fucked up. Tomorrow, the last act of the scam was set to begin. He didn't want Zorro's ass dragging through it. The Mexican gave no signs that he'd even heard the warning and swaggered out through the rain to his Ford.

Amazon stood for a moment at the window, then he stretched out on the couch and lit up a joint.

He had brought the *Carteles* with him from dinner; from time to time he would pick it up to examine the late Ramón's face. That Ramón Ramón had been killed made him extremely frightened for himself. And he would stay frightened for the next two days. The hawk was on the wing, and Henry Amazon was about to abandon his cover and make a very long run across a very open space.

At 10 P.M. Thursday Wanda Lamar took Hog Wissle to bed just to prove her newfound friendliness. It was, she told herself, all part of her strategy.

Hog stripped his clothes off in a flurry and let them lie where they fell. Wanda was slower, and she could feel his eyes all over her while she folded her skirt.

When Wanda turned back to the bed, Hog was lying on top of the covers. He began licking her breasts clumsily and tried to ease his finger between her legs. After several short minutes of that, Hog then climbed on top of her. Wanda asked him to go slow, but the warning fell on deaf ears. Hog began thrusting as soon as she helped him inside. She tried again to slow him down, but by then it was too late. Hog was grunting and sweating at an accelerating pace, so Wanda Lamar faked it and let out several moans. Then Hog blew his wad, went completely limp, and rolled off.

"Oh, Hog," Wanda purred.

The agent lit a cigarette and blew out a deep puff. "You liked it, huh?" he asked.

"I loved it," Wanda lied.

Hog fucked Wanda twice more before he said the shift was about to change, and he had to get back to his post. It would be best to keep up the appearances that regulations demanded. But, he added with a pinch at one of her tits, they were good friends. Wanda could count on Hog. He was her man now. Hog didn't tell her, but Wanda was the kind of woman he'd always fantasized about but had never before laid. She was visible proof that he was indeed the genuine stud he imagined himself to be.

She kissed him good-bye. Wanda had come no closer to getting off the second and third times than she had the first. She lay awake in the dark for several hours after Wissle's departure. Eventually she thought about the room in the San Marcos where Ramón Ramón had been captured. This time, instead of Ramón, the cops were holding Henry Amazon, her new target. The picture Wanda had of Amazon was an old one, the way he'd looked when they first met almost ten years before. Just like Ramón, he called Wanda Lamar a bitch and a cunt and said she was as good as dead. In the shy Amazon's mouth the words had little menace. Instead they simply sounded convincing. Wanda Lamar was indeed as good as dead. When she was, it would all be Judy Rosenberg again. Only Wanda's karma remained, she told herself, and it would come to a head shortly.

Some time before dawn Friday morning the rain lessened and then stopped, but Wanda Lamar was sleeping too deeply to notice.

23

When Wanda emerged from her half of the suite on Sunday to start work, Hog was waiting in the outside room with Garcia Huahilote and two other Mexicans. Hog greeted the snitch by grabbing her ass ostentatiously. Wanda heard suppressed chuckles and cluckings from the rest of the narcs. Obviously, Hog had passed the word of his conquest along. Wanda Lamar just smiled at him, rubbed his arm, and then pushed his hand away. It was, she said, time to get out on the street.

Wanda commenced looking for Henry Amazon at nine o'clock with Wissle thirty yards behind her, carrying his two-way radio in a flight bag. The Friday sky was covered with smudge-colored clouds, but dry.

Since Amazon was a much less social type than Ramón Ramón, Wanda's list of places to inquire was noticeably shorter. Once again it began at Tonebar's Veracruz Café. Hog stayed across the street while she went inside.

Tonebar was minding the grill behind the counter. He turned when he heard the door open. The greasy-looking proprietor acted like he was in a very good mood.

"Wanda," he called out, "*quiubo?* You musta come back for that breakfast."

"No, Tonebar," Wanda answered when she reached the counter, "I didn't."

"Then you still looking for Ramón. You never found him, huh?" Since Tonebar didn't read, he as yet knew nothing of Ramón's recent death.

The mention of him passed a shadow over Wanda Lamar's face, but it was so quick Tonebar wasn't even sure he saw it. "I gave up on that hunt," Wanda lied. "Now I'm trying to find someone else."

"Who you lookin' for now?" the cook asked. Before Wanda could answer, he turned around to tend something on his stove.

Wanda waited until he was done. "Henry Amazon," she began again. "Have you seen him?"

"Henry Amazon? Boy! You really goin' backward in time, Wandita." Tonebar followed the remark with a large wink and several chortling sounds.

Wanda feigned good-natured embarrassment. "It's important," she insisted. "Does he ever come in here anymore?"

Tonebar wiped the sweat off his forehead with a corner of his apron. "Not in months," he answered. "I don't think Enrique is even around these parts any more."

"How about that Zapotec he used to run around with? The one they call El Chorizo." Tonebar just broke out in laughter at the mention of Jesus Mapassa's lascivious nickname.

"Come on, Tonebar, enough of the humor. Have you seen him?"

"Maybe it was Monday the last time. Maybe Tuesday. It's hard to remember."

"Do you know where I could find him?"

"He drives around and parks a lot."

El Chorizo's career as a low rider had begun after Wanda had left town three years earlier, and this was the first she'd ever heard of the Indian's driving habits. "He's got a car?" she asked.

"You been gone a long time, Wanda, I'll say. Chorizo's got two of 'em. Two trucks. The one he drives in mostly is one of those Ford pickups. Or maybe it's a Chevy. I just cook. I don't know those kinds of things."

"How about the other?"

"I only seen it once. I think it was a Dina, one of those big flatbed kinds with double wheels on the back. Painted green."

"And he just drives around and parks?"

"Sometimes he takes girls with him."

"Does he drive the same place all the time?"

"*¿Quién sabe?*" Tonebar answered. "I never drive with him." The cook found that funny and blurted out more laughter.

Wanda waited patiently for Tonebar to continue. When he didn't, she asked, "Where does he park?"

"All around, I guess. I seen him a few times down on the whore street and some more times at the park where the *mariachi* bands hang around. That little strip of grass by the Santo Domingo Cathedral, too."

Having extracted all the information she thought she was likely to get, Wanda Lamar took a couple of minutes to tie the conversation off and return to the street. Up the block Hog caught up with her and she gave him a report. Amazon himself hadn't been around, but she had gotten a line on an Indian who would know right where to find him.

By early afternoon Wanda's list was exhausted. Her search increasingly focused on locating that Indian and his truck. During that part of the search she rode in the backseat of Garcia Huahilote's sedan; Hog and the Mexican sat in front. Mostly the narcs talked to each other as though she weren't there. Occasionally Hog reached back to rub her thigh.

* * *

319

Henry Amazon had spent Sunday morning with El Chorizo collecting the fuel for the airplane's return trip.

Zorro CeAttle didn't wake up until almost two o'clock in the afternoon. The Mexican had not returned from his visit to the whorehouse until 4 A.M., and then he'd been dead drunk and pleased that he'd ignored Amazon's warning. Now Zorro found his *gringo* partner in the sitting room, drinking coffee. The Mexican took a cup sullenly. His head was throbbing, and the pain made him mean.

Henry Amazon was not in his best mood either. Ever since he had read the *Carteles* the night before, his mind had been swarming with images of disaster. Zorro's behavior had irritated him, but he tried to restrain himself.

"You alive enough to listen?" he finally said with a slight edge on his voice.

Instead of answering Zorro just waved his hand at the *gringo* in a disdainful gesture of agreement.

"I want to tell you what's coming down from here on in," Amazon continued.

"*Qué milagro,*" Zorro interrupted sarcastically. "You finally gonna tell me the plan. We been at this for two months, and you finally gonna tell me the plan. *Muchas gracias, señor Enrique.*"

Henry Amazon let his partner's obnoxiousness pass for the moment.

"At four thirty," he continued, "I'm calling R.W. in the States for our last check. If his end is together, he flies south on Monday. After I talk to him, I call Gomez Gordo and let him know. At five we meet El Chorizo in the city and send him and the gas out through the roadblocks to the east Valley. I'll follow at seven thirty, and you follow at ten. You know that second village after the turnoff in Tlacolula?"

Zorro made another motion with his hand.

"We're all gonna meet at the second culvert outside of there. The second culvert." Henry Amazon paused to make sure his partner got the message.

Zorro was insulted by the gesture.

"Next," Amazon went on, "we meet Rascón at the spot we went to

320

yesterday and load his dope. Afterward we pick up the other half nearby. Then we stay out there and baby sit it until it's time to show up at Gordo's around five the next afternoon. The plane will land as close after dark as it can make it."

"How come we gonna stay out there all night?"

Henry Amazon had anticipated that Zorro would gripe about camping out. "The dope's got to be guarded," he said with a matter-of-fact tone.

"So why not wait to pick it up until Monday?"

"Because the time don't work right, that's why, *mano*." Amazon's irritation pushed its way to the surface. "You can't take two deliveries and load up a plane in time to get it back into the States while it's still dark, unless you meet the dope when the sun's out, and I am not about to do that. Movin' it during the night is risky enough."

"Maybe to you," Zorro snapped. The Mexican started to say more, but Amazon didn't let him. The American slammed his fist down on the coffee table.

"That," he exploded, "is all that matters. Do you *sabe, cabrón?* I make the plans, and if you want your split, you follow them. That's the way it works."

Zorro stared resentfully, and Amazon stared back. Finally Amazon spoke up.

"Right now you got work to do."

"What work is that, *mi jefe?* Zorro said *"mi jefe"* with a snarl.

"You got to buy five tarps." Amazon pulled some money out of his pocket and tossed it into his partner's lap. "They all have to be top quality, and you can't buy more than two of them in any one place. You also have to be back here by four thirty."

"How come I—" Zorro started to complain about being used as an errand boy, but again Amazon interrupted.

"Because you don't get up early enough to do nothin' else."

Zorro withdrew into sullenness, finished his coffee, and headed out the door.

Alone in the bungalow Henry Amazon waited nervously. He anticipated that there might be difficulties getting an international line, so he placed his call to R.W. through the hotel switchboard at four. At four thirty, when Zorro returned, it still wasn't connected. The two partners sat in the sitting room. The Mexican seemed to enjoy Henry Amazon's discomfort. Already the *gringo* was falling behind schedule. By four forty-five Amazon knew he wasn't going to be able to hook up with El Chorizo at the appointed time. At four fifty he decided to tell Zorro to go along in his place.

"He'll be parked along that strip of grass on the side street by the Santo Domingo Cathedral," Amazon instructed the Mexican. "You tell him to get movin'." Even though he didn't yet have his pilot's go-ahead, Henry Amazon figured he could always drive out and fetch the Indian if the plan had to be changed. *"Muy pronto,"* he added.

It was five o'clock on the nose when CeAttle's Ford pulled out of the Modesto's courtyard, and the call to R.W. still hadn't gone through.

Wanda Lamar found Chorizo shortly after Zorro did. She spotted the Zapotec's green Dina as the Hunter Squad car was cruising north on the Alcala past the Santo Domingo at 5 P.M. The truck was parked in the side street south of the cathedral, and at first Wanda didn't identify it. She'd been looking for the pickup, and the flatbed only registered as an afterthought when the narcs' car was even with the cathedral itself.

"Pull over here," she told the driver, Garcia Huahilote.

"What's up?" Hog asked.

"I think I saw the Indian's second truck back there. Parked in one of the spots Tonebar mentioned."

Garcia Huahilote wheeled over to the curb on the other side of the cathedral steps. The walkway blocked any view of the cross street where Chorizo was. "Stay out of sight," Wanda warned as she got out. "You'll freak him." With that she headed back for the cross street.

Wanda Lamar wasn't sure it was indeed El Chorizo until she was across the steps, approaching on the driver's side. Wanda noticed the truck was half loaded with what looked like oil drums. The Mexican she had seen with Henry Amazon was standing at the driver's side. El Chorizo started his engine and Zorro backed off as the flatbed pulled out and headed down the street. Wanda hurried to catch the Mexican before he left as well. Her breasts bounced as she trotted. Zorro saw her coming and slipped his shades off. Wanda walked the last few steps up to where he stood.

"Aren't you the one I saw with Henry Amazon the other day?" she asked.

"Let me introduce myself," Zorro smiled, bowing his head in an exaggerated Latin manner. "I am Zorro CeAttle, at your service."

Wanda smiled in return. "Wanda Lamar."

"*Mucho gusto.*"

"I'm glad I caught you," Wanda continued. "I need to find Henry Amazon. Since you two were together in the Monte Alban Tuesday, I thought you might be able to help me."

Zorro let his glance stray all over Wanda's body. He was not about to connect this woman with Henry Amazon. He'd taken too many backseats to the *gringo* already. Now Zorro was going to be the man in charge and immediately latched onto the idea of taking Amazon's woman for himself. Maybe he would tell Amazon about it later and watch his eyes squirm. It would be a nice note of humiliation to end their partnership with.

"I might," Zorro answered. "We're partners. Why do you want to see Enrique?"

"Something personal."

The *mestizo* questioned her answer with a lift of his brows. "You're a friend of his?"

"From a long time back," Wanda explained.

Zorro CeAttle now adopted an expression that made it clear he was considering the proposition with a certain distrust. "Well," he finally said, "I might be able to help you . . . but I don't know. Enrique don't like me telling people where he is, you know?"

323

Wanda used her friendliest manner. "He won't mind me knowing," she tried to reassure Zorro. "*Cierto*. We were good friends."

"Maybe what you say is true, *señorita,* but I don't got no way to be sure. *Comprende?* Maybe you and I should get to know each other better first. So I know I can trust you."

Wanda had seen the pass coming. Three days ago, she might have been confused by it, but today she had a strategy. Zorro's move fit right into it.

"Sure," Wanda said softly. "I'd like that."

Zorro said nothing and concentrated on trying to bring his eyes romantically to bear on hers. For the first time Wanda noticed how purple the Mexican's looked.

"How about tonight at eight?" she suggested. "At the fountain in Juarez Park."

Zorro liked the location's implications. Juarez Park was a known strolling and necking place for Oaxaca's lovers.

"Eight o'clock," he answered, "if the *señorita* will excuse me?"

Zorro then returned to his Ford and drove back for the Modesto. When he rejoined Henry Amazon, he made no mention of his encounter with Wanda Lamar.

Amazon said his call north had gone through and everything was advancing as planned. Gordo had been notified. Now the two partners just had to wait somewhat uncomfortably together in the bungalow until it was time for Amazon himself to head east out the Pan American along the same track as El Chorizo and his gas truck.

Back at the parked Hunter Squad car by the cathedral, Wanda Lamar commenced the riskiest part of her strategy. Meeting Zorro gave her leverage, and now she intended to use it to the hilt.

Wanda slid into the backseat, closed the door behind her, and didn't answer when Hog spoke up.

"Was it him?"

Garcia Huahilote pulled the sedan into traffic.

"What happened?" Wissle pressed.

Wanda Lamar looked up, and her voice was hard. "What's it worth?" she asked.

"What do you mean, what is it worth?"

"Just that."

"Cut the bullshit, Wanda," Hog snapped. "I said what did you find out?"

"And I said what's it worth? No bullshit, Hog. I found out plenty, but this time I'm not letting you in on it until I get something in return. Straight business. I learned my lesson once."

Wissle adopted a pleading tone. "Come on, Wanda. I can't make any deals with you. Only Purd can do that. Why don't you—"

Wanda interrupted. "Then let's go see Purd," she said.

"Hey, you don't want to make trouble with that old fart. Trust me, honey. I'm looking out for you." He ran his hand along Wanda's leg, but it made no difference.

"Let's go see Purd," she repeated. Her renewed frostiness had Hog backpedaling, and she intended to make the most of it. Rejection clearly drove him up a wall.

Hog had no choice but to get on the horn to Purd. "Hunter One to Command," he called on the walkie-talkie. "Do you read me?"

The set in his hand crackled and then came alive with Purd's voice. "Command to One. I read you."

"I got a problem with the snitch. Can I meet you at the Trocadero?"

"At the Trocadero," Command answered. "Roger and out."

When Wanda Lamar and her two keepers reached the hotel, Purd was already in the suite, waiting. Seeing the flustered look on his junior agent's face, he guessed right away that some kind of game was being run down. He didn't like it at all.

Wanda took a seat on the couch, and Purd turned on her. He was standing immediately in front of Wanda, five feet away. At first she didn't look at him.

"All right, Wanda," Purdee opened, "suppose you tell me what the problem is."

"Henry Amazon is around and in business," she said, without looking up.

"How do you know?"

"I met his partner."

"What's the partner's name?"

"He's a Mexican."

"What's his name?"

Wanda kept her eyes on her feet and didn't answer.

Purd hooked his hand under her chin and forced it upward. His voice, full of bellow until now, turned suddenly softer. "What's his name?"

Instead of capitulation she taunted him with another hint.

"I got an appointment to meet the Mexican again," she said, "tonight."

"Where?"

Again Wanda went silent, and Purd dropped back into his bellow. His face was getting pink. He would not tolerate this kind of shit from a snitch. "I said where?" The voice was full of menace.

"What's it worth?" Wanda asked.

"What'd you say?"

"What's it worth?"

"Whatever I decide it is, little lady," Purd growled. "You don't set no prices here. Ole Purd does that. You do good work and maybe I'll let you go. Keep this bargaining shit up and I'll send you back to the Mexicans."

Wanda read Fletcher's remarks as a bluff and treated it that way. She knew Purd wanted her information very badly. "Then send me back to the Mexicans."

Senior Agent Purdee Fletcher didn't answer right away.

"If you want Henry Amazon's partner," Wanda offered, "I can give him to you. You give me my papers back and enough money for a plane ticket to the States, and he's yours. Otherwise you can just do what you're gonna do."

Purd was furious. Ole Purd Fletcher had never let a snitch twist his tail, and he wasn't about to start now.

"You must not have heard me," he said in his soft voice. "So I'll repeat it. Things don't work that way. You and me are playing under Ole Purd's rules—first, last, and always. You just tell me what you know and then we'll see what it's worth."

"No way."

As soon as the words were out of Wanda Lamar's mouth, Purd's free hand whipped into the side of her face. With one thick paw already nestled under her chin, it was like teeing up a golf ball. The blow knocked Wanda bleary for a moment.

"You got a name to tell me?" Purd demanded.

When Wanda looked up with runny eyes and shook her head no, the director of Oaxaca's Hunter Squad brought the back of his hand across the bridge of her nose.

Purd was about to repeat himself when Hog Wissle moved from where he'd been leaning against a wall and grabbed Purdee by the shoulder. Purd looked at him in obvious irritation.

"What?" he growled.

"Could I talk to you over here for a minute, Purd?" Hog asked in a low voice.

Purd reluctantly agreed, and the two of them huddled on the other side of the room.

"Look, Purd," Hog opened, "you don't have to beat her. Let me have a shot at talking to her alone. I've gotten to know how she thinks. I can get it out of her. You got her scared now. Just let me work on that. Hard and soft, you know? The technique'll work."

Purd puzzled on the proposition while he lit a cigarette. He had been impressed with Wanda's newfound stubbornness and didn't particularly want to break her. On the other hand, he was going to do whatever it took to get his hands on Amazon. Old Purd had too much riding on this not to.

"Okay," he finally agreed. "You get her for ten minutes. But I want results."

Purd then returned to Wanda. "Look, little lady," he said, "Hog here thinks maybe you'll listen to sense from him, so I'm gonna leave you two alone for a little bit. Then I'm coming back, and if you aren't ready to tell me everything you know, I'm gonna make you wish the Mexicans already had you. And that's a promise. You got Ole Purd's word on it." Fletcher then left the room and went down to the Trocadero bar for a quick drink.

Hog took Wanda Lamar into the bedroom and closed the door. As soon as it slammed shut, he swung her around by the arm so she was facing him. "What the fuck do you think you're doing?" he demanded.

"I think that's obvious," Wanda answered. None of her coldness had receded.

"This is the goddamn dumbest thing I ever seen. Purd's gonna grind you up. You don't got to put yourself through this. Don't you see? I meant that friends stuff. I'm lookin' out for you. You got to trust me."

"Sure, Hog, like you trust me. What a bunch of shit. Some friends. You trust me so much you won't even let me carry my own papers." Wanda's attack was flustering Hog, and she pressed her case. "What about that, huh? Explain that one to me, friend."

"That's just the way things are," Hog sputtered.

Wanda Lamar pulled away from him. "Not for me."

Hog pursued her as she walked across the bedroom. "You got no need for papers. What does it matter? You got to be here until we catch Amazon. Then it'll all get sorted out. Besides," he added with something of a little boy's voice, "I thought we had something goin' between us. Where you gonna go to get it better than I give it to you?"

Wanda's immediate temptation was to cut Hog to the quick, but she resisted in the interests of strategy. It would be better to play with his ego, so she softened her antagonism.

"Don't you understand, Hog? It's the issue. I like you," she lied, "I like you a lot. But I want to be my own person, not somebody's slave. If you won't even let me stand on my own two feet, then you don't want me to do anything but get used by you."

From the look of genuine anxiety on Hog's face, it was apparent Wanda's approach was working. "Come on, Wanda," he answered, trying to hold her by the arms again, "it's not like that between you and me."

"Then how is it?"

"We're tighter than that."

"Is that so?" Wanda snarled, pulling away again. "Well, if we're so fucking tight, how come you won't even give me my goddamn papers?"

"It ain't up to me, Wanda," Hog pleaded. "Don't you understand that?"

"Bullshit. You carry them right in your own pocket day in and day out." Wanda pointed at Hog's jacket where Wanda's papers were kept. Since Wissle was Wanda's immediate keeper, they were his responsibility.

"Purd would never allow it."

That answer told Wanda that it was time for the final push. She switched into a much more intimate voice and reached out to touch Hog's hip. "But, Hog," she said, "Purd doesn't have to know."

Hog said nothing for a while and looked away. Wanda rubbed him sympathetically. When he turned back, he grabbed her arms again. "And if I let you carry your own papers, you stop this bullshit and tell us what went on today?"

"Those plus the price of a ticket north."

Hog let her go. "Ticket north?" he whined. "What's this ticket north shit? How friendly is that?"

"I didn't say I was going to use it," Wanda soothed. "I just ought to have that possibility. How are we ever going to figure out if we're right for each other if I'm not able to do anything else? Or maybe," she added with a fresh hint of coldness, "that's what you want."

"No, that's not what I want."

"So, show that you trust me, Hog, that's all I'm asking. So I know you're serious."

"You won't tell Purd."

Wanda suppressed a smile. "It'll be between us," she said. Wanda moved closer to him so the top of her chest brushed against the bottom of his. "Our own little secret."

Hog Wissle pulled back and took Wanda's passport and tourist permit out of his jacket. Then he counted three hundred dollars of his own *pesos* and handed all of it to Wanda. "Now," he asked with a smile, "do you believe I trust you?"

"I do," Wanda answered, moving closer again. "And I won't forget." On her own initiative, she kissed Hog on the lips and wormed her tongue into his mouth. He responded by grabbing her tit, but after a few moments Wanda stepped away. "Purd will be back," she explained with a look of caution, "and we don't want him to guess."

Hog agreed, and after Wanda straightened her dress, they went back into the sitting room where Garcia Huahilote had remained and resumed their previous positions across the room from each other.

When Purdee Fletcher returned, he fully expected that he would have to whip on Wanda some more. Purd was surprised when Hog informed him that she was ready to talk. He said nothing of the deal that had been struck.

"Is that true?" he asked Wanda.

Wanda nodded with a defeated-looking expression. Like Hog she made no mention of their arrangement.

"So talk."

"Amazon's partner's name is Zorro CeAttle. I'm supposed to meet him at the fountain in Juarez Park at eight o'clock."

"What does this Zorro character look like?"

"I'll point him out," she answered without hesitation. "Then he's all yours."

Wanda had only the final stage of her strategy to go.

24

The last time Henry Amazon saw Zorro CeAttle was at seven thirty on Sunday night when he drove away from the Modesto to meet Chorizo past the roadblocks in the east Valley. Since he planned to return the next night when the load was on its way, Amazon left his suitcase in the bungalow. Zorro was scheduled to follow in exactly two and a half hours.

"See if you can make it on time," Amazon said to his partner. "The plan's important."

"*Sí, sí, mi jefe,*" Zorro responded derisively. "Whatever you say."

As soon as Henry Amazon's rented VW bus was out of sight, Zorro left the hotel. After a stop for a quick drink near the *zocolo,* he headed for Juarez Park and his appointment with the *gringa.* He was looking forward to it immensely. The *mestizo* with purple eyes figured to take Wanda somewhere for a drink and then back to the Modesto. There he planned to get into her pants before heading out to join Amazon.

When Zorro arrived at the park, he circled it slowly. Juarez Park was the size of a long rectangular city block, dotted with graceful trees and walkways. At the center was a large fountain with a tiled pool.

The park was lit sparsely, but well enough for Zorro to notice that Wanda was not yet at their appointed meeting place.

She, however, saw him. She was in the backseat of Garcia Huahilote's car, parked halfway down one of the adjacent side streets. Hog was next to her, and Purd and the Mexican were in the front seat. Wanda recognized Zorro's car right away.

"That's him," she blurted.

"The Ford?" Purd growled.

"That green one," Wanda answered. "I don't know what kind it is."

Purd had Huahilote radio the Hunter squad's other two Mexicans. They were stationed on a side street across the park and reported that they had the car in view. It was parking.

"Tell them to keep the suspect in sight," Purd instructed. "But don't close in until I give the signal. Make sure they understand that. Wait for the signal."

When the message had been broadcast, Purd stepped out onto the sidewalk. Hog and the Federale did likewise, leaving Wanda alone in the car.

"Take your cuffs," Purd told Hog before they headed up the street, "and chain ole Wanda there to the seat until we get back."

"What?"

"Goddamn, is Ole Purd surrounded by deaf people? I said chain her to the fucking seat. We can't spare anybody to stay with her."

"She won't go anywhere, Purd. Come on."

Purd had about had it with his partner. "Look," he hissed in a stage whisper, "you chain her and stop dicking around. Then catch up with us and don't be obvious about it." Purd turned on his heel and motioned Garcia to advance on the other side of the street. Both of them set off at a brisk walking pace. Zorro was on the far side of Juarez Park, locking the doors on his Ford.

Hog turned back to the Hunter Squad vehicle where Wanda Lamar had been listening to his conversation with Purd through her open rear window.

"You're not going to do that, are you?" she complained.

"Keep your voice down, Wanda. Goddamn, this is a police operation." Then he opened the door and stooped down with his handcuffs. "I got to."

"Bullshit."

Hog clicked one cuff to the frame on the front seat and reached for Wanda's leg. She pulled away.

"Goddamn it, Hog, if—"

Hog interrupted by grabbing her ankle.

"You son of a bitch," she sputtered. "If you do this we're through."

Hog snapped the other cuff around her ankle but only tightened it one notch. "Look, Wanda," he warned, "you got to stop trying to shove me around. I'm the one wearing the pants here. You got what you wanted so back off." He wiggled the cuff to show how loose it was. "It's on the first notch. It couldn't be looser." In fact, the cuff slipped over her ankle bone and fell like a bracelet on top of her foot.

Wanda Lamar reached over and felt at the shackle with her fingers. From the amount of space around the edge of the opening, she could tell her foot would slip through with a little work. Her mood changed immediately.

"I'm sorry, darling," she said, straightening up again. "I guess I've just been anxious. Take care of yourself. I'll be waiting for you." She squeezed Hog's arm, and he rubbed the inside of her leg in return. Then he pulled away and got ready for business. While he knew she was still watching, Hog checked his thirty-eight and then advanced up the sidewalk at a lope.

Wanda could have cared less. When Hog had taken twenty steps, she had her sandal off and her hands on the cuff. By the time he had reached the corner where Purd was waiting, Wanda's foot was through, and she was loose. At that point Purd directed Hog to move on from the corner to the right wing. The plan was to make a loose net completely around the suspect and then squeeze it closed. Zorro was halfway to the fountain when the entire five-man Hunter Squad moved into the park, covering all angles of exit.

Wanda jumped out the car's back door. She had her sandals in her hand and ran barefoot in the opposite direction. She was carrying a shawl over her shoulders, a purse with a shoulder strap, and nothing else. She headed at a gallop for the first-class bus station three blocks from Juarez Park and reached it five minutes before the departure of a Cristóbal Colón express to Guatemala City, Guatemala. Wanda bought a ticket.

Fourteen hours later she would pass across Mexico's southern border and enter Guatemala on an eighteen-day tourist visa. She would then wire her trust fund under the name Judith Rosenberg and two days later depart on the weekly Delta Air Lines flight direct to the States.

Meanwhile the scene in Juarez Park was its usual muffled self. The night was pleasant, and several couples were sitting on benches, none in the immediate vicinity of the fountain. The concrete pathways were dotted with puddles left over from the storm. When Zorro reached the park's centerpiece, he sat on the rim of the pool and lit a cigarette. At first he didn't notice the five men approaching him from five different directions. Zorro was horny and thinking about screwing the *gringa*. He was also thinking about how he'd drop the news on Henry Amazon.

It didn't strike Zorro that something strange was going on until the closest narc, one of the Mexicans from the second car, was thirty yards away. Zorro had risen to look around for Wanda, and this time the five men stood out. All of them had their hands in their pockets, and two were *gringos*. Zorro reacted to the danger like a cat.

His first move was into his boot for his automatic. The closest Mexican spotted the motion and opened fire. His initial round ricocheted off the fountain in the general direction of Garcia Huahilote, advancing on the opposite side. Garcia thought the fire had come from Zorro and returned it. Zorro in turn squeezed off a round at the closest man, who fired twice more and set off an answering burst from Hog Wissle. One of those bullets passed over Zorro's shoulder and struck the closest Federale in the middle of the forehead. As soon as he went down, Zorro CeAttle sprinted in that direction. Zorro was weaving and firing across his body. One of his shots sent Purd diving for cover behind a tree. By then Zorro had escaped the net.

Hog Wissle and Garcia Huahilote were in immediate pursuit some forty yards behind. At the edge of the park Zorro whirled and fired twice more. While the gunfire sent Hog sprawling behind a bench, it hardly phased Huahilote. When Zorro sprinted on up a side street that ran a short block and then made a T, Huahilote was only twenty-five yards behind. Zorro was fumbling a fresh clip into his weapon as he ran. Halfway up the short block, the pursuing Mexican agent stopped to take aim and fired twice.

The second bullet shattered Zorro CeAttle's left arm. He staggered visibly and seemed to look around.

A two-story house three quarters of the way through demolition was nearby. He headed for the cover there, stopping once to turn on his pursuers. Garcia Huahilote was twenty yards back and coming. Zorro fired three times, and the agent dove into the service entrance of a bicycle shop. Huahilote was able to get off two return shots before the suspect reached cover, but neither of them had any effect.

Inside the doorway of the demolished house Zorro hid behind a mound of rubble. Breath was coming in gulps and his left arm felt like it had hot coals inside. When he checked the street again, Huahilote was making a run for a truck parked almost directly across from Zorro's doorway. Zorro fired twice.

Hog had reached the scene by now, and when his thirty-eight answered Zorro's, the smuggler threw himself back behind the rubble. The third bullet fired by Wissle ricocheted off a pile of *adobe* to Zorro's right, rebounded sideways, and passed through his neck, neatly severing his spinal cord at the third vertebra and paralyzing him from the Adam's apple south. Zorro pitched forward and fell face down in a foot-deep pool of water left standing by the previous day's rain. The spot where he tumbled was hidden from the street.

Out there Purd had caught up with the others. He stopped next to Hog at the corner of the T. Purd was wheezing.

335

"Where is he?" Purd demanded.

"In that broken-down house."

Purdee Fletcher took charge immediately. "I'll give you cover fire," he said between gulps of air. "You get down past Huahilote and take him from the side."

"Done," Hog answered, preparing to dash out into the open.

Purdee grabbed his arm. "Remember, he can tell us a lot. I want him alive."

Hog nodded and then spun around the corner. As he did so, Purd stepped out from cover and cut loose with four rounds from his pistol. They slammed off the rubble with a high, whining sound. After a brief pause at Huahilote's station Hog took off along the sidewalk again. This time the Mexican agent provided cover fire. When he'd flanked the demolition project, Hog cut across the street and flattened himself against the house next door. By now, the gunfire had drawn the attention of the authorities, and an approaching Traffic Patrol squad car wailed somewhere nearby. On a signal from Hog, the other two agents opened up again. As they did, Hog Wissle sprinted up to what had once been the house's window, stuck his pistol inside, and pointed it at where he thought the suspect was.

"Freeze, motherfucker," Hog shouted.

There was no response.

At first Hog Wissle thought Zorro wasn't there, but then he noticed two feet sticking out from behind a short pile of bricks. Hog turned back toward Purd. "He's down," he shouted.

While Wissle kept the pair of feet covered, Purd ran across the street and in the door. He spotted Zorro and was the first one to pull the smuggler's face out of the water. The Mexican made a desperate slurping sound.

"He's still alive," Purd yelled at Hog. "Help me."

The scene was now lit by the flashing red cone of the Oaxaca Traffic Police cruiser arriving on the street. The two *gringos* bundled the unconscious Zorro out to the car and flung him in the backseat.

"You come with me," Purd shouted at Garcia Huahilote, "and you," to Hog, "bring up the car."

Purd jumped in the backseat next to Zorro. In an instant the police cruiser squealed away with its sirens blaring to Oaxaca's hospital.

Hog loped back to where they'd parked before the gun battle.

The first thing Hog noticed when he got there was Wanda's conspicuous absence.

Hog caught up with Purd Fletcher in a waiting room on the hospital's second floor. Zorro CeAttle was already being operated on down the hall. Garcia Huahilote was on the first floor, filling out all the official forms. Purd was pacing back and forth, smoking one Camel after another. He was anxious that Zorro survive long enough to be questioned.

"It's about time," Purd snapped when Hog pushed through the swinging door.

"The nurse downstairs wasn't sure where you were," Hog explained. "I didn't know until I ran into Garcia."

"Bring the woman up here," Purd instructed. "I want to talk to her some more."

Hog neither moved nor answered.

"Jesus H. Christ," Purd exploded, "have you gone deaf again? I said bring me the snitch."

"I can't," Hog responded sheepishly.

"You can't?"

"She wasn't at the car when I got back there."

Purd smashed his cigarette in one of the waiting room's standing ashtrays. "I told you to chain her up."

"I did," Hog stammered. "I just must've left it too loose."

"I don't believe it. Ole Purd doesn't have a partner; he's just got a permanent fuck up."

"I'm sure she just went back to the hotel. She was a little queasy about all this."

"Then go get her," Purd roared.

Hog left immediately and didn't return for more than two hours. Wanda Lamar was not back at the Trocadero.

337

At the moment he made that discovery, an enormous sinking feeling began welling up in Hog's stomach. It would only increase as time wore on. He checked several restaurants where he knew she liked to eat, but no luck. When he finally rejoined Purd, Hog knew he'd been played for a colossal chump.

"Where is she?" Purd demanded.

"She wasn't there."

Purdee Fletcher shook another Camel cigarette out of his pack and lit it with his Miami Beach Zippo lighter. He was trying to calm himself. Visions of Amazon's escape had been haunting Purd throughout the wait. "Well," he said after his first exhale, "you'll just have to find her. She's out there somewhere. She doesn't have the equipment to get out of town."

It was at that point that Wissle mumbled out an explanation of the deal he'd struck with Wanda earlier in the day. Purd made him repeat it in a louder voice. By the time he finished, a thick blue vein was protruding from Purdee Fletcher's forehead.

"You dumb, insubordinate jackass," Purd screamed. "You idiot. You fucking mushbrain. She's the only one that even knows what Henry Amazon looks like. And you just sent her on her way."

Hog cowered.

Purd lashed out at one of the standing ashtrays with his giant wing tip and knocked it tumbling across the room.

"What is it, Hog?" he fumed. "you just got shit between your ears, or what?"

Hog said nothing.

"Answer me, goddamn it."

"I guess so," Wissle stammered.

Purdee Fletcher advanced to less than a foot away. "Well, get this straight, Mr. Guess So. Your ass is cooked if she's gone, so you better get it out of here and find her. Take Garcia with you, and I don't want to see you until seven thirty tomorrow at the office. We meet there, and the woman better be with you. Otherwise, Ole Purd's gonna have your badge, and that's a fact."

Hog clattered out the waiting-room door, but Purd was sure it would come to nothing. Wanda had suckered Hog, and that in itself was evidence that she would be hard to catch. Purd's hopes all rested on Zorro now.

By eleven thirty the *mestizo* was in the recovery room, breathing on his own but still both paralyzed and unconscious.

By 1 A.M. Henry Amazon was seriously considering that something might have happened to his partner. He had expected Zorro might hang him up, but now it had extended to a point where the Mexican was in danger of missing the meeting with Rascón. Since Zorro also had no knowledge of the spot they were headed to after that meeting, he was in danger of missing the entire first night of the scam as well. The only place he could catch up with it would be the next afternoon at Gordo's. Amazon wouldn't have put it past Zorro to behave that way, but even for him, that was pushing things a little far.

Whatever the explanation, Amazon could wait no longer. He and Chorizo were parked off the road outside of the Fuenteses' village. He walked back to Chorizo's truck.

"Looks like the Mexican has hung us up one more time," Amazon said through the Dina's open window.

Chorizo was visible as the glowing ash on the end of a cigarette. He flipped it away in a sizzling arc over the *gringo*'s shoulder. "What'd I tell you about that *hombre?*"

Amazon ignored the comment. "We got to go. If we wait any longer, we'll miss our appointment." He turned back to his VW with a swift gait.

At the appointed wash Henry Amazon stopped and walked back to the Indian's truck again. "This is the place," he whispered. "You back in first and then wait. I'm going to leave my wheels up there." Amazon pointed to a wide spot on the other side of the culvert. When he rejoined the Indian in the Dina cab, they backed down to the spot Amazon had shown Zorro on Thursday. There he told Chorizo to kill the engine and got out. After three steps deeper into the wash he heard a voice on his left.

"*Buenas noches.*"

Amazon shined his flashlight at the sound. Rascón was standing there.

"*Buenas noches.*"

It took half an hour to inspect the *mota,* seal the boxes for travel, and load them onto Chorizo's flatbed. Once there they were covered with heavy tarp and tied down behind the fuel drums. Amazon paid Rascón in stacks of twenty-dollar bills, and the Indian melted into the surrounding hillside. Chorizo's truck lumbered back to the road afterward, and Amazon fetched his rent-a-car and led the way back to their original meeting place. When it was apparent there was still no sign of Zorro, Amazon wheeled around and headed back the direction they had come. It was three thirty Monday morning, time for them to get to Cucaracha's and get settled before the sun came up. Whatever Zorro was doing, Henry Amazon told himself, it was much too late to turn back now.

Amazon and Chorizo repeated their backing maneuver at a wash near The Cockroach's. This time Amazon led the caravan in his VW. Cucaracha's wash, wide like the first one, only rockier, wound away from the road and disappeared into the foothills with a right-hand turn. The right turn was followed by a left, and then the streambed climbed.

It was wetter than the spot where they'd met Rascón. A stream flush with runoff occupied the center of the wash, but it was small enough that Amazon's rent-a-car could straddle the current and maintain firm footing. At the point where the bed began to climb the slope, a huge mound of cut cane and tree limbs was piled on the right. Amazon stopped, and El Chorizo did likewise. "This is where we leave your wheels," he explained.

Working quickly in the dark, the two men used the tree limbs and cut cane to cover the Dina. Then they both got in the VW and continued backing up the streambed. The footing here was dicier, and several times the VW had to take a second run at a stretch. After they had climbed some forty yards, the wash flattened out again for ten yards and then became impassable. Here an almost solid ceiling of tamarinds covered the streambed. Henry Amazon parked. The Cockroach's cave was some fifty more yards up the steep incline to the right, but the Indian had already moved the *mota* to a lean-to only ten yards above the loading spot. When Henry Amazon climbed up to it, the old Indian was asleep with his pistol in his lap.

Amazon nudged The Cockroach and shined his light in the Indian's face. Cucaracha sputtered awake. "Some guard you are," he joked.

"Tortuga," the old man cackled. "You're late."

Amazon shrugged. "Everything here?"

"Everything."

Henry Amazon shined his light on the eggboxes under the lean-to.

"Did you find the cane I cut for you?" Cucaracha asked.

"I did," he answered, turning down the slope. "It worked just right." Amazon sounded distracted.

It took twenty minutes for Chorizo, Amazon, and the old man to transfer the boxes into the bed of Amazon's rented VW bus. His original plans hadn't called for hauling anything in the rent-a-car, but Zorro's absence forced a change. The boxes reached the roof, and only the front seat remained empty.

Henry Amazon paid Cucaracha five thousand dollars American cash. "That was good Kind you grew, old man," he commented as he handed it over. "As sweet as I've ever smoked."

Cockroach handled the bills with a good deal of excitement. *"Gracias, Tortuga,"* he said. *"Muchas gracias."* For a moment there was an embarrassed silence as the Indian figured out how to leave gracefully. "You gonna stay out here till tomorrow?" he finally asked.

"Just like I said."

"Well, the lean-to is dry," Cucaracha commented.

"Muchas gracias."

"And when you hear Garcia Garcia Garcia and The Scorpions of the Valley," the Indian continued cryptically, "know that I am thinking of you."

With that the old man and the smuggler parted company forever. Cucaracha headed up the slope without waiting for a response or even looking back.

Now there was nothing to do but sit and let time pass. Amazon and Chorizo decided to sleep in shifts.

25

Purdee Fletcher spent all the dark hours of Monday morning at the hospital waiting for the wounded suspect to recover enough to talk. At 4 A.M. an English-speaking doctor informed the waiting American that the patient's eyes were open. If he would ever talk, now was the most likely time.

When Purd walked into the room, Zorro's eyes were indeed open and on full purple, but he was unable to move them from side to side. Being underwater so long had demolished large sections of his brain, and at that moment the Mexican smuggler seemed to be using up its last visible shreds. The intelligence still in his head wanted to know where the rest of him was but could only come out with faint gurgles in his throat. Purd bent over so Zorro's lips were almost against his ear, but he still couldn't understand. When the sound stopped, the narc asked his first question.

"Where's Henry Amazon?"

Zorro blinked his eyes. The name Amazon had gotten through even though the *mestizo*'s mind was not up to fully processing it.

343

"Can you hear me, Zorro? Where's Amazon?"

It was impossible to tell what Zorro was thinking at the time or even if he was thinking at all. He responded with more noises that seemed to rush out of his throat instinctively. These sounded more like words, and Purd pressed to hear.

The only ones he could decipher were *truck, culvert,* and *out of Tla.* ... The statement ended on that syllable.

"Where?" Purdee pressed again.

Zorro couldn't answer. There were no words left in his brain. He could see a picture of an airplane but couldn't make words. The sound of its motor drowned everything else in the *mestizo*'s fractured head. Pressing his lips together, he tried over and over to duplicate the sound. The result was a flapping of lips that buzzed and sprayed spittle on the side of Purd's head.

The narc backed away and wiped himself off with a handkerchief. "What?" he asked again from a distance.

The request was useless. Zorro's eyes were still open, but there were no more noises. The Chihuahua *mestizo* had made his last communication with the outside world.

Purdee stuck around the hospital until the sun started up Saturday morning, and the uselessness of his vigil was overwhelmingly apparent.

Out on the street he flagged a cab to his office in the Judicial Federal headquarters over the funeral parlor. Purd concentrated on reviewing the information that had accrued to him during the course of the night. He knew from the wallet found on Zorro that Henry Amazon's partner also went under the name Lacandone and passed as an American. The suspect's car had yielded little. It was registered at an address in New Mexico that Purd suspected was phony as a three-dollar bill. Aside from a half-empty bottle of *mescal* and a few tarps they found in the trunk, the automobile was empty. The rest of what Purd knew amounted to the last words of Zorro CeAttle and the story told the day before by Wanda Lamar. She had said the Indian's green truck was half-loaded with oil-type drums, and this Zorro had been in a hurry when he sent the truck off. Purd figured the drums were either full and used for refueling an airplane or empty and used to hide *mota* for a trip north by ground transport. Either way Amazon's henchmen seemed to be doing something in the near future. Purd wished that he still had Wanda to ask more questions, but that, he needed no reminder, was unlikely. Wanda Lamar had either skipped clean or gone to cover deep enough that she'd never be found before whatever was about to happen had happened. Purd had an hour and a half before his forces would have to be deployed for Monday and, thanks to Hog, he was stuck having to just make his best guess and act accordingly.

At the office Purd listed on a tablet, in longhand, all the words he'd picked up from Zorro. First came *truck,* then *culvert,* and *out of Tla.* . . . Purd underlined this last syllable several times and guessed that somewhere in there was a place name. He stopped to consult his Oaxaca state map, but the number of places starting with those three letters had exceeded twenty when he stopped counting. Then Purd returned to his pad and tried making an intelligible syllable out of Zorro's final lip sound. Purdee Fletcher repeated it over and over again out loud.

It wasn't until fifteen minutes before the Hunter Squad came straggling into his office that Purd put the noise together with the scam he was chasing. He had been thinking that Zorro's utterance sounded like a fly buzzing and, when picturing a fly, snapped *airplane* and wrote the word down. Coupled with those mysterious drums, Purd also came up with *airplane fuel.* By the time his detachment assembled, Purdee Fletcher had taken his guess.

Purd opened the agenda by making cold acknowledgment with his eyes in the direction of Hog Wissle that the junior agent had not in fact returned with the woman. But he said nothing openly about it. Purd just wanted Hog to dangle at a distance with no recognition whatsoever. When he spoke, it was about the hunt for Amazon.

"What we've got here," the pear-shaped Purd began, "is an airstrip operation. It belongs to the violator Amazon that Ramón Ramón told us about. That Mexican we shot was part of his operation. The two things that are clear are that they're doing business and doing it soon."

The Hunter Squad listened with a somewhat sullen look. Garcia Huahilote was sullen from lack of sleep; the other Mexican was sullen because his partner was dead, and Hog Wissle was the most sullen of all. He was crushed, embarrassed, and resentful all at the same time. Purd ignored him and spoke with a flat, businesslike tone. Hog would get his in due time.

Zorro's car, Purdee continued, had contained no personal belongings. To Ole Purd that smelled like a rented room somewhere that might include a suitcase full of more clues. Huahilote and the remaining Mexican would begin checking hotels. They were to start on the south side of town and check each place for either a Henry Amazon, Zorro CeAttle, or his alias, Luis Lacandone. In the meantime Agent Wissle, as Purd made a point of addressing Hog, would observe the two airline departures from Oaxaca International that morning to make sure Wanda Lamar wasn't on them. After that he was to begin checking rent-a-car outfits. Ole Purd would man the office and stay in radio contact. Fletcher closed the meeting by turning back to his desk and listening to everyone straggle back out. His eyes burned, but he wasn't about to sleep.

Of Monday's Hunter Squad deployment Hog's rent-a-car effort would bear fruit first. By 1 P.M. he would report that Amazon had put a deposit on a Volkswagen bus, Oaxaca license ZZP 633, the week before and had yet to return it.

By 4 P.M. the other half of Purd's command would have worked their way across the city to the Modesto. Once there Purdee Fletcher would find the last clue he thought he needed.

Sometime past noon Henry Amazon and the Indian El Chorizo consumed a bag of cold *burritos* and several warm beers for lunch.

346

Then Chorizo decided to grab a little more sleep. Amazon climbed down to where the VW was parked to listen to the weather report on his rent-a-car's radio. The sky had scudded up again and was showing gray everywhere he looked. Amazon worried about the possibilities of rain. Station XEOA carried a regular meteorological update just before Garcia Garcia Garcia and *The Scorpions of the Valley Show*, and Henry Amazon found it.

The first thing he heard was the Spanish announcer's words for "trailing edge of the Pacific storm. It may look wet," the announcer continued, "but it's not likely to prove it. Rain is only a twenty percent possibility, and most of that is expected in the inland mountains and not over the Valley itself. And, to end on a note for you Garcia Garcia Garcia fans," the voice chuckled, "the moon tonight is scheduled to be full. With a little luck you may even see it once or twice." The voice got louder and filled with flourishes. "When that happens . . . watch out. Now to tell you more about everything, yourself included, here's the crazy himself, your favorite and mine, Garcia . . . Garcia . . . Garcia."

With the last "Garcia," The Scorpions of the Valley took up with their *mariachi* theme song, and the host came on the air howling like a wolf.

"Ooooooooooooowwoooo, Owoo, Owoo. It's me, moon lovers, triple G with my Scorpions: Luis, Luis, Ramundo, and Little Red. Got lots of people who are gonna sing today and let you know what is goin' on. From Tehuantepec to Tlalpan, Yagul to Yalalag, this is where you find it."

Henry Amazon lit a cigarette. He was a little too antsy to sit and listen to the radio, but on the other hand there was little else to do.

"Well," Garcia continued, "I can see we got a live one today."

The audience clamored in response.

"All right, all right. To get things started we got a special treat. On the weather they're talking about stormy nights and the full moon, so Garcia's got a guest from the other side of Tlacolula to start things off

347

who's right down that alley. He looks for buried treasure. Let's say hello, folks."

The audience roared.

"Now, sir, step right up to the microphone. That's right." There was a clunking sound as the invisible guest ran into some of the studio machinery. That was followed by more audience sounds, and then Garcia returned to the air. "Just whose treasure are you looking for, *señor?*"

"Cresensio's, *don* Garcia."

Henry Amazon's ear perked up at the voice. It was an old man's, laced with *mescal*, and familiar.

"You mean the bandit from the days before Juárez?"

"The very same, excellency."

Amazon reached over and turned the volume up. "I don't believe it," he said out loud. "Cockroach fucking did it."

"Digging for treasure must be hard work," Garcia offered. "Very hard work. How does an old man like you keep going?"

"By singing my name song, *don* Garcia. Every day."

"And what," Garcia Garcia asked with a tone of expectancy, "is that?"

"*La Cucaracha,*" the old Indian answered in a hesitant voice.

"What?"

"*La Cucaracha,*" he said in a louder voice.

Garcia Garcia Garcia repeated it at top volume. "*La . . . Cuca . . . racha.*"

On the last syllable The Scorpions began blasting out the melody. That was followed by several awkward moments of hawking and spitting while The Cockroach cleared his voice.

"*La Cucaracha,*" he finally commenced shakily, "*la cucaracha,*"

> *ya no quiere caminar,*
> *porque no tiene,*
> *porque le falta,*
> *marijuana que fumar.*

When the word *marijuana* came out, the audience noise boiled over and dominated the broadcast. They knew that General Cortez de Corriente prohibited unapproved usage of the words *marijuana, revolucion,* and *communista* on the radio and cheered the old man for putting one over on Garcia.

The host regained control immediately. The music switched to The Scorpions' theme song, The Cockroach's voice disappeared, and Garcia came back on in a monologue. "I guess it takes all kinds," Garcia commented, "but I think that old man has a problem. Maybe you got one too. Maybe it's in your teeth. If it is, I know a doctor who can help you out. Dr. Ruiz Principe is a dentist you know you can trust. Just tell him Garcia—"

Henry Amazon switched the radio off. Since this was his last Garcia Garcia Garcia show, Amazon wanted to end on the note of the old man's victory. It was nice to see someone south of the border end up doing what they set out to in the first place.

He considered it a good omen.

The longer the afternoon wore on, the more he felt like he was going to need one. Amazon's worry focused on his terror of riding out in the small plane in Zorro's absence and would stay riveted there for much of the remaining wait. Inactivity only exacerbated the worry, and it was with a final sense of relief that Amazon woke his Indian driver at half past three.

"Wake up," he told Chorizo. "We got to leave for Gordo's soon."

Purdee Fletcher was informed that both the shot-up *mestizo* and Amazon himself were registered at the Hotel Modesto at four Monday afternoon. It was four thirty before the senior agent actually arrived on the scene. By then the bungalow had been completed searched. All it yielded were suitcases and clothes.

"Nothing," Huahilote reported when Purd asked what they'd found.

"We'll see," Fletcher said on his way into the bedroom. "A place ain't searched til ole Purd's searched it himself."

349

Purd sorted through the clothes, stripped the beds, and dumped drawers. He picked through ashtrays and lifted the carpet. It wasn't until he got to the sitting room and emptied the wastebasket there that Purd found something he could use. At first the contents seemed inconspicuous. There were cigarette butts, several old newspapers, some dead flashlight batteries, and a piece of stationery that had been crumpled into a ball.

The stationery caught Purd's eye right away. He uncrumpled it carefully and examined it, flattened out on the coffee table. The letterhead belonged to a plumbing supply house, and Purd sensed right away that the ball-point markings on it were a map. The drawing's most obvious feature was the right-angled intersection of two apparently major roads. One of those led out to a square marked T. The other, past a circle to a right-hand intersection. The mouth of the triangle they formed was a squiggly line passing one small square and through another and then connecting the large square marked T with the main artery running past the circle. There were two locations marked with an X. One was on the hypotenuse road leading across from T. The other was up the right-hand squiggle leading off the top of one of the perpendicular lines.

Like the rest of the Hunter Squad Hog was out in the courtyard, having a smoke.

"Wissle," Purd shouted, "get in here."

Hog scurried in.

"Bring me my map out of the car," he instructed, "and bring Garcia back with you."

When the two of them returned, Purd unfolded the Oaxaca state map and began looking for road arrangements like those on the stationery. There were several approximate right angles, but the only one leading to anything sizable and beginning with a T was the intersection of the Pan American toward Tlacolula with the highway to Ixtlán and Veracruz. Purdee also found a line coming out of Tlacolula. It ran past one village and into another. At that point on the official map it ceased being a solid line. From there across to the Ixtlán Road it was

350

just two thin broken borders, but it was indeed a road, completing the triangle.

"Garcia," Purd called.

"¿*Si?*" Huahilote was standing some ten feet away.

"How many roadblocks are there between here and Tlacolulu?"

"Tlacolula," the Mexican corrected. "There's two."

That checked with the cross-hatches on the Plumbing Supply stationery as well. The first three letters also matched with the last syllable Zorro had made. Purd burst to his feet, scooping all the maps up in his hand.

"Saddle up," he said.

"Where we goin'?" Hog asked.

"Tlacolulu," Purd snapped. "You're driving me. Garcia and the other Mexican follow." With that Fletcher bowled his way out of the room with the others in tow.

The Hunter Squad would stop at both roadblocks along the way to Tlacolula to question the officers in charge about a green flatbed with oil drums or a VW bus, Oaxaca ZZP 633, driven by a *gringo*. It would be well after six o'clock before the task force reached the mouth of the road leading out to Fuenteses' village. By then darkness would be falling rapidly.

Before the narcs left the Modesto, Henry Amazon's caravan had reached the parking lot outside Gomez Gordo's restaurant. Just as they'd arranged, The Fat Man was waiting there next to his Chrysler. Unexpectedly, his daughter, Dolores, was with him. She was sitting behind the wheel of the car. Henry Amazon stopped his VW nearby and slid over to his passenger window when Gomez Gordo approached. The short, fat frame was draped with a lime-green leisure suit.

"*Buenas tardes.*"

"*Buenas tardes,*" Amazon answered. "What's she doing here?" He made a motion with his head at the Chrysler and Gomez's daughter.

351

"She wants to see the plane come in and out," Gordo explained. "She does it a lot with me. Teaching her the business, you know?"

Henry Amazon nodded, and The Fat Man continued. He'd been looking back at the truck behind Amazon. "I thought you said there was goin' to be three cars? Where's that Mexican?"

"Who knows?" Amazon answered. "I take it he hasn't been up here?"

Gordo said he hadn't, and Amazon checked his watch.

"Well," he went on with some disgust in his voice, "if he were coming, he would have come by now. We just do it without him."

"That doesn't bother me," Gordo offered.

"It means a little change in plans."

"What's that?"

"I'm gonna have to leave this," Henry Amazon motioned at his rent-a-car. "You think one of your people could drive it back down here and call Hertz to come and get it?"

"No problem. Dolores will do it after you leave."

"Then let's go."

Gomez Gordo skittered back to his Chrysler on his little feet and climbed inside. Dolores squealed out of the lot, and the VW and the truck kept up as best they could. When they reached the airstrip turnoff, the Chrysler was already stopped there among the line of soldiers sealing the neck of the side road. Gordo was talking across his daughter to the lieutenant at the window on the driver's side.

"These are my friends," he said with a move of his tiny fingers toward Amazon's bus and Chorizo's Dina. The Fat Man then handed a thousand dollars American to Dolores, who passed it on to the officer. "All of these vehicles," Gordo added, "will be coming back out later. We don't wish to be disturbed in the meantime."

"*Sí, don Gomez, muchas gracias.*"

With that Gordo's daughter led the caravan ahead. The boxes in Amazon's VW were obvious, but no one at the roadblock seemed to care. Most of the privates were lounging in the grass and talking to each other. The lieutenant only smiled and waved him through.

Once at the runway he had little to do but wait for darkness and the plane that was scheduled to arrive soon thereafter. Henry Amazon did so morosely. His stomach was tingling, and his legs felt weak. It was nothing more than a matter of a few hours now, but they passed like molasses.

26

The Hunter Squad cars clattered through the Fuenteses' village during the last of Monday's light. Long shadows fell across the streets, but Purd kept Hog pushing the pace. Turkeys and dogs scattered in their wake, people jumped into doorways, and those who witnessed the law's passage crossed themselves immediately.

The guesswork Purd had been engaged in all day was building up for more. Once through this Indian settlement, Fletcher was back at the limits of his knowledge. Purd knew Amazon had marked some spot on the approaching road with an *X*, but he did not know why. The only thing he knew about the road was Zorro's word *culvert*.

Purd had also reached the limits of his own endurance. It had been thirty-six hours since he'd slept, and his head felt thick. His body was loggy as well.

Outside of the village Fletcher had his men follow up the culvert clue and stopped at each of them in turn. Purd told his Hunter Squad to look for any signs of activity. Footprints, tire tracks, anything that

354

showed people were around in one direction or another. Purd knew he was grasping blindly but felt there was nothing else to do. By the time his party had crossed over the first ridge and begun checking the culverts on the other side, they had to use flashlights. Night had come down in a final rush, virtually snuffing out all their immediate surroundings. There were holes in the clouds to the east where the moon shone through, but none near them. After several minutes fumbling around looking for something, Purd's men began to grumble audibly about the waste of effort involved, and Hog was chief among them.

"Now what do we do?" Hog finally blurted.

"We keep looking, goddamn it." The vein in Purdee Fletcher's forehead was beginning to swell again. "They're doin' something out here, and there's got to be a sign of it."

"You're off your gourd, old man. Do you know that?"

What Purd did know was that he was through taking lip off his junior agent fuck up and started to say so. He was interrupted by something he heard. Purd's head cocked suddenly.

"Shut up," he said.

"What?"

"I said shut up. You'll hear it. Turn those damn cars off." The Hunter Squad autos were sitting on the road with their engines running. When they'd been turned off, the seeming silence around them escalated into a legion of night sounds. Floating on top of them all was a dull hum that seemed to be approaching. For a moment Purd just listened to it. The hum droned in and out, always returning just a little louder than it had been before.

Then Purd started scrambling up the embankment to the car. At the top he cursed himself. He'd come to the wrong X first. In a moment the two narc cars wheeled away for the Ixtlán Road, as fast as they could go.

When the pilot R.W. picked up the beacon from Oaxaca International on the radio of his twin-engine Cessna, he knew he was more or less right on target. R.W. had been in the air for over seven hours. By his calculations he was now crossing the Oaxaca Valley northwest to southeast. He switched his set to the channel he and Amazon had arranged ahead of time and broke radio silence.

"This is Pigeon calling Nest," he called. "Do you read me?"

The radio answered immediately. The voice was full of crackles but sounded like Henry Amazon. "This is Nest, Pigeon, I read you. Recognize. Repeat. Recognize. Over."

R.W. then responded with his half of the recognition code. "Cowboy. Repeat. Cowboy. Over."

"Indians, R.W.," the voice relaxed. "What do you need?"

"Give me a flash. Just so I can line myself up."

Amazon had Gordo's men switch the runway lights on for a moment and then off again.

R.W. spotted them to his right and adjusted his course. "Again," he requested.

The second flash of lights was dead ahead, some five minutes away. Darkness and radio silence followed for a while until R.W. called back. "This time turn them on and leave them that way."

The landing lights of his Cessna twin-engine came on when it was almost on top of the runway. As the plane touched down, the airstrip lamps came off again, and it taxied to the end of the dark strip, guided by the two narrow beams of light poking out the underside of its wings. Henry Amazon was the first one to reach the plane when its engines had finally shut down. R.W. was climbing out of the cockpit.

"How'd it go?" Amazon asked.

"Nothin' to it," the pilot answered.

It was another ten minutes before Henry Amazon told R.W. that the Mexican had failed to show and that Amazon himself would be the passenger on the trip back.

R.W. laughed, but Henry Amazon did not find the subject funny. He looked wan and acted surly and distracted, like a man who didn't want to face what he was about to do.

* * *

It took an hour to get the Cessna aircraft ready for the return trip, and during it all Henry Amazon's mood remained intense and unchanged. While Gomez Gordo's ground crew pumped fuel under R.W.'s supervision, Amazon and El Chorizo stacked the boxes of Kind in the cargo compartment. Henry Amazon went through all the motions like a man walking in his sleep. All of Amazon's conscious deliberations had been captured by the small seat next to the pilot's. The prospect of flying north strapped to it terrorized him as deeply as anything he could remember. Amazon pictured the chair as a narrow sling dangling over an endless elevator shaft. Throughout the loading process his hands were cold and sweaty. His stomach churned.

When the Cessna twin-engine was refueled and loaded, R.W. had the ground crew push it to the very back edge of the strip so he would have maximum runway to take off from. While they were doing so, Henry Amazon rejoined Gomez Gordo and his daughter in the shack where the radio was kept. Gordo noticed Amazon's mood.

"What's the matter, Tortuga?" he asked. "You look like a man who's about to be hanged. Is being rich gonna be that bad?"

Amazon brushed the question aside. "It's those little planes," he explained. "Can't stand to be in them."

Gomez Gordo laughed in a noticeable shifting of suet. "You must be in the wrong business then."

"Could·be," Henry Amazon answered. "Could be."

Without delving any deeper into the subject, he set to paying everyone off. He counted The Fat Man's money out on the table, twenty thousand dollars in all. When Gordo was done recounting the bills, Amazon tossed the keys to his VW rent-a-car on the table next to the cash. Gordo handed those to his daughter.

"She'll take it back to the restaurant as soon as you leave," he reassured the *gringo*.

"*Bueno*. We'll be off the ground in five minutes." Amazon then ducked through the doorway and went back outside. Gomez Gordo and his only daughter Dolores followed shortly.

357

By the time they did, Amazon was paying off El Chorizo. The wad of bills included a twenty-five-hundred-dollar bonus.

"You earned it," he told the Indian.

"Muchas gracias," Chorizo answered.

Somewhat at a loss for what to say, Amazon grabbed the Zapotec by the shoulder. "It's been good, *compadre*. Real good," he finally offered.

"It has," Chorizo agreed. The Indian stubbed at the ground with his boots. "You ever coming back?"

"No," Henry Amazon told him flatly, "I'm not."

The words were final enough that nothing followed. Henry Amazon squeezed the Indian's shoulder again and then turned for the plane.

The only sound in the night was the chatter from the direction of Gordo's huddled ground crew. R.W. was waiting for Amazon to strap himself in before turning the engines over. At the cockpit door Amazon started to look back and then bolted inside and cinched his seat belt down over his lap.

The first thing R.W. did was show his passenger where the plastic air-sickness bags were kept. Amazon grasped one between his hands and rumpled it like worry beads.

By then Purdee Fletcher and his two-car Hunter Squad were rapidly approaching the second *X* on his map. Purd knew time was short and made his next guesses on the run. Since the restaurant they passed was the only building within several miles, he assumed it was what had been represented on the Plumbing Supply stationery by the circle alongside the Ixtlán Highway. He told Wissle to be on the lookout for a road coming in from the right.

Hog swerved down the first one they saw.

As soon as he did, the turnoff was blocked by the blare of search-lights and headlamps from two Army trucks. Shadows of helmeted men carrying rifles rushed out at the car, and Wissle had to slam on the brakes. The tail end slid around somewhat and was almost clumped from behind by Garcia Huahilote's car. For a moment every-thing was chaos. Purd was staring at a *mestizo* enlisted man holding a submachine gun stuck in the open passenger window.

"Tell 'em we're on their side," Purd fumed at Hog.

Hog did, but none of the soldiers moved.

The situation was cleared up by the lieutenant who approached the driver's door.

"Tell him we're the drug police," Purd rattled at Hog. Every second was crucial, and this wait might blow their chance. "We got to chase a suspect up this road."

Hog again did as he was told, and the lieutenant in turn asked for identification. Both the agents handed their badges over. The lieuten-ant was courteous but seemed unconvinced.

"I am pleased to meet you," he said, "but these documents say you are both Americans. What, may I ask, is your legal authority?"

To clear that question up Garcia Huahilote was summoned from the second car, and the three of them huddled with the officer in charge on the roadway. The soldiers waited with their guns at the ready several steps away. When it was clear to the lieutenant just who these police were and what operating authority they in fact had, he answered their first question.

"You cannot go up here," the lieutenant explained. "My orders come from General Cortez de Corriente himself. Until they change, you can't go past."

"Goddamn it," Purd swore when the response had been translated for him. "Doesn't he understand? We're the police. *Policía.* We got a big fish we're chasin'. We're on the same fucking side."

Hog conveyed Purd's sentiment, but the officer just shrugged.

Purdee Fletcher bit his lip and tried to control his emotions. His head was throbbing.

"Well," he asked Hog with a voice sounding forcibly restrained, "can he tell us if Amazon is even up there? Tell him the suspect's in a Volkswagen bus and give him the license."

Hog translated the question and then its answer. "He says," Hog told his boss, "that he would be glad to give that subject consideration if he got some consideration too."

"What in the name of Jesus does that mean?"

Garcia Huahilote offered that Purd should give the man some money.

The news infuriated Purdee, but he quickly produced a twenty-dollar bill for the lieutenant's inspection. From the way the Mexican looked at it, Purdee Fletcher knew to produce another. With it in hand the lieutenant said he had indeed seen the VW bus come through.

"Well, then let us go after it," Purd blurted. No one translated the statement.

"That car will be back out soon," the officer continued to Hog. If the police wanted the *gringo* driving it, they could wait between here and the restaurant and catch him then. The highway was out of his jurisdiction. After proposing this compromise, the lieutenant also made it clear that for a hundred dollars more he would be sure no one told the *gringo* that the police were waiting for him when he drove out.

When that was translated, Purd's fury leaped out full bore. "Jesus fucking Christ," he screamed. To vent the rage, the pear-shaped *gringo* kicked the car's dashboard. "What kinda goddamn country is this?"

Purdee Fletcher started to say more, but the reappearance of the sound he'd heard while looking for the first *X* stopped him. The buzzing was nearby and made by twin propellers. The engines were winding up, and Purd could picture the plane trembling as it waited to launch.

At that point Purd resigned himself to making the best deal he could. Since Henry Amazon's rented car was scheduled to return the way it had come, Purdee Fletcher assumed Amazon would be in it. Even if he couldn't touch the strip, Ole Purd could still bust the man himself.

Purdee Fletcher paid the hundred dollars and withdrew his Hunter Squad to their own roadblock in a blind corner a mile down the hill toward Gomez Gordo's restaurant. He also told his forces that the suspect was considered dangerous and would most likely have several armed bodyguards. Since the narcs totaled only four, each of them was instructed to use his gun at the first sign of trouble.

As R.W.'s Cessna twin-engine charged toward the bank of lights at the far end of the runway, Henry Amazon stuffed the air-sickness bag between his knees and held onto the sides of his seat with both hands. *Mota* boxes were stacked to the edge of their seats, and the space he and the pilot were hunched in made him claustrophobic. The plane vibrated and picked up momentum. He held his breath as they lifted off, plunged through the runway glare and into the dark beyond.

The twin-engine had been airborne for thirty seconds before hitting the first updraft. It rose four hundred feet in two seconds, clattered through several bumps and was then wrenched upward again. R.W. had some trouble keeping the aircraft in hand. This heavily loaded, the controls were mushy. When the plane finally evened out, he turned to his passenger. The pilot expected Amazon to be hunched over, losing his lunch in the plastic bag.

Instead Henry Amazon was as calm as R.W. had ever seen him. The transformation seemed absolute. He was looking out at the blackness below with a big smile on his face. Then he turned to the pilot and began to sing.

"*La Cucaracha,*" Amazon sang, "*la cucaracha, ya no quiere caminar . . .*" The roar of the engines overtook his voice, and R.W. lost track of the words. Amazon kept singing. R.W. throttled back.

"*La Cucaracha, la cucaracha,*" Amazon repeated, "*ya no quiere caminar . . .*"

The ground below was indistinguishable from the air itself.

Shortly after the plane departed, Chorizo followed Dolores Gordo down the dirt track connecting the strip to the Ixtlán Road. The Fat

Man's daughter was at the wheel of Henry Amazon's rent-a-car. Dolores had been driving automobiles for two years but had never driven a Volkswagen Kombi before. Her reactions in it were slow and unsure. The VW bus rolled between the line of soldiers near the highway in silence, and the green Dina followed likewise. Both turned back toward Oaxaca with the Indian some twenty yards behind. The moon had finally poked through in places, and the caravan slithered across splotches of glow. At the end of one of them Gomez Gordo's only child turned a blind corner and shortly came face to face with Purdee Fletcher and his Hunter Squad.

All Purd's men were on a hair trigger while waiting, and Ole Purd himself more than anyone else. The strain was telling on him, and his body ached all over from being pushed past its limit. He was the first to identify the silhouette of the VW bus in the moonlight at the corner.

Purd had stationed the Hunter Squad cars side by side across the road's two lanes with their as-yet-dark headlamps pointing uphill. The two Mexicans were posted outside the drivers' doors to man the light switches, and he and Hog made up the position's flanks. The Mexicans were armed with M–16s and the *gringos* with handguns. Fletcher didn't order his men to illuminate their position until a flatbed truck had turned the corner behind the VW. That confirmed the identification as far as Ole Purd was concerned.

"It's him," he shouted. "Turn 'em on."

The sudden glare panicked Dolores Gordo. She was only forty yards away. To her this looked like two cars rushing straight at her for a head-on collision. Dolores swerved instinctively for the shoulder to her left and slammed her foot at the brakes. It missed and landed on the accelerator. The Kombi leaped ahead out of control, and Purd interpreted the move as an attempt to run for it. By all later accounts he was the first one to fire.

A wave of gunfire and muzzle flashes rippled down the Hunter Squad line as soon as Fletcher cut loose. Dolores Gordo was hit six times. The rented VW swerved and assumed an inexorable path to the edge of the drop. A portion of the gunfire then switched to the truck behind. Chorizo had figured out what was going on by then and come to a full stop. He intended to put the truck in reverse and back out of danger as fast as he could. He was hit with eleven different rifle rounds. His Dina crashed into the wall of the cut and stalled. El Chorizo was dead when it stopped. The car originally rented by Henry Amazon flew into the *barranca* with Dolores Gordo at the wheel.

Purd had no way of knowing who the VW driver was, but he was sure he'd nailed Henry Amazon. The lardy *gringo* ran over to the edge while the Volkswagen was being smashed to bits on the rocks below.

"Gotcha, you son of a bitch," he yelled into the dark drop. "Gotcha."

On Wednesday night Henry Amazon drove a motorized mobile home to a motel in Oklahoma City. His Toyota Land Cruiser was attached to the back end with a tow bar. Fat Albert was in a room there, rented under an assumed name. Albert had a suitcase full of twenties and hundreds, divided into packages of five thousand dollars apiece. Amazon spot-checked several of the currency bundles at random and then counted the total number. It was the full one million five hundred thousand dollars Fat Albert had promised. After Albert had in turn counted and inspected the boxes of Kind outside in the mobile home, Henry Amazon took his suitcase and threw it in the Land Cruiser. The last time Fat Albert saw him, he was headed west.

What Amazon had just finished caught up with him a little way outside of town. For no apparent reason he had an attack of weakness that left his legs limp and his steering unsure. The fear he'd been riding seemed to be disappearing with a final whiplash. Henry pulled off the freeway for a while to let the tremor pass. Eighteen-wheelers roared by, and he leaned against his Land Cruiser and smoked a cigarette. A nearby billboard announced a Howard Johnson's thirty minutes ahead. When he'd gotten himself back together, Henry Amazon headed there for the night. The only bag he had with him was full of money.

The next morning Amazon headed farther west and disappeared. He would never go south of the border again. He was someone else now, someplace far away.